...and engaging. It's so good!'
BA Paris

'This darkly comic novel... has the
potential to become a cult classic'
Daily Mail

' is isn't a book for the squeamish or the faint-hearted
... think Bridget Jones meets American Psycho'
RED

'Filthy and funny... a compulsive read'
Sunday Times

'You MUST read this book especially if you like your (anti)
he es dirty-mouthed, deadly dark, dark dark. I adored it'
Fiona Cummins

'This anti-hero is psychotic without
doubt... incredibly funny'
SHOTS

Makes Hannibal Lecter look like Mary Poppins...
this is going to give me a serious book hangover'
John Marrs

'If you like your thrillers darkly comic and
outrageous this ticks all the boxes'
Sun

'SO dark, SO laugh-out-loud funny, the world through
Rhiannon's eyes is perfectly, acutely observed. Brilliant!'
SJI Holliday

C J Skuse was born in 1980 in Weston-super-Mare. She has two First Class degrees in Creative Writing and Writing for Young People, and aside from being a novelist works as a Senior Lecturer at Bath Spa University.

Also by C J Skuse:
The Alibi Girl

Sweetpea Series:
Sweetpea
In Bloom

For Young Adults:
Pretty Bad Things
Rockoholic
Dead Romantic
Monster
The Deviants

DEAD HEAD

C J SKUSE

ONE PLACE. MANY STORIES

HQ
An imprint of HarperCollins*Publishers* Ltd
1 London Bridge Street
London SE1 9GF

www.harpercollins.co.uk

HarperCollins*Publishers*
1st Floor, Watermarque Building,
Ringsend Road, Dublin 4, Ireland
This edition 2021

1
First published in Great Britain by
HQ, an imprint of HarperCollins*Publishers* Ltd 2021

MIX
Paper from
responsible sources
FSC™ C007454

This book is produced from independently certified FSC™ paper
to ensure responsible forest management.

For more information visit: www.harpercollins.co.uk/green

This book is set in 10.7/15.5 pt. Sabon

Printed and bound in Great Britain by
CPI Group (UK) Ltd, Croydon, CR0 4YY

For Alex, Josie and Joshua

Three for Three

How can I be substantial without casting a shadow?
I must have a dark side too if I am to be whole.

CARL GUSTAV JUNG,
FOUNDER OF ANALYTICAL PSYCHIATRY

Wednesday, 22 January 2020 – Barnes & Noble, Fifth Avenue, New York City

1. *Space invaders – arm overspill, leg overstep, sole of shoe overhang*
2. *Woman on her phone coming out of Sephora who barged into me and told me to apologise. Have wheelchair, must have attitude it seems*
3. *Cab drivers who stink of beefy crotch sweat*
4. *That jowly cuck news guy Guy Majors*
5. *Grandpa Joe – you lazy, lazy bastard*

You can smell Bryan coming. He's the store manager. He bounds onto the makeshift stage with all the elegance of a dying rhino – grey trousers at half-mast, stain on hurriedly bought tie, pustules along his chin, greasy hair scraped into an elastic band by fingernails caked up with newsprint and old cum.

We're on the mezzanine. Twenty lines of chairs in the endless Biographies section. It's standing room only. I'm at the back, facing the aisle between a woman with a bulky handbag and a MAGA-capped Hulk Hogan lookalike with more earrings than actual ear. At the front, behind two vacant stools and mic stands, is a huge poster of the book cover with my face on:

THE SWEETPEA KILLER:
The True Confessions of Rhiannon Lewis

They've gone to town on decorations. Paper lei garlands draped over bookshelves, fake roses dangling from jutting Barbra Streisand memoirs, fake petals scattered around the carpet. Everyone on seats or standing is carrying a copy of the book.

My book.

Wow wow wow, fellas. Look at the old girl now, fellas.

They're giving out iced biscuits too. Flower-shaped – nice touch. The tray is empty by the time it gets to me, of course. Typical. God forbid someone nips out the back to open another packet and refill it.

I spent the best part of my twenties trying to get a book deal. And now I have a bestselling book out with *my* face on the cover and *my* story within the pages and it's been at the top of the (non-fiction) bestseller lists for the last four months. The only problem is I can take none of the credit. No glow radiates on me.

Opportunity has knocked and, once again, I'm fucking out.

Not *one* of those Best Book Awards or Author of the Year awards or invitations to New York Fashion Week has *my* name on it. They all have *his* name on it: Freddie Litton-Cheney. The man whose name is on the cover *above* mine. He is the author – I am merely his muse.

'Hey, everyone, thanks so much for coming out on this freezing night,' Bryan laughs nervously into his mic. 'A few more minutes and we'll welcome our special guest to the stage.' He reads out some fire regs and notices of upcoming events with Michelle Obama and that owl who saved the kids from the barn fire, before bouncing off, black T-shirt patchy with sweat.

Clearly there's an issue. The star turn has thrown a wobbler over the blue M&Ms or the wrong puppies they got him to play with in the green room while he waits. Nevertheless, all gussets throb with anticipation.

Freddie asked me once why I wasn't milking my fame more, back in the days when Craig had just been banged up for my crimes and I found myself basking in 'his' reflected glory. I'd been offered a shit ton of telly work and magazines to tell my story as Girlfriend of a Serial Killer. Could have earned thousands. He said I was a headliner – *I* should be centre stage, like Deloris Van Cartier in *Sister Act*. And now here I am, centre stage – and everyone's throwing flowers at my understudy. I couldn't answer him then. I can now.

Bryan gets a message and bounds back on and through his sheen of sweat announces:

'OK we're ready now so please put your hands together for tonight's guest. We are *so* privileged he's been able to stop by on his tour of the States, and he's fresh from a recording of *The Ellen Show* too, I'm told—'

Cue the chorus of 'woo hoos' and palpable hum of excitement.

'—and he has to fly to Chicago straight after this event—'

'Woo hoo' squared.

'Mr Freddie Litton-Cheney!'

And on he bounds, with infinitely more elegance and poise than old Cum-Nails Bryan. Freddie's in his highly polished Tom Ford loafers, a tailored cream suit and trousers so tight you can see the dead presidents on his pocket change. His grin is predictably shit-eating and as knicker-wettingly seductive as ever and I can almost hear the distant explosion of a thousand ovaries.

No wonder he's a star.

'Thanks so much, everybody.' He nods with a polite British wave, before manspreading widely atop his stool so The Bulge cannot be ignored. Every one of us is now pregnant with his child. Even the chairs.

He shakes hands with Bryan – poor bastard – but to his credit doesn't wipe it off afterwards. Hulk Hogan next to me and a couple of younger women further along are fixed on Freddie's face. Awestruck. That's the expression. After all, the man they are looking at is the man who has *met* a serial killer. The man who has *hugged* a serial killer. The man who has *the* number one bestselling book *about* said serial killer.

And that serial killer is little old *me*.

'So Freddie, how are you enjoying New York City?' asks Bryan, slurping up some rogue drool as a few dandruff flakes float from this thatch.

'Oh, it's great. I've been well looked after by my publisher—'

Freddie informs the crowd that he has already done a tour of major news networks, which produces a third 'woo hoo' from a woman in a neck brace on the Frow. He has quite the following. A whole herd of leather trousers gaze up at him – all snap-happy with their phones, all hair-did specially. The fact

Freddie has been happily married to another man for years, with whom he has two children, doesn't put them off. Every hand gesture, every hair flick is to be admired. Every time he says something mildly suggestive, they yank off their knickers and several sodden Tena Ladys fly at his face.

OK that's a lie, but I'm sure they're one neat vodka away from doing so.

'You've heard all about the book already of course,' he says, 'but part of the reason why I'm doing this tour—'

International fame and a fat stack of cold hard cash?

'—is that I want to give people the chance to ask me any questions about it, about Rhiannon herself and the time I spent with her—'

I choke back a guffaw. He doorstepped me twice and bought me one ice cream. Our conversation ranged from our favourite doughnut to reasons why *Back in the Habit* is the best *Sister Act* movie. We're hardly besties.

'—I'm interested in what everyone's views are on Rhiannon and the whole story, having read the book. Have y'all read the book yet?'

I don't know why he's saying 'y'all' like he's some hickory-smoked banjo strummer from the Bible Belt – he's from Torquay. Anyway, a chorus of 'Yeahs!' follow and he grins. Once upon a time that grin could have supplexed me into a mattress and skewered me like a kebab. Now it just irritates.

Bryan invites Freddie to do a reading from said book. And I have to stand there listening to him putting the emphases on all the wrong words so my jokes fall flat and it's all I can do to stop myself getting up, grabbing the mic and doing it myself. I can't *bear* it when people tell jokes ineffectually.

After the reading, Bryan asks a series of tedious questions which are basically segues into his own book about serial killers and his time working with them – he'd visited Ted Bundy's cousin's niece once in jail or something. I drifted off to a nearby shelf to flick through a Patricia Highsmith biography, only half-listening.

I perk up when the convo swivels back to me.

'The British media dubbed Rhiannon "Little Miss Vigilante" and "Ripperella". Are those fair nicknames, do you think?'

'Yeah, I guess so,' Freddie smiles, teeth a-twinkling, and you can almost hear the elastic snapping on each pair of knickers on the Frow. 'I think Rhiannon would have liked those names.'

I didn't.

'A lot of readers have reported that they found themselves rooting for her as they read the account, myself included actually—'

Yawn. Nobody cares, Bryan.

'—did *you* root for her as you were reading her diaries for the first time?'

'Yeah, for sure,' says Freds. 'I can see why people took to her. She was kind to animals and children and the vulnerable. She once saved a woman from being raped. She's extremely popular in the UK, still is. There was a survey on British TV, not long after the story broke – 90 per cent of the respondents said they wouldn't call the police if they met her.'

'That's extraordinary,' says Bryan, with no meaning behind it because he's too busy getting lost in his notes for the next question. 'But there were a few particularly shocking killings, weren't there?'

'Dean Bishopston for sure, yeah. He was merely a taxi driver in the wrong place at the wrong time. And AJ Thompson, the father of her baby. He was only 19. They did nothing wrong.'

'But just because the other people *did* do wrong, the guys in the van, the old pederast, it doesn't mean they deserved to die, does it?'

A hush descends. My eyebrow involuntarily rises as though it's trying to grow an extra ear to hear Freddie's answer to this one.

'Nobody *deserves* to die, of course,' he says on a long exhale, 'but in Rhiannon's mind, sex offenders and paedophiles were fair game.'

'Was she raped herself?' asks Bryan, escalating the chat with admirable aplomb. 'Was that why she held sex offenders in such particular disdain?'

'If she *was*, she never mentioned it in the diaries,' replies Freddie. 'It could explain a lot but I have no evidence to suggest that, no.'

'What about the grandfather?' calls out an achingly thin woman with red hair three rows from the back. 'The one she watched die in the river?'

Freddie looks in the woman's general direction. 'That can't be proven, madam. She certainly didn't divulge such information to me.'

'What kind of vibe did she give off?' asks Bryan. 'Were you scared in her company?'

'I didn't know what Rhiannon had done when I met her. I thought she was simply Craig Wilkins' girlfriend and he was on remand for multiple murder. I thought she was a victim. I felt sorry for her but no, I wasn't scared of her.'

Bryan's practically rubbing his crotch by this point. 'What was it like when you got that mail with her diaries in?'

'It was an ordinary morning, a few days into the New Year. My husband had gone off to work. I was taking our kids swimming and the postman rang the door. I had a parcel and I left it on the dining table.'

'You didn't open it up right away?'

'No, I assumed it was some books I'd ordered for my husband for his birthday. They were coming from Australia.'

'Right, right.'

Two mentions now of the husband but the Frow don't seem to have noticed. One brunette is visibly unbuttoning her blouse.

'When I got back, I made the kids lunch and we settled down to watch a film – *Coco*, I think it was. I put the parcel in the wardrobe and forgot it.'

Cue audible gasp.

'I know, it's crazy, isn't it? But my husband's birthday wasn't till February so I thought I'd wrap it up nearer the time. About two weeks later, the parcel fell out of the wardrobe while I was packing away some blankets and I opened it to have a look at the books. Instead it was these two handwritten diaries. On the front it said "The True Confessions of Rhiannon Lewis, aged 27/28".'

Another audible gasp.

'And it began on New Year's Eve 2017 with her realising her boyfriend Craig was having an affair. It went on to talk about her life in minute detail, and included the murders of various people. Planning it, doing it, covering it up. I couldn't believe what I was reading.'

'Wow, that's completely *amazing*.'

'I read them in two days. I barely slept. From the first chapter when she killed that guy by the canal and sliced off his penis, I was stunned—'

That bloody penis, it never stops coming up. The media's always obsessed by that, even though there was only one. I haven't severed a cock since but even so some magazines still insist on calling me The Slicer which sounds pretty cool, but others call me Lorena Bobbitt Two, Cock-A-Doodle Daisy or Buffy the Wangpire Slayer, which doesn't even work. The first thing they ALWAYS mention is that fucking dick.

I HAVE DONE OTHER THINGS. Now I know how Daniel Radcliffe feels.

'So was it just the diaries she sent you? The full confession we all know?'

'And a postcard,' says Freddie.

'What did it say on the postcard?'

Freddie smiles, a secret smile. 'The postcard said, *When you're shoving your foot in the door, make sure you're wearing a big shoe.*'

There follows a light-hearted but confused murmuring in the audience.

Freddie explains. 'It relates to the last conversation we had. I told Rhiannon I was leaving the *Plymouth Star*, the local newspaper I used to work for, but that I still wanted to get "a foot in the door" of journalism.'

'So she helped you?' asks Bryan, swatting away a fly that seems hella interested in his left ear. Probably a doughnut parked in there for later.

'Rhiannon Lewis has changed my life,' says Freddie and the room goes silent. So quiet you can hear a fake petal fall. 'She wanted her story to be told and she assigned *me* to tell it. My husband said I should take the manuscripts straight to the police. It was evidence after all and there was her ex-boyfriend

Craig Wilkins, looking at a life sentence for the crimes on those pages. We had an argument about it because I was so keen to get the story out there—'

And make shitloads of money off it—

'—but in the end I did the right thing. I gave them to the police, but not before I'd made copies. I couldn't do anything with them at that point because I'd fall foul of sub-judicial procedure but as soon as the CPS made the decision to charge Rhiannon in absentia, I took the risk.'

Bryan scratched his temple. 'They had a trial in the UK, didn't they?'

'Yeah, they had a trial with a jury and they sentenced her to life, with a minimum forty-year tariff. They issued a warrant for her arrest—'

'—but they never found her,' Bryan clarified.

'Quite.'

'I don't get how they had evidence to jail her without her being there to go to jail,' said Bryan, like it was the most ludicrous thing he'd ever heard.

'They had enough evidence – a written confession in her own handwriting, bearing details only the killer could possibly know. They just didn't have *her*.'

'Ah right. So eventually, you were allowed to release the book?'

'Yeah, once she'd been confirmed as deceased, there was nothing stopping me. The rest is history.' He beams up at the humongous poster.

*Her*story, you mean. Prick.

'That's incredible,' says Bryan. 'So your book went on sale globally in September and it's sky-rocketed, hasn't it?'

'Yeah, it's caught fire.'

'Correct me if I'm wrong but it's been published in thirty-four countries, is that right?'

'I believe it's thirty-six now. And we've sold the film rights too.'

'Oh wow,' says Bryan. Cue gasping, flailing and a rapturous applause.

Yawn.

'It's been life-changing. I can pay my bills without worrying now, myself and my husband have new cars, our kids are in good schools—'

Freddie talks with ease, enthusiasm, and occasionally expressive flourishes of his arms. Piano player's hands. Creative fingers. His eyes are alive and passionate about his subject, which in this case happens to be *moi*.

Twenty hands shoot up into the coffee-thick air of the bookshop as we come to the Q&A.

'How do you think she got out of the UK, Freddie?' whines a Roseanne Barr-esque woman with purple hair, fifth row from the front.

'I don't know for sure,' says Freds.

'Neither do the cops!' a Metallica-beard dude shouts from the back.

'Well, quite,' Freddie chuckles. 'According to the police, the last phone signal that came through on her mobile bounced off a transmitter on the Western Esplanade in Southampton which suggests she left from Southampton Docks, doesn't it? But there was no record of anyone called Rhiannon Lewis boarding a cruise ship at the terminal. She simply disappeared.'

'Did she catch a ride on some smaller boat?' suggests a small guy near me who had been watching videos of himself dicking about with his cat on Tik Tok before the gig had got going.

'There were theories that she was hiding in Portugal or Spain with one of her dad's cronies. There were sightings of her in Africa, Thailand, Buenos Aires as well but there was no telling what was true.'

Old Lady Chunky Blue Heels on the aisle shoots her bingo wing up. 'What do you think made Rhianna murder in the first place, Mr Cheney?'

Rose West Fucking Wept – my name's on the cover of the damn book she's bought and she *still* can't say it right.

'Could be any manner of things,' says Freddie. 'We could speculate that it comes from the brain injury she suffered when she was six. Her father was a vigilante and she used to watch him at work in wild fascination for his violence – and this was from an early age, remember.'

Cue serious faces all round, one batting of eyelids and several lost little headshakes. Poor kid, poor *poor* Rhianna.

'Studies have shown that children with weak or dispassionate relationships with their mothers often lapse into patterns of violent crime—'

He's talking like a criminology YouTuber. I'm briefly impressed.

'—or you could surmise that she was just a bad seed.'

'Amen,' says Old Lady Chunky Blue Heels.

A woman with a beaky nose and Pot Noodle perm gets the roving mic. 'Did you get to interview her sister? Do you know how she feels about it all?'

'No, she wouldn't talk to me,' says Freddie. 'She wanted no part in this story. Which is ironic when you consider her role in it.'

Another Texan throwback pipes up. 'I read that most serial killers don't just stop killing – that there may be a cooling-off period but that they never stop because it is a predilection which cannot ever be curbed or rehabilitated. Now what I want to know and what you might be able to tell me, sir—'

There's always one. It's as certain as the scrawny autistic kid will win *Countdown* – the guy who takes as long as he pleases to ask a question.

'—in your opinion do you think she carried on killing people after she left the UK, sir? Because we don't know anything about what she did after killing that woman at the farm shop up until the point she—'

Freddie butts in. 'Yes, I do. I do think she carried on killing.'

The lesser-known *Carry On* film.

'Rhiannon Lewis is a killer. That's what she did, that's what she *enjoyed*. I've spoken to a number of criminal psychologists while working on the book, and they're all in agreement: there is no way she stopped after Sandra Huggins. She got better at hiding it, that's all. And herself.'

Another arm shoots up. Guy with big cheeks and a stained Jeffrey Dahmer T-shirt gets the mic. His hand's been up a while. He'd cream his jeans if he knew I was in the room.

'Why d'you think Rhian left her story for you to tell, Mr Litton-Cheney?'

'I think I got lucky,' he replies. 'If it hadn't been me, it would have been someone else. Maybe at the newspaper office where she used to work.'

Mmm, no, he has me wrong there. I wouldn't piss on anyone in that office if they were thirsty, let alone give them the scoop of the century.

Woman in yellow coat with too-red lipstick and smokers' mouth creases shoots up a hand. 'I didn't appreciate all the cursing in the book,' she complains. 'Was that your input or hers? Some of it was quite disgusting.'

'It's all hers,' Freddie smiles ruefully.

'Why does she have such a filthy mouth?' the old bint quacks on.

Freddie laughs. 'I don't know why you're more offended by that than her killings, madam, but I guess the amount of rage Rhiannon carried around with her could help to explain it.'

A chorus of giggles follows, like he's offered a wittier *bon mot* than Oscar Wilde. He hasn't, the malodorous cockswerve. Getting *my* laughs. But I might rescind that insult if he defends me again to one of these nobs.

Old man hand goes up. He's bought a stack of books about the Civil War and hasn't bought Freddie's yet. This is clearly a subject too beneath him to spend good money on but he was in the bookshop anyway and it's a free event so he thought, *Why not*? 'That last murder in the dairy – why was it so disproportionately brutal, do you think?'

It was a farm shop but thanks for listening.

'Well, she had just given birth,' says Freddie. 'I think it may have been a hormonal surge. She'd been tracking Sandra Huggins for some time.'

My chest clenches with the mention of the birth but I sweep it away quickly, thankful that one of the Frow blondes, who's had so much facial surgery she looks like she's been set on fire and stamped out, finally gets her time to shine.

'Hey, Freddie.' Cue inexplicable giggle. 'It's so great to meet you.' Another giggle. 'We met when you were doing a signing in Austin last week—'

'Oh yeah, I remember you, thanks for coming along.' He clearly doesn't remember her at all. I'm better at reading people's real meanings now. His tongue paints the lie while his eyes shield the truth.

'Could you tell us what you working on now?' Another inexplicable giggle.

'Uh, I have a few ideas in the pipeline that I'm working on but to be honest with you, this one has taken over my life somewhat.' He scratches his eyebrow. 'There's so many people who want to hear Rhiannon's story and in lieu of Rhiannon herself, it has befallen me to tell it.'

Hmmm, chin rub. Sounds disturbingly like he's run out of ideas. Hardly surprising since *I* was the one who gave him *this* one.

I want to ask him a question, but refrain from doing so because that's who I am now: reticent. Quiet. Calm. As invisible as mist. There but not there.

Pretty soon the Q&A comes to an end and Bryan announces where Freddie will be sitting to sign books. Everyone rushes off. A tall Trump pout-alike with tits to her knees pushes me out of the way to get in front, her too-fat-for-rings fingers clutching my story like a portable life support machine.

I retrieve my bag and my box from under a table of half-eaten iced biscuits and pass a stand with the few remaining books on. I pick one up. On the central pages there are pictures – me and Craig on some night out, me with the PICSOs – People I Can't Shake Off – me looking bored next to Elaine at some prayer evening, banging a tambourine. Joining WOMBAT

– the Women of Monks Bay and Temperley – had been a brief and ill-fated attempt to get good with God. I didn't last long before they kicked my ass out.

A line snakes back from Freddie's signing table. I take the book to the tills.

And I wait. Listening to the chatter. Theories. Opinions. Did my mother hit me? Did I actually kill my own dad? Why did I use so much cling film when I chopped AJ up and buried him in the flower beds – didn't I care about the environment at all? I watch Freddie, sipping his Huel, interacting with his fans, posing for selfies, kissing cheeks, baptising babies, curing cancer.

My turn comes. I stand before the table and slide the book towards him.

'Hey, thanks for coming.' He smiles easily, looking up briefly before opening the front cover, readying his pen. 'What name was it?'

I clear my throat. 'Deloris.'

'De-lo-ris,' he writes.

'—Van Cartier,' I add in my best American accent.

He slowly looks up at me, his smile vanishing as colour drains from his cheeks. His pen hovers but after a moment he hands the book back trying not to look directly at me. I don't take it from him until our eyes meet.

He stares until he blinks. His brow sweats. Gotcha.

'Thank you,' I say. 'Fancy meeting me for a drink? If you've got time.'

His mouth hangs open, but snaps shut quickly. 'I h-h-have a flight.'

'Ah, no worries.' His fingertips press down on the page he's signed. 'Hey, be careful, don't smudge the ink.'

The lady behind me giggles, gazing at Freddie adoringly. She doesn't hear our conversation because my voice is set to a volume only he can hear and everyone else is gossiping too loudly. He reaches for his drink again.

'There's a bar down the street. Sluggers. I'll be in there.'

He nods as the giggle bitch urges me out of the way so she can have Freddie to herself, starting with some interminable anecdote about how she's making a special pilgrimage to attend every event on his US tour. She asks for a selfie and a 'cheeky smooch'. She's a Brit. Ugh. They're everywhere.

Freddie stares at me as I walk away from his table, a trickle of sweat snaking down his temple. I wouldn't have been surprised to see a trickle of piss escaping the confines of those tight tight trews.

I head straight out into the icy wind howling up Fifth Avenue towards Sluggers which is dark but atmospheric and I grab the last booth, furthest away from the TV monitors booming out some baseball game – the Cincinnati Cocksuckers versus the New England Bollockheads or something.

I don't have to wait long. As sure as huevos is huevos, Freddie walks in half an hour later, breathing heavily as if he ran here.

'That was quick,' I say as he approaches my booth. I close his book that I've started reading and push his beer towards him.

'Told Bryan I wasn't feeling well.' He slides in opposite me. He hasn't taken his eyes off me.

'Take your coat off then, if you're stopping.'

He wriggles himself out of it with some difficulty because, like everything he wears, it's a size too small. Still can't catch his breath. His eyes drift to the square box beside me. To my bag, my folded-up coat. Back to me.

'So... how have you been?' I ask.

It takes him ages to speak and when he does, it's almost too quiet to hear. 'You're dead. You're... *dead.*'

I check my pulse in my neck with two fingers. 'Nope, still here.'

'They identified you. *Seren* identified you. They shut the case. But ... you're *here.*'

'Yes, Freddie.' I remove Richard E. Grunt from my pocket and make him do a wave. *'I'm here too, Freddie,'* Richard squeaks.

Freddie's eyes go too wide. He still hasn't touched his beer.

'I didn't drug it, if that's what you're worried about.'

He nods, looking down at the bottle. 'I don't understand this. You look... like a different person.'

I pocket Richard and sip my cocktail. 'Yeah, I kind of am.'

He peeks under my Yankee cap, looks around my face, down to my denim dungaree dress and roll-neck. 'I didn't recognise you.'

'That's the general idea.'

Freddie goes into the kind of blink overdrive you only do in a sandstorm.

I sip my drink. 'Mmm, this is lovely. It's called a Pink Panther. Vodka, pineapple juice and grenadine. Did I tell you about the time I was on the dole and I got a job dressing up as the Pink Panther giving out leaflets on Weston-super-Mare seafront? Only lasted a day. Five pounds fifty-seven an hour to climb into a sweatsuit a million nonces had wanked in? So not worth it.'

'Rhiann—'

'—no, no no, don't speak the name that shall not be spoken, Freddo.'

He leans in as a home run is scored and loud booming cheers go up around the bar. 'How did you do it? How?'

'Wouldn't *you* like to know?'

'I have money. From the book. I've put it to one side. I did everything you wanted me to. Changed your friend's name, your solicitor, your dad's friends—'

'Didn't matter anyway. They still arrested Heather *and* Marnie for "aiding and abetting". Never caught Keston though.'

'No. He vanished.'

'We're good at that. I was glad Marnie and Heather didn't do jail time.'

'They both spoke up for you.'

'I know. Good friends. The PICSOs all sang like canaries. Hashtag bad friends. Still, it's nice when the trash takes itself out.' I drained my Pink Panther and signalled to the waitress for another one.

'You seem… happy. Confident. Sort of settled.'

'Shouldn't I be?'

He shakes his head and sinks a few gulps of his beer. Wipes his mouth. Looks back to the bar. Looks back at me. 'Am I dreaming?'

The cluster of fat, baseball-capped men around the TV screens whoop at something and there follows a hasty symposium on whether the referee's decision is correct or not. Someone didn't hit a ball right or something.

'I can get it to you, the money. A fake account or something—'

'That's not why I'm here.'

'It's not?'

'Nope. I'm on a layover. Had some time to kill before my connection. Brought a present for someone…' I tap the top of the box, 'and I was walking past the bookstore when I saw the poster in the window. Thought I'd stop by and say hello. Complete coincidence.'

'A layover from where? Where do you live? Where have you been?'

'I could tell you some stories but you have a flight to catch.'

Freddie takes a deep breath, checks his Breitling Chronomat watch – ten grand's worth – lets the breath go. 'I'm going to miss it.'

'Not if you run. You can get a cab right outside—'

'No,' he says, staring me down. 'I *am* going to miss it.' He fumbles for his phone and clicks into his voice recorder app.

'No, Freds,' I say, holding down his hand. He looks at my hand like a tarantula's crawled into view.

'Can I at least make notes?'

'If you must.' He fumbles in his knapsack for a pen and a battered leather-bound journal, opening it out to a brand-new double page, smoothing it down and breaking the spine. 'What do you want to know?'

'Everything,' he says, eyes flicking towards the box again. 'Absolutely everything.'

PART 1: Europe

Wednesday, 22 January 2020 – Sluggers Bar, Fifth Avenue, New York City

'I had to get to Madeira. Bobby Fairly had it all worked out from there.'

'Bobby Fairly, Bobby Fairly,' Freddie mutters, furiously scribbling in writing I recognise from my *Gazette* days as shorthand. I never did shorthand. They wouldn't pay to send me on the course. He riffles through a list of bullet point reminders. 'There's no Bobby Fairly mentioned in your confession.'

'Well, there wouldn't be. He wasn't integral to my former story. He'd been a friend of my dad's from his boxing days.'

'A vigilante like Keston Hoyle?'

'No, Bobby was a money man. Funded my dad's gym, sponsored him and Keston when they boxed for the county. Sent care packages to Dad in jail, all sorts. Probably cos Dad had something on him. Bobby was one dodgy fucker from what I've learned. Anyway, I found his number in the shoebox of trinkets I'd saved from my parents' house before I sold it.'

'Did you know him?'

'I met him once, when I was six. Before Priory Gardens. We'd gone on holiday to Madeira and stayed at his hotel – me, Mum, Dad and Seren. I have flashes of memory from that week – me and Seren playing on pool noodles pretending they were horses. Eating cake with green bits in. Going down a hill in a big basket. A dead lizard in the bath. I didn't kill it.'

'Right, OK,' says Freddie, turning back to his half-empty page.

'So Bobby lived on Madeira and I called him to arrange it a few days before the end of the year.'

'Just get here and I'll sort everything,' he'd told me. He didn't even ask what I'd done – I said it was a Code Red and he understood. He was Northern. Sounded like Shaun Ryder's asthmatic grandad.

'And I'd like an American passport.'

Cue the sharp intake of breath, the clicking of tongue, the cogs whirring. 'Right, well that'll be one fifty.'

'One hundred and fifty pounds? That's reasonable.'

Cue the throaty laugh. 'That's *grand*, love. A hundred and fifty *grand*.'

'GRAND?'

'Well, yeah.'

'One hundred and fifty GRAND? That's nearly all my money!'

'That's what sanctuary costs nowadays. That includes a new passport, your place to stay while you recuperate from your surgery and yer—'

'*Surgery?*' I shrieked. 'You mean I have to go full Mickey Rourke?'

'If necessary. And we're fast-tracking it, so that's what it's gonna cost.'

'Fuck me pink and slice me sideways!'

'Do a BACS transfer – get it done today, then it'll come out before New Year. In't meantime, get disconnected. Close all your digital doors.'

'Yeah I have. Just my phone to go.'

'Get rid. Cut up your credit cards 'n'all. We'll set up the odd account to plant some disinformation. I can get that going today. Make it look like you've gone to Argentina or Uzbekistan.'

'Why would I go to Uzbekistan?'

'Don't matter, does it? We're planting false seeds. The police'll be rattling every cage fo' yer, including mine eventually.'

'OK so I googled some flights from Exeter Airport and there's one to Madeira leaving—'

'—no, no, not a flight and not direct,' he interrupted. 'A cruise. That's what you want. Anything leaving from Southampton via Madeira for two weeks or more. And book it for *two* people. You and your husband,'

'Book a cruise for *two* people for *two* weeks? That'll cost a fortune!'

'You said money weren't a problem. I mean, faking your death would be cheaper if you wanted to go down *that* road—'

'—no, I don't want to die. Not yet anyway.'

'Right, so book it.'

'Won't they be suspicious of a lone woman getting off a cruise midway?'

'Not if you book a *partial* cruise, no. Tell them you want to sail to Madeira, then hop off and say you and your husband intend to rejoin the ship at, say, Barcelona or somewhere. No, Italy. *Rome*, Civitavecchia. By the time you're due to rejoin the voyage, you'll be well gone and the dibble won't have a clue. How up the shoot are yer?'

'Do you mean my pregnancy? I'm thirty-three weeks. Ish.'

'What's that in English?'

'Nearly eight months.'

'Pad it out for now so you look dead fat. And we'll need to get documents sorted for it when t'time comes. Any friends or family?'

'No, I don't have any.'

'You must do.'

'Well, there's Seren and Marnie but—'

'Don't go near their social media and don't google yourself. Once they know you're gone that's something they'll monitor. The dibble have got software that'll intercept key words and search patterns. They'll tap into any search they think you'll make.'

For a crusty, he was quite internet savvy. I was impressed. He'd clearly talked someone through this before. 'What will happen exactly when I get to you?'

'I'll sort it, don't worry. I'll make some calls today. You get yourself to my gaff. You can play purser on my yacht while you lie low, get your sea legs and then we'll get you gone. All right, cock?'

'Gone where?'

'South America, most likely. I've got a few contacts who owe me favours. I'll see what I can sort out. You changed your image yet?'

'I bought a wig and some lenses for my passport. Keston got me an Australian one. If I go somewhere remote, I might not *need* surgery though?'

'Oh, you will. If you're as hot property as you say, and you want to re-integrate, you're gonna need a new face. It don't hurt for long. You have to wear bandages for a few weeks. You'll look hangin' for a bit but once they come off, you'll look and feel mint. Like, brand new and that. You'll still feel like yer a hundred and fucking eighty but you'll look dead good, swear down.'

'Great.'

'But before that, the more immediate stuff is a case of adapting. You've got to change every habit for a new one, swear down. Become someone else quick as you can, like.'

'How? How do I change every habit?'

'Do the opposite of everything. Change your shopping habits, the food you eat, the food you *don't* eat. 'Ast any hobbies and that?'

'Gordon Ramsay programmes. Sylvanian Families. Sadistic torture.'

'Anything that can mark you out as Rhiannon Lewis you've got to jettison, dead quick. What sort of scran do you like?'

'Maoams. Pancakes. Pop Tarts. Anything in Nutella. Coffee.'

'Not anymore. Get into all that wellness bollocks – edamame beans, protein powder, kombucha, all that sorta crap. I know it sounds painful, believe me I couldn't get me underpants on of a morning if I haven't had a Full English but needs must. Quit alcohol 'n'all, get into that green shit they're all drinking. You educated?'

'Eight GCSEs, three A Levels, degree in—'

'—not anymore. Act dead thick. Wouldn't know shit if you swallowed it.'

'Fucking Hell's bells.'

'And stop swearing. And stay away from anyone British and from CCTV. Try and change your accent 'n'all.'

'I've been practising Australian. I watched the end of *Neighbours* today.'

'Good. Watch *Home and Away* 'n'all. And that film wit' her whose face don't move. Keep working on it. Once your story breaks, all ears'll be pinned back for a British voice, especially a bird on her own.'

It all seemed like a lot of extra work. 'Fu-dging he-ck.' Polite swear words tasted like arse in my mouth.

'The price for freedom is everything you once were, Rhiannon. Text me when you've booked your cruise and lemme know what date you get here. Ditch your phone. And don't call me again.'

'Are you sure you can get me gone?'

'Consider it sorted. Just get to my gaff. And do the transfer, there's a good girl.'

'OK. Thanks,' I mewed, still uncertain about the patronising prick but unfortunately that prick was the one prick from which my future hanged. Bobby had enough dodgy contacts to keep me and the baby hidden forever.

'But you didn't take the baby with you?' says Freddie, mid-scribble, smoke emanating from the nib of his Visconti ball-point.

'No. She arrived early on 27 December, the day Bobby

28

received my money. The day *before* I was to set sail on the *Flor de la Mer*. I had to leave her behind.'

He nods. 'This was before you killed Sandra Huggins?'

'Yes. Just before.'

Freddie clears his throat and flicks through his notes. 'You got your solicitor to sign her over to Claudia Gulper, is that right?'

'Yeah. I was so hell-bent on turning old Huggins into a one-woman Red Wedding, the baby was a mere obstacle. Once she was gone, I could let rip.'

'Do you regret leaving her behind?'

A gnawing began in my chest. A biting, vicious little pain I try to push down. 'You're a serial killer who has just hacked a woman to pieces and stuck her head on a large singing Santa, on the same day you've given birth and abandoned your baby at the hospital. You're all alone having fled the UK with leaking nipples, an aching vajoodle and police hot on your arse who will throw the key away if they catch you. How do you *think* I was feeling?'

Monday, 31 December 2018 –
at sea – one day to Madeira

1. *Hen parties on cruise ships*
2. *Stag parties on cruise ships*
3. *Old people on cruise ships who take their sweet time
   to get around cos they know they've only got the
   buffet and the grave to get to now*
4. *Other people on cruise ships, including the captain
   whose boring updates keep cutting into my naps*
5. *My sister, Seren*

As it turned out, I'm not a great traveller.

The baby blues kicked in the moment the ship left
Southampton. And those fuckers kick *hard*, lemme tell you.
I became a smelly, sobbing zombie who stayed in her cabin
for the most part, eating junk, bleeding from my loosy goosey
and watching re-reruns of *Friends* – the older episodes before
Phoebe's wig, Chandler's weight fluctuations and Rachel's
constant nipples.

I was all at sea, emotionally, physically, literally. From
the time I boarded the ship on 28 December to my port of

sanctuary, I had four days. Four days to wait it out. Four days to stay as invisible as possible. Four days to bide my time and pray the British police force was as slow and inept as I'd always hoped they would be.

My cabin became my own sort of womb – all-encompassing. Safe. Cool and calming, absorbed from most noise, save tannoy announcements, the low hum of the distant engines and the occasional smattering of Mediterranean rain on my sloping window. I was on Deck 9, Room 510 at the front or the 'forward' and my stateroom overlooked the helipad, underneath the radar.

Just the way I liked it.

But it was purgatory with a travel kettle and tiny soaps. I told the room steward – Gabriel with the ridiculous biceps and chemical-toilet-blue eyes – that I had sea-sickness which explained why I wasn't joining in with the New Year's fireworks up on deck. The only thing that could tempt me outside was a visit to the on-board pharmacy for more king-sized pantyliners to mop up my endless womb leakings. I had nobody to talk to, save Richard E. Grunt and The Man in the Moon, but they never talked back. It's not like Alexa – you can't ask a question and get an instant answer. After a while, I stopped trying.

My third day at sea, sick of the *Friends* theme tune and feeling like a lump of clay, I managed to wash and ventured a walk around the *Flor de la Mer* at the ass crack of dawn. I couldn't get my bearings at all – it was a confusing puzzle of corridors, lifts, spangly staircases, auditoriums, fountains, casinos, designer shops, clubs, pubs, pools, pizza shacks, sushi restaurants and cafés, linked together by a chaotic swirl of blue carpet.

My body was not mine anymore. It had stretch marks in new places, sags in others, unexpected leaks everywhere. I couldn't look in a mirror without wanting to smash it. I had aches and pains and constant mind fog. My anger – the scaffolding that kept me upright – had disappeared.

There was no more yearning to hack down every Tom Dick and Harriet who pushed past me in the line for bagels. No desire to do anything other than sob and sleep. Had the old me slid out along with Ivy's afterbirth? I didn't have a clue. I located the Business Centre in the bowels of the ship and bought myself some Internet access – $17.00 for the day, I shit you not. I needed to google my post-partum symptoms to check they were all normal. And for the most part, they were. I ticked every box:

1. *'After pains as your uterus contracts back' – tick. I was popping paracetamol like Maltesers.*
2. *Night sweats – tick*
3. *Absence of libido – tick. Normally I can get turned on watching the Yorkshire Vet ram his arm up a heffer but since Ivy, Gobi gusset.*
4. *Perineal discomfort – tick. 'Try wearing loose clothes to give it an airing and lukewarm herbal sitz baths to soothe the area,' the website suggested. I had to sit my vadge in a bowl of herbs? FML*
5. *Burning piss – tick*
6. *Sore porn-star tits – Tick. They ached like hot boulders.*

7. *Constant tiredness – tick*
8. *Piles like The Borrowers are stabbing your arsehole with tiny knives – tick*
9. *Incontinence when you sneeze – tick. I always dreamed of being in TLC when I was a kid, little did I know that it meant the Tena Lady Club*
10. *Persistent sadness – tick tick tick tick BOOM.*

All the other advice was to do with the rapid changes to 'the new mum's life' – the sudden sense of responsibility. Breastfeeding. Adjusting to the baby's unpredictable sleep pattern. Dealing with the demands of visitors who all want to *see* the baby. Of course I had none of this but there wasn't a section on Dealing with Giving Birth But There *Being* No Baby.

And that was the worst symptom of all: I missed her. And I couldn't understand why. I was a serial killer, for fuck's sake. Days before I had chopped a woman to pieces and stuck her head on a singing Santa. Serial killers don't *have* feelings. Rose West needed shovels, not cuddles. It takes a lot for me to cry. Even when *Britain's Got Talent* wheels out the hydrocephalic magician who's lost his mum to cancer and they play 'Snow Patrol' when Simon hits the Golden Buzzer – I'm dry as a bone. *Craig* is the one who always buries his head in *What Car?* so I can't see his quivering lip.

But Ivy, apparently, was the difference.

I googled Seren while I was in the Business Centre. I knew I shouldn't have but I wanted to see her face. To see some shred of home. In an ordinary world – in that damn parallel universe where I imagine the correct version of me lives – Seren would be on the end of the phone giving me advice and parcelling up second-hand onesies.

But we weren't in that universe – we were in this one. And I'd given Ivy up so I could keep on killing. And my sister was the one who'd called the cops.

Seren had no online presence to speak of but her nine-year-old daughter Mabli's got a vlog where she talks about her pets and does the odd children's book review and sometimes she'll appear in the background, folding washing or dancing along to a song. I must have watched twenty videos. Most of them were Mabli talking about various pets dying on her. Hamsters, guinea pigs, fish. She was fed up with creatures she loved dying. I felt that.

I googled Wherryman and Armfield too, the solicitors where Heather Wherryman worked – the only person who could tell me what I needed to know, that Ivy was OK. I still had her business card in my purse. My fingers itched to dial her number.

But deep down somewhere, a little thought owl was unravelling from its deep winter's sleep and flapping its wings.

Don't! it squawked. *Don't do it! Too soon! Too soon!*

And, of course, the pesky owl was right.

Aside from a few barflies propping up the counters and the distant trill of jazz coming from the Chill-Out lounge, there didn't seem to be anyone else about as I wandered, through the meandering corridors, up and down deck, as lonely as a twat.

Until I stood at the railings on the top deck, looking out onto the blackest sea, allowing the cold to seep through my clothes, my bones, and a woman in a grubby blue dressing gown appeared, carrying a crying baby.

The sound of that shrill screaming tore right through me. And I couldn't find any anger to divert it either. The sound took me straight back to Ivy. And quicker still to Priory Gardens where my mind got stuck. It took me to smashing glass. Shouting. To our childminder's screams as she scurried upstairs. To the Fireman Sam theme trilling along behind Antony Blackstone as he launched himself at my friends. To that look in his sweaty eyes as he brought his hammer down. To waking up and seeing him hanging up there, swinging back and forth from the wooden eave. To the blood I woke up tasting.

It all started *there*.

'She's still alive! This one, she's got a pulse. It's faint but it's there...'

'It's all right, Sweetpea. You're all right now, nothing can hurt you.'

'Can't seem to settle him,' said the woman in the dressing gown.

I tore back inside the ship like I was a crying toddler myself and the cabin was my dad's open arms. But I got lost. I must have gone to every deck but they all looked the same. I got so confused I couldn't even remember my room number. All I wanted to do was collapse onto my bed and scream.

Chest thumping, mouth dry, legs drained, piles stinging, I gave up and sat as gently as I could on a sofa beside the elevators in the Entertainments Quarter. I was opposite a small cinema – The Classics Lounge – open twenty-four hours. I went inside the empty theatre and settled into a seat at the back. It was Kevin Costner films all night long. *Waterworld* had just started.

I woke up as some wolf was shot dead. Totally different movie.

The sleep did me good. I was at least level enough mood-wise to blend into a snaking line of tourists who were headed up to the main restaurant. There's no such thing as a good time to hit the buffet on a cruise, I learned. There's always an assortment of besandalled old funts coughing around the pancake station, jostling for the strips of bacon that have actually seen an oven and the corners of French toast that don't look like they've been gang-banged.

There were so many people – I wasn't more than an arm's length away from anyone at all times – and yet I'd never felt so alone. Luckily, this feeling of loneliness never lasts long for me because human beings are, basically, cunts. All of them. Eventually. They *are*. You wait.

I must have walked through at least three farts and saw an old man eating half a grapefruit like it was a vagina. It totally curbed my appetite. I found a table to myself, as out of the way of the throng as I could get, and I watched the families congregating.

A man I'd seen walking around the top deck a few times, who I'd dubbed The Man Who Walks, was sitting alone, shaking pepper onto eggs and sausages, gearing himself up for another exhausting day of ambulation. He glanced up at me before looking away.

Misery loves company. But this old misery thought he was a prick.

I was interrupted by a *Breaking News* bulletin on the TV wall opposite.

TENERIFE PLANE CRASH LATEST: Over 200 feared dead

The tickertape along the bottom of Sky News spat out various titbits of information – how the passengers were mostly British and the British Embassy was helping to locate families.

Nothing about Sandra Huggins. Nothing about me. Nobody gave a shit. I watched the other passengers, enjoying their waffles, sipping their coffees, admiring the dolphins.

And I thought: why the hell was I running? What was there to run *to*?

Keston Hoyle had been right: Ivy was my future. And I had given it away to spend a lifetime on the run, killing people who didn't even matter. I had a mouthful of pancake and I couldn't swallow it. I took it out and placed it on the side of my plate. I wondered if I'd have the courage to jump overboard. To dive down into that freezing blue mass and call time on this waste of a life.

But on Day Four the sun rose and the engine shuddered as we pulled into the port of Madeira and dropped anchor. I'd made it to Bobby Fairly's island. Sanctuary. A chance of a future, however alien it felt. And I had already paid him so I at least had to find out what I'd bought, didn't I?

I probably should have topped myself when I had the chance.

Tuesday, 1 January 2019 – Madeira

1. *Couples who indulge in gross amounts of PDA*
2. *People who say they genuinely prefer Scandi Noir to normal Noir. No you fucking don't.*
3. *Influencers. Do I need a reason?*
4. *People who aren't ready to order/pay after a long-assed wait in line*
5. *Pushy bellhops – I've carried my own bag across the continent. Why do you get £20 for carrying it up one flight of stairs?*
6. *The entire British government*

I packed my rucksack, made myself as plain as possible in my white-and-navy holiday shorts and T-shirt combo, brown contact lenses and Sally Bowles wig, which was growing ever more ropey with the salty wind, and headed outside my cabin to whatever life Bobby Fairly had bought me.

The corridor was deserted but for my room steward, Gabriel, folding towels on a cart. He was from Austin, Texas and called me 'Darlin'' a lot which I kinda liked. Time was if you called me 'Darling' or 'Sweetpea' I'd have held a knife to your carotid, but it didn't bother me so much at that moment.

'I'm from Brizzie,' I said, trying out my best Australian accent when he asked me where I was from.

'Brizzie?' he replied.

'Brisbane, Straya?' I said, and his gaze lingered a mite too long. I couldn't tell if it was a *Christ what a terrible Australian accent* gaze or if he'd seen me on a news bulletin.

But then he said, 'Well, have a nice day, Hilary from Brizzie.' And he winked at me. A definite fuck wink.

He was built like Anthony Joshua and ordinarily, I'd have invested in some shameless flirting, but on this occasion there were no gussy flutters to speak of. My piles were throbbing and I'd had a terrible night's sleep. When I had managed to lose myself I'd dreamt about Ivy as a tiny pink butterfly I couldn't catch.

I walked with my head permanently tilted through the corridors, going over my new identity in my mind in the best Aussie accent I could muster.

Hilary Sharp, pleased to meet ya. I'm a ditsy, gym-obsessed clean-living Australian gal born on a sheep farm in Coober Pedy in South Straya. My folks are Moira and Alf Stewart, my brothers are Chris and Liam and I love surfing and barbies and we have a pet kookaburra called Chook...

I didn't even believe me. I just had to get to Bobby and everything would be all right.

But as the lift doors opened on Deck 7, I bumped straight into the couple I'd spoken to when I first came aboard – Ken and Gloria Prosser from Yorkshire. I'd even had my photo taken with them on the gangway. I had hoped that the sheer size of the ship and the number of passengers meant I almost certainly wouldn't come across them again.

Clearly, Fate had other plans.

'Oh hello, petal!' shrieked Gloria, tottering into the lift towards me in her white-and-gold strappies. 'We thought you'd gone overboard!'

'I've... been in the gym, mainly,' I said, phasing in the Aussie accent and affecting my most angelic Bindi Irwin smile. 'Toning myself up so I can load up on the old carbos.' I was thankful for the sunlight streaming in which meant I could reasonably put on my sunglasses to hide my lying bitch eyes.

'Frightened your husband will have gone off you?' Gloria chuckled.

It was only then I remembered what I'd told them – that I was meeting my husband in Madeira. I couldn't even recall if I'd given him a name.

'Yeah,' I said. 'He works out a lot too. We're both real gym... kangaroos.'

'You'd get on with our Ryan,' she said, rolling her eyes as they stepped into the lift beside me. 'Our son lives in the gym, don't he, Ken?'

Ken was studying the day's itinerary, half-moon glasses perched on his nose. 'Yeah, he can't get enough of it. Got muscles like the Statue of David! He's in there now, in't he, Jayde?'

I noticed the woman who'd got into the lift behind them, holding a sleeping baby and gripping the hand of a young boy in a dinosaur onesie picking Smarties from a tiny box. Jayde had black skin, a sparkling, Beyoncé-esque smile, and she wore what I would have worn as Holiday Mum – grey bandeau maxi dress that waterfalled where it didn't cling. She was fucking stunning but I couldn't help staring at the baby in her arms, whose chubby cheek she was stroking. Jayde was everything I wanted to be and everything I wasn't.

'Who's this then?' I said, desperate to seem like the least freaked-out woman around children ever, gesturing towards the baby in her arms.

'This is Sansa and Tyrion,' she replied, scruffling the Smartie boy's hair.

'Pleased to meetcha,' I said, wincing at my own shite accent. '*Game of Thrones* fan, are ya?'

Jayde rolled her eyes. 'Not me, my husband.'

In that parallel universe, there was me saying, 'Mine too! Craig watches it all the time. Fancies that redhead bird married to the Jonas brother.' I'd be nursing our infant daughter and bemoaning my hella predictable spouse and we'd have compared tit milk or something. As it was, the only thing *I* was nursing was the prize for Worst Australian Accent Ever.

Ty shook his empty Smarties box. 'Grandad said I'm being a little shit.'

'Nice,' I laughed. The lift took an arrogantly long time, collecting people on all different floors, but eventually stopping at Deck 16 and the Caravel Breakfast Room. The buffet was already at full steam ahead.

'You coming, luvvie?' said Ken, stepping out.

'Oh, I wasn't going to breakfast. I've had a protein shake instead. Toning up,' I said, patting my sucked-in belly. 'I was heading down to the gangway.'

'You won't be able to disembark yet, love,' said Gloria taking Ty by the hand. 'Might as well get some proper scran inside you. Or steal a couple of croissants at least to have during the day. It's all free.'

'*Pre-paid*,' laughed Ken, jingling his change in his trouser pockets.

'Why can't I disembark?'

'They've got to get the OK from the port authority to get people off and even then it'll be the excursions first. Are you on an excursion today?'

'Er, no.'

'You'll spend hours in't assembly point queue if you go now.'

Ugh, I thought. Fuck My Fake Life.

'Best stay with us, Harriet,' said Ken. 'We'll show you what's what.'

They couldn't even get my *fake* name right. 'It's *Hilary*,' I said. People don't fucking listen, do they?

Anyway, I was stuck there until the Deck 3 gangway was opened so I decided that I could do worse than have the Prossers for an invisibility cloak.

'Fair dinkum, that'd be ripper,' I said, stepping out of the lift before the doors could clang shut behind me.

I Purelled my hands at the hand-wash station and followed Jayde's shining back towards a newly cleared window table with a high chair at one end. 'Glo said you were meeting up with your husband today, is that right?'

I heard the question but I was too fixed on the baby watching me over her shoulder to answer. Eventually, it filtered through. 'Yeah. He's been working out here. I'm meeting him in Madeira and we're travelling round for a bit before we go to the UK. His parents live there. We'll stay with them a few months before going back home to Brizzie.'

It was less an answer, more an alibi.

'What's his name?'

42

'Bruce,' I said, as she deposited Sansa into the high chair. I'm amazed I didn't say Mick Dundee. Thank God she didn't ask what he did on Madeira cos I couldn't think of anything other than 'wine.' He was a 'wine thing'.

'I've really missed him,' I said with a meek Princess Di head dip. 'He works so hard, so I don't have to. He likes a more traditional home life.' I shrugged, happy-go-luckily.

Ugh, I hated 'Hilary' already. I wasn't a Hilary. Hilarys are small and cute and do Pilates and volunteer at Cats Protection. They wear 'pinnies' and have Cath Kidston purses and won't suck a cock in case it smudges their lipstick. I hated this Hilary with her 'gym kangaroo' ebullience, over-toothy grin and homogenised homelife.

And it was only going to get worse. Bobby was going to have me under the knife so I would look even *more* like someone I wasn't.

The price for freedom is everything you once were, Rhiannon.

Gloria returned with the cutlery and glasses of orange juice, taking her seat opposite me and she couldn't help a cursory look down my front – ketchup stain. Bit of string cheese. Dried-on chunk of onion, all from room service bar snacks from the past few days. This was not chiming well with the gym bunny health freak Hilary lie. I had to do better.

'They've got a nice salon on here,' she informed me. 'You could... freshen yourself up for yer fella.'

I gazed at Sansa who was dipping her doll's leg in her yoghurt. She was so beautiful. She had her mum's eyes. I wondered if Ivy had mine.

'Yeah, good idea. I'll get my hair done, I think.' And a whole new wardrobe. And personality. And face.

Three-year-old Tyrion was a rebellious delight. He was the spiller of salt, the tapper of cutlery, the toucher of what he wasn't supposed to and the asker of questions.

Mummy, why has that man got such a big belly?

Mummy, who is the lady sitting with us?

Mummy, why is the water wet?

And on and on and on. For some reason he took to me, moving my face around every time I tried to talk to anyone else. Sansa sort of stared, half-asleep but taking everything in including occasional slurps of doll-leg yoghurt. She was fascinating. It got easier to be around her the longer I had to be. As long as she didn't squawk or cry, I was good. Mood = level.

Ken brought me back scrambled eggs on toast and an orange juice, not that I'd asked for them, and I had to hear all about Gloria's cruise exploits – Zumba classes, the new gel nails that kept coming off, the massages and a flower-arranging class where she'd tried making a 'double-ended feminine spray'. I didn't do the obvious joke because I was Hilary now. The words 'double-ended feminine spray' held no meaning for straight-laced frilly vanilla-y Hilary at all.

'You done any classes yourself yet, Hilary?' she asked.

'No,' I said, resisting the urge to shudder. 'I'm hoping to, though.'

'There's a line dancing class tonight at eight if you're interested.'

Rhiannon was figuratively vomiting into a bucket – Hilary was smiling inanely. 'Do you know, I've always wanted to try that,' I beamed.

When she wasn't extolling the virtues of cruise life, Gloria was pecking at Jayde – *She doesn't need it at the table, love. She's not strapped in properly, love. Ty, you don't need any more jam, petal, that's quite enough isn't it?* Jayde barely said two words until Ken and Gloria went up together to get teas and coffees. Rhiannon wanted a coffee – Hilary opted for green tea. Ugh.

'It were a Christmas present, this holiday,' Jayde confided in me. By the look on her face she might have said *I want to fucking die*.

'Crikey. You're four days in. Think you'll survive three weeks of this?'

She laughed, ruefully. 'Well, there's always overboard, isn't there?'

'Them or you?'

She laughed and rolled her eyes. 'Don't tempt me, please. So what's Australia like? I've never been.'

Thankfully there was a PA announcement about excursions so sadly I couldn't regale her with tales of a country I knew nothing about.

'Are you doing an excursion today?' I asked her, inhaling the hum of cooked egg from my plate and trying not to vom as the thought of aborted chicken babies on toast flitted into my mind.

'Not by choice. They want to do a walking tour through the "mosaic-patterned streets of the old town". Kids are gonna love that, aren't they? Ken wants to do the Valley of the Nuns this afternoon, whatever the fuck *that* is.'

'Might be fun?' I said, giving my untouched plate to a passing waiter.

She eyeballed me. 'I'm dying for a smoke. It's not worth it with her watching me like a hawk.'

'Where's your husband?'

'Where he always is, in the gym. He's coming out with us today though.' She painted on a smile. 'It'll be a lovely day, I'm sure.'

The tannoy called out, 'Excursion Groups A to F to your Assembly Points, please.'

'That's us,' said Jayde and set about getting the kids' things together. 'Might see you tonight in the dining room?'

'Yeah!' I said spryly, handing her Sansa's floppy bunny, like Ivy's pink bunny I'd nicked from her incubator, only grey. Another dart to my chest. I couldn't get off that boat quick enough.

Bobby's place was 'within walking distance', according to a map, so I walked to the Hotel Extasis, which was perched in the foothills of Ponta do Sol. But it took me over an hour to climb up there, encumbered by my bag and baby-belly-sans-baby and I was sweating cobs and panting like a bloodhound.

The hotel had a beautiful frontage, covered in a kaleidoscope of African daisy, bushes of camellias and blinding yellow mimosas swaying in the warm breeze. For a split moment in the time/space continuum, I thought everything was going to be OK. *I* was going to be OK. Sanctuary at last.

I crossed the cobbled courtyard on the shrieks and giggles of two little girls running around the pool up on the terrace. The noise chilled me – it was me and Seren, years ago. Same ages. Same colour costumes. I wondered if it was a sign that everything was going to be all right.

I soon learned it was a sign that everything was about to turn very bad indeed.

I was ushered into an office behind the Reception to wait

for a woman called Dannielle and within moments, a 50-something perma-tan on vertiginous heels in a too-tight business suit tottered in. Her name badge read Dannielle Fairly-de Souza, General Manager. She was Bobby's daughter.

'Hiya,' she sighed, plonking herself in the swivel chair behind the desk. She looked pissed off, like I'd dragged her away from something important, but as it turned out, it was her permanent way. 'You're Hilary, are you?'

'Yeah. Bobby said to meet him here. Where is he?'

'He's dead,' she replied, no fanfare. She sat back in the chair with a mechanical creak and folded her arms as best she could in her too-tight jacket, her face working on the prize for Least Grieving Daughter Ever. 'Sorry to break it to you 'n'all that.'

I couldn't catch my breath so I held it where it was. 'Dead?'

She nodded. 'New Year's Eve. It weren't a shock. Best medics in Portugal been telling him to change his lifestyle for years. Cut down on't smoking, boozing, the 10 gram of coke every day. Didn't listen though, did he? Still, he went happy. Face wedged between the buttocks of an underage whore.'

My bowels nearly fell out. 'Oh. My. God.'

'Yeah. And now I'm left sorting out *this* dog's mess.' She flipped over a stack of paper on the desk in front of her.

'He's... *dead*?' I said again, completely forgetting to be Australian.

'Had to import a super-size coffin for him 'n'all, cos of his girth. He was such a sex maniac I doubt they'll be able get a lid on. Not that we've got clearance to bury the bastard yet cos the undertaker's got a backlog with that plane crash.' She rolled her eyes. Even an international tragedy was a personal inconvenience. 'You on't run then, are yer?'

'Yes I am. Shit.' My mouth had gone all dry and it was hard to get the 's' out. Sounded more like 'thit.'

'What were it, sex, drugs or murder? I'm guessing… sex?'

I shook my head. It was all I could do.

Dannielle sucked in her breath. 'Well, I can't help yer. I'm in enough shit of me own.'

'I've paid for it, he's had my money!' I cried. 'He said he'd sort it for me. Did he leave you any instructions or… a new passport? You knew my name.'

'Nope, he just said he had a "pregnant girly called Hilary" coming in't New Year.' She looked down at my stomach. 'Where is it, yer baby?'

A black flower stretched out and bloomed in my chest. 'She's gone.'

Her face darkened. 'Oh right. You poor lass.' Her mouth went to say something but she bit it back at the last second. 'I'd assumed you were one of his many lovers and the kid was yet another half-sibling.'

'No I'm not. Last time I saw Bobby I was about six. He knew my dad. He said he could get me a job on his yacht.'

'Where did he say you were headed, Venezuela or somewhere, was it?'

'Yeah, South America. Maybe.'

She leaned back. ''S'where he sends most of his "shipments".'

'You mean I was going on a boat filled with drugs?'

'Yep. Count yourself lucky. Yacht's been impounded by Portuguese police. If you *had* been on there they'd have taken you in 'n'all. It were a floating opium den. It'll be the end of my salon. No smoke and all that.'

'Fucking hell.'

'I *am* sorry, love, for what it's worth. How much did he fleece you?'

'A hundred. And fifty. Thousand.'

'Oh fucking hell. I'm sorry. And about the baby too. You've had a tough time of it, by the sounds. And a wasted journey.'

'Well, what the hell am I going to do?!' I shouted.

This was my one basket full of eggs, and every fucking one was smashed.

I knew this would all come back to bite me on the arse. I should have trusted Keston. I should have gone with *his* plan.

I'm not a panicker, not normally, but since Ivy, all bets seemed to be off. At that moment, with Dannielle Fairly creaking that chair back and forth and telling me she was sorry and that I'd had a wasted journey, panic was properly setting in and I started hyperventilating. The faded grey of the windowless office walls pressed in on me. No air con. Stifling. Suffocating. No way out.

'Fuck. Fuck. Fuck. Fuck. Ffffffff-FUCK!'

'Hey, come on now, it's all right,' said Dannielle, bouncing out of the chair and tottering round to my side of the desk.

I was in full can't-catch-my-breath mode. 'Isn't there… anything you can do? He was going to sort it. I've… *paid* him. Where's it all gone?'

'A lot of people paid him, love. It's probably gone up his nose.'

'Where do I go? What am I going to do?'

'Lemme get you a glass of water.' She scampered out, returning moments later with a large tumbler of clear brown liquid that definitely *wasn't* water. 'Here, get this down yer. It'll help wi't shock.'

49

I took the glass with a shaking hand and gulped it back, wincing at the taste. Whisky – ugh. But it did calm me somewhat. She tottered round to her side of the desk and opened a drawer, pulling out a bag of mobile phones with chargers tied to them with coloured elastic bands.

'We haven't sorted through all of Dad's offices yet. There might be something left for you somewhere. Gimme a few days. Can you do that?'

'Yeah. I guess.'

'Where did he call you from, here or the Funchal Palm? Or the Eden Suites? Or the Casa de Oro?'

'I didn't know he *had* other hotels, I thought this was the only one.'

She jotted down a number and taped it to the back of one of the phones, before handing it to me. 'If I find anything I'll call you. It's fully charged.'

'What do I do in the meantime?' I said, still shuddering from the scotch.

'Hold tight. Keep yer head down. I can't say how long it'll take and that's if I *do* find anything. My dad weren't the most reliable man in the world but he never usually let his mates down. I know some of his associates. I'll see what's what but don't hold yer breath, all right?'

I can't even remember saying 'thank you' as Dannielle shoved the rest of the phones back in the desk drawer and escorted me outside. Back through Reception. Back towards the ship. Back towards inevitable capture.

I stared at the phone – an iPhone 4 with a cracked screen – and started the long walk back down the hill to the town, finding a small square halfway, thriving with stalls and boutiques.

I sat on a vacant bench beneath a tree, shaking all over, despite the heat. I gripped the phone hard. At this point I guessed my only option was to hope Dannielle would come through.

There was a few grand left over from my inheritance that Keston had wired to an offshore account, and I still had access to it, despite the ATMs on the ship charging a fortune per transaction. My anxiety on a rolling simmer, I walked across the square to a small dress shop, scoping it for Hilary-approved outfits – I had to think old school Britney. Pre-pleather Taylor. Pink, white and fluffy, florals and fake smiles, Capri pants and cock-teasing.

I milled around the shops all day, in and out of boutiques and a small pharmacy where I managed to get pile cream, administering it in a blue-tiled toilet in a back street. The place stank of cheese but the relief was immediate.

Later I found a hair salon that was willing to install tumbling twenty-two-inch hair extensions all over my head. It was run by a small group of women who didn't speak any English and by the time I returned to the dockside, I looked like a much better, cleaner, more carefree version of the person who had disembarked the ship that morning.

The Prossers were spilling out of a taxi in the car park as I walked through the dock gates towards the terminal building – Ken and Gloria were swinging Ty, Jayde was pushing Sansa in the buggy and Ryan Prosser looked like he'd walked off the cover of *Men's Health*.

'Hi, Hilary!' Jayde called out. 'I barely recognised you, you look amazing!'

'Thanks,' I said, flicking a clump of extensions over my shoulder. 'I fancied a change.'

'You look gorgeous, petal, have you had a good day?' asked Glo.

'Where's Bruce?' asked Ken.

I beamed my bestest Hila-beam, allowing it to falter slightly. 'Oh, he's had to stay on. He's going to have to meet us in Barcelona instead. No biggy.'

'Aww, I were looking forward to meeting him,' said Glo.

'Yeah, you will in a few days. No dramas.'

Ryan Prosser extended a hand in greeting. He had caramel curls and muscles that belonged in the Uffizi Gallery with the other works of art. He looked like AJ but older, good-lookinger and with a bigger bulge. If I'd been in Full On Ho Mode, I'd have been locked on to Peen Land, no question, but childbirth and the pressing issue of life on the run had a lot to answer for.

Ty held out his little pudding hand to me too and I took it gladly.

'You can come line dancing tonight now, petal, can't yer?' said Glo excitedly. 'I can't get any of this lot to come with me. And we'll set another place on our table at dinner. No need for you to be lonely at least.'

'Thanks, Gloria,' I said. 'That'd be... bonza!'

And they swooshed their big family cloak around me and gathered me in. Exactly like I needed them to.

Wednesday, 2 January – Cadiz

1. *People who refer to their other halves as their 'partner in crime'*
2. *Fat celebrities who lose a shitload of weight then whack it all back on a year later after the workout DVD's done the rounds*
3. *German bodybuilder in the gym who manspreads at the pec press machine right in front of my rowing machine. Today his cock fell out of his shorts. And he knew it. And he smiled.*
4. *Fake-assed bitches on reality shows – hair, tits, nails, lenses. Even though, technically, I am the bitches. And this is my reality show.*
5. *That rap twat, 6ix9ine*

I did go line dancing with Gloria. I had no excuses not to. And lemme tell you, if you ever want a laugh, go line dancing. If you want a bigger laugh, go line dancing with a serial killer who's trying to appear normal by line dancing.

The sight of myself in the studio mirror boogying my scootin' boots, throwing down hoes, turning Monterrey and heel-toe steppin' with hitches and kicks almost pushed me over the edge into endless hysterics.

It wasn't lost on me how ridiculous my life had become in such a short space of time. But the experience further cemented my vanilla façade and that was all that mattered. Not that the Huggins murder had made the news yet – it was still all Brexit and plane crashes. And I have to admit, I was kind of relieved. Another day under the radar was a chance to get even further from the UK.

The itinerary and *Cruise Letter* had been slipped under the door when I got back to my cabin, serving to remind me where I was and how long I had left. After all, this wasn't a holiday – it was a countdown.

Next stop Cadiz, then Gibraltar. After that came Cartagena, Valencia, Mallorca, Barcelona, Marseille, Genoa, Florence, Rome, Sardinia, Naples, Sicily and finally Malta where the ship would turn around and head back along the African coast via Tunisia. Back towards the UK.

I had about two weeks to find asylum or be in one.

And I don't like uncertainty, I never have. I like plans, expectations, safety. I like being at home. I like gardens. Planting something and being there long enough to watch it grow. I like knowing what country is going to be outside my door every time I open it. But I was stuck there on that floating tin can for the foreseeable – aimless. Rootless. And no amount of checking that phone screen was going to hurry along a miracle.

Not that I could let the Prossers in on any of this. As far as they were concerned, I was Fair Dinkum and a fantastic new travelling companion who got a round in when expected, was brilliant with children and answered the easiest pub quiz questions about pop music and soap operas (even though I knew the Caravaggio one *and* the square root of sixty-four).

For the Cadiz stop-off, I stayed with them on the ship all day. I won the bingo twice and shared my congratulatory bottle of wine with my new family. I got in the ball pit with the kids and joined in with the balloon-twisting workshop and mini golf and ice-cream-eating competitions.

At dinner, helped along by said wine, I regaled them with tales of mine and Bruce's wedding in Bora Bora (it had come up in the pub quiz) and duetted with Ken on 'It Takes Two' at karaoke. But by early evening, even though my face was pointed towards the Russian acrobats during 'Putin on the Ritz', all my thought owls had flown to the big question marks in my head:

Where was I going? Who was I now? How long could I keep this up?

I pretended to have a headache and excused myself. I went up to the deck and gazed out at the endless sea, listening to old school Simply Red pumping from speakers, watching couples in sandals, walking hand in hand. Men with belly overhang getting in a late swim with their leathery wives.

Mums. Dads. Sisters. Boyfriends. Families. A woman holding a baby against her shoulder. A dad holding a baby against his neck.

I missed Ivy. I missed her so much my womb would contract whenever I thought about her. And though I tried to push past it and be all No Dramas like Hilary, sometimes life sucks the fucking nice right out of you.

The Man Who Walks, for instance, ambled past and

I attempted a Hilary 'Hiya' and he blanked me. And in a flash, I could see myself pushing him towards the hand rails and upending him overboard.

Ooh, I thought. There she was, briefly: Rhiannon, red in tooth and claw. Hiding in the shadows, waiting for her moment. You can lead a whore to Malta but you can't make her quit wanting to toss people overboard.

I tried to ping Dannielle Fairly a text but it wouldn't send. No signal at sea, it would seem.

I went back to my cabin and flicked on the TV. *Breaking Bad* was on – it's quite good once Walter White stops fucking coughing. I ordered room service – a burger, a mojito and a bowl with 'mixed herbs' – thinking I'd give the sitz bath a try.

Where I splitz, I sitz.

I told the steward it was for my sinuses. I boiled the kettle and I sat there in the middle of the floor watching bald white people shoot each other over bags of blue crystals while bathing my hoochimagooch. When I went to bed, it felt numb. *I* felt numb. Inside and outside.

And numb was an improvement. On this occasion, numb was good.

Thursday, 3 January – Gibraltar

1. *Parents on cruise ships whose kids take the decorative carrot goldfish on the salad before I can get to it*
2. *Waitress called Vicci, which could rhyme with Ricky or itchy but I'll never know cos I'm not speaking to her again. She didn't laugh at my Poseidon Adventure joke.*
3. *People who slam doors without a thought for those in the next cabin*
4. *Outside broadcasts on morning TV – when the presenters go outside to test supercars or barbecues. Get back on your sofas, you pricks.*
5. *People who Instagram Every. Fucking. Moment. Of. Their. Holiday. 'Here we are, walking up some stairs. Here we are, walking back down the stairs. Here we are, eating breakfast – toast today lol.'*
6. *The Real Housewives of Anywhere*

The following day the ship docked in Gibraltar but seeing the Prossers talking to another family in the endless buffet queue outside the Caravel, I ducked out and headed for the quieter Brigantine restaurant. Irritatingly, a lot of other fuckwits had the same idea and the queue was twice as long.

When I did finally get in, people attacked the buffet like vultures, taking handfuls of whatever was on offer. I couldn't get near anything, save the last croissant and a glass of tepid juice. I took them both outside to eat.

The speakers out on deck were playing Carpenters classics that day. 'Ticket to Ride'. What a mournful song that is. I don't remember it being quite so depressing when the Beatles did it but I suppose they weren't in the throes of anorexia. There weren't many people around, save an older couple in M&S summer gear chatting over quoits. Friends laughing. Happy holidaymakers. The *Titanic*, pre-Iceberg. Thoughts of Kate Winslet flinging herself off the starboard bow flittered into my head as I chewed my stale croissant. I wondered if I should do the same.

Who was I kidding? I'm too arrogant to kill myself.

The dulcet sounds of an old posh woman bollocking two kids drifted down from the upper deck – the Diamond Deck.

'Do you *see* any Giant Jenga up here? No. So go back down to the youth area. This is for Diamond Class passengers only and *your* parents are *not* Diamond Class. I can tell by your mother's leggings.'

Two boys loped down the small stairway, past the 'Private' sign, and disappeared inside the ship. I set down my crumby plate on a sun-lounger and climbed the steps. There wasn't much up there – a grass-roofed cocktail bar, a few sun-loungers and a hot tub shaped like a Martini glass.

'This is for *Diamond* passengers,' said the same bored drawl.

A dumpy old woman with a stern expression lay on

a sun-lounger, draped in chiffon, piña colada in hand. I flashed my pass like a homicide detective, covering the gold bar with my thumb. That was the only difference between the classes – her pass had a diamond, mine a gold bar. 'I *am* Diamond Class,' I said. She closed her eyes and gave herself to the sun's rays.

'Not a fan of kids then?' I said, perching on the lounger next to her.

'Can't stand the little fuckers.'

'You not seeing Gibraltar today?'

'No. Once you've climbed a chunk of granite in the battering wind and had your nuts pinched by an ape, you've seen all Gibraltar's got to offer.'

Her face bore the expression of someone who'd lived a thousand years and was half past give a shit with it all, like the old Countess in *Downton*. Like every wrinkle was a folder full of memories. There was a wheelchair parked beside her lounger and a gold sequined scarf hanging on the back.

The Man Who Walks appeared at the top of the steps. He opened the gate, closed the gate and kept on walking past.

'Ugh, I can't stand that guy,' I said, eyeballing him.

She saw him too. 'Why? What's he done?'

'Nothing. He just walks. I've never seen him sitting down, even in the dining room. He circumnavigates this bloody ship like a hamster in a wheel.'

'He's lost.'

'Buy a fucking map then.'

'Without his *wife*, I mean,' she added, sipping the remains of her drink. 'They've been coming on this cruise for years. She died last summer. Aneurysm.'

'Why does he still come on the cruise?'

'Doesn't know what else to do, I presume. He's grieving.'

'We're *all* grieving. We don't all lap a ship fifty times a day like a prick.'

'Oh dear, we did get out of the Mediterranean on the wrong side this morning, didn't we?' I hadn't realised I was being myself – and my un-Australian self at that – until she'd called me on it.

'Sorry,' I said. 'I'm having a bad day.'

'Don't apologise, it's refreshing. There's enough bullshitters. People who bid you "good day" but wouldn't piss in your mouth if your teeth were on fire.'

I decided I liked her. I liked being myself in her company. It was a risk, of course, but I've always been a risky pixie.

'There you go, Caro,' said a waiter, placing a fresh piña colada on her table and removing the empty glass. They shared a conversation where I learned that she knew most of the staff by first name and they all knew her.

'Been coming on this ship a long time?' I asked when he'd gone.

'I never leave,' she said. 'I've been on here for eleven years.'

'You *live* on the ship?' She nodded, her wattles quivering. 'Why?'

'Can you think of a better place to live? All you can eat and drink, 24-hour entertainment, medical care, a new vista every morning.'

'What about your home?'

'*This* is my home.'

'No, your house, your family?'

'I don't have any.' She picked up her book from the table.

I'm normally wary of older people in case they start having a stroke or need something wiped but this one looked safe-ish. Maybe I could become her companion, like the granddaughter of the old bag in *Titanic*. Cue the 'It's been 84 years' GIF. My parasitical suckers twitched.

'I'm Hilary,' I said, remembering my Aussie accent and phasing it in. I read the cover of her book – *The Countess's Courtesan* by Vaughan Dempsey-Newhall. 'Why do you never get off the ship?'

'I don't need to,' she replied. 'There's nothing to be seen that I haven't seen a hundred times before. Things don't tend to improve with age.'

Maybe *I* could do that, I thought, cruise forevermore. Maybe the crew could become a family of sorts. But I remembered my tumbleweedy bank account and shot that particular thought owl out of the sky.

'How much does it cost to live on a cruise?'

'I'm not sure.'

'You must be loaded.'

'I am. And I *don't* need a lady's companion if that's what you're thinking so if you've somewhere else you have to be—'

'No. I'm only… killing time,' I said.

'Until what?'

For the first time in a long time I told the truth. 'I don't know. I have no idea what I'm doing.' And all my thought owls flew to Ivy. That day marked her week-old birthday.

'Just enjoy your holiday then,' she said, focusing on her book, mouthing the words as she read them.

'Read a bit out to me,' I said, lying back on my lounger.

She flattened the pages and cleared her throat. '*Her love*

ignited a fire inside me,' she read. *'I'd never beheld a countenance as bright as hers, and in that moment the Earth slipped away and my body took flight as her hungry fingers penetrated my sex.'*

'Whoa,' I said. I looked at the cover again. 'Is it lesbians?'

The woman smiled broadly. 'Oh yes. It's marvellous. He doesn't usually write for lesbians, this chap. He does these awful romance novels for bored housewives about a haddock fisherman-turned doctor who fucks all his patients. But this series is his best by far. It's *Downton Abbey* but with lesbians.'

'Are *you* a lesbian?'

'Yes, I suppose I am. Though I did love my husbands too.'

'Husband*s*?'

'Well, I loved four of them. One and three were shits. Five was a shit without me *realising* he was a shit. Two was a Nazi spy so he was a shit to everyone else. Four was gay himself. I think it's called *bi*sexual. That's probably what I am.'

There was a red calla lily on the front of the book, looking unavoidably vaginal. 'May I?' She handed it to me and I thumbed through the dog-eared pages. 'You've read this more than once, haven't you?'

'Of course. What else do I have? I'm too bloody arthritic for physical pleasure and I haven't got the patience to keep learning the WiFi password.'

'Big print,' I said, gesturing to the pages.

'I'm losing my sight,' she murmured, closing her eyes towards the sun.

'I'm not surprised.'

She grinned, wiggling her eyebrows. The grin was catching. 'It's more than that though,' she said. 'It's full of that passion, the ardour one doesn't experience often when one gets to a "certain age". It captures that febrile intensity of reconciling with the yearnings of one's body.'

'Blimey.'

'*I* had that once. For real.' She picked up her drink and sipped half of it away. 'It's terrible in one way, once you've had it, because nothing ever matches up to it. The rest of the time you're... treading water.'

'Who with? Which husband was this?'

'Oh God, no, not a husband. A *waitress*. On Capri. I met her on my second honeymoon.'

'You had an *affair* with a waitress on your honeymoon?'

'Yes.' Her eyes twinkled. 'And a rather torrid one at that. We were there for a month. My husband was working in Naples.' She set down her glass and made a face. 'Jordan's a dear chap but he never puts enough rum in these.'

'So tell me more about this waitress.'

'Beatrice,' she smiled, like she could still taste her. 'Beatrice Genovesi. I knew it the moment our eyes met, she was it. You hear young people talking about "it" all the time – The One. Well, she was *my* One. And I was hers.'

'So why didn't you ditch the husband and run off with this Beatrice?'

She looked at me as though I'd spat in her eye. 'Because it was 1955. And I was married with two children by then. You didn't just *leave*. You didn't do whatever you wanted and fuck the consequences.'

'I'd have fucked those consequences till the cows came home,' I scoffed.

'Yes well, different times. We quickly became best friends,

then lovers, then soulmates. But I went home with Geoffrey and that was that.'

'You never saw her again?'

'No.'

'Are you seeing her when we go to Naples? There's a Capri excursion, I think.'

'No,' she repeated, picking up her drink. And she left it at that.

'Is she the reason you drink piña coladas for breakfast?'

She didn't dignify that. I went back to the book. It was only when her glass clinked against her ring I realised she'd fallen asleep. The page had fallen open on one of the hot bits, the horny housekeeper talking about the Countess being 'the most sumptuous oyster she'd ever cracked open.'

. . . she was naked with herself when she was with the Countess. Shame had fallen from her shoulders like a silken robe... a gorgeous new thrill rippled inside her, a hot, molten feeling of utter serenity.

Ooh.

. . . like her body was a dolphin shooting into the sky. The excitement. That silver thrill of knowing one had that power: to have conquered oneself. In finding the Countess, she had conquered the living death that was life.

That's how it feels, I thought. To kill someone. I know it wasn't the point of the plot – to put a serial killer in touch with her murderous lust – but that's the effect it had. It was describing how *I* felt when I took someone's life. When I sensed their last breath leave them. Caro telling me about her first love had inadvertently brought me back to mine. Killing was my The One. It was how I'd felt after suffocating Derek Scudd.

After knifing Gavin White. After mounting Troy Shearer and stabbing him through the heart in that alleyway. After slicing Sandra Huggins to bloody bits.

. . . she was a better person with her love beside her. With her skin on hers. When she was her own true self. Happier. Settled. And her rage and her fretfulness quelled to a calm, undulating sea.

'Fucking hell,' I said. I'd missed that feeling. I wanted it again. I didn't want to be numb anymore. Treading water. Scared. When I was Rhiannon, nothing scared me. Nothing *could*. I wanted that back.

And I thought: if I could control it this time, I could have the best of both worlds: Hilary for business, Rhiannon for fun. My heart started thumping. I headed back indoors and got the lift down to the Business Centre. I bought another twenty-four hours of internet and logged onto PlentyofCatfish.com.

It was like coming home – even if home was a cesspool of mansplainers, swipe rights, dick pics, DM sliders, thirst traps, leave-on-reads, slow fades, foot fetishists, golden showers, garage flowers and over-proteined poon hounds with ass acne and Harley Davidsons wanking themselves blind over *Top Gear*. But home has always been where my heart is.

Friday, 4 January – Cartagena

1. *Kris Jenner – aka the queen who spawns the silicone eggs*
2. *Ken and Gloria – the couple who've been everywhere, done it all and know everything. Except that their shipmate is a serial killer.*
3. *Parents who allow their toddlers to shriek at random intervals*
4. *Parents who bring all eight children on holiday with them and hog the mini golf course. Why do people keep on having kids anyway? The last one not pulling in the followers on Instagram like she used to?*
5. *Parents in general*

Fuckboyee: Are you in Alicante?

HillsHaveEyes69: No. Am in Cartagena. Come to me, baby.

Fuckboyee: Where dat?

HillsHaveEyes69: Get a map.

Fuckboyee: OK I'll see wot I can do. Won't be til late afternoon tho. Can't wait to see you. I rly enjoyed last night.

HillsHaveEyes69: Yeah, it was great wasn't it?

Fuckboyee: Can't wait to be inside you for real!

HillsHaveEyes69: Mmm. Me eiths.

I waited an age for a response. Watched a YouTube video of two men attempting an enormous fry-up in a hollowed-out loaf and did a Buzzfeed quiz to pass the time – Which Member of BTS Is Mostly Likely To Help You Change A Tyre Based on Your Krispy Kreme Preference? (Jungkook, obvs.) Anyway, eventually I got a bite. My old hunting ground – PlentyofCatfish – was its usual cavalcade of incels and desperados, lots of whom were married and at least one of whom was in prison but would still 'blow my back out' given half the chance.

Ahhh, so many Mr Darcys, so little time... *smitten blinky eyes gif*

The little fishy that bit was a loathsome patch of cunny fungus called Liam or 'El Fuckboy' as his profile suggested. He was on a stag weekend in Alicante, along the coast from Cartagena, and looked like a younger, gone-wrong Lewis Capaldi. His photos were the usual – one in sports gear before a big mirror, one astride a garish red motorbike, one with a drugged-up tiger cub in the Far East and one in a suit at a party, probably his own wedding.

According to his profile, he was 25, from Chepstow, and

a Sagittarius. We chatted back and forth, at first sober, testing-the-water messages like *Where are you from?* and *What box-sets have you binged recently?* but before long he was asking me my bra size and sending videos of him water-skiing with a Go-Pro attached to his cock. I didn't send anything back – he had to make do with words for the time being.

Nevertheless, within hours, he was ravenous for me.

Fuckboyee: Babes we need to hook up. I'm gonna bury myself in you.

I had no intention of sleeping with him – my foof was still the last battered cod under the heat lamp – and though my soreness *was* subsiding, I'd apparently waved my libido goodbye at Southampton Docks. I just wanted Liam to test out a theory, the way Einstein needed chalk and a blackboard.

And the theory was this: if I could kill again, I could feel like my old self again. I'd get that familiar rippling inside, like Caro's book had said. That dolphin-surge thrill of removing life from another's body. If I could kill again, I could handle all the other stuff – the boring saddo fluffy pink Hilary stuff. I could make my heartache disappear.

Liam texted me at first light on the iPhone 4. At least some fucker was:

Fuckboyee: Good news, babes! I got two hours free this arvo. Where we meetin so I can sex u up? *tongue out emoji*

HillsHaveEyes69: Laguna Rosa? It's pink – my fave colour!

Fuckboyee: Lol. Where dat?

I'd seen it advertised at the Excursions Desk and I knew it would be a good spot – a large pink-coloured lake, the kind of place Instagrammers go to risk their lives getting selfies. It looked romantic, quiet, and better still, unpoliced. I booked one of the last tickets for the afternoon tour.

HillsHaveEyes69: Torrevieja? Be so romantic *heart eyes emoji*

Fuckboyee: Ah yeah cool I heard of that. Be good for The Gram. I'll GMap it. All rightee, see you there 'bout four-ish?

HillsHaveEyes69: Can't waiteeeee *open-mouthed smile emoji*

Fuckboyee: Wait, have you got skins?

HillsHaveEyes69: I'm on the pill. U can cum as U are *blush emoji*

Fuckboyee: Fuck, I've got a semi on thinkin bout u! Can't wait to smash that pastie! Catch u later baby *six lines of kisses* *aubergine emoji* *peach emoji* *heart emojis agogo*

HillsHaveEyes69: Catch u later babeee *smiling devil emoji*

I planned to stay on the ship until my excursion was called, maybe catch a morning stretch class, try out the zip wire or join in with the bean bag toss. Unfortunately, Fate had other plans again.

There came a knock on my cabin door – it was Gloria Prosser.

'Hiya, you coming out to play? Jayde and Ryan have taken the kids to the water park so us oldies are hitting the shops. You're welcome to join us.'

I couldn't think of any excuses. Not a single one. So cue the boo-boo. 'That'd be ripper, thanks, guys! I'll go grab my bag.'

In the absence of Jayde and Ryan, the Prossers had invited their cruise chums along – Lynette and Dennis Hall, two dehydrated ex-farmers from Devon, and Eddie and Shona Callahan, retired firefighters from Orange County. Brexiteers and Trumpians alike – they were people I'd normally cross motorways to avoid. As it was I was stuck in Gammon Central. I had to go Full Throttle Hilary.

'That's a brilliant observation, Dennis. I agree, totally!' I found myself saying when he went on some rant about migrants paying for healthcare.

'You're so right!' I beamed at Eddie. 'Mexico *should* pay for the wall!' He high-fived me with his sweaty paw. I wiped it on Gloria's cardigan, mid-cringe.

'Oh, I hear you, Shona, I hear you,' I said with an Amen hand as she started on about how we should all be doing our bit to reduce plastic and save the planet. She'd already fucked the planet by birthing five kids so it didn't actually matter how many times a day she swilled out her tampon. Still, Hilary earned their trust and that was all that mattered.

I had vowed to take a bag full of the essentials whenever

I left the ship, on the off chance I got the call from Dannielle while the phone had full signal, but the call didn't come in Cartagena. The screen remained blank all day.

The town was a searingly hot but tranquil little place, filled with old buildings, marble streets lined with palm trees and a marina of bobbing boats. Everything smelled like sun cream and the heat deepened my tan as we walked around, touring Mercia Cathedral before Gloria dragged everyone shoe shopping.

It was a dull but fairly relaxing day – until I saw the five police officers gathered outside the Punic Wall museum. *Policia Local Cartagena* written on their blue-and-yellow jackets, dicing bands on their hats, guns poised. Mirrored sunglasses so nobody could see who they were looking at. They didn't seem to be interacting, just waiting. Waiting for me?

Any second I expected that tap on my shoulder and the inevitable '*Disculpe señora, está bajo arresto*' but the moment never came. They didn't pay me much mind at all. Still didn't stop me stressing about it and looking at my phone every five minutes.

I took the opportunity to text Dannielle Fairly. She didn't appreciate it.

> I said don't hold your breath. I've got 99 problems here, Hilary. Hold tight.

The Gammons didn't pay me much mind either. They never looked behind to see if I was there or asked what I wanted in the coffee shops, or offered to pay – I wasn't the little girl on the pool noodle being reminded to keep my water wings on anymore. As far as they were concerned, I was there but not *there*. Like the sky. Or the third Jonas brother.

After our third 'little rest stop' of the day for refreshments and a slice of pizza so dry the point had curled up like the end of a Turkish slipper – we nipped into a supermarket for room provisions – six cans of Spanish lager and Gloria's Valium from her handbag while she was in the loo. I deposited The Gammons on hired beach-loungers and once they were safely all asleep, I gave them the slip to catch the 2.00 p.m. minibus to the Pink Lake.

The ride there was torturous, as is always the case when I'm crammed into a clanky, moving box loaded with dickheads and their hot farts. There were fourteen of us – three pensioners, three Fiat 500 Twitter types, two sets of couples in their 30s, three of the loudest children I'd ever met and me – the serial killer. The kids had the worst names – Kasidy, Braxxton and Swayze, and they were so dosed up on Haribo Tropifrutti that sitting down was an impossibility. I like children normally, but I didn't like them. If the bus had crashed and I was the only one conscious, I resolved not to help.

Our rep Chrys with a 'y' – like 'y' can't anyone spell their fucking name anymore? – informed us along the way of what we could expect from the Pink Lake – information the guy who sold us the tickets hadn't.

'Now Laguna Rosa is a *salt* lake so although it might look like a giant milkshake, it's not nearly as inviting and is actually full of bacteria which gives the lake its pink hue. So sadly you can't go for a dip, I'm afraid.'

'What?' said a pensioner with flip-top glasses. 'Not even to paddle?'

"Fraid not, no. You can sit beside it and have your picnics, take as many pictures as you like, or do a mud pack – the mud on the banks is great for your skin actually – but no swimming. It's pretty lethal.'

Great, I thought. So we've driven nearly an hour to sit by a salty pink puddle covering ourselves in muddy pathogens? Ugh.

It *looked like* something out of a science fiction movie but was still kind of beautiful. This huge pink pond, surrounded by long grasses, stretched as far as the eye could see, rippling on the breeze. All around the edge, deposits of salt had stacked up like drifts of warm snow and after making some salt castles I discovered it stings like shit so I had to wash my hands in lager – the only liquid I'd brought with me. I located a space in the long grass, away from the throng, and texted El Fuckboy to let him know I'd arrived.

He *did* arrive, more fool him, an hour later. He wore long navy shorts and trainers, and a T-shirt with the fucking Smurf thing on from that film I hate but Craig loved – *Avatar*. He didn't wait long to start kissing me, one hand venturing down towards the holy triangle.

'Babes, I'm so glad you came!' I lied, with my sparkliest Hilary smile.

'You too. And you're right, you *do* look like a fat Cheryl Cole!'

His tongue was like a tiny cold worm and it took all my concentration not to gag as slipped it in my mouth. 'Do you want a drink?' I said as I pulled away.

'Yeah, I'm just so hot for you,' he laughed. 'Had a semi on all day thinking about this!'

'Ah, that's really lovely. Well, let's cool off for a second, yeah?'

Luckily, the worm took my bait and downed a can of the super-strength Spanish lager I'd brought, emitting a belch, and slinging the can behind him.

'Now, where were we?' He leaned over.

I reared back. 'Nah-uh, not yet,' I grinned, removing his hand.

'You gone frigid on me?'

'I'm not as horny as you yet. Be patient, little grasshopper.'

'Grass-what?' he laughed, removing his shirt. 'Come on, babe, I've got a fucking rod on here.'

'Not yet,' I chuckled, pushing him back again.

'Oh, come on.'

'No, I said,' the sparkle fading from my Hilary beam.

'Pleeeeeease? Shove your hand down here.'

'No, honey.'

'Go on… a little bit… right there…'

'Will you fucking woo me first, BITCH!' Rhiannon smashed through Hilary's glass façade and almost shattered everything.

He leaned back. 'Whoa. What the hell was that?'

I exhaled, long and slow. 'I'm so sorry. I can't take you in dry. You'll hurt me. I need warming up first, baybee. OK?' I fluttered my eyelashes.

'So lemme put me hand down there. *That'll* warm you up.'

He came back on me, body pressed against mine, supplexing me into the grass, fingers creeping down the waistband of my shorts. He reached knicker elastic. Creep, creep, creep, went the digits, down, down, down, almost hitting pube, almost on maternity pad…

'I need a drink,' I said, pushing him off. 'Do you want another one, hun?'

'Yeah, go on,' he said, defeated.

'You can start undressing, if you like, while you're waiting.'

This placated him as he finally stopped fucking with me and undid his laces – giving me long enough to slide a couple of pills into his open can. Quite a few pills, actually. A whole blister pack, if you must know. I'd had them ready and rattling in my shorts pocket most of the day.

'Fancy a dip?' I said, handing him the can.

'Nah, s'full of salt, innit?' He necked the lager.

'Oh yeah,' I said, pretending to sip my own.

Liam stood and made his way over to the shore, plunging his foot straight in. "S'fucking freezing 'n'all!" he laughed.

I looked around for signs of Chrys the rep or the old man with the snort or That Prick Swayze who'd pulled my hair on the bus, but everyone was hidden by the long grasses. There were orgasms coming from the east.

He sank the dregs of his second can, tossing it into the scrub. He lay down on my towel and turned to me. 'Get yer knickers off then.'

I stroked his chest. 'You have to take this slowly. Make love to me.'

His breathing deepened. 'Shit, that's hot.' His face moved towards my mouth and I held his head away, turning my lips towards his ear. I nibbled. 'Mmm, say more stuff like that, baybeeee...'

I stroked his chest, all the way down his happy trail and into his shorts. My face inadvertently winced as I wondered what breed of crab I was going to catch if those pills didn't kick in soon.

His breathing deepened as the cold wet worm licked my neck. 'Mmmmmmmm,' I feigned.

I clamped my thighs together and reached inside his shorts, taking hold of his springy little knob, already moist with precum. Bloody DNA.

'It's gonna go off in a min...' he breathed as I kissed him and that stupid worm invaded my mouth again. 'Give it a tug. Or nosh it off if you like.'

And they say romance is dead, eh? It soon would be.

He picked at the spaghetti straps of my vest and pulled one down to reveal my boob. 'Wow, your tits are huge!'

'Mmmm,' I said, struggling to summon the will to go on living and biting back the pain as he squeezed each breast in turn. Oh Christ, I thought, what if they leaked? How would I explain that? But Lady Luck for once was on my side that day as without warning he fell back on my beach towel, laughing.

'What's the matter?' I said, looking down to the tittage to see if they'd betrayed me. They hadn't.

'Fuck, I'm wasted, man. You'll have to get on me.'

I didn't move. I posted my boob back inside my vest and lay on my side, watching. Waiting for something else to happen. 'Do what?'

'Reverse cowgirl. Hop on. I'm ready.'

Voices wafted over from the scrub. Couples, frolicking. Phony Braxxton swinging a vuvuzela. A woman in an orange bikini running to the lake and filling up a bottle, sprinting back into the grass, presumably to chuck it over someone. Liam's arm was over his face and his breathing grew laboured.

'Are you all right?' I whispered.

'I dunno.' He tried to sit up but collapsed back down. 'Fuck.'

He got to his knees before stumbling forwards onto his face before twisting around violently, eyes rolling back to the whites, fitting fully and bodily, like I'd plugged him in to a socket.

'*Gnnnnnnnnnnnn,*' he went, on and on, like a washing machine on spin.

'Oh shut up,' I seethed, climbing on top, pinning him down, legs to legs, arms to arms, face to face, as he shook rigidly beneath me, foam seeping from his mouth, eyes wide, pupils at full stop. I held myself hard against him and willed that rush into my bones – the surge. The magnificence. He was dying. He was dying and *I* was on top of him, all powerful. Taking his life.

'*Gnnnnnnnnnnnnnnnn,*' he growled.

'Die against me, you pig, fucking die against me,' I muttered.

His death rattle spluttered out as his last breaths released into my hair. And his whole body stilled, one limb at a time. And his heart ceased to thump. And his eyes stayed wide.

But I didn't get it – the surge. That expectant cliff edge before the almighty orgasm. I strained and I shuddered and I willed that delicious surge of adrenaline to come until sweat beaded on my forehead. But it was not there. I did not fall. I did not cum. 'Ugh.'

I got to my feet, yanking out my towel from under him. 'You can't even fucking *die* properly,' I hissed, tucking the towel beneath my arm. I checked around for detritus, submerged Liam's phone along with the lager cans in the lake, and walked to the bus, shaking. Like a normal person.

Who the hell was I? This wasn't Hilary and it definitely wasn't the old Rhiannon. I was stuck in some hellish limbo where nothing felt good. I'd never felt this way before, even when I was pregnant and stymied by Ivy's little do-gooder voice – I'd still wanted to kill. I'd been desperate to. Now, I didn't even want to kill. I didn't know *what* I wanted. It was all Ivy's fault. She'd done this, trying to make me a good person. Now I was neither one thing nor the other.

Serena Williams was never the same after she had a kid. Jess Ennis stopped winning gold medals. Amy Schumer stopped being funny. Now it had happened to me. What a waste of time and effort. Liam had been my US Open, except there was no umpire to rant at. There was nobody at all.

Saturday, 5 January – Valencia

1. *Celebrities who endorse weight loss products*
2. *Celebrities on cruise ships who still think they're the big I Am*
3. *Flip-flops, the people who wear them, make them and who will one day, eventually, die in them if I get my way*
4. *Ken, Gloria, Dennis, Lynette, Shona and Eddie – aka The Gammons. They've dubbed themselves 'The Crazy Gang'. The 'craziest' thing they've done is order a shared pudding with a sparkler in it. And the sparkler had gone out by the time the waiter brought it over.*
5. *Talking of gammon, Jon Hamm*

I googled some true crime podcasts when I got back on the ship that evening, taking out another mortgage for twenty-four hours of WiFi. Everyone listened to podcasts these days, I didn't think that would signal a red flag to authorities. On one podcast the discussion was *Do serial killers ever simply stop killing?*

One criminologist concluded that *it may be possible for*

some killers to find alternative outlets and killing becomes less of a necessity. They may indeed become dormant. See The Golden State Killer, The Green River Killer and BTK...

Interesting but I *had* no other outlets, aside from the odd line dancing lesson, film marathon and scenic tour with septuagenarians. She continued:

The killer may have found a worthwhile occupation or started a family and the sources of stress that once were may have disappeared...

I *had* no worthwhile occupation and though I *had* started a family, I'd abandoned it. The sources of stress – my friends, my boyfriend, my in-laws, my job – had all gone, along with my dog. I had nothing and nobody left. So *this* was what it was going to take to make me stop killing? An empty life?

Some serial killers diminish their fury when they form happy human bonds, as in the case of The Green River Killer when he got married...

I sat at the computer in the Business Centre, watching the clock ticking down. Craig took my 'happy human bonds' and blew them up Lana Rowntree's fart box. *He* had been my chance of a normal, happy life but the second he'd got with her, everything collapsed. It was her fault. His fault too.

Who was I kidding? It was all *my* fault.

On the way back to my cabin, I passed the gym – a place I should have been frequenting as Hilary, having bought myself a new baby pink Adidas tracksuit that made me look like a pig in armour. I lingered by the door. There was no one in there – the ship had left dock, bound for Valencia, and most passengers were at dinner. Sky News flickered on the end TV.

There was a picture of my face on the screen. And on the tickertape:

HUNT FOR FARM SHOP KILLER: LEWIS HAS LEFT THE COUNTRY

I clicked the door open and went inside, stepping up on a treadmill.

Cue grainy CCTV shot of me striding across the farm shop car park with Sandra Huggins' blood dripping from my hands. They'd made the connection. I was officially a wanted woman. Cue serious-faced newsreader with severe eyebrows and ladybird brooch. I checked no one was around and turned up the volume on the middle TV.

'Avon and Somerset police are still hunting for 28-year-old Rhiannon Lewis, the prime suspect in the murder of Jane Richie before New Year. The force today released new CCTV images of Lewis calmly leaving the farm shop on the A30 near Monk's Bay after murdering the 48-year-old shop assistant. It is now believed Lewis had given birth earlier that day, and it is feared the baby has come to harm as well.

Detective Inspector Nnedi Géricault from the Major Crime Investigation Unit in Bristol believes Lewis has left the country...'

I clicked on my treadmill. I started walking.

'Someone out there knows Rhiannon Lewis's whereabouts and we believe she did have connections in the criminal under-world through her late father Tommy Lewis, a known villain in the South-West in the 1990s. Early indications suggest that she has left the country. We are following every possible lead.'

Liar. *She* knew who Jane Richie was – the alter ego of

Sandra Huggins, paedo nursery nurse extraordinaire. She knew *exactly* why I'd done it. I pushed up the speedometer and walked faster.

'*Does this twist in the investigation mean a possible exoneration for Craig Wilkins, who is on remand charged with five murders?*'

'*We aren't ruling anything out.*'

'*Given the possibility that Lewis herself carried out Wilkins' crimes, and that three victims were sexual deviants, was there a similar motive in Jane Richie's murder? And can you tell us anything about Lewis's baby yet?*'

Suddenly I was running.

'*Someone has been murdered. We need to focus on finding the culprit before she can hurt anyone else. That is our priority. Regarding the baby, we believe that the child was born before Lewis left the UK and we remain concerned for the child's safety. That's all I can say about that at this time.*'

'*DI Géricault, thank you for your time.*'

Géricault scratched her chin briefly with her three-fingered hand. I was running hard by this point, pumping my arms, losing my breath, 8.7 speed, almost full pelt as another picture of me flashed up on the BBC News 24 channel – an old one from a PICSO evening out where I'm sitting in a booth in the China Palace, grinning in an enforced group photo. I'm cheersing and my eyes are all thin and, arguably, a bit evil. I could see why they'd used it.

I pushed my legs as hard as they would go until I had no more breaths to keep up with them and slowed the numbers to a brisk walk, propelled by the thumping of a hip hop track on another TV.

Adrenaline. The thrill of seeing my face up there on the screen. The thrill of knowing this hadn't been in vain. That even though the police wanted me, they didn't have a clue where I was. I was still in the driving seat.

And I felt better; the sweat beading on my face felt like it had pushed something out of me. My lungs had been blown up to their full sizes and all my toxins had been squeezed out into the air-conditioned room. I stopped the belt and stared at the four TV screens ahead. My face on two of them. My name on the tickertape. I'd finally made it. I was famous.

But a sinister new thought owl was incoming – an evil black bird with a sharp, pointed beak, slicing through the horizon with razor-sharp wings: why did Géricault say they 'remain concerned for the child's safety'? They must have known about the adoption. Claudia must have given a statement. Why hadn't someone come forward to refute that at least? Heather? Claudia? They knew I hadn't hurt Ivy – that was why I left her. Why would Géricault say that? And where the hell was my confession?

That bird got blacker and louder in my head as the night went on.

The next morning, I was in no mood for the bustle of the main dining room at breakfast so I ventured up to the quieter Diamond Deck instead, sneaking into an area called Park Avenue; a glass-covered walkthrough filled with trees and plants, interspersed with quiet cafés. I wanted to stew and sulk some more about what Géricault had said about the baby and the presence of green things and floral smells immediately cooled my jets. I ordered a flat white and sat at a table next to a huge ornate bush, allowing a bird of paradise flower to graze my cheek. It was a tiny pocket of calm amid a cluttered brain.

Raised voices filtered through my peace.

'Your children race up and down that dining room every morning and it's got to stop. Nobody else will say anything but I've got nothing to lose.'

'They're kids, what do you expect?' a man in a Homer Simpson 'Big Daddy' T-shirt laughed. His belly moved independently of the rest of him.

'I *expect* you to behave like a responsible parent and exact some discipline for the sake of the other 2,499 passengers on this vessel.'

'They're on holiday, love. Why don't *you* lighten up and have one?'

'Apart from anything else, there are hot drinks being carried around—'

'—oh, so now you're worried about them being scalded? Look, I've been polite up to now but if you push me any further Mrs—'

'—what will you do, hit me? Go ahead, make my century.'

The man bent down, placing his hands on the arms of Caro's chair, gurning his face right next to hers. 'Don't come near my kids again.'

She frowned. 'Why protect them now? The damage is clearly done.'

'You OK, Caro?' I asked as Homer retracted his fist.

She threw me a glare obviously meant for Homer. 'Yes, thank you. This gentleman was just leaving. He hasn't eaten in a while. Must be feeling faint.'

Homer looked daggers at me but walked away, still pissing

and whining, calling Caro all the names under the disco ball, including 'dry old snatch'.

I sat on the edge of a planter with my coffee. Caro returned to her cocktail and flipped over the book she was reading, a different one to the other day but with the same big print.

'You didn't need to save me.'

'I know.' I kicked my heels against the metal planter.

'Do you mind not making that noise?'

I stopped kicking. 'I read your book when you were asleep the other day. Lesbo *Downton*.'

'Oh? And what did you think?'

'It was good. It sort of… turned me on a bit.' Her eye twinkled, despite itself, but she didn't look up. 'Are you going into Valencia today?'

'No. There's nothing to do there. You?'

'I might. We could go together. I could keep you company.'

She looked up. 'Why would I want you to do that?'

'Someone to talk to?'

'You're hardly the Peter Ustinov of raconteurs,' she sniffed. 'And I thought you were Australian?'

'I am,' I said, trying to affect my most Kylie Minogue lilt. I'd become so comfortable around the salty lil witch that I'd forgotten who I was supposed to be and carried on being who I was. 'I *am* Australian. Fair dinkum.'

She afforded me a slight eyebrow. 'Your accent's somewhat muddled.'

I deadass didn't know how to respond so I said 'Mmm' and took a deeper interest in the flowers. I decided to phase out my Bindi Irwin act with Caro. With her at least, I could risk being halfway more myself.

'Strange girl.' She went back to her book.

'We had one of these in rehab,' I told her, patting the planter.

She eyeballed me. 'Are you a drug addict?'

'No.' I maybe should have lied, but I didn't want to around Caro. 'I had brain damage when I was a kid. Had to learn to walk and talk again. I went to this rehab place in Gloucester where they had this garden – some charity built it. And it had all these flowers and herbs in that you could eat off the stem. I always feel peaceful around plants.'

'So do I,' she said. 'But these are all fake.'

I raked my hand through the soil. 'Real soil but fake plants?'

'Mostly, yes.' Caro didn't say anything for a whole minute – she sipped the rest of her cocktail, set down her glass and reversed her chair out from under the table. 'Come along.'

'What?'

'We're going into Valencia, aren't we?'

'You said there was nothing to do there.'

'Well, we can do nothing together, can't we?'

'But you never get off the ship.'

'And *you'd* never read lesbian pulp fiction before the other day. So there's a first time for everything.'

We didn't bother with any excursions or escorted activities – instead we took a taxi into the old town, found a bar and got absolutely shitfaced. Turns out it was one thing the 87-year-old and I had in common – we both liked to drink. Not to excess, just to that point where nothing matters and if your arse caught fire you'd just laugh and carry on drinking.

Agua de Valencia became the third entity in our relationship. Fresh Valencia orange juice, cava, vodka and gin. And it meant every word of it. We found this great little dive bar, cool from the midday scorch, its walls covered in signed black-and-white photos of famous Spanish people who'd visited over the years – I didn't recognise any of them. We stayed there for hours, drinking AdV and talking about our lives.

Well, Caro talked and I listened and drank.

I learned she'd been a model in her twenties having been scouted when she was a secretary for a woman's magazine in London. Her five husbands read like a spotters guide of red flags. Charles, the First, was a photographer who beat her up. George, the Second, was 'born the wrong side of the royal blanket', and had a double life as a spy for the Nazis – he ditched her after their second child was born. Henry, the Third, ran up gambling debts she had to pay off when he croaked and Number Four, William, was shagging her brother, even on the day their baby was born. Clive, Number Five, monitored her calls, tracked her car, and ran over her dog. After that, she gave up on marriage and went cruising.

'Don't you miss your children?' I said.

'Every day. But it hurts me to think about them. So I try not to. I've only been in love once in my life. *True* love.'

'Your little side dish on Capri, you mean?' I leaned forwards so my chin rested on my folded hands.

She sat back, stroking the side of her glass. 'We *will* meet again, some sunny day.'

'How did you know you were in love with her?'

'When you're in love, you feel like anywhere they are, that's your home. Safety is like a prison sometimes – I experienced that in a couple of my marriages – the trick is to find safety with an open door that neither of you want to walk through.'

'I don't get why you've never visited her,' I said. 'If you haven't been off that ship in eleven years, you must have passed Capri loads of times.'

'Sixteen times.'

'And you've never wanted to go and see her? The love of your life?'

'It was fifty-odd years ago, Hilary. She wouldn't remember me.' Caro's smile faded. 'She might even have... passed over.'

'You could find out,' I said, resting my heavy head on my hand.

'I like to remember her as she was,' said Caro. 'I don't want to go to Capri and find a grave. That would be too awful.'

'Have you never even googled her?'

'Wouldn't know where to begin. But I'll tell you this, Hilary,' and I knew she meant what she was about to say cos she put down her glass. 'There's not a day that goes by that I don't wish things had been different. That the world had been kinder to the idea of us. That I'd had more courage.' She put her hand to her neck and pulled out the square pendant that hung under her dress. She fumbled for the clasp, took it off and handed it to me.

I studied the image – it was a square cameo, the softest blue with two white figures almost-kissing on top. Two figures with hair blowing in the wind and ripples of sea and a crescent moon in the background.

'Beatrice's father used to sculpt cameo jewellery. She was going to take over the business when he retired. She made it for me.' I handed the pendant back to her. She tucked it inside the collar of her dress. 'You ever find a love like that, you fight for it. Promise me.'

'Yeah, right.'

'No, I mean it. You do what you have to do but you fight for it. Fight for him, her, whoever they are.'

'I doubt it'll happen for me somehow.'

'Why do you say that? Anything is possible.'

'Nah, not for me.' I drained my glass.

'Promise me,' she said again. She wasn't going to take no for an answer.

'OK, I promise,' I scoffed. 'What if I did some googling for you and found out where Beatrice lived now?'

'No, don't go to any trouble.'

'It wouldn't be any trouble. Can I look for her and find out if she still lives on Capri?'

'Why do you want to?'

'Because I do. I want to do something for you for being my friend.'

'You don't have to do anything for me. A friend is a friend, it doesn't require invoicing.'

'She might be a way off the ship for you.'

'I like living on the ship.'

'Yeah, but you're lonely. Beatrice is your home. You should go home. I would if I could.'

'Why do you say that? Why can't you go home?'

'I just can't.'

'A man?' she guessed. 'You'll find someone else.'

'How do you know?'

'Law of averages. They'll appear, right when you least expect them. Maybe right when you most need them. That's how I met Beatrice.'

'But you lost touch with her.'

'No – *I* let her go,' she explained, pouring herself another AdV from the carafe. 'You have to be better than you want to be, I've found. And I needed to be happier in myself to be better. Your mind is a garden, your thoughts are the seeds and you choose what to plant there – good or bad. I only planted bad seeds. And I lost her.'

I didn't want to believe it, but I knew she was right. I remembered what Bobby Fairly had told me – *The price for freedom is everything you once were, Rhiannon*. I had to be better than I wanted to be. I had to be more Hilary. There had to be some good to extricate from the wreckage of Rhiannon.

Caro topped up my glass. 'Oh bollocks, let's finish this one awf, shall we? Could be dead tomorrow.'

'You'll outlive us all,' I said.

'Not with this fucker in my chest cavity I won't.'

It took me a few moments to understand. 'You're *dying*?'

'We all are. I'm just further along the conveyor belt.'

And I didn't mean to but I snapped and threw my glass to the floor where it shattered into a million pieces.

'Well, there was no need for *that*, was there? That's just childish.'

'I WANT TO BE FUCKING CHILDISH!' I shouted. 'Everyone leaves me.'

'Well, I apologise for getting breast cancer to piss you off but there we go.' She patted juice from the table with her napkin. 'Who else has left you?'

'Everyone. My baby… I lost my baby.'

'When was this?'

'Recently,' I said.

'You're still grieving. It will take time but you'll get there.'

'What if I don't?'

I wanted to spill all the fucking tea, tell Caro everything, like the child she had called me, desperate to confess bad behaviour. Ask her advice on what Géricault had said at the press conference. Ask why they were suggesting I'd hurt my baby when all I'd wanted was her to be safe. But despite how pissed I was at that moment, I knew telling Caro too much was a one-way ticket to the slammer. So I kept schtum.

'We all feel love, so we all feel pain,' she said.

'No, *I* don't. Not until now.'

'Of course you do,' she said again. 'You love your baby. I love all my children, despite what shits they became. If any one of them needed me in their lives, I would step off this ship in a heartbeat. I would stop the world.'

'Would you?'

'Yes.'

'I dunno if I experience love the way everyone else does. The brain injury I got – my sister said it smashed all the love out of me. I don't deserve love.'

'Of course you do. Maybe your sister underestimated you?' Caro suggested. 'Maybe love has smashed all the hate out of you?'

What, like a reverse *Breaking Bad*? Was I breaking *good*? A tear rolled down, landing in my glass with a *plink*.

Caro sat back, glass rested against her necklaces. 'There's love, right there. Hurts, doesn't it? It's the greatest feeling we were given the capacity for but it's also the most painful. I think I would rather experience it than not.'

I drank and drank until the angry flame for Ivy dulled and went out. I drank until I was happy and laughing about every single little stupid thing. I didn't care if the entire Spanish police force marched in and loaded me into a straitjacket and a Hannibal mask.

Old Moneybags paid our bar bill, thank God, and I wheeled her chair outside where the sun was still beating down and the day wasn't done with us. 'Do you want to have a mooch round the square before the ship leaves?'

'Oh no thanks,' she said. 'I need another church like I need another tumour in my tits.' And we were laughing again. 'I'm hungry,' she announced. 'Let's go and find something stodgy to mop up all this booze.'

The rest of the afternoon, we wandered about the old town laughing at hats on souvenir stalls, eating churros and free samples of roasted snail, tapas and Spanish sausage. I couldn't be arsed to be Hilary so I let the act slip and went a little more Rhiannon. There was something about Caro which made me feel like I could be more myself – to a point, anyway. After lunch we flagged down a cab large enough to accommodate Caro's wheelchair and went to Jardin Botanico – the botanical gardens.

It was my kind of place – parkland, flowers, stray cats everywhere. But I felt so ill. I puked in a bush and lay down on a bench groaning.

'I'm never drinking again,' I said, my head spinning like a top. I'd gone from spoilt child in the restaurant throwing food to pissed teenager on a park bench in one hour. Around Caro I had regressed.

Caro parked her chair next to me. The giant trees offered a cool shade from the scorching sun, and every so often a cat would appear and nuzzle our legs or snuggle up in the flower bed to sleep. One sat directly in front of us and licked its own arse clean.

'I wish I could do that,' she said.

'Yeah, me too. I'd never need another man again.'

There were a few beds in bloom, quite odd for January. Caro said Spain had a warm winter which explained it. 'The flowers don't know what month it is – all they know is warmth so they come out.' A welcome smattering of almond blossom sprinkled down on us as a breeze blew through the grove.

Caro read from the leaflet as we walked round. She didn't need her chair the whole time and she'd get out when she felt like it to stretch her legs. Except when there was an ice cream kiosk in sight and then she was straight back in it so we could jump the queue.

'There's an orchid house too. Cacti and succulents, we've done them. Greenhouses, done. Ponds. Palms. Ooh a physic garden! This way, come on.'

We came to a small area near the back wall marked *'Plantes Medicinales'*. Raised beds packed with shrubs. Caro knew what they all were from studying the little signs. I knew nothing because it was all in Spanish.

'So what have we got here?' she said, bending over. She plucked a sprig of lavender and held it against her face, inhaling it deeply. 'Mmm, no better smell.' She handed it to me. I smelled it too. If I hadn't felt so sick and headachey from all the alcohol I'd consumed that morning, I'd have agreed.

'Spearmint, Echinacea, yarrow, sage. Evening primrose. Oh, I adore primroses. They're my favourites. We used to go picking them as children. You're not allowed to these days.'

'I used to take that for my bitch fits. PMS.'

'Evening primrose? Did it work?'

'No, not exactly.'

'Arnica. Peppermint, lemon balm, marigold, rosemary, St John's Wort. That's mmm, that's witch hazel.'

'Can you bathe your vadge in these?'

'What?'

'Nothing.'

Caro rolled herself towards the next section – '*Plantas Peligrosas*. Have a guess what that means.'

'Plants they use to make Pellegrino?'

'*Dangerous* Plants,' she said with a twinkle. 'Henbane, Manzanilla – apple of death. Strychnine, Brugmansia – Devil's Breath – Belladonna and Hemlock too. That's how Socrates died, hemlock.'

'Oh right.'

She fumbled around in her handbag and produced a pair of small white gloves, pulling them on before bending over and tearing up a couple of sprigs of hemlock, wrapping them carefully inside a clean hanky.

'What are you doing?'

'Picking some. If it gets too much I can boil this up in water and knock it back, can't I?'

I wandered on behind her as she took sly cuttings of all the most poisonous plants in the garden, all of them bearing yellow '*No tocar!*' warning signs and each one with several more exclamation marks than the last.

'You won't be allowed to take them back on the ship,' I told her. 'How are you going to get them through security?'

'I'm an old, disabled woman. Officials tend to rush me through because I hold everybody up. Carry on, I say. Use their own prejudices against them.'

I got that. And I'll admit it was useful having Caro in

a wheelchair. People gave us the best tables, pushed us to the front and generally ignored us wherever we went. But I still didn't like her taking the plants.

'Ooh look at these.' We came upon a small tree whose beautiful trumpet-like flowers drooped towards the ground like they were bowing. '*Los trompetas de angel* – Angel's trumpets,' she announced.

'Pretty,' I said.

'Pretty lethal,' she chuckled. 'These are the most dangerous flowers here. A botanist did a talk a few months back on the ship – they contain some terrible toxins, like atropine. They look beautiful but they're killers.'

Kind of like me, I thought.

'We should take a few,' said Caro, reaching out to the blooms.

'Are you insane?'

She plucked some of the flowers and wrapped them in a hanky.

'No,' I said, standing my ground. 'Put them back. Put it all back.'

'What?' she said, turning round to face me.

'I don't want you to take any of it,' I said. 'I don't want you to die.'

She removed her gloves and tossed them in a litter bin. 'It's not something *you* have any control over. Every day I become frailer, more scared. What have I got to live for? Sitting in a wing-back chair, pissing myself to *Judge Rinder*? You have your life ahead of you.'

'No I don't.'

'Of course you do, silly girl.'

'I don't have anything. Or any*one*.'

'That's silly talk—'

'—why can't you live as much as you can for now? Then go home and die there?' I bubbled with rage.

'Because my home is the ship.'

'Your home should be on Capri. With Beatrice.'

'Capri is in the past.'

'*The past can hurt, but you can either run from it or learn from it.*'

'Is that Rousseau?'

'No, it's the baboon from *The Lion King*. But he's right, isn't he?'

'Yes. And your baboon knows what he's talking about,' she laughed.

'So you just want to die, is that it?'

'I didn't say that.'

'I might die as well too then.'

'You're drunk and vulnerable, I'm not listening to this.'

'I'm serious. I don't want to live. I wanna die as well. We'll do it together.'

'You're young enough to get over your baby. You'll bounce back.'

'I don't *want* to bounce back. So if you eat that stuff,' I marched over to the hemlock and poised my hand, ready to pluck, 'so will I.'

'No, don't touch it!'

'I will, I swear.' My hand hovered underneath it. My head swam – I was still so nauseous. 'I thought you were my friend.'

'I *am* your friend. We've had a lovely day, haven't we?'

'But why do you have to die?'

'Cancer isn't terribly negotiable.'

'I know. My mum *and* my dad died from it. They both decided OK, *that's enough treatment. Nothing else worth staying around for. I'm off now.* Not a thought for anyone else. And you're the same.'

I zoned in on a bed of lantana flowers, pinks and yellows in bloom too early. I staggered over and tore into them, ripping their heads off left right and centre, throwing them at Caro, wrenching and kicking them asunder.

'You're a fucking. Selfish. Bitch!'

Petals flew, the air filling with the sweet scents, until all around me were bare, brown stems and spikes. When I was done, I traipsed back through the pink-and-white carpet towards a bench and slumped down. My hands were covered in small red cuts.

Caro walked towards me. 'Look at the mess you've made.'

I felt a hand on my chin and another on the side of my face, forcing my head up to look at the torn-out roots, the pink-and-yellow petals scattered around. I closed my eyes, my eyelids crushing out two tears. She reached into her sleeve, pulling out a clean handkerchief, drying my cheeks with it.

'You need to stop hating yourself so much. Leave it behind. Start anew. All this anger, it will only lead to no good.'

'Maybe no good is where I belong,' I huffed.

'Don't talk rot,' she said, cupping my face. 'You have to start letting her go, my darling. For your own sake.'

I watched the last of the petals floated to the ground with the others. I looked at my hands, covered with little bubbles of blood. I rubbed them all over my face, smudging it all over me. I still. Felt. Nothing. No pain at all.

Caro looked sternly at me but my stare was unwavering. Slowly, she reached inside her bag and pulled out what she'd taken, throwing them down one at a time, upon the dry earth.

'What now?' I sniffed.

'We shall get some plasters for your hands and a cold flannel for your face… and we shall go home.'

Sunday, 6 January – Mallorca

1. *People who still don't know what to do with an apostrophe*
2. *The idiot savant in the nightly quiz who keeps winning. For fuck's sake, get a girlfriend and give somebody else a chance to win a baseball cap.*
3. *The Jonas Wives*
4. *Football fans who act like Match of the Day pundits but haven't kicked a ball since they were teenagers – e.g. Ken and Dennis*
5. *Adam Levine*

I could see the newspapers now:

NIPPED IN THE BUD: Killer Turns Soft

FROM SWEETPEA TO PANSY: Murderer Admits Baby Dulled Killer Instinct

DEAD HEAD: Badass Bitch Gives Up Bloodlust For Bootees

Caro tried hard to snap me out of my malaise, inviting me up to the Diamond Deck for a dinner and jazz evening. It was a whole other world. Clean, quiet, beige. Each dining table had its own personal member of staff in attendance and there was a complete absence of noise and/or children. It was like a soundproof haven, separate from the rest of the ship.

Even so, I couldn't lift myself out of my doom. Caro would have got more conversation out of her still-bleeding filet mignon.

'Do your hands still hurt?'

She'd given me a pair of navy silk gloves to wear to repel queries about the scratches. They stung like hell but only when I was reminded. 'No.'

'More wine?'

'No thanks.'

'How's your steak?'

'Fine.'

'What would you like to do tomorrow? I have a hair appointment first thing but we could take a taxi into Palma afterwards?'

'I don't need you to babysit me.'

'There's a good chiropodist in Palma actually. We could go and have pedicures together if you want to. How about that?'

'I'd rather have a smear test done with rusty instruments.'

'Whatever tickles your fancy.'

'Don't worry about me tomorrow. I'll be all right on my own. You go and have your hair did and your feet felt.'

She carried on chewing her filet. 'We don't have to explore at all. We could stay on board. The pool on this deck is much less busy. No children, none of those silly pool noodles to keep tripping over.'

The reminder kicked me in the heart. 'I think I'll have an early night.'

'Are you sleeping at the moment?'

'No, but I can watch TV.'

She rooted around in her handbag for an age, eventually pulling out a small bottle of pills. 'One will suffice.'

'What is it?'

'They're prescribed, but they can knock you out. When you've had a good night's rest you'll be able to think more clearly.' I reached out for the bottle but she held it away from me. 'Oh no, I'll administer, I think. Come along.'

She placed her scrunched-up napkin on the table and set about standing up. A waiter appeared beside her with her wheelchair, without even being asked but she flapped him away and reached for her stick instead.

'Where are you going?'

'To tuck you in, of course.'

'What about the jazz?'

'Nobody needs jazz at the best of times. I want to check you're safe.'

Most people would have left me well alone after my botanical gardens meltdown, but for some reason Caro cared. And that made me want to care about her too. I let her escort me back to my cabin and wait for me to do my ablutions and change into my PJs, and tuck me into my bed.

'Here you are.' She handed me a pill and a tumbler of water. I knocked back the pill – it tasted like chalky ink – and the drink. She took the glass and turned off the TV. 'I'll call for you before my hair appointment.'

'You don't have to. I'll be all right,' I said.

'Don't turn that TV back on. Start counting sheep jumping over fences.'

I remembered my mum saying the same thing to me once, even though she and Dad had been stupid enough to let me have a TV in my room. They let me have anything I wanted. Maybe that was my trouble.

'How many sheep do I have to count?'

She hobbled towards the door with her stick. 'As many as it takes. I'll see you in the morning.'

'Nighty night,' I called out.

The last thing I remembered was seeing the hind legs of Sheep Number 57 disappearing over the fence...

I awoke to my floating home shuddering – it was 9 a.m. We'd docked in Mallorca. I'd slept for twelve hours. The pill had been magic. I was still in the same boat, aimless, with stingy hands, a pile that wouldn't quit, a knackered twat and no sign of any messages on the cracked iPhone but my overall mood was level again. A reset button had been pushed. Another day. A sunny day.

I washed and dressed in my new red maxi dress and baby pink Converse and put some flower slides in my hair for extra girly effect – in the mirror, I was Hilary. Inside, I was Rhiannon.

I headed for the gangway, the endless corridor stretching out before me. And the more I walked, the more I thought: I haven't been given the right opportunity to test my theory. Liam, the libidinous scrote in Cartagena, hadn't been the right test subject. He wasn't a strong enough target, just an oversexed gusset monkey in head-to-toe Sports Direct. Any man's meat.

What I needed, more than anything to be sure as sure could be that my basic instinct had indeed been replaced with vanilla ice cream, was a sex offender. A paedophile. A rapist. And the more I walked, the more I thought.

Hmmm – to be a Good Girl doing Good Deeds or a Bad Girl doing what Bad Girls Do? Cue the distracted boyfriend meme.

The sight of an abandoned dinner tray on the floor outside one of the cabins served as the perfect opportunity to make my decision. There was a steak knife on the tray, greasy blade, flecks of meat between the teeth, partially hidden beneath a folded white napkin and a dying anniversary rose. Nobody else was around.

I knew beyond all doubt, once the knife was in my hot little hand, that this was my chance. Killing again, the way I liked to kill, would bring me back to life.

And I did what any wrong-minded cruise passenger whose ship has docked in the party capital of the Balearics would do: I went down to the Business Centre and googled 'Sex Offenders on Mallorca.'

As it turned out, Mallorca was a veritable Deliveroo of sex offenders. I had opportunistic rapists near the Drach Caves, migrant wolf packs near Valdemossa, paedophiles at Porto Cristo, flashers on golf courses, a guy in a blue parka upskirting women on the promenade at Cala Pi, and a British teacher in Paseo Maratimo, charged with hiding cameras in a school toilet.

Only problem was – I didn't know where any of these men were. If there was a paedophile trailer park, like there is in Florida, I'd have forged a plan – ventured down there at midnight with a full petrol can and a match – but I only had nine and a half hours before the ship set sail again – there was no time to stalk or strategise. I had to go on instinct.

One of the links took me to a recent Twitter thread where opportunity knocked a little louder. A woman called Tracey had gone to Playa des Carbo with her family and a homeless guy flashed his penis at her young daughter. The man had a warning from the beach patrol but he was back a day later, in the dunes 'moaning and groaning obscenities' within earshot of playing kids.

But even *I* knew that the odds of the same guy turning up in the dunes on the exact day *I* happened to be there waiting for him were not in my favour, especially out of season. And I didn't fancy the long bus ride to the beach to waste my time. Instead, I went through the checkpoint gates and got a taxi into Palma, where I sat in an outdoor café near the beach and ordered several herbal teas and coma-inducing salads. I watched the passers-by, looking for a target to lock onto.

But I couldn't get a bite. It wasn't exactly surprising, just disappointing.

It got to 1.00 p.m. and I was getting increasingly fed up and the steak knife grew ever-heavier in my bag. A bus operator opposite one of the cafés was giving 25 per cent off half-day excursions to Alcúdia, the monastery at Valdemossa and the Caves of Drach with pearl factory pit-stop, and I remembered something on one of the online threads about a sex pest near the Caves of Drach. It was worth a shot. I had to get something out of the day.

So I bought a ticket.

The bus trip was a bumpy, drawn-out affair interspersed by the odd goat grazing on a rocky outcrop and complaints about the faulty air-conditioning. Our tour guide – Margaretha – was clearly on commission from the pearl factory where we stopped for a pee break because aside from Rafael Nadal, it was all she could talk about. *Did you know Rafael Nadal's home is over this hill? Did you know Rafael Nadal built a tennis school over there? Did you know you can all get 5 per cent discounts on earrings at the Majorica factory where it is rumoured Rafael Nadal buys all his pearls?*

A blonde perm in a too-tight pink jacket and shorts constantly pecked at her husband in the row in front of me. Her pale legs were covered in purple blotches like two hunks of *jamon* after a street fight and her stilettos were so high she walked down the aisle like Mr Tumnus. Bardot, her name was (apparently) and his was definitely Gareth – I say definitely because of the myriad orders she barked at him – *Have you got the antibac, Gareth? Could you get me a water, please, Gareth? Will you peel this apple for me, please, Gareth? Could you push me off the coach and roll me under the wheels, please, Gareth?* Poor git.

Actually no, *stupid* git. He's got what he paid for. I thought about stabbing *her* but I couldn't summon the enthusiasm. Besides which, she seemed like a squealer.

Anyway, we got to the Drach Caves and filed off row by row and I kept the old antennae out for sex pests, nonces and unattended erect penii. Clearly Lady Luck was shining down on me because it didn't take long for opportunity to knock. On one of the other buses that pulled up next to ours in the car park, I zoned in on three lads and their behaviour towards two skinny young girls. One of the lads, short and neck-beardy, kept twanging their vest straps in the queue for tickets. Another, in a basketball vest, kept leaning over and saying things which made the boys laugh – the girls had no reaction at all.

I forced myself into the line behind them.

They would not leave these girls alone, even as one of them turned around and said, 'Would you stop doing that, please, And there came the inevitable 'We're only having a laugh, babe, chill out.'

I tapped the tall, curly one on the back to ask him if he had a cigarette.

'Nah, sorry, love.' The other lads turned around and dogged me up from my feet to my face. Clearly, they didn't like what they saw. Too old. Too much belly. Not a fuckable enough mouth. They started again on the young girls.

'Is it cold inside the caves, do you know?' I asked them in my Hilary twang. 'I forgot to bring a cardy.'

The curly one turned again. 'Dunno, never been before. You here alone?'

'Yeah,' I said, spinning him a line about being dumped before me and my girlfriends came out here. 'They didn't want to come today. Too hungover.' I giggled, the way a Hilary would giggle. 'I'm Hilary, by the way.'

'Conan,' Curly Hair replied, looking more vegetarian than barbarian. He pointed out the other two who afforded me the merest of nods before returning to their phones. 'These are Trav and Ethan.'

'Nice to meet you all. What is it, Lads on Tour?'

'Summing like that *hur hur hur*,' Conan chuckled, keeping

one eye on the girls in front who'd moved as far as they could forward in the line. I wasn't quite sure where to go next in my line of questioning but, the boys were happy as long as one of the following was happening:

1. *I laughed at their jokes;*
2. *I flirted back;*
3. *My tits were on show at all times;*
4. *I asked them questions about themselves and agreed with any and all opinions they offered and*
5. *I paid them compliments about their clothes, muscles, and/or hair.*

And so I did. It was exhausting but I did. And by the time we reached the cave entrance, the lads were fully focused on me and *not* the young girls.

Conan was the one who bit hardest on my fishing line – Trav had a girlfriend, whom he was constantly texting, and Ethan was too much of a pig-ignorant funt to pick up on any of my hints.

The caves themselves stank of hot meat. Conan and I exchanged relationship stories – he told me about his 'nagging bitch ex-girlfriend Claire,' while I regaled him with tales of Craig and his inability to keep his yoghurt squirter out of Lana. Our conversation then took a sour turn.

He leaned in. 'Well, not being funny, but it might have been the weight, love.'

'The weight?'

'Can I speak frank, right? We don't like our women too heavy to handle, know what I mean? You've got a gorgeous face. And if you went down the gym, you could lose that tummy in no time. I can show you some exercises I do.' He lifted his shirt to smack the scrawniest, whitest set of abs I'd ever seen. Like a fleshy pink cheese grater.

'Wow, you're stacking some muscles there, aren't ya?' I said, stepping down into the second chamber and stopping to look at yet more badly lit dripping calcium deposits.

I could hear our guide Margaretha distantly banging on about karstic precipitates and paleoclimatic variations and pointing to some rock up ahead that looked a bit like Dumbledore riding a pig. Talking of which...

'I went out with an overweight girl once,' said Conan, pushing in front of me to get a look at Piggy Dumbledore. 'She was funny but they always are, aren't they? They overcompensate. No, I'm not saying there's anything wrong with it, like. But you can always tell with fat girls where their priorities lie – the fridge!'

I laughed like a drain – blackly and emptily. 'You're so right!' I giggled, scanning his body for the right sinewy parking space for a blade.

But there was something even more amiss about Conan – something beyond being a habitual douche-canoe. No, he was wired, for want of a better word – and through the absence of any scent of alcohol on his too-close breath I deduced it was drugs. Uppers, ecstasy or speed. He constantly touched his nose and had this swinging jaw habit going on.

He held up his bicep to show me the fruits of his efforts. I could barely see it. 'Feel that. Go on.' So I did. He flexed. It was like a plum on a twig.

'Wow. So hard.'

'That's since November. And I can bench nearly 40k.' He lifted his shirt to show me another flash of cheese-grater abs.

Please stop. My penis can only get so erect. 'That's dead impressive.'

We shuffled forwards and I wasn't so much blood-lusty by this point as utterly bored. I sort of wanted to kill him but in a way that wouldn't take that much effort. I thought about pushing him into one of the deep pools surrounding the walkway but there were too many people around who'd help.

'Men don't make passes at gals with fat asses,' he announced, laughing like he'd invented it. Negating his point, he pinched my arse cheek.

I chuckled, forcing a smile. 'You're so clever.'

Now normally, although people like this grab hold of my ire and twist it round like a fucking dishcloth, I don't kill them for it. Let's face it – if I killed every single person who pissed me off I'd have been in jail since I was six. Conan happened to be in the right place at the wrong time.

He also happened to feel up one of the 14-year-olds' butts in the darkness of the caves when I happened to be looking his way.

And the girl stood there, looking at the sights beyond – more calcium deposits and a stalagmite that looked like Danny DeVito – not exactly letting Conan touch her but not stopping him either. Until she moved along towards what I can only assume was her mother and Conan started on her friend who, pleasingly, threw him a glare until he backed off.

Giving up on the girls, Conan leaned in to me. 'Where you staying?'

'In town. Why?'

There came the lusty whisper. 'Do you wanna go back to your hotel?'

'No forget that,' I said. 'There's a little cove we passed on the way here, up the road, through some woods.' I unfolded the map I'd been handed on the bus. I showed him the general direction of where it was. *Plenty of secluded areas*, it said. 'We can go there.'

'Our bus leaves in two hours,' he sniffed.

'Won't take long, will it?' I gave him an obligatory hair twiddle and wink. 'We can be back before the buses leave.'

He didn't need long to think about it – he was already pitching a tent for me. *Boys do get hard-ons for girls who like lardons.*

'Yeah, all right.' His breath went ragged. 'Come on, dirty girl.'

I was so honoured that the majesty of Conan the Vegetarian saw it fit to grace my fat fuck of a foof with his majestic cock but that's exactly what he wanted to do. What a privilege for a chonker like me, eh? Shame I hadn't shaved – it had been months since my last sweep round with the No No. I usually have a rule – no No No, No Noo Noo. But on this occasion, I had absolutely no intention of letting Conan cum into my mentions.

We sneaked out of a side entrance and up the winding lanes from the cave complex and he found it hilarious that I was out of breath and sweating by the time we arrived at the woods. I ventured to brush my hand against his in the hope that he would hold it. And he did. And even as he walked and I was perspiring because it was a hot day and all hills, he still kept on about my lack of fitness.

'If you went to the gym you could tighten all this,' he said, seeing fit to drop behind me and play bongos on my buttocks. 'You'd have more stamina. You'd be burning off fat, instead of, you know, a load of cakes.'

'You're right,' I puffed. 'And do you know what, I'm going to get on the treadmill when I get back to my hotel. I'll use *your* body as my motivation.'

He grinned widely. 'Thanks!'

We walked through the woods to where the trees thinned out but the ground was all sand and shards of bark. I kept losing my footing and he raced on ahead. I didn't want us too out in the open.

'Stop,' I puffed. 'Wait for me.'

'Come on, slow coach. I can see the sea, it's down there.'

'Where?' I said, coming up behind him.

'Down there, look,' he said, stopping and pointing down the slope. 'See?'

I withdrew the knife from my bag and plunged it into the back of his neck and he gargled and heaved. I pulled it out, then stuck it back in to sever his vocal cords and into his back again and again and again. It was like being back at school, being with my parents, being with Craig: normality. Safety. Not thrilling, just familiar. This is what I know. This is what I do.

This is what Home is.

I stabbed him seven times till he fell forward onto his knees. I was about to push him down when he scrabbled up and stumbled into the brush, faster than I could run.

'Fuck!' I cried out, dashing after him.

He stumbled and grabbed out for something to keep him upright. His bloody fingerprints on every tree. He wouldn't get far – his legs kept buckling. I slowed. He grabbed out for fallen branches, handfuls of sand and dry leaves, and he kept turning to find me, gaining on him. There were people on the beach below, families splashing. If one of them saw...

Saw me coming at him again. Saw him stumbling. Saw me pushing him forwards, pinning him down and plunging the knife into him eight more times. Making certain that this time he wouldn't get back up again.

'That's the thing... about fat girls, Conan,' I puffed, dodging a spurt of aortic blood, 'you can't live with 'em, and you can't... fight 'em off.'

Soon all the struggle left him and he stopped, face down in the dirt. I turned him over, feeling a flicker of a pulse, sand stuck to his bloodied face, eyes fluttering. I couldn't lie on top of him – there was too much blood – so I lay down beside and watched that last little light go out. Lying like a lover on the sand, waiting for her paramour to bring her to ecstasy.

I prepared myself for the rippling; flames igniting my rocket to the stars.

But there was no rippling. No flame. It was sex with no climax. In out, in out, in out – then just out and I left it dripping on the cool sand. He got his, I didn't get mine. The disappointment was crushing. I lay beside his body for the longest time, nauseated. Agitated. I started digging.

'What you doing?' said a little voice.

'What?' I flicked around. A small girl had appeared, around five years old, in a pink-and-blue striped swimming costume, carrying a little yellow bucket and spade, scraping curls out of her face with a sandy hand.

'Are you digging a hole?'

'Yeah.'

'Can I help?'

'No. Where are your parents?'

'Mum's down there. My dad's playing football with my brother.'

'Go to your mum.' Conan's brown leather wallet slid from his pocket.

The girl dropped her bucket and some twigs fell out. I had her full attention. 'Did you bury *him*?' Conan's foot was sticking out of the sand.

'Yeah.' I pushed a wall of sand over him to cover the foot and flicked some more over a dribble of blood which had seeped out from under him.

'Are you cold?'

'No.'

'Bye,' she said picking up her bucket and the sticks and coming towards me, leaning over to see Conan's face, but I got in the way to spare her from the full sight. She disappeared back where she'd come from, the breeze catching the slightest hint of coconut from her full head of curls.

I didn't know why she'd asked me if I was cold but I realised then I was shaking. It must have been shock. I'd felt the hate but I'd also the guilt, immediately, when she'd appeared. I kept seeing Ivy's face on hers. Ivy seeing what I'd done to her dad. My Ivy. My baby. This was what I'd wanted to save her from.

What the fuck had happened to me inside a week? I should

have been jubilant – I'd rid the world of another predator. But where was the rush? Where was the orgasm I'd had after killing Sandra Huggins and had strode out of that farm shop feeling like the whole world was a marble in my fist?

It was not there anymore.

I'd reached the end. I couldn't go forward or back. I had this overwhelming feeling of futility. I was a nothing. A spent force. A dead head.

Keston Hoyle's words as he'd pointed at my belly screamed into view.

That's your future in there. That's the one good thing you have. You'll realise that when she's born.

This was no life. And whatever it was, I didn't want to live it anymore.

I waited in the dunes for the little girl to come back with her mum or dad. For Trav or Ethan to come looking for Conan and find me, sitting beside his cold body with a bloody knife in my hand. For anyone to appear and ask what I was doing. Call the police. Call someone. Take me in.

I was ready to tell them: I am Rhiannon Lewis. I have killed again. I will come quietly. I had never been more ready for anything.

But nobody came. Nobody came looking.

And eventually, as the clouds regrouped above me and the beach emptied, I buried Conan's body in the sand with the knife. I walked down to a secluded part of the shore, tossing the phone and thumbing through the wallet, finding a student union ID, a debit card, a photo of some woman with her tits out and a small baggy of powder. I pocketed that and slung the rest.

I don't remember a single other thing that happened that day. I must have got back onto our bus because I got back onto the ship. I must have snorted the cocaine but I can't remember when. The next thing I knew, I was waking up, in my own bed, in my own cabin.

And all I could smell was shit.

Monday, 7 January – Barcelona

1. *Christian rock bands*
2. *People on social media warning others of triggering in news articles*
3. *All those virtue-signalling Instacunts sipping cocktails but Sending Thoughts to those caught up in the Tenerife plane crash disaster*
4. *Gamers so addicted they'd rather piss than pause*
5. *Logan Paul*

I opened my crusty eyes to see Caro, sitting in the chair beside me, thumbing through a leaflet called '*Olé* For Barcelona', and shaking her head.

'Why does it stink of shit?' I croaked.

'Because you've shit yourself,' she replied without hesitation.

Apparently, I had passed Caro in the corridor outside my room where she'd been calling for me on and off all day long. She had noticed my nose was bleeding. Apparently she had followed me down into the gym where I had got on a treadmill and run seven kilometres.

Apparently, I had bought myself the most expensive drink at the juice bar – the Sunshine Superfoods Smoothie – because

I needed 'to rid myself of my toxins and replenish my Hilary' and she had followed me back to my cabin where I had promptly thrown it all up again in the sink and got into my bed and talked her ear off for hours until I'd fallen asleep.

Apparently, at God knows what hour, I'd run out onto the deck and stood beside the railings deep-breathing until she had coaxed me back in and tucked me into bed. I remembered a sensation of being suffocated.

But that wasn't the worst of it. The worst of it was that I'd shit myself.

I'd actually *factually* shitted myself. Myself, I had but shat.

'Tell me you're kidding,' I croaked, picking off a rogue crusty blood clod from my inner nostril.

'I'm afraid I can't,' she said, pulling at a stray eyelash and flicking it to the floor. 'It was one of the many fluids you covered yourself in over the course of last evening.'

'Have you been here all night?'

'Yes.'

I felt around the bed – no evidence of shit on my hand and yet I could still smell it on me. 'I've never done that before. Ugh.' My stomach lurched and my head banged. 'Who cleaned me up?'

'You managed to undress yourself and get into the shower and I monitored you. I asked your room steward to launder your clothes.' She pointed to a clean pile of fresh laundry on the desk.

'I don't remember. You shouldn't have done that.'

'It was either that or incinerate them. I told him you had a milk intolerance and ate the wrong ice cream.'

My hair was slightly damp. There was a bunched-up sodden

towel behind my head that I'd been using as a pillow. 'You saw me naked?'

'I didn't have much choice. It was either that or leave you lying foetal on the carpet stinking of your own excrement.'

'Did you… touch me?'

'No. I did not.'

'I don't know why I asked that.'

'Because I have intimated to you my preference for women,' she sighed. 'But trust me, anything naked covered in its own excrement does not excite. It bears as much allure as a farm-yard animal.'

Shame slithered over me like snakes. 'I'm going to have another shower.'

There came no argument from Caro. A *shushing* sound her-alded the appearance of that day's *Cruise Letter* and she got up, waddling over to the door to retrieve it. When I emerged from the bathroom, she was still there, sitting at the dressing table.

'I'm clean,' I mewed, standing beside my unmade bed like I was ready for a choirgirl audition. The room smelled slightly less shitty but a vague odour lingered like an embarrassing reminder.

'Just in time to catch breakfast,' said Caro, standing up.

'I don't want anything.'

'You can sit and watch me eat mine then.'

We went up to the Diamond Deck breakfast room and I joined Caro at her usual table overlooking the garden. Still no signal on the iPhone, even though we had docked. A waiter came over to take our order.

'Two freshly squeezed orange juices and some ham and cheese croissants, I think this morning, please, Martin.'

'I said I didn't want anything,' I reminded her.

'They're not for you,' she replied with a definite bat of eyelid. Martin poured out coffee into respective cups, taking the order to the kitchen.

'Thanks,' I said. 'For helping me last night. When I shat.'

'It's nothing,' she said, sipping her coffee.

'No, to me it's something. I know I'm in a state. I know I need to sort myself out.'

'You can't think too clearly when you're grieving,' she said, buttering a breakfast roll for me and one for herself. My son died when he was 29.'

'How?'

'The official cause was bacterial endocarditis. He was a heroin addict.'

'Christ.'

'We hadn't been speaking. His body was found three weeks after he died by his landlord, who'd only troubled him for the rent. Not one caller, not even his mother. I've carried the guilt with me all around this world. And it will accompany me into the next. Whenever someone you love leaves you, or you leave them, it feels like they've taken a piece of you with them. And the place where that missing part is, it always hurts. I know an addict when I see one.'

'Me? I'm not an addict.'

'Oh, I think you are. You're addicted to something.'

'I'm not.' I checked around, lowering my voice. 'Before last night, I'd never touched hard drugs before. I met up with a guy in Porto Cristo and he… gave it to me. I've had a few spliffs but I've never snorted anything.'

'So why last night?' She batted her enormous eyes at me.

'It's none of your business,' I snapped. 'We're not family. You're not my grandmother. I had two of them and they were both cunts.'

'Strong word,' she said, without batting a wrinkly eyelid.

'They were always lecturing me too. I don't need a lecture on how bad drugs are, OK? I know. I woke up and smelled the shit I was covered in.'

'Drink your coffee.'

'I don't want coffee. I want green tea.'

Within a heartbeat, Martin had been summoned to remove the offending cup and brought me a fresh pot of White Monkey Paw Green Tea, which he informed me was 'hand-crafted using a 3,000-year-old scorching method in the Fujian Mountains' and served with a tiny pot of heather honey.

'Thanks,' I said quietly, stirring my pot and leaving it to settle. There were so many elephants galloping about the room I could barely hear myself think. Caro said nothing. It said everything.

I turned my attention back towards the garden through the window. An elderly man using an electric wheelchair was wheeling around, following the curve of the path, talking to the plants.

'I know what it's like to lose someone you loved and feel powerless over it,' said Caro as Martin brought the croissants and juice. 'I see you going through the same pain I was in, the same pain my son was in. And I want to help. That's all.'

A tear betrayed me, scuttling down my cheek before I could stop it. Caro reached across and dabbed it away with her napkin. The smell of Chanel Number 5 and the sudden heat of the dining room and sizzle of fresh bacon swilled around my head and instantly I grew nauseous and I had to get out. 'I need some air.'

I didn't think she was going to follow me out on deck but she did. I perched on the edge of a planter as the buzz of her wheelchair approached. The breeze whipped my hair extensions and blew them all around my head. I grabbed them by the handful and tucked them inside my T-shirt.

I stroked the leaf of an agapanthus, only to find it had a serial number on the stem. 'They're fake. They're fucking fake,' I said, trying to tear off one of the leaves. 'There's no smell at all. Even the stems are plastic.'

'Well, you can't expect flowers to bloom all year round, can you?'

'Why bother? Why bother to plant them at all?'

'Because they make people happy. *Some* people anyway.'

'Yeah, well. The boot that fits one always hurts another, doesn't it?'

'That's misquoted – and it's a shoe,' she said.

'It's not a real garden. There's nothing real here. It's all fake. It's all plastic.'

'Some of the plants are real. Those are,' she said, pointing to a palm with wide green fronds. I got up and went over to sit next to that instead. Stroked a leaf. Inhaled it. Tried to imagine I was somewhere else. Except there was nowhere else to go, even in my imagination.

'Let's go into Barcelona today,' said Caro. 'I'll organise a car to take us round. We can go and find a real garden, one you're not going to demolish, perhaps?'

Dad used to do that, linger when I was in a strop, trying to find ways of making me smile, of bringing me back to life. He usually managed it with the promise of buying me a book or Sylvanians or taking me with him to watch him and his mates thump the crap out of a paedophile. But Caro wasn't my dad or my mum or Seren. She didn't really know me and owed me nothing.

'I'm going back to bed.'

'No you're not. I won't let you.'

'Why don't you leave me alone? You will eventually anyway.'

'I'm not going anywhere.'

'You're going to die.'

'Eventually, but not today.'

'Trust me, I'm no company.'

'Is that what you want? Solitude? To wallow in it?'

'I don't know *what* I want.'

'Right. Let's go into Barcelona.'

'What for?'

'To look at the sights, the architecture. And to eat until it fucking hurts.'

And that's what we did. I'd forgotten how much I love food – it's my most favourite thing, official. And until men taste as good as carbs, ever thus shall be. Caro's room steward organised a hire car to meet us outside the cruise terminal and it accompanied us the whole day, taking us into the city, giving us a guided tour from the comfort of an air-conditioned back seat, and dropping us off and picking us up as directed, mainly cafés that 'looked nice'.

We found a small café selling hot chocolate pots with churros and bought a fistful each. We sat outside and I ate seven of the buggers, savouring every mouthful, even the ones I downed so quickly they burned my tongue.

'I act a whole different type of fat for Spanish pastry,' I said, swinging my legs beneath my stool.

'I noticed,' she replied. There was chocolate on the tip of Caro's nose. It amused me greatly not telling her.

Finally with a full signal, I checked the iPhone for a Dannielle message. *Nada*. But after a while, I stopped looking and fell into Barcelona's warm embrace. Me and Caro became tourists – taking pictures, strolling around ancient monuments and staring up open-mouthed into the clean blue sky at the nightmarish majesty of La Sagrada Família.

'What a magnificent building,' I said, staring up high into the sky at the lethal-looking spires.

'Waste of bloody money,' said Caro.

That response was par for the course, as I soon learned. Things I found beautiful– Casa Batlló, Casa Milà, Park Güell – Caro found ugly or dull, and vice versa.

But slowly, so slowly I barely noticed, I felt better. Diverted. Distracted. I bought a unicorn keyring and a fresh fruit smoothie and irritated Caro with my slurping noises. It made me laugh. It was like spending the day with Marnie when we'd gone shopping in Bristol and walked around the museum and had freak shakes. Being with a friend tipped my world back in the right direction. It reminded me of something Daisy Chan said to me once at the *Gazette* – in time, with love and patience from others, you do get better. She'd been talking about her anxiety and anorexia, but maybe it applied to me too.

As the day went on and the happier I became, the gloomier Caro got. Like she was absorbing the bad mood from me.

'He was a turd as well,' she huffed as the limousine

circumnavigated the Columbus Monument twice so I could take pictures.

'The guy who found America?'

'He didn't *find* America,' she snipped, 'America was already *there*, being lived in quite happily by millions of native people. He struck a lucrative deal with Spanish royalty so he could plunder any land his ship happened across and force the inhabitants into slavery. He was a selfish bastard. That should be called *Monumento a un bastardo egoísta*.'

We ambled through the winding streets of the Gothic quarter into an enormous covered food market called La Boqueria. We sat at a counter, and Caro did all the ordering in Spanish. We tried samples of everything on offer – dried and fresh fruits, jamon Iberico, olives, salted anchovies, fried sardines, baby squid, fish still fucking breathing they were so fresh (not such a turn on), oysters, cheeses, gelato, pintxos, hot sandwiches. You name it. When she was happily feeding her face, I saw my chance.

'What was your son's name? The one who died.'

'Simon,' she replied.

'How did he get hooked on drugs?'

'The usual. Moved to a city, mixed in with some bad apples, lost his job.'

'Why did you two fall out?'

'He'd only call for money. And when he stopped calling me, he'd call my eldest, Sarah. She soon washed her hands of him but I abandoned him first. I do that. Some therapist teased that out of me in the Seventies – someone gets too close, I abandon them before they can abandon me. I did it with each of my children. Comes from being adopted, apparently.'

'You were adopted?'

'My mother left me for a man who wasn't my father. My own father couldn't cope and put me up for adoption. This was in 1946, you understand, just after the war. He was old by then. His idea of a bedtime story was to tell me about his time as a PoW.'

'Sorry.'

She flapped her hand. 'Tish and pish, I'm not looking for sympathy. But it does explain why I left all five of my marriages early. And why I left Beatrice. I loved her more than anyone I'd ever met.' Her head bowed. 'But I couldn't be sure I deserved her. So I left.'

'But you said society wasn't so accepting in the Fifties—'

'—oh, bugger society. Society could fuck itself in the eye for all *I* cared,' she snapped, wiping her hands roughly on a tissue. 'If I'd wanted to stay with her, I would have. Irrespective of marriage. Irrespective of society. I'd have *stayed*. But I didn't feel that I deserved her.'

'I bet she felt differently.'

Caro laughed, a rueful laugh dampened with lemon juice. 'It's a vicious cycle. You don't think you are worthy of love so you keep it at bay. But you still want it. I had a succession of flings after her – I treated all of them dreadfully for the simple fact none of them was Beatrice. I always called time on it before they had the chance to. After a while, you suffice yourself with being alone. You'll never break your *own* heart.'

'But Beatrice *didn't* break your heart. You broke *hers*.'

'I'm sure she got over it.'

'I bet she didn't. Is that why you live on the ship? So you don't have to put down roots anywhere?'

'Roots?' she said. 'Oh, I've never given them a chance to grow. Once you've been yanked out of one place, it's difficult to thrive anywhere else.'

'Great,' I said, downing as much churro as I could get in my mouth in one go, and even then I coughed some out onto the table top.

'That same therapist told me something which helped me reframe Simon's loss. He said that when a woman grows a baby, she retains some of that child's cells forever. Your baby has left some of her cells inside you where you can never lose them.'

Tears came thick and fast at hearing this.

She gripped my hand. 'I shouldn't have said that.'

'No,' I sniffed. 'I like that.'

'The point is that the bond will always be there. There will always be a part of her with you. Always. And nobody can take that away.' She dried my cheeks with her silk-soft palms. 'Come on – final stretch. Let's see what that misogynistic old prick Picasso's got to offer us, shall we?'

For the last part of the day, we walked around the white rooms of the Picasso Museum. Well, I walked, Caro insisted on using the chair so that we got priority in the queues and elevators. She was almost a more manipulative bitch than I was. No wonder I liked her so much.

I lost Caro on the way round, eventually finding her on a bench, staring at a painting – a 1897 oil on canvas called *Science and Charity*. Three figures around a dying man's bedside – a nun carrying a child and a doctor checking the dying man's pulse on a timepiece. The man's face was yellow, eyes hollow. Like Dad's when I last saw him.

'The old legs are starting to pinch now,' she said. 'How are you feeling?'

I followed her gaze to the painting. 'You're dying and you ask how *I'm* feeling after my coke-induced tantrum?' I scoffed.

'It was more than a tantrum, Hilary. You could have killed yourself.'

'Yeah, well. Thanks for today.'

'You're welcome. I have a chiropodist's appointment tomorrow.'

I frowned. 'Is that important?'

'It means I won't be able to be with you in the morning. But you could come with me and have your feet done if you'd like.'

'No thanks,' I said, plaiting the mane on my unicorn keyring. 'I'll take my chances with the verrucas. Never been keen on having my feet felt.'

'Come and find me at lunchtime. I'll be free then.'

'Don't worry about me, I'll be OK. I'll join a macramé workshop or go pole dancing or something.' She smiled. I looked towards the painting she was still staring at. 'What's the fascination with that one?'

'I was just thinking. About things. About death. How it will be.'

'If you want, I'll do it for you.'

She turned to me, her milky green eyes flicking round my face. 'What?'

'I did it for my dad when he was in pain. If that's what you want.'

Her mouth opened but no sound came out. She stared back at the painting, chewing on her bottom lip for a long time. 'Your own father?'

'Yeah. He was in hospital, having end-of-life care.' She reached for my hand. 'I wouldn't if he hadn't wanted me to. He was my hero.'

'Oh, Hilary,' she said. 'That's awful.'

'No it's not. I did it for him, not me. I didn't want him to go.'

'I don't *want* to be like this. I don't want *that* to be my only option.'

She was silent for minutes, staring at the painting. I was silent too. I rubbed at the little rainbow heart on the backside of my unicorn keyring. I thought about buying the matching pencil topper in the gift shop window.

'I was in Croatia once, in a restaurant with my husband…'

'Which husband?'

'Number Two. And he *was* a number two as well. Anyway, we were watching this cat with three legs, climbing a wall. And it fell off, directly into a cactus. And it yowled and screamed and scurried away, covered in spines. I went outside to see if I could help it. But by the time I got there, it had run directly into the path of a speeding car. I saw it on the road. And I stood watching this cat twitching for the longest time before it died.'

'Well, this is cheering me up no end.'

'It made me think – where there's life, there's hope. Being alive is enough. We strive for perfect – perfect children, good career, finding The One. But the most important thing is, fundamentally, we're *here*, we're *breathing*.'

We both looked back at the painting. 'Until we're not.'

'Precisely.'

'Wouldn't you like to see Beatrice again though, before you die?'

'No.'

'But what if she still loves you?'

'She doesn't.'

'She does.'

'She doesn't...' she snipped, eyeballing me. 'Why do you keep arguing?'

'Because she told me,' I said.

Tuesday, 8 January – Marseille

1. *Snooty assistant in the ship shop who'd played the role one too many times and now her face was stuck like that*
2. *Room steward Amanda who always seems to be outside my cabin door ready to clean. The most ubiquitous woman since the Fiji Water Girl*
3. *Meghan Markle's sister*
4. *Man on the harbourside who threw a plastic bottle into the ocean*
5. *People who have no personalities outside of their relationships with their spouses – e.g. Bardot and Gareth. Also...*
6. *People who name themselves glamorous names like Bardot but don't live up to them*

I'd found Beatrice on the morning of the Mallorca trip while I was googling sex offenders. In between waiting for pages to load and checking my niece Mabli's latest vlog about her new micro pig and finding Twitter posts about paedophiles I knew would trigger me – I do that sometimes – I'd absent-mindedly put the words 'Beatrice' and 'Capri' into the search bar.

Caro had mentioned Beatrice's maiden name was Genovesi so I started there. There was a jewellery store on Capri called Genovesi which had changed hands in the Seventies but the owners had kept the name. Beatrice's father had sculpted cameo jewellery and though he was long dead, I followed that line of inquiry and Google Translated a message to the current owners asking for any information. They got back to me later that afternoon.

Beatrice and her husband Rocco had sold the store in the Seventies and moved to the outskirts of Rome. Taissa had told me their married name was Pelagatti – a thankfully rare surname – and that was where her knowledge went cold. I widened my search for Pelagattis in or near Rome and sent several people with the surname the same message.

I'd all but forgotten about it, until the morning we docked in Barcelona and a notification pinged through on the cracked iPhone. My heart skipped a beat, thinking it was from Dannielle Fairly, but it was a guy called Enzo Pelagatti. He'd contacted me in English, saying he was a student in Rome and that his grandmother had been called Beatrice Genovesi in the Fifties. He'd spoken to her and she remembered Caro and would love to see her again.

His actual words were: '*Beatrice vuole vedere il suo amato Caro più di ogni altra cosa al mondo.*' Or rather, 'Beatrice wants to see her beloved Caro more than anything in the world.'

So I set up a meeting for when the ship docked in Rome. A little knowledge and a search engine goes a long way these days so it was piss-easy all in all, but Caro was acting like I'd scaled Everest and found Beatrice resting on the south-east ridge. All the way back to the ship she cried.

'I can't believe you found her. I can't believe I will see her again. You are a wonderful person, Hilary, truly wonderful.'

'It was nothing,' I beamed, my head swimming with goldfish.

'No, this is everything. This is unbelievable.' But as the car journey went on, she grew quieter, more thoughtful. She stared more out of the window and picked at fingers. 'She'll be old,' she said, more quietly than she had been talking. 'I only remember Beatrice being young.'

'Well, I hate to state the obvious but—'

'I know I'm old too,' she snipped, 'but in my head, she's twenty-five.'

'*My beloved Caro*, she said,' I reminded her. And she smiled like I hadn't seen her do before – all broad and unashamed.

Her face lost about twenty years in that car ride. There were signs of the younger woman beneath. And weirdly, it made me happier. Not molten happiness, no orgasmic happiness, just happiness. Contentment that I had done something good for someone who'd shown goodness to me. And that lasted for the rest of the day.

Sad, innit? Even serial killers need cuddles.

Talking of which, by this point I was all over the news at home:

FARM SHOP KILLER'S AXE FRENZY: WHAT WE KNOW

FARM SHOP KILLER IS CELEBRITY CHILD HERO: Rhiannon Lewis was sole survivor of Priory Gardens Massacre

FARM SHOP KILLER MAY HAVE KILLED BABY TOO: Killer was eight months pregnant before murder

HOW DID THE DEADLY DUO GET
AWAY WITH IT FOR SO LONG?

Flicking through the news channels got me all angry again. Nothing was momentous enough, nothing was loud enough. On all the channels I was the third or fourth news item down. No biggy, just some little isolated murder in some little town no one had ever heard of. The main news was all Brexit chaos, Donald Trump's latest Twitter faux pas, the Tenerife plane crash and which Brits had won big at the Golden Globes. And why were they calling us a deadly duo? Like Craig was Clyde Barrow and I was his infatuated, simpering little Bonnie, still on the run. Why was he still the Charles Manson figure and I merely his brainwashed hippie acolyte? Fucking cheek.

One paper said he was on suicide watch.

God, it all felt like such a waste of time and effort. And where was my confession? I'd posted it on Christmas Eve – even with the holidays it should have reached you by now. Yet still nothing. I was still an also-ran in the contest for Most Evil Female in History, behind Rose and Myra.

No man had done *my* dirty work though – I'd done it all by myself. And what thanks did I get? No sodding thanks whatsoev.

There was still nothing from Dannielle Fairly either and my insides churned and bubbled and spat like a vat of acid. My good deed and all my good feelings of finding Beatrice floated away on the steam from the ship's funnels as we pulled out of port at Barcelona, headed for Marseille.

By the next morning, El Fuckboy had made the news too. His picture popped up on the *Daily Mail* website.

MISSING BRIT WHO VANISHED DURING ALICANTE STAG PARTY WITH FRIENDS, MAY HAVE 'COME TO HARM', SAY POLICE

A British man who travelled to Spain for a week-long stag party with his friends 'may have come to harm' detectives have said last night.

Liam Challoner, 25 from Chepstow, travelled to Alicante on 3 January for the short break. Gwent Police Major Crime Team are working with Spanish authorities to investigate the circumstances of his disappearance.

'Liam's family is understandably concerned about his disappearance,' said Detective Chief Inspector Lloyd Williams. 'Going this long without contacting family or friends is out of character and Liam's phone has been off since 4 January. The family are being supported by family liaison officers and are being kept informed.'

'We would like to hear from anyone who has seen him, or has any information about his whereabouts in Spain or any other location since Friday, 4 January.'

Challoner was reportedly staying at the Hotel Estrella in San Gabriel with twelve friends, after arriving on 3 January for a seven-day holiday to celebrate his friend Jack's forth-coming wedding.

Liam is white, 5ft 9in, of medium build and with short brown hair. He has distinctive tattoos on both his calves (see pic) and was last seen wearing a white T-shirt, long red shorts and white trainers.

Anyone with information is advised to call this special police hotline...

It was a matter of time before police made the connection – the killer who absconded from the UK at Southampton, jumped on a ship bound for the Mediterranean, killed this guy in Cartagena, then another on Mallorca. But it was taking so long. I'd never been the most patient pea in the pod but coupled with the uncertainty of my situation and my endless heartache for Ivy, it was maddening.

The last thing I needed that day was lunch with The Gammonati. Unfortunately, Jayde played the emotional fiddle on my doorstep first thing and Hilary, being Hilary, could hardly refuse.

'Will you join us? You can bring Bruce along, we'd love to meet him.'

It dawned on me that I'd told them all 'Bruce' would be joining me in Barcelona – now that time had passed. I had to come up with Bruce.

'He's a bit crook. Touch of sea-sickness. Or too much grog yesterday. Better count him out.'

'Oh, OK. Well, me and the kids could use some sanity around that table – otherwise it'll be all racist jokes and judgement on my mothering skills. And that's just from my in-laws! Save me, Hilary. Please!'

Caro had informed me she was booked up all morning having chiropody and blood pressure checks so I had absolutely no excuses lined up and I needed to keep up my act.

'Sure, no probs. I'll meet you in the tea lounge this arvo, no wuckas.'

It was the usual suspects around the circular table – the distended old bollocks Eddie and Dennis were puce with gammony hysterics about some joke the comedian had told at last night's cabaret. Lynette, Gloria, Ken and newcomers Gareth and Bardot offered trite chat and nods in all the right places.

'Here's another one for you,' said Dennis, wiping his eyes and opening up last night's folded menu on the back of which he'd scrawled a couple of the 'best' jokes. 'How are women and fried chicken the same? Take away the legs and the breasts and you're left with a greasy box to put your bone in.'

Eddie joined in. 'What's the difference between a clit and a cell phone? Nothing because every cunt has got one!'

Jayde covered Ty's ears as Eddie's voice carried over louder than everyone else's. She didn't say anything and so neither could I. I found myself bubbling with rage like at work when I'd overhear Linus taking credit for my suggestions. I wanted to march over to Eddie, cut out his tongue and wedge it between his wife's vegan baps.

Shona was no less irritating. Quite apart from the fact that she looked like Momo, we had to endure her diatribes about how 'we could all do more to reduce waste'. I fixed my stare on the saggy belly under her shift dress which had birthed five whole-assed kids before diverting my attention to alcohol to stem the need to hand the surly faced Moomin her own arse.

The children were the most enjoyable company, as ever. Jayde allowed me to feed Sansa and get her out of the high chair because she wanted a cuddle and me and Ty were having a funny conversation about what shoes would sound like if they had voices.

'So all trainers are cockneys, of course,' I told him, 'so Daddy's feet would sound like, "Awright, geezer, how's yer father and all that malarkey, awright?" And Nanny's shoes would sound all hickory-smoked and Karen-esque like, "I was at this here McDonald's and I was just disrespected. I said, 'I want the McRib meal' and this bish looks me up and down and says, 'Well, it don't look like you need it.' 'McScuse me, bish?'"

Ty chuckled. 'What do my shoes sound like?' He pulled his leg out from the table and stuck it out to show me – a little black-and-white Nike high-top.

'Oh, well, you have the coolest shoes in the world so they're like...'

And what followed was the world's worst impression of Stormzy, from which I will spare you. Still, Ty thought it was hysterical and I had to draw on all my shoe knowledge and perform every accent I'd ever done to keep the laughs a-coming. Gareth butted in, trying to engage him in peekaboo behind a menu – a pathetic attempt to cash in on my blinding limelight but Ty was having none of it – he knew where the real comedy gold was. So did Sansa. We had this little game where I'd pretend I had too much air in my cheek and she was the only one who could puncture my bulging cheek with her tiny fingertip. She laughed her arse off when the noise came out.

'You're going to make a brilliant mum someday, Hilary,' said Jayde, beaming at her little girl's smiling face.

That pulled me up sharp – I laughed it off before teaching Sansa how to stack her sandwich squares into a little house where her peas could live.

'Did you get yer bum pinched in Barca, girls?' asked Dennis, apropos of nothing, clanking more nasty gold than Post Malone, sawing through his T-bone and our innocent merriment.

'No, actually,' I replied. 'Did you?' My food arrived – Hilary had opted for a shredded kale power salad with a lemon and tahini dressing. Rhiannon had wanted a double cheeseburger.

'You wanna watch them Latins. Most of them are sex pests,' he said with some authority on the matter, it seemed. 'Our Kelley got fingered by some Arabs when she went to Morocco. In one of them souks.'

'Well, you know what they say – get fingered in a souk, your bad louk.' It was such a shit joke but I was in the saltiest mood and well up for pushing the envelope till it cut someone. Rhiannon was slowly bleeding from all my pores. This was dangerous territory – everything was ripe for the joking.

I caught sight of my room steward, the angel Gabriel with the ridiculous biceps too big for his uniform, walking across the dining room with a tray of empty glasses. We locked eyes and I got another wink for my efforts.

Incredibly, something stirred south of the border.

He was around AJ's age, 19, and I was reluctant to go for a teenager again. It'd be all skateboards and Fortnite dances and hours of ineffectual clit play. Actually, I take that back – AJ was pretty good at sex for a 19-year-old, both dead *and* alive. And I wondered if Gabriel could be the missing link in terms of refreshing the parts serial killing couldn't reach.

'What's Bruce up to today, Hilary?' asked Gloria.

'Oh, catching some zees mainly, I was saying to Jayde – he's a bit crook, think he had a bad prawn for room service last night. He could do with a couple of days rest and relaxation. Been working so hard. Poor fella.'

Ugh. I resented every beige word coming out of my mouth. I wanted to stand up and scream THERE IS NO BRUCE. HE

HASN'T GOT THE SHITS AT ALL, I MADE HIM UP! I'M HERE ALONE, ON THE RUN, HAVING CHOPPED A WHOLE-ASSED WOMAN TO PIECES. AND SHE AIN'T THE ONLY ONE!

But I didn't, obvs. Or this would be where my story would end.

Gabriel started laying the table nearest us, sex vibes coming off him in waves. It was a boost to realise I *could* still have that effect on a guy – I'd figured after childbirth nothing would want to come near my vajoodle again, even doctors. But now the after pains had subsided and my tits no longer felt like pulsating zeppelins, a new vista had opened up. I hadn't had a crumb of dick in months and it felt like feeding time.

'You wanna stick close to yer husband when you go on these excursions, Hilary,' interrupted Ken, meaty clods between each of his lower bicuspids. 'Especially the closer we get to Africa. Who was that lass we know, Glo, who ran off with a porter at that hotel?'

'Oh yeah, Dick and Daphne's daughter. Went to Ibiza on holiday, met this chappie, never came home. Got trafficked. Last Dick and Daphne heard she were living with a tribe, wearing togas and drinking ox blood.'

Lynette sniffed. 'It's awful, isn't it? Women aren't safe these days.'

'I think *you're* pretty safe,' I said but she pretended not to hear me.

Gareth and Bardot weren't riveting company either. He was clearly a former incel, liberated from his mother's spare room, who looked like the kind of guy who'd give you some depressingly vanilla sex but you could always rely on him to put the bins out. He'd look at Bardot every time he offered an opinion, conditioned to check what he'd said was OK, like she was some kind of human autocorrect. I imagined her as Cleopatra in Ancient Egypt and him as one of her lowly servants, covered in honey to keep the flies away from her. They'd been on my bus to the Drach Caves – the awful day I shat myself and killed that skinny bloke. I wondered if Gareth needed liberating. Perhaps it was time to jump into my phone box and twirl into my blood-stained cape. I tested the water.

'So tell me, Gareth, have you done any of the shows yet?'

Bardot answered for him, of course. 'Yeah we've done *Cats* and the *Anchors Aweigh* pirate show on deck the other night, that was good.'

'Have you been on any excursions, Gareth?'

'Oh yes,' answered Bardot. 'We did the light show in St Michael's Cave on Gibraltar and the walking tour of Cartagena and the Drach Caves. We didn't get off at Cadiz cos we wanted to stay on board for the art auction.'

'Have you used the spa facilities yet, Gareth?'

'He's not allowed,' chuckled Bardot. 'Not until I can trust him with the Visa again.'

'Oh, you should,' I said. 'They do leg waxing, teeth whitening, arsehole bleaching. I'm think of having either a Brazilian or a Clit-ler – where they leave a little Hitler moustache above your slice. And my arsehole needs bleaching. Do you bleach your arsehole, Gareth? Or do you pour it straight down her neck?'

Neither of them got the joke, which was fine by me but it did create another awkward silence. I decided to perform a little Bard-ectomy – going straight for the tumour. 'Bardot, remember when I asked for your fucking opinion? No, neither do I!'

Within seconds, she had flushed hot red all up her scrag neck, gathered her bag and coat and flounced out, as well as she *could* flounce in the vertiginous heels she'd shoved her trotters into. And Gareth, being Gareth, made his apologies to the others and scurried after her like the mouse who would never roar.

I looked at Jayde, expecting her to be laughing, but she was looking down, avoiding my gaze. She didn't look well at all. Pretty soon she made her excuses that Sansa needed a sleep (she didn't) and she and the kids got up, with much argument from Ty.

'No, Mummy, I stay with Hilly! No, Mummy, I not going, get off me!'

'Ty, NOW please, we're going, stop it.'

And he was hitting her and kicking for all he was worth but Jayde was having none of it and off they marched on a lingering echo of his piercing screams and kicking Stormzy feet. There was nothing I could do because Jayde was his mum and I was just a tourist, in every sense of the word.

That left me with concentrated Gammon extract – I silently hoped the ceiling above them all would cave in and Dennis would get the jazz bar piano implanted in his skull.

But of course nothing happened. Nobody got crushed, there were no sudden piano entrances or vomitus bleeding from the mouth like on *Downton*. Nothing ever happens unless I *make* it happen.

Gabriel appeared again, walking back across the dining

room with his massive biceps and his third fuck-wink so far. And I winked back.

By two o'clock, we were in my bed, going at it like a rodeo. I had been concerned that my foof wouldn't be up to the job since giving birth but Gabriel made all the right noises and I'd felt all the right inches so maybe there was life in the old girl yet. Once I'd cum for the second time, I lay there on his thumping great chest as his cock pulsed against his leg and the last trickles of spooge left him.

'Woof! That was awesome, thanks, darlin'!' he said, and once he'd got his breath he bounced out of bed and climbed back into his uniform.

'Oh, you're not staying then?'

'Nah, I should be working. It was good though.' He reached inside his trouser pocket and pulled out his phone. He showed me a picture in his album of some woman asleep with her arse out.

'I did her on the last cruise. Recognise her, from that girl band?'

'Uh no, I don't,' I said, squinting.

'She used to be in that group. Five girls. She was on here touring her solo stuff. I had her every which way but loose.' He shoved his feet into his shoes without untying the laces.

'Oh right,' I said, handing back the phone. 'So your thing's been up her as well as me. Delightful.'

He guffawed. 'She preferred it in the ass.'

'Even better.'

He kissed me again when he had his shoes on and as he pulled away, I held onto him.

'What's up?'

'Hug.'

'Baby, I have to go.'

'I know, I know. Just hold me for a couple of seconds. Please.'

And he did. I saw Craig in my mind. I breathed against him. I'd missed it. The closeness of another body, dead or alive. Someone with heat and a heartbeat and regularly inflating lungs. But he pulled away. He didn't get it.

'See you later,' he said.

'You will?'

'Yeah. I clean your room once a day so I'm bound to,' he laughed, striding across the carpet without another look.

The bed felt cold but not because of his lack of warmth. Gabriel wasn't what I'd wanted, but I was getting closer to it. Whatever 'it' was.

I washed and changed into my virginal broderie anglaise vest top and shorts and went up on deck to watch the ship pulling out of port, heading for the next stop: Genoa. Seven days remaining. I breathed in, breathed out. I checked the cracked iPhone 4 – still as silent as the grave, but there was one bar of signal remaining. I chanced a call Dannielle Fairly. Good or bad news, I had to know.

There was no answer. I left a message:

'Hi, it's Hilary. Just wondering if there were any developments, anything at all to report. I need… something. Anything. Please.' I hung up.

Caro wasn't back at her cabin yet and the upper deck was fairly quiet with most people having hit the dining rooms or catching a show. A message *bing!*ed through around two minutes later, straight to voicemail.

'Hiya, love,' came the Mancunian caterwaul. '*Yeah, I found Dad's file with the information in – I'm waiting to hear back that the fella's expecting yer – he's got a bad connection where he is. Bit remote. Give me a few days and I'll let you know the address—*'

'What address?' I shouted down the phone. 'Where am I going? Aren't you even going to tell me which fucking country?'

No, she didn't. She warbled on and on about how hard it had been to find the envelope Bobby had hidden, how they still hadn't released his body for cremation yet and how she'd never known such admin when a person dies.

'Oh cry me a fucking river, I don't care, just tell me WHERE, Dannielle?' I cried. 'WHERE AM I GOING?'

'*You've lucked out though – Dad's done all right for yer. Place looks reet nice. So yeah I'll call yer as soon as I've heard back and let you know when he'll be expecting yer and all that, all right, love? You take care now.*'

I called her back immediately but the ship was already fully at sea by then and all signal had been lost. I walked a lonely, uncertain circuit right around the top deck, chewing it over, trying to pick the bones out of what she'd had said. A 'reet nice' place but a 'bit remote'. Where could it be? South America, like Bobby had said originally? Afghanistan? Australia?

I found the longer I walked, the less I wanted to leave. I wanted to stay on the ship, in the cabin, in my little bed. Sightseeing with Caro. Playing with Ty. This was the only home I had. The angry bubbles popped and fizzed in my stomach. Everything felt wrong – bowling shoes wrong. *Point Break* remake wrong. Bounty-in-the-God-Tier-of-Chocolate-wrong.

And you know what that means.

The only other person about on deck at that time was The Man Who Walks. He was leaning against the railings like I was, newspaper tucked under his arm. Wrong place, right time.

'Hello,' I said, leaning on the railings next to him.

'Oh, good evening,' he said, with a polite nod, and he attempted to step past me but I blocked him. He wore a lemon shirt with a glasses pocket, tucked into white trousers and his shoes were grey and neatly tied with bowed laces. Everything about him was clean and pressed and even. Including his face.

'You were thinking about your wife, weren't you?'

He frowned. 'Sorry, do I know you?'

'No. I heard you lost your wife, though. I lost someone too.'

'Did you?'

'A baby.'

'Oh. I am so sorry,' he said, relaxing his stance. I copped a glance at the paper – an English one, a few days out of date. 'Was this recently?' He didn't seem to know where to look but at least he'd stopped trying to leave me.

'Few weeks ago. I came on holiday to perk myself up. It's scary and painful but we must go through it, mustn't we? It's OK to grieve.'

'Yes.'

'Do you want to see your wife again?' I asked.

'Someday. I know I will. Does that seem silly?'

'Not at all.'

'Good.'

'That day could come sooner than you think.'

'What do you mean?'

'None of us know when we're going to die. All you have is today.'

'Wise words from someone so young.' The newspaper relaxed in his grasp, fluttering on the sea breeze. 'I'm John, by the way.'

'Oh,' I said, shaking his extended hand. 'Hi, I'm Rhiannon.'

Wednesday, 9 January – Genoa

1. *People on Twitter who dog whistle for sympathy with 'I'm not going to tweet for a while' posts because of their mental health then forty mins later respond to a shortbread showstopper on the series opener of Bake Off.*
2. *People who climb cliff faces with no safety equipment. Oh, fucking fall off already. Your only skill is not dying.*
3. *Social media feministas with husbands giving it the full Burn Your Bra act in public while maintaining the safety net of a traditional patriarchal relationship. Oh yeah. I see you.*

Dead Boy in the Sand, tra la la la la.

Conan's body had been found, according to a Spanish news channel. There was footage of the stretcher being wheeled out of the woods near the Drach Caves. No link to me thus far. *Olé, olé,* I get my way.

Caro came calling first thing with an opening gambit that usually set the cat chasing pigeons around my ribcage – 'Would you like to join me for breakfast? I'd like to talk to you about something.'

This kind of request was usually followed by *Do you know anything about this bleach in my water bottle*? Or, *Any idea how the fire started*? Or, *Is that you covered in blood in that news bulletin*? but I was strangely serene that day. Almost balanced. Dead calm, like the sea.

We were in the lift on the way up to Diamond Deck – Caro in her gold kaftan and sandals, me in my hot pink shorts, virginal white daps and floaty florals – when she elaborated.

'It's about this meeting Beatrice in Rome…'

'Oh,' I said, with more than a hint of relief. 'Yeah, Enzo suggested 2.00 p.m. in a café by the Pantheon—'

'—I don't think I can go,' she said. 'I don't think I can meet her.'

'Why not?'

'I never asked you to arrange a meeting, Hilary.'

'I know you didn't.'

The lift doors opened onto the main deck. There were loads of people hanging around the railings, as usual, waiting to see the ship come into port.

'We can cancel if you want but I don't know why you would want to. She's not going to reject you, you know.'

'How do you know that? How do you know she isn't having the self-same conversation with her grandson that we're having now?'

'I don't,' I say. 'I just hope.'

'Those days with her – they belong in my head. It's the place I go to when I need it. It's *my* paradise. And I don't want it to be sullied by modern let-downs and grief.' She caught sight of herself in the window, but quickly looked away. 'This is not how she knew me.'

'What do you expect me to say? Do you want me to blow smoke up your arse and call you young and vivacious and still bearing a passing resemblance to Kaia Gerber in a certain light?'

'No,' she laughed. 'Who's Kaia Gerber?'

'Oh, some foetus with no tits and famous parents, it's not important. What *is* important is you meeting Beatrice. Could be your last chance. You don't want to be a painting in a museum that people feel sorry for, do you?'

'No, but—'

'—right, so shut up moaning, get your knickers on and let's go into Genoa shopping and we'll buy Beatrice a nice gift. Maybe even find you an old Italian apothecary who can cast an anti-ageing spell on you or something.'

'Don't be silly.'

'I think we're both in a silly mood.'

'Anyway, we're not in Genoa. Did you not hear the announcement?'

'What announcement?'

'On the public address, first thing. We're still at sea.'

Out on deck, Elton John was blaring out and I was expecting to see a port and heaps of shipping containers and cranes and a terminal building, but there was only sea and the ship had stopped dead in the middle of it. Passengers were craning their necks over the railings.

'Someone's gone overboard,' said Caro as we walked past the two-person-deep lines for railings towards the Diamond Deck staircase.

'Oh no, that's awful,' I said, trying to pack my face with the same amount of concern as her. I probably just looked like I was trying to stifle a fart. 'Anyone we know?'

A passing deck hand – Devonte – filled us in on the deets.

'Yeah, it was some time last night,' he said, pointing up to the Jumbotron above the kids' pool – a photo of the passenger, taken in happier times, raising a glass at some bleary-eyed, grey-gravy Christmas piss-up.

'Goodness me, it's that poor chap!' cried Caro, her hand to her mouth the way people always do when they're genuinely shocked. I did the same, more to hold back an ill-timed laugh.

'His name's John Carraway,' said Devonte. 'Did either of y'all see him last night at dinner? We're trying to piece together his last movements.'

'No,' said Caro. 'I think the last time I saw him was yesterday morning, walking around the pool. I was at bridge all evening.' She looked at me.

'Yeah, I was...' Shagging my room steward before actively encouraging the old funt to go shark-side, if you must know. But to save face I said, 'At the squash tournament.'

'We've sent out three rescue boats. Something's been spotted nearby,' said Devonte, 'and we've informed the coastguard so we just gotta pray now.'

'Yeah, that always helps,' I said piously.

'It's sad.'

'*So* sad,' said Caro.

'It's a sad, sad situation,' I added. But Caro looked at me again with an expression I couldn't read.

At breakfast, I caught her looking at me in the same way as I scrolled through Mabli's latest vlog post on the iPhone 4. Her micro pig had got out onto the road and been hit by a car. Kid couldn't catch a break when it came to animals. And when I looked up, Caro's steely greys were on me like magnets. 'What?'

'You don't seem all that concerned about John Carraway.'

'I'm not,' I said. 'I don't even know the guy, do I?'

'I suppose not.' She sipped her coffee, flicking through her *Cruise Letter*.

'So should I cancel Beatrice if you've got cold feet?'

'I don't have cold feet. I just don't think it's a useful idea for us to meet.'

'*Useful*? What do you mean *useful*?'

'Well, it's not as though...' But she couldn't finish the sentence.

'I know what you're going to say. "It's not as though we'd have much of a future together anyway because I'm dying and we're all old and stuff."'

She was about to argue but stopped herself at the last moment. 'That's exactly what I was going to say, yes.'

'Well, don't look at it as this important meeting which could impact how you spend the last days of your existence – look at it as meeting an old friend for lunch. An old friend who wants to see you. That's all.'

'You seem different today. Sort of happier.'

'I am,' I said, chewing toast. Caro looked out to sea and I nicked her *Cruise Letter*. 'So what are we doing then? There's a hop-on, hop-off bus tour of Genoa, a peek at Cinque Terre, a hike through Portofino, a coastal hop ending with the pretty markets of Alassio... Alassio.'

The name rang a distant bell. I couldn't think where I'd heard it before but the name stuck in my head like a cocktail stick.

'We can do Alassio if you want,' said Caro, scooping out her grapefruit.

Alassio was where Marnie's family had come from. She told me once that's where she would go if she ever left her *Übermensch* husband Tim.

I wondered if I could go to Marnie instead of waiting for Dannielle to come up with the goods. At least I knew Marnie. At least I knew she loved me. Well, she hadn't told on me. Yet. As far as I knew. I could go to her.

I spent a good hour seriously considering it, all through breakfast and when I got back to my cabin to pack my bag for the day but—

Realistically, calling on Marnie was not a great plan, for three reasons:

1. *I'd left her husband down a deep, dark well to die a slow death. However much of a prick he had been to her, she wouldn't have wanted her baby's father to die like that. Marnie was a good person which was why, despite how much I liked her, we could never truly be friends.*
2. *If I did get caught, she'd be an accessory for hiding me. And I didn't want anyone else to pay for my crimes, least of all her.*
3. *I wanted her to be happy. And free. And safe. Like Ivy. And the best way of achieving that was to ensure I was nowhere near her.*

As I was leaving my cabin, the announcement came over the PA system.

'*Everyone – this is your captain. We regret to inform you that the Genoa excursions have had to be abandoned today while we search for the passenger who has tragically fallen overboard in the night. We will remain at sea for as long as we can. Our rescue boats are out searching the area for him…'*

You won't find him, I thought. I weighed him down.

'These are exceptional circumstances. For anyone who had a shore excursion booked, the cost will be refunded to your Sea Pass cards and we will be putting on extra entertainments while you remain on the ship…'

Great. More line dancing and volleyball tournaments for the win.

'…a revised Cruise Letter *will be posted into your cabins within the hour. We hope you have an enjoyable day aboard the* Flor de la Mer.'

I sat on the bed. A window of opportunity had opened but I had slammed it in my own face. Yet another infamous boo-boo. Not only could I *not* get off the ship, I couldn't get any damn phone signal either, and for who knew how long? Dannielle could have found my one-way ticket out of Europe and be desperately calling me to make arrangements for all I knew. I was getting antsy in my massive maternity panties.

Meanwhile, I was stuck on the ship, in a Wonka-a-Thon in the Classic Lounge with shrieking children. Ivy was on my mind again and I needed to be where children were not but I was stuck on a ship full of them.

I ventured to the nearest child-unfriendly space – the gym.

There weren't many people about – two middle-aged lumps in full make-up chatting on neighbouring treadmills, a 60-something woman who'd gone so hard with a tan towel she'd changed race, and a Russian guy doing bench presses and swearing at the FTSE index tickertape on Sky News.

There were full-length mirrors all over the place so every-where I turned I couldn't avoid the sight of my strangely shaped new body – my bigger arse, giant tits and disgusting stomach. All the treadmills were facing the mirrors – like what kind of arrogant gimp chooses to watch themselves flap about?

I chose the one treadmill facing the only blank wall and a TV showing *Babe: Pig in the City*. I stayed there for two hours – sometimes walking, sometimes running – and as the credits rolled I felt slightly better about things; sweaty, but less frustrated. Tired, but less angry. I remembered Mabli saying in one of her videos about her hamsters running their wheels all night long 'to get their stress out'. It had worked for me too.

Of course when Ryan Prosser appeared, towel around his shoulders, loose-fitting vest and bulge-prominent shorts, new emotions crept into view. He spotted me and lifted a hand to wave and I carried on pedalling my recumbent bike, pretending I was concentrating.

Sandra Huggins' murder was the third item on Sky News, after the plane crash and 'the worst cold snap to hit the UK in years'. I tilted my cap to cover my eyes. They didn't call her Sandra Huggins – they called her Jane Richie, her alias. No link to her paedophile past. Police were on the hunt for the 'sadistic killer' who'd ended her life with an axe.

There were tickertape updates of the 'grisly find' in the quiet West Country town. Drone shots of motorists slowing on the dual carriageway to hang out of cars taking selfies with forensics teams. A white tent. Yellow evidence markers where her blood had dripped from my coat. Pieces of her being carried out in bags by police officers in HazMat suits.

And finally, an update from an officer who wasn't Géricault

– some keen-bean detective sergeant fresh out of the academy called David Stone. He stood outside the police building where they'd interviewed me.

'*We can confirm that an arrest was made today of a woman who has confessed to organising the adoption of Rhiannon Lewis's baby…*'

Which meant Heather Wherryman.

'*…we can also confirm that the baby is safe and well and in good hands. It appears Lewis gave birth and handed her over before she left the UK…*'

Which meant Claudia Gulper.

'*And can you confirm whether you are any closer to catching Rhiannon?*'

'*We are following a number of lines of inquiry but it is too soon to say…*'

Which meant no. I couldn't stop my mouth from stretching into a wide smile. *Safe and well and in good hands.* That was all I needed to know. They had a small fridge in the gym with fresh flannels rolled up in neat stacks. I was dabbing myself as Ryan sauntered over to grab one himself.

'Hey, Hilary,' he said, one fingerless-gloved hand around an isotonic drink. He'd generated enough sweat on his cotton vest to float a lifeboat. 'I saw you deep in concentration there so I didn't want to disturb.'

'Ahh cheers, yeah, trying to work off some choccy biccies I had earlier,' I said brightly, almost bouncing with renewed energy.

'We've been hitting the chocolate a bit lately too. Jayde gets pissed off with all my training but I don't wanna stop it cos it makes you lazy.'

'I agree,' I said, wiping my brow. He was shifting about on his feet and I have learned that this is a tell that people are trying to get away from you. I didn't give him the satisfaction of dumping my ass like his beautiful bitch wife had done at lunch the other day at lunch so I got in there first.

'Well, have a good one, catch you later!' I was halfway to the door.

'Hang on a sec,' he said, as my face flashed on the screen behind him – a different photo where Craig had been cropped out at the *Gazette*'s last Christmas party. Lana was in the background, drinking WKD.

'What's up?' I said, feet pointing in the direction I needed to go – out.

'Jayde wanted to apologise for leaving you in the shit yesterday. She said you'd gone to lunch with her and she had to go. She wanted to explain.'

'Oh no wukkas,' I said, with a flap. 'My language can be a bit much when I've blown the froth off a few. I'd avoid me too if I had the chance!'

'No, no, it wasn't you,' he said urgently, still shifting awkwardly. 'We had a bit of an emergency – Jayde miscarried.'

'Miscarried?' I said, my whole body flushing through with ice water. The little fridge towel was warm in my hand. 'She was pregnant?'

'Yeah.' Ryan looked down. 'Only eight weeks. We weren't going to tell anyone yet...' His face changed – he was crying. 'It was awful. She's being a warrior as usual and I'm the mess. I haven't left her side till now – she made me come down here and... I can't focus. Anyway, she wanted you to know she's sorry she left you.'

'It doesn't matter, Ryan,' I said quietly. The picture behind him was of my face again, square on, green eyes, unmistakable.

'I wanna take her and the kids into Florence tomorrow when the ship docks in La Spezia. Try and give them a nice day. Would you come with us?'

'Come to Florence with you?'

'Yeah. No-Mum-and-Dad day,' he smiled, wiping his cheek roughly with the back of his hand. 'The kids have been asking after you – Ty keeps on about his "Best Friend Hilly".'

My chest glowed from the inside out. 'Yeah, I love that little dude.'

'And, well, anything you can do to perk Jayde up, would be magic too. We'll pay for your ticket, of course. Unless you've got something on?'

I pulled the cracked iPhone 4 out of my tracksuit. Having a full signal was reason enough to leave the ship and going on an excursion but with the Prossers in toe would at least afford me some kind of anonymity. 'I'm free as a kookaburra, mate. Course I'll join you. Wild roos wouldn't keep me away.'

Another wave of emotion had taken him over and he was rolling with the tide. And it took me a few moments to realise this would probably be the moment to hug him. So I hugged him – more for me than for him. And he gripped on tightly – definitely more for him than for me.

Thursday, 10 January – Florence

1. *People on social media who are all: 'Eight days till my wedding!' 'Eleven months till our holiday!' 'Eighteen more years till my kid puts me in a care home!' 'Ten more minutes till I drive a stake through your ear.'*
2. *Anyone who uses a selfie stick*
3. *Anyone who wears sandals with feet that look like they've been dug up by an archaeologist*
4. *Snap-happy blonde on the bus to Florence who had discovered her iPhone had a camera – 'Ooh an Italian drainpipe', 'ooh some Italian monument', 'ooh an Italian tramp having a shit in a doorway.'*
5. *Our excursion leader Doreen – 'You understand where we meet, yes?' 'You hear time we back at bus, yes?' 'You enjoy yourself, yes?' I didn't know which were questions and which were direct orders*
6. *Learner drivers – here's your first lesson. Use your fucking accelerator*

The ship docked in La Spezia at 8.30 a.m. for the day's excursions to Florence. But even when the iPhone had achieved full signal, there were still no messages from Dannielle Fairly. No voicemails, texts, no nothing.

Tu piezza di merda!

Fottuta stronza inutile!

Spero che tuo padre morto si alzi dalla tomba e faccia una merda nella tua vasca da bagno!

At least I had enough signal to look up Italian ways of saying she was a useless bitch and that I hoped her dead dad rose again to do a shit in her bathtub.

Sunny with a chance of rain, said the *Cruise Letter*. Turned out it was pissing down in La Spezia, with 'a chance of brightening up later' said the weather channel so they had that ass-backwards. Nothing on that sodding *Cruise Letter* was true. It also said the on-board entertainment was 'among the best in the world'. That's if the best includes acrobats who can't balance, comedians who aren't funny and singers who couldn't hit a note with a shovel.

In my opinion, obvs.

When I got up to the Diamond Deck breakfast room to show Caro the latest message from Beatrice – a picture Enzo had scanned in showing both women younger and in bikinis on rocks as the waves sprayed up behind them – she was nowhere to be found. She wasn't in her stateroom either.

'She left early for the wine excursion,' her room steward informed me as he sorted through towels on his trolley.

'Caro doesn't *do* excursions,' I frowned.

'That's where she said she was going.'

If I didn't know better, I'd have said Caro was avoiding me. I hadn't been able to find her the night before either. So much for seeing me through my pain and helping me out. She'd ticked that particular box now, had she?

Nevertheless, I was booked on the Florence Museums tour with the Prossers and I had a job to do. I had to go into Super Turbo Hilary mode with extra sprinkles to help them over their miscarriage. I didn't disappoint.

I bought Ty a colouring book for the two-hour coach ride into Florence and regaled Ryan and Jayde throughout with jokes, anecdotes and tales of Bruce's suspected food poisoning which meant he was still laid up in bed with the shits. Ty loved all the fart noises. And despite the air-conditioning on the coach being as effective as being breathed on by a small dog for two hours, generally I was a jokey, sparkly delight to be around.

I owned that coach journey. I was Hilary Sharp, commander of them all, general defender of children and animals, mother to an abandoned child, wife to a non-existent husband, Australian when she remembered.

And I would have my gelato, in this life or the next.

Jayde seemed OK, as far as I knew. Well, she didn't cry. But I'm about as good at gauging emotions as I am at windsurfing, so who knew? As for myself, I was much more serene now – in a genuine, bouncily happy Hilary-esque mood now I knew Ivy was well. An emotional roadblock had been cleared and I could see a road beyond it again.

The moment the coach stopped in Florence, Hilary was sucked right up the drainpipe and Rhiannon emerged, like Pennywise's balloon.

My expectations of Florence had been sizeable – Michelangelo's *David*, the Palazza Vecchio, the Uffizi, the Duomo, the best pizza on earth, the best gelato in all Italy – and I'm pleased to say they were all met.

By somebody who isn't me.

Because *my* experience of Florence was this – fucking tourists.

Not literally fucking tourists – just fucking tourists. Every fucking turn.

If you weren't being pummelled and pushed out of the way by tourists over-eager to get their fifty-eighth Instagram shot of the Ponte Vecchio or a bench where some syphilitic pre-Raphaelite once got railed, you were being harassed by street hawkers thrusting selfie sticks and shit watercolours in your face. I say You, I of course meant Me.

The one highlight was a text from Dannielle Fairly. It said this:

Tenoch Espinoza, Hacienda Santuario, Camino Cabo Este, Rocas Calientes.

WHAT DOES THAT MEAN? I sent back, but again, nothing was clarified. It looked like I was going to a Spanish-speaking country at least. Bobby had mentioned South America, so that narrowed it down. I tried not to think about it until I got more info. Tried to lose myself in the priceless art all around me.

The statue of *David* was impressive – I'll give Florence that. He was taller than I'd imagined and we were reliably informed by our guide that 'in Michelangelo's day, a small penis was thought a thing of great beauty.'

'Yeah, in the days before they gave women an opinion,' I heckled. Well, *Rhiannon* heckled. Hilary would never have said such a thing. It made me laugh though, even though nobody else did.

Actually, *one* person laughed – Jayde Prosser. She and I wandered around the Uffizi together, Ryan bringing up the rear with the double buggy.

'Thanks for coming with us today,' she said. 'It means a lot.'

'*De nada*,' I said. 'How you goin' today?'

'I'm good. Now that *he's* stopped treading on eggshells around me and Ken and Glo aren't with us. We needed a day without them.' She looked behind us to check that Ryan wasn't listening in.

I wanted to tell her about Ivy – that I knew how she felt, that she could confide in me, as a fellow mother. But I stopped myself. Because I wasn't a mother. I'd given birth, yes, but I hadn't stuck around for the hard part. I had no idea what Jayde was experiencing. Her baby was dead. I knew mine was still alive. I had hope. Jayde was hope-less.

And a strange sensation came over me – I wanted to hug her. I didn't get it often, but I held my arms out and she took the hint and we hugged, in the middle of the gallery. We pulled away and I wiped her cheeks with the balls of my hands like Caro had done for me in Valencia. And I said:

'When a woman has a baby inside her, she keeps some of its cells forever. Your kid left cells inside you where you can never lose them.' I gave her another hug. 'You're going to be fine, I promise. C'mon, let's go check out some more bums and willies.'

And Jayde beamed her Beyoncé beam and suddenly, Florence became more enjoyable than I thought it could be.

Me and the Prossers stood at the back of the throng every time our tour group stopped for an explanation and made rude jokes and observations like the naughtiest kids in class.

We saw *David* several times, plus Botticelli's *Venus* and Artemisia Gentileschi's *Salome Beheading Holofernes*, and a million and one tits, but once the kids needed nappy changes and started grizzling for food, the screeching started and I ran out of enthusiasm for art.

The Prossers left to find the toilets while I stayed in a crowd looking at a wooden shield in a glass case with an image of a horrified woman in the centre – Caravaggio's *Medusa*. I found myself standing in front of a guy, who I'd singled out earlier as being One to Watch. He carried that air of wrongness – an air I'm always so good at sniffing out. Greasy hair, darting eyes, baggy jeans. I could smell him – old milk and cigarettes. As the crowd hemmed in around *Medusa* and her horrified face stared down at me, I felt a pressure against my arse.

Tickling. His fingers.

Funny how they always gravitate to me, isn't it?

He stopped tickling and rubbed around my buttock region for a bit, clearly enjoying the fact I was trapped; penned in by sweaty humans as more and more crowded round the glass case, remarking on the craftsmanship of the shield, the aghast expression on *Medusa*'s face, the snakes spilling out of her head. And ever so *slowly* I reached behind me, made gentle contact with his wandering hand, held the first two fingers and with one quick jolt, snapped them right the fuck back. *Crack!*

His howl filled the already-crowded space and he quickly dropped away, as did the bodily pressure around me. While all eyes were trained on him, awaiting an explanation for the sudden and prolonged screaming he'd seen fit to fill the stuffy room with, I slipped out, quietly on a sweep of floaty florals, joining up with the unwitting Prossers outside.

We carried on walking around the exhibits but it was soon clear that none of us were appreciating it as much as we were the thought of a good gift shop and some decent cakes. We did bond over our mutual love for the *Teenage Mutant Ninja Turtles*, I suppose that was culturally appropriate.

'I used to fancy Raphael,' I said, to the guffaws of both Prossers and Ty, even though he didn't know what we were laughing about. 'I don't *still* fancy him,' I blanched as Tyrion insisted on holding *my* hand instead of Daddy's.

'You wanted to *bang* a cartoon turtle?' Ryan guffawed, drawing several snooty looks from tourists with earpieces in.

'Well, he was the hottest one. Oh, come on, don't tell me you never got wood for Daphne from *Scooby Doo* or She-Ra.'

'I didn't. But Jessica Rabbit, *now* you're talking. At least she's human.'

'Yeah, but she shagged a *rabbit*.'

'He had a good sense of humour, Old Rodge. It's not all about looks.'

'Says the guy who spends half his life flexing before a full-length mirror,' scoffed Jayde. 'I used to fancy Baloo.'

'*Jungle Book* Baloo?' said Ryan, incredulous.

'Yeah.'

Ryan threw me a look and I caught it and threw one back at him.

'Hey, the heart wants what it wants,' said Jayde. 'He was so cuddly. And that deep voice. And he could dance. That bear had some serious *moves*.'

Ryan seemed surprised. 'I never knew you were into chonks.'

'I'm not, as a rule. There was just something about Baloo.'

'Silly Mummy,' Tyrion giggled. Ryan picked him up and threw him over his back in a fireman's lift and we headed off out into the crowds.

Our coach gang was supposed to meet back outside the gold jewellery store on the corner of the piazza at 4.00 p.m. so we ditched the guided tour and made our own way around the rest of the city.

I enjoyed my time with the Prossers, talking to their kids, making up stories about hunched creatures living in the bell tower of the Santa Croce and the horses who drew the carts of lazy-assed tourists through the streets. I got to carry Sansa for a bit when she didn't want to go in her buggy and her parents were getting tired of holding her. I never minded and I liked smelling her head. We played the full cheek game again and counted pigeons together – the child was a genius with numbers by the time I'd finished with her. I tried not to close my eyes and imagine she was my Ivy – I really did.

We each took it in turns to mind the pushchair full of bags while one of us dipped into a shop to investigate souvenir shot glasses or designer leather goods but for all the fun I had, I wasn't part of their family. It made my teeth itch to see how happy they were as a unit, the four of them. Swinging Ty between them. Ryan with Sansa on his shoulders, her holding onto his ears. Taking licks of each other's gelato. Happy human bonds. I read the message from Dannielle again.

Tenoch Espinoza, Hacienda Santuario, Camino Cabo Este, Rocas Calientes. No reply to my message with further explanations.

Around an hour before our meeting point at the gold shop, we stopped for refreshments in an outdoor café overlooking the square. Rhiannon wanted a pizza, every flavour cannoli and a proper hot chocolate – Hilary ordered grilled sea bream and a papaya and mango frullato.

'On us,' said Jayde as I fumbled in my bag for my purse. 'No arguments.'

Bardot and Gareth were paying when we spotted them. Gareth was fumbling about in his wife's handbag for the money – well, I'm guessing it was money. Certainly wasn't to find his fucking balls.

'Hi guys, you having a good time?' asked Bardot, specifically to Jayde and Ryan without so much as a glance at me. I was playing funny faces with Ty. I mimicked Bardot's face and he fell about his chair laughing.

'Yeah, good thanks,' said Ryan. Gareth got out some caricature they'd had done of him and Bardot by a street artist – the guy clearly had talent. He'd depicted Bardot as some sort of devil with smoke emanating from her nostrils. She wasn't amused. Gareth smiled. A lot.

It wasn't their fault, Ryan and Jayde's. They were distracted, getting directions for an artisan chocolate shop nearby. But it did mean that I was the only one who had focus. The only one who saw her coming.

A shabby blonde with fierce black eyebrows and chipped nails. I'd seen her lingering outside the church when we'd arrived and the only reason she'd piqued my interest was because I can smell a wrong-un at ten paces. It's one of my gifts, along with ready-made sarcasm and terrific hand jobs.

There wasn't a discernible trait to set her apart from any one of the thousands of other people I'd glanced at that day – it was an instinct. She was up to something. Ready to pounce on

166

a handbag, was my first guess. I watched her like a razor-eyed hawk.

'Do the face again,' Ty whined opposite. 'Do it, Hilly.' He'd climbed on his chair and was bending down to his plate picking off the flakes from his sfogliatelle. We were by the rope separating the café from the busy square.

And the woman was floating closer to the café, pretending to be on her phone but her eyes weren't on it – they were on us. Our table. Sauntering. Eyes flicking up like a crocodile's. My fingers lengthened. My heart pounded. With no further warning, she reached across the café ropes and snatched Ty by the waist, hoisting him up and disappearing into the crowds before anyone else saw what had happened.

But Rhiannon saw her. Rhiannon knew exactly what was going on. And before Hilary or anyone else could stop her, she was gone, pushing through the tourists, buffering people out of the way, listening out for Ty's cries, keeping a fixed view of the blonde head as it got further and further away.

I desperately kept my eyes on the pilfering prize. The woman was so fast, and a few hours on a treadmill for the first time in fifteen years wasn't cutting much ice when it came to stamina. But somehow my body responded, flooding me with the adrenaline I needed and pumping it furiously into my limbs. As the tourists thinned out and the streets narrowed, the woman slowed to a jog up a cobbled street, away from the shops, encumbered by her heavy screaming cargo.

She thought she was home and dry. My feet were light. I grew closer. She got slower. She had her hand over his mouth but he was wriggling violently. She hit him across the face. Shouted in Italian to shut him up.

My breathing was fast. She didn't hear me coming.

I reached out and grabbed her blonde hair hard in my hand and yanked her backwards, forcing two fingers into her eyes. 'DROP HIM NOW.'

She dropped Ty instantly – I could hear him crying but it was like the sound was underwater. All I could concentrate on was her and inflicting as much pain as I could.

She wriggled and jiggled in my arms and screamed and bit down on my skin as I thrust my arm tight into her neck and pressed down.

Ryan was there, scooping a bellowing Ty into his safe arms, sweating and puffing.

'Oh my God, oh my fucking God,' he cried. 'I thought we'd lost you.' He cuddled that little boy so tightly. A true dad.

But I was having a party. The blonde woman's knees buckled as she sank to the ground, the tighter my arm became around her throat. When she was weakened, I thrust her forwards to the cobbles and pulled her round to face me. I mounted her. Nothing was going to stop me now. Nothing could.

It was back – that molten feeling. That urge. The wetness between my thighs as I strangled her. This potential paedophile who'd stolen my best friend. The rippling, crippling can't-do-anything-else-but-kill thrill sizzled all the way through me. Oh, how I wanted her. So badly. Just like Derek. Like Sandra. Like Troy and Gavin and Daniel and those men at the quarry.

This was fucking paradise.

I straddled her body and smashed her head back onto those cobbles, again and again. And I whispered in her ear: 'You die now. You fucking die now.'

I squeezed her neck, making her squirm and gasp as my

own face ignited. And the life force seeped away from her the tighter I held on. She was dying in my hands. Her breaths became weaker. Veins bulged in her skin, eyes bulged. And it felt exquisite. I loved it. I was home again. The thrill was too much. An orgasm heightened and rippled through my body.

She was almost there, almost dead beneath my fingers.

'Let her go! Hilary – you've got to let her go! You're killing her!'

But Hilary wasn't my name. That's why I didn't hear him at first. Right then, I only knew Rhiannon.

He was too strong and pulled me back with his free arm until me and him and Ty lay on our backs and the woman was disorientated and gasping, scrambling to her feet, coughing and stumbling from alley wall to wall, bleeding all over her face, clutching her neck. She glanced back, briefly, before tripping over her feet and running off, vanishing round a corner.

And I lay on those cobbles, staring up at a narrow blue sky. Shaking.

'It's all right, it's all right,' Ryan soothed.

He thought I was scared. He thought I needed placating as much as Ty did. But I wasn't scared at all. I was shaking with ecstasy. I felt like I had been lost but now I knew where I was going. I finally felt like myself again.

Thursday evening, 10 January – at sea

1. *That roving reporter on Up at the Crack when she does her reports from a mega loud factory so her foghorn voice grates even more than usual*
2. *Holidaymakers who hold their tablets above their heads to take pictures*
3. *People who go to Italy but don't like the food – aka Eddie Callahan. What the fuck is there not to like? Carbs and cheese. Fair enough if you've got an intolerance but for fuck's sake.*
4. *The whole cast of Stranger Things*
5. *Davina McCall. You're fit, we get it*

The irritating thing about being a hero when you're an on-the-run serial killer is you have to play it down. Despite the glorious pride and excitement that fizzed in my chest like shaken cherryade, I couldn't dine out on my daring rescue of Ty. I couldn't crow about it as much as I wanted to. As much as *Rhiannon* wanted to. I had to dial up the Hilary Act for this one.

Jayde hadn't stopped crying since we got on the coach. 'There were loads of witnesses,' she sniffed. 'They'd be able to give a good image of her.'

'We should tell the cops,' Ryan whispered into Ty's sleeping head as the coach juddered back along the endless motorways out of Florence. 'They should be told, in case she tries—' He buried his face into his son's hair.

I was sat behind them, alone again, naturally.

'Guys, look, I can't stop you from going to the police and reporting it but please don't mention me. Say Ryan got him back, leave me out of it.'

'But you *saved* him,' Jayde wept, cuddling a sleeping Sansa closely. 'Ryan said if it wasn't for you...' Now *she* couldn't finish her sentence either. 'I can't think about it.'

'They might give you a reward,' said Ryan, more to the back of the seat in front of him than to me.

'I've *had* my reward,' I said. 'He's back safe. I don't need anything else.'

And I meant it. I sat and watched the countryside ribbon past my window, sunshine streaming in, bathing my body in warm gold, my gusset still damp from the beautiful moment I thought I was killing her.

Maybe I *had*. Maybe she'd gone around the corner and collapsed. A bleed on the brain. I liked to think so.

At the ABBA tribute dinner and dance in the posh Schooner Restaurant that evening, after we'd all watched the ship pull out of La Spezia, bound for Rome, talk of my heroism had spread like a fire in a trickle of gasoline. Before long, people were lining up to say 'well done' or buy me drinks. Dennis flexed big time and bought me a pearl necklace from the ship shop.

'That's $200's worth of Majorica pearls, that is,' he announced proudly so everyone in a three-metre radius could hear. He'd left the price on the box as well, in case anyone missed it.

'Thanks so much, Dennis. This is... lovely. I can't think of anyone I'd rather receive a pearl necklace from.'

He blushed, as Lynette piped up, 'You more than deserve it. It's a shame yer young man couldn't come down. We'd like to meet him.'

'Bruce? Yeah, he had a bad prawn. Can't seem to shake it out of his system, the poor lamb. Maybe tomorrow.'

Sansa was in a high chair, being fed bits of turkey and chunks of potato by Ken and Gloria. Jayde and Ryan were either side of Ty who was sitting there like a little prince, being kissed every so often, his every whim being catered for, his every toy out on the table, every question answered.

'Mum, why did that lady take me?' 'Dad, why did that lady smell funny?' 'Daddy, why did Hilly hurt the lady?' 'Is the lady dead now?' 'Nanny, can I have the cherry in your drink?' 'Grandad, what's an ABBA?'

It made me happy *and* sad to see them all fussing over him. Happy, sad, violent, calm – I was like a bubble in a spirit level, impossible to get dead centre.

'Well, I've said it before and I'll say it again,' said Gloria, folding her napkin. 'This wouldn't have happened if he'd been on reins.'

'Mum, we were in a restaurant,' said Ryan, buttering Ty a fifth bread roll. '*Sat down* in a restaurant.'

'Even so, these buggers can strike when you least expect it. You've got to give them no leeway—'

'—we'll have to get the kids down soon – it's already past their bedtime – but will you join us for breakfast tomorrow, Hilary?' said Jayde.

'Sure,' I said. 'I'd love to. Thanks.'

Eddie and canyon-gash Shona came over from a neighbouring table and set down a large piña colada before me – more ice than colada. I made a face.

'That's your poison, isn't it?'

'Yeah. But I don't like ice. Cos there's human shit in ice, isn't there? I read this article online—' Their faces fell and I remembered who I was again. 'Thank you so much, you're such kind people!'

Egos smoothed, all was forgiven. 'Well, we wanted to say well done saving the boy today, darlin'. You done real good.'

'Oh. Thanks, Eddie. Shona. That's so kind. Kind kind kind.'

Eddie held up his hands like he'd just saved ten orphans from a fire. 'Small price to pay. Glad the boy's back where he belongs.'

Ty stood on his chair. 'I got kidnapped today,' he told Shona's pendulous milkers.

'I know, Honey, you are so brave,' she said, holding his face between her hands. 'We're sure glad you're back though!'

'Me too,' said Ty, reaching for another bread roll and stuffing it in his face. 'I don't have to clean my teeth tonight cos brave soldiers don't have to.'

Happiness swelled in me all night long and I found that the more people were nice to me, the less I resented them. Kindness kills the hate. It fills you up. Happy human bonds. But I had got the message loud and clear that day: to exist in this life now, I couldn't be Hilary *or* Rhiannon in entirety. I had to be both of them. Hilary for business, Rhiannon for pleasure.

We rounded off the evening with a Nineties boyband reunion show in the main theatre. One of them had found God and refused to do the thrusting but it didn't stop their front row of 50-somethings frothing at the crease.

'You were so brave,' said a voice, sidling up to me – Bardot. 'Saving Ty.'

'He needed saving. So I saved him,' I said. 'Pity I can't do the same for your husband. More difficult when it's a grown-assed man.'

'Now look, I don't appreciate—'

'—save your breath,' I interrupted. 'When I want to exchange pleasantries with a despotic hambone who can't even peel their own apples, I'll WhatsApp you, 'K?'

It felt good to make her cry. I laughed in her face for a good two minutes as we stood there clapping the encore. She didn't move – she just took it. But as I turned away, Ryan Prosser was watching me, holding a child's milk bottle. He gestured towards the door and I followed him out.

'Where's Jayde and the kids?' I asked as we emerged out onto the deck.

'She's putting them to bed. I'm supposed to be warming up Sansa's bottle. Listen, about today, I can't stop thinking about it.'

'I've told you, we're cool. I ran after her, rugby-tackled her to the ground, you grabbed Ty and she ran off, never to be seen again.'

'You'd have killed her,' he said, his voice quivering on the salt breeze. 'If I hadn't dragged you off her, she'd be dead.'

'And?'

'Is that all you can say?'

'What do you *want* me to say? Ty could be on some boat to fuck knows where now with fuck knows who doing fuck knows what—'

'Don't you dare say that—'

'Say what? The truth? You're having a go at *me* for beating the bitch dry when I was the one who saved him? You wouldn't have caught her.'

He shook his head. 'That's what worries me,' he said. 'You saw her first. You saw her before anyone else... did you know her?'

'You what?'

'Did you know her? Did you know she was going to do that?'

I laughed. 'You think I truck with women who steal children?'

'I don't know *what* to think. But what I saw – in that alley today – it scared the living shit out of me. And the fact you're around my kids...'

'You reckon I'd hurt them?'

'I don't know, do I—'

'—well I wouldn't. Ever.'

'I know what I saw and I don't want that around my family. I won't go to the police because, yeah, as you say, you saved him. I'll make some excuse to Jayde about breakfast tomorrow, why you can't join—'

'—what excuse? What are you going to say to her?'

'I'll say you're busy with your husband. An early excursion he booked as a surprise or something. Where is he, by the way?'

'I told you. He had a bad prawn. He's in our cabin.'

He folded his arms. 'Is he.' It wasn't a question. 'Is *he* English too?'

'What?'

'Your Australian accent has disappeared.'

Big boo-boo. I stood there, stinging like a smacked arse.

He pointed at me, his eyes black. 'Don't come near my family again.'

I reared back. 'That's the thanks I get, is it? Your son could have been Maddie McCanned today and I get a load of filth for saving him?'

'You're a psychopath,' he hissed, pulse thumping, black eyes searching.

Ty and Sansa's faces flittered through my mind. I put my hand to my own neck, with one swift move tearing off the pearl necklace, my hero present, sending the pearls bouncing to the deck. 'Swine don't wear pearls.'

And I turned on my heel and I headed back to my cabin.

I was so frustrated that even though I'd tried my fucking best to be Hilary at all times on that boat, and even though I was the hero of the day, he could still see the scumbag beneath. Hilary wanted to cry. Rhiannon wanted to hurt something. So we compromised. We slammed some doors, stabbed a pillow with a plastic knife, watched *Downton Abbey* and ate room service sliders until we both vomited violently into the sink.

Friday, 11 January – Rome

1. *Airport security. At any airport. Anywhere.*
2. *People who take FOREVER to eat their in-flight meals and leave their bread roll till last*
3. *Air stewards*
4. *People who are afraid of flying – don't fucking fly then*
5. *Rita Ora. Enough already.*

I stewed about Ryan Prosser's verbal bollocking all night long but I didn't do what I normally did – go out and catfish some pervert to make myself feel better. Only because I couldn't though – we were in the middle of the fucking sea for a start. Instead, I waited until first light and went up to the Diamond Deck and knocked on Caro's door – no answer. There was a slim chance she'd gone to breakfast early so I headed for the dining room but she wasn't there either. Martin, who'd served us before, knew my question before I asked it.

'She's still in the Medical Bay,' he told me. 'After her fall.'

'What fall?'

'Down some stairs, I heard. Didn't you know?'

'No, I didn't. I haven't seen her for a couple of days. What stairs?'

'I'm not sure. Medical Bay's on Deck 2. Give her our best, won't you? We've all been worried about her.'

I could smell the bullshit before I even entered her cubicle. She was reading her *Cruise Letter* and seemed surprised to see me.

'Been sliding down bannisters again?' I said. The room was windowless, fitted with that shiny, corpse-blue linoleum you only ever see in hospitals.

'I fell,' she said, folding up the *Cruise Letter* and wincing as the Iranian doctor prodded her ankle. 'It's probably broken, isn't it?' She glared up at him.

'No, there's nothing broken, Mrs Wellesley. Just a bit of bruising. I'll give you something for the pain so you can enjoy the rest of your holiday.'

'I'm not *on* holiday,' she said. 'I live here. And if they didn't switch doctors so bloody often you'd know that.' She flapped him away. 'Pass me my handbag.' He did so. 'Now go away. I want to talk to my friend.'

The doctor made his excuses, wrote up his notes on the computer and left us to it. Caro clutched her bag against her and sat there, staring at me.

'Why did you do this?' I asked her. 'We could have cancelled. You didn't need to go full Madonna at the Brits.' I pulled the visitor's chair across.

'Who told you I was here?'

'Martin. He couldn't believe I didn't know.'

'Why? We're not related.'

'That's not the point. Why have you been avoiding me?' We were closer to the ship's engine in the Medical Bay but I could still hear a pin drop in that room over the distant hum. I could hear Caro's throat as she swallowed.

'Because I am scared.'

There was a newspaper folded up on the counter behind. I wondered for a split second whether she'd seen the story, recognised my face. Whether my number was up. She secured her stance on her stick before looking back at me. 'Scared of what?' I asked.

'Scared of dying. I didn't want to show you that... weakness, I suppose. Knowing that Beatrice still loves me, knowing there's another possibility of a life for me makes me realise how precious life is. And I've been a stupid, scared old woman, going through the motions on here all these years, drinking myself into oblivion, deluding myself into thinking I was living the good life. All I've been doing is *avoiding* it. Literally going round in circles.'

There was a hubbub outside the door and I got up to open it an inch. Several staff members were clustered around an elongated blue sack, fumbling it down the stairs, taking it into the next-door cubicle and barking orders in at least two different languages. I didn't understand it. Caro did.

'They've found Mr Carraway.'

'Oh,' I said.

'Is that all you can say?'

'I told you, I didn't even know the guy.' I pulled the iPhone out of my pocket to quickly change the subject. 'I'll cancel Beatrice. I clicked onto Facebook and began typing a message to Enzo. Outside the room, some stewards chattered, leaving the Medical Bay one by one on several creaks of the main door. All went silent. Caro put her hand over my phone, rose to her feet before steadying herself and grabbing her stick from a hook on the wall.

'Where are you going?'

I followed her out into the next cubicle, where she stood beside the zipped-up body of John Carraway on its gurney. She stood beside the bag for a while, probably five minutes, not saying a word.

'Shall I unzip—'

Caro placed her hand on mine as I undid his zip. 'No. Don't.'

I hid my disappointment.

She stood silently, her hand on mine. 'I told you that being alive is enough,' she said eventually. 'That fundamentally, just being here, is enough. And it is, for the most part. Life has been kind to me. But I know it isn't worth living for if there's something your heart aches for. I want to see my beautiful Beatrice. I want to hold her and not let go... until I have to.'

There was a hollow *plink* as one of her tears dropped to the body bag.

'*Where there is life, there is hope*. That's what you told me. You're still alive, she's still alive. Maybe that's enough. So come on – let's go get her.'

The Prossers walked along the opposite gangway. They didn't see me – I had my big floppy hat on. Neither Ryan nor Jayde looked happy. I didn't know if that was to do with me or the fact they were staring down the barrel of another day with Ken and Gloria. Either way, I didn't care. What I *did* care about was Ty and Sansa. Ty was playing up, refusing to behave, and Sansa screamed in her pushchair. My two little friends. That was the last I ever saw of them.

I knew as soon as our car dropped us off at the Circus Maximus in the centre of Rome that day, I could not go back to that ship.

We passed a news stand. There were a few British tabloids facing out:

RHIANNON LEWIS: THE FULL CONFESSION

It took my breath away. My face was on the front of a national newspaper. *Me*. Not Craig, not the victims, not Trump or Boris or some model's iCloud fappening. Me. It put something of a spring in my step.

I manoeuvred Caro's wheelchair away from the newsstand and we blended in with a snaking line of tourists heading for the Colosseum. Halfway there I heard a *ping!* behind me, though whether it had come from my cracked iPhone 4 in my bag or someone else's phone, I couldn't make out. I couldn't wait to get it out and check, in case Dannielle Fairly had sent me the last piece of information – where I was going, but we'd been constantly told by our driver to keep our belongings close in case of muggings and I didn't want to take the risk of losing it.

Rome was even more packed with tourists and school groups than Florence, which I should have expected because, again, travel agents are lying ass-hats.

You could spot the Brits a mile off – we were the only ones sweating. Me and Caro couldn't get close to the Colosseum so after a brief ice cream, we walked to the Forum, onwards to the Trevi Fountain and the Spanish Steps where the car picked us up and took us nearer to the Pantheon, as near as he could get due to several closed roads. Angela Merkel was in town for a conference, apparently. It was opposite the Pantheon in a little café that Beatrice had wanted to meet us with Enzo.

Caro took a deep, rattling breath as we got out of the car.

'You OK?' I said.

'I'm OK,' she breathed out. 'Now we're here, it doesn't seem so fearful.'

There were more newsstands, dotted all around the Pantheon, all in different languages that I couldn't translate but I could guess:

SERIAL KILLER BRITANNICO IN FUGA NEL MEDITERRÁNEO

'You're quiet,' said Caro and I pushed her in her chair across the piazza.

'Hot and bothered,' I said.

'Yes, let's find this café and get some drinks.'

The closer to the Pantheon we got, the more I didn't want to stand still in case somebody recognised me. The city was small and stifling and every direction I turned there were British accents and newsstands.

EL ASESINO EN SÉRIE BRITÁNICO PODRÍA HABER MATADO A 20 PERSONAS

All eyes were on me and, unlike the evening before at dinner, I didn't like it. The hair extensions and the lenses and sunglasses and floppy hat were not enough to make me invisible anymore. My head itched, my eyes stung where I'd rubbed sun cream into them and the sunglasses pinched my bridge. I was Top Story. People would be actively seeking me out, especially the Brits.

CONFESSION DE RHIANNON LEWIS: JE SUIS UN TUEUR EN SÉRIE

I mean, yeah, I was famous, something I'd always wanted, but I couldn't enjoy it at all. I was a sitting duck. A fish in a barrel. A babe in the woods. All it would take was for one person to notice me and the long arm of the law would swoop down and embrace me in its chokehold forever.

At 1.30 p.m., we reached the café – La Piccola Casa Della Tortain. We had to queue and wait for a table for four on the terrace. A TV flickered inside, showing round-the-clock news. My picture again, a photo booth shot taken at Lucille's birthday party three years ago. Footage of me being interviewed on *Up at the Crack*, trying not to look at the presenter's schlong. More pictures from my Facebook page. Drone footage of police at the farm shop. Sandra's bits and pieces taken out in covered boxes. A bloody axe in a see-through bag.

I became fidgety and unsettled – the café was small and the outside tables too close together. There were British voices all around me – Scouse accents, Brummies. Two blonde women definitely catching glimpses at me whenever I caught a glimpse of them. I desperately wanted to check my phone.

The waitress brought us our drinks – a strawberry smoothie for me, piña colada for Caro. When Caro went in search of a toilet, I saw my chance.

And I did have a message. From Dannielle. It simply said:

Go. Now.

I immediately dialled her back. On the tenth ring, a woman answered. And she didn't sound at all happy.

'Yeah?'

'Dannielle? It's Hilary...'

'Oh, thank fuck for that, where've you been? I've been ringing for ages.'

'We only got into port at eight – I don't get a signal at sea and the WiFi's too expens—'

'—never mind that now, are you at the airport?'

'What airport?'

'Any airport. You need to be on your way, lady. They're on to you. You've got to get out of Europe before they find out what cruise you were on. Your confession's broke.'

'Yeah, I saw some headlines. You haven't told me where I'm supposed to be going, though.'

'Yeah, I did, I told you. Hacienda Santuario.'

'Where? What country?'

'Oh, did I not say?' And then she told me.

I stopped short of saying the word out loud at that moment, observing that the two blondes had definitely stopped talking and were listening in. 'Right. So what do I do?'

'Are you near an airport?'

'Um, I'm in Rome today.'

'Right, get to the Leonardo Da Vinci Airport and get on the first flight out. Book return Business Class for two people.'

'Why two people?'

'It'll throw off any suspicion, as will a return ticket. Business Class passengers are less likely to be interrogated. Look, I have to go. We've got the police coming again at four. You'll stay with Tenoch for a bit until you get yourself sorted, he'll arrange a new passport for yer, an American one, and that'll get you into the States. OK? Destroy the phone as soon as you can, preferably now. Make sure you write down that address before you do.'

'But what if I'm recognised on the way to him?'

'You're on your own, Kid. I've done my bit. Good luck.'

When I got off the call, I checked Twitter: I was trending in the UK. There'd been a hastily produced *Panorama* on TV last night:

United Kingdom trends

1 #MondayMotivation
2 #TheRhiannonLewisStory
3 #NationalSausageWeek
4 #MentalHealthAwarenessWeek
5 #loosewomen
6 #RuinAFilmByAddingUpYourBum
7 #RhiannonLewis
8 #serialkiller
9 #CraigWilkinsIsHot
10 #StabMeRhiannon

Caro returned from the toilets, beaming.

She was smiling, for the first time that day. 'We came here once.'

'What?' I said, distracted.

'Me and Beatrice. One Sunday at Pentecost.'

'Oh right,' I said, scrolling through BBC News, Sky News, Al Jazeera, Fox, CNN – the story hadn't reached America yet but British news channels heaved with information from the diaries.

'We attended mass with the rose petals,' Caro continued. 'I've only just realised why she wanted to meet us here. It's where she told me she loved me.'

They listed all my victims, one after the other.

Pete McMahon. Dad. The guy in the canal. The Man in the Park. Julia Kidner, my childhood best friend. The Blue Van Rapists. Derek Scudd. Dean Bishopston – the poor, innocent taxi driver.

'They drop them through the hole in the top, the *oculus*.'

'Drop what?' I snipped, looking up from my phone.

'The rose petals. Thousands of red rose petals.' Caro looked out across the square at the enormous grey monolith of the Pantheon. 'The choir sang Veni Sancte Spiritus. And I wanted to kiss her. But we couldn't do that of course. Instead she whispered it – she loved me. And I whispered it back.'

AJ Thompson, the father of my baby. The Fortune Teller. Lana Rowntree. Patrick Edward Fenton. Troy Shearer, who'd molested Marnie on our night out in Cardiff. Tim Prendergast, Marnie's husband.

'It's overwhelming when someone you love says they love you back,' said Caro. 'It is the most wonderful thing.'

'Yeah,' I said. 'It must be.'

There was mention of the men I'd catfished, men I'd lured to cutting flower symbols into their skin, men I'd blackmailed about their pervy videos to the point of suicide. How I'd planted evidence to frame Craig.

'It colours your world differently when you are loved like that,' said Caro. 'Nothing else matters when you have something so rich and true in your life.' She smiled at me, broadly and unapologetically.

'I can only imagine,' I said.

The area around the Pantheon crawled with police. Police in doorways. Milling among the crowds. Talking into CB radios. Brandishing guns. And it felt like each and every one of them was looking my way.

'I'd never have let her go,' I said. Caro sipped her piña colada, letting out a deep, lingering breath. 'You'll be loved like that someday.'

I clicked onto a fan forum that had already been set up in my honour. *We Love Rhiannon Lewis*. There were seventy-eight members already. Seventy-eight people all purporting to love me. Caro said something I didn't catch.

'Pardon?'

'Pass me the menu.' But before she could take it, she locked eyes with someone behind me. 'Oh my word, there she is!'

Two people – a boy in his early twenties, and an old woman in grey trousers, a flowing white blouse and a Fedora, were walking directly towards us. The woman had long grey hair streaked down her back and she walked with a stick like Caro, but a little faster. Caro was already on her feet, moving towards them as fast as Beatrice was moving towards us. Beatrice clocked Caro and handed her stick to Enzo, raising both hands to her mouth.

Caro hobbled around the chairs to get to her. The second

they made contact they embraced the years away and for minutes, all I could hear were the sounds of them both crying. When they pulled out of their hug, Beatrice held Caro's face before her own and sobbed incoherently.

'Oh, *mia bella* Carolina, *ti ho aspettato così tanto tempo! Non ho mai smesso di amarti!*'

And they kissed, unashamedly, unhurriedly and unflinchingly like it hadn't been sixty years without one another, merely a day or two apart.

Three police officers started clapping and whistling. I looked at Enzo – he had tears in his eyes. Quite a few people around did. Two waitresses in the café were sobbing and a man in acid green shorts dried his eyes with his vest. The only one not crying or cheering was me. Because what I was seeing was not a love that I could ever experience. Love for me was brutal, strangulating and blood-spattered. Love had no heartbeat. It was cold and blue and dead.

The two women broke away but continued to hold hands. Caro brought Beatrice over to our table, wiping her eyes. 'Hilary, this is Beatrice…'

I held out my hand. 'Nice to meet you, Beatrice.'

She shook mine with both of hers. '*Grazie mille per avermi riportato la mia Carolina. Grazie, grazie.*' They couldn't stop staring at each other. I didn't quite believe what I was seeing. Or maybe I didn't *want* to believe it. She and Enzo sat and a waitress brought over a lunch menu.

They chit-chatted easily, in English and Italian, and not once did they stop holding hands. That damned parallel universe floated into view again – the one in which I persuaded Caro to stay in Rome with Beatrice and she asked me to live with them, to run errands, bake cakes, or mop floors. I was happy in this universe with my two new grannies. Grannies I actually liked.

I was clinging onto something I could never have and knew I had to go. 'Just nipping to the loo,' I said.

Caro looked up. 'Do you want me to order for you?'

'Yeah. Prawn linguine. And a beer. Thank you.'

And I walked away from the table, watching her and Beatrice smiling and holding hands like the old friends and young lovers they once were. I wanted to stay. But I couldn't.

They didn't need me anymore. And as I melted into the crowds, for once grateful for the many people swarming and jostling around me, I was gone.

I got a taxi to the airport and, thanks to all Merkel's cordons, it arrived thirty minutes before the Alitalia desk closed. I bought the last return Business Class seat on the 20.40 flight. And that was it – that was most of my money gone. I had nothing else, apart from my Hilary Sharp passport, the clothes and bag on my back, my little pig dad, Richard E. Grunt, and the pink bunny I'd taken from Ivy's incubator. It didn't even smell of her anymore. It was a self-check-in desk, but when I scanned my boarding card and ran my passport through the scanner, it beeped and a red light came on.

Please wait for assistance.

'Oh fucking hell,' I seethed, standing there like a complete twunt, my rucksack getting heavier by the second, my mouth completely dry. This was it. This was Hand on the Shoulder and 'Come With Me, Miss' time.

A short shiny guy in a too-tight waistcoat slid on over. 'Sorry, madam, let me help you there.' He took the passport and flattened it out, running it through the scanner. He checked my boarding card. Another red light.

'Sorry, it does this sometimes. New system.'

I bit the inside of my lip until I could taste blood.

He slid it through again. A choir of angels sang – a constant *beeeeeep* and a green light. My heart came out of arrhythmia. I couldn't believe it.

He handed them both back to me. 'There you are, madam, sorry about that, you're good to go. The lounge is up the escalators and first right. Please show your boarding pass at the gate and they will let you in to use the amenities. I hope you have a pleasant journey to Mexico City.'

'*Grazie mille*,' I said, trying the 'th' sound so I sounded Spanish.

Luckily the security check was as effective as Epstein's suicide watch, and once I was over the first hurdle there was no further passport check even when my underwire maternity bra set off the alarm. No pat downs. No eye contact. Almost like I'd requested it. Do terrorists never fly Business Class? They should – you get away with murder.

Once inside the lounge, relief flooded into me like cool water. It was a welcome only the richest travellers got – trays of champagne, canapes, unobtrusive soft jazz on the PA system, air-conditioning, offers of foot massages, and the cleanest toilets I've ever seen. I felt sorry for the cattle schlepping along through the gates of Economy, mooing their dissatisfaction.

On the way to the gate, there was a shop with a newspaper

stand. The French and Spanish newspapers were all over it. Not so much the Italian ones. There wasn't time to stop and take a closer look but I got the gist:

ASESINATO EN SÉRIE OCULTOS EN EL MEDITERRÁNEO: La policía cree que ella escapó en un crucero desde Southampton

Translation: SERIAL MURDER IN THE MEDITERRANEAN: Police believe she escaped on a cruise from Southampton.

I was waiting for it, always looking over my shoulder at the tooled-up police on the way to the gate, but nobody stopped me. There was a curt smile from the steward as I stepped aboard the plane and turned left.

And soon I was reclining in my leather seat, sipping complimentary Krug, chowing finest pork sword in a delicate jus prepared by a Michelin-star chef and rifling through a travel kit of soft pyjamas, blindfold and Kiehls vanity case. It was only then that I could truly breathe out.

I took one last look at the address Dannielle Fairly had supplied me: *Tenoch. Espinoza, Hacienda Santuario, Camino Cabo Este, Rocas Calientes...* Mexico.

Opposite me sat two honeymooners, holding hands in their recliners, reading the dinner menu. She leaned into him, butting her forehead playfully against his to make him laugh. Money could buy me all the freedom and luxury I wanted, apparently. But it couldn't buy me *that*.

It wasn't until they turned the lights off that it dawned on me: when they came back on, I'd be the other side of the world.

Chance to wipe the slate clean. Tenoch would arrange another passport and then there would be no more Hilary Sharp *or* Rhiannon Lewis. Nobody would know who the hell I was.

Least of all, me.

PART 2: Mexico

Sunday, 13 January – Aeropuerto Internacional Benito Juárez

1. *People who try to ram enormous carry-on bags into overhead lockers*
2. *Everyone on planes who stands up the second the seatbelt sign bings. You honestly think your bag's gonna be first off?*
3. *People who studiously take note of the safety demo on flights – what good is a whistle and an oxygen mask when you're crashing 500mph into a mountain?*
4. *People at airports who hog any plug socket to charge their phones – a woman at Los Cabos found the plug to a departures board and removed it so she could juice up her Samsung*
5. *Paris Hilton*

Crowded airports are concentrated Hell on Earth.

After changing some money for Mexican pesos and paying a ridiculously high fee for the privilege, I had to wait six hours for my connecting Aeromexico flight to some tiny airport out in the super sticks – the nearest one to Rocas Calientes at the southern end of the Baja Peninsula. I spent most of this time eating, pissing and nodding off on an uncomfortable metal seat that had a small puddle of jizz beneath it.

Then, quite suddenly, a miracle. A beam of sunlight speared through my malaise.

'Hey,' said a deep voice. 'Is this seat taken?'

'Go ahead,' I said, taking out the book I'd bought from a newsstand to pass the time. I stole a glance at the guy who'd spoken to see the most beautiful face I'd ever seen. No book in the world could've torn me away.

'Good book?' he asked, sitting down and putting his feet up on his case.

'Probably,' I said, opening it up. 'Shame I can't understand a fucking word of it.' I showed him page 1.

He laughed. 'You're English and you can't speak Spanish?' The way his brows furrowed sent an arrow straight through me. 'May I?'

I handed the book to him and sneak-scratched my itchy extensions. He started reading.

'Bloody cheek,' I muttered, folding my arms and hate-watching the Paris Hilton interview twittering away on the overhead TV. After a time, the book plopped back down on my lap.

'Yeah, you're not missing much.'

He cradled the back of his head in his hands, attempting to sleep despite the hurly-burly of the busy airport. He had closely cropped black hair, large brown eyes and looked like he'd stepped off a page in a calendar of Mexican Hunks. After a few brief exchanges with the people on the other side of him and opposite, I realised he was part of a huge Mexican-American family, going on to some party if the myriad gift bags of presents were anything to go by.

'Can't stand her,' I said, nodding up at the TV as Hilton banged on about being so misunderstood by the media. 'She's so... meh. Like, you ever get that when someone is so over-exposed you don't even see them anymore?'

He snorted, one unshaven cheek resting on his fist. 'Yeah. She's definitely on The List.'

I snapped my head round to look at him. 'You have a *list*?'

'A *metaphorical* list. I'm not some maniac, I promise.'

'Oh,' I said. '*I* am.'

'What, a maniac?'

'Quite a big one.'

'Cool,' he sniffed. I swallowed, mouth arid. 'That's good. Maniacs tend to be the most interesting people.'

'Do you think so?'

'Oh yeah. My aunt Salomé's a maniac. She's the most interesting person in the fam. She's done time in jail, smokes weed, hates people, makes art.'

'She doesn't sound too cray.'

'She uses her *flujo menstrual* in her art. You know, her period blood.'

'Oh. Fairly batshit then.'

'Yeah,' he laughed. 'She sold one of my pieces recently. Didn't make much money but I was so amped somebody bought it.'

'I won't ask what *you* dipped your brush in.'

A middle-aged woman in tight white jeans and a floaty top tottered over and gave him a passport and boarding card, barking at length to him in Spanish. He snipped back at her and took the passport, posting it in his jacket pocket. She threw me a curt glance, before rejoining the birthday party, all chit-chattering away over Paris's sex-tape trauma.

'My mom,' he explained. 'She thinks I'm still 13, not 33.'

'I have a list too,' I told him when she'd gone.

'Really? Who's on yours?'

'Be quicker to tell you who *isn't*.'

He smiled again and Oh. My. God. His resting bitch face didn't exactly do him a disservice but when he *smiled*, the overcrowded smelly Hell around us turned into Ko Samui, complete with cocktails, palm trees and cutely squeaking dolphins. 'Where are you from?'

'San Diego. We got relatives in Rocas Calientes. We meet there a couple times a year for special occasions.'

'What's *this* occasion?'

'My cousin's twenty-first. What brings *you* here?'

'Just visiting,' I said. 'My uncle lives in Rocas Calientas too.'

'Oh cool.' That was his chance to push the relationship up a gear; suggest we should hang out together, that he could show me around, grab a beer or a light supper, maybe rail me senseless up against some smooth-skinned variety of cactus. But he didn't – he started watching Paris Hilton again and I lost him.

I entered into a fantasy about that movie *Cocktail* – that was set in Mexico, wasn't it? – where Tom Cruise works in a bar and meets that curly-haired chick. And before long they're going on daytrips to waterfalls and banging by moonlight. That could be us, I thought. Me and Future Husband.

Actually, it wasn't set in Mexico at all that film, it was Jamaica.

'There's a cool art district in Rocas,' said Future Husband. 'That aunt I was telling you about owns Galería de Salomé Casta. You should check it out.'

'Yeah, I will.' If he'd said she owned the local museum of used tampons and turds I'd have promised to check it out.

'There's a cool rooftop bar, overlooking the art walk. And you have to do Campo A Mesa – it's this organic restaurant surrounded by all the produce and livestock they use in their cooking. It's up in the hills. I hang out mostly at Sal's. Or at the hotel where we're staying, the Holiday Inn. It's the biggest one on the beachfront, you can't miss it.'

Was that a hint? I thought. Was he implying that's where he'd be if I fancied seeing him again? He played his cards close to his magnificent broad chest. I couldn't see it under his clothes but a girl can dream. And I *did* dream. I dreamed of doing unspeakable sexual athletics with that body in the forty-seven minutes we were sitting there, forearm hairs kissing.

A guy who looked like him from *Jersey Shore* with the eyebrows and the ridiculous bling, took a seat on the other side of me with an oversized carry-on and rifled through the pockets. His movements were too loud for me and Future Husband to continue talking so we stopped and sort of looked at each other. He was fuming as much I was. After a while, it became funny and we were both smiling. Jersey Shore eventually found some gum and posted four pellets in his mouth, proceeding to chew and pop while texting.

'Gum snappers,' I sighed.

Future Husband looked at me. 'Huh?'

'The list. People who snap gum.'

The penny dropped, right into my pants. He gestured

towards the woman on his left, not a relative, some redhead. 'People who sniff a lot.'

I looked across at a couple of barefooted backpackers, flip-flops in hand, studying a departure board. 'People who go barefoot on public transport.'

He chuckled, nodding towards one an older male relative having a coughing fit. 'People who cough without putting their hand over their mouth.'

'People who *do* put their hand over their mouth but don't disinfect it after.'

He gestured towards a seated man opposite wearing a brown suit and mismatched green Crocs, doing a crossword. 'People who wear *those*.'

'People who barge in front of one another at the baggage carousel like if they don't get to their suitcase first they're gonna burst into flames.'

'That dude picking his nose,' he said, signalling towards another backpacker, also in Crocs, this time purple.

'That leathery old twadge checking her lipstick,' I said.

'That dude hitting his kid.'

'The dude who left the puddle of jizz under this seat.'

He craned to look under my chair, bursting into laughter. 'Holy shit.'

'No, it's definitely jizz.'

We found a multitude of irritants and tourists to bitch and laugh about – Woman With Hairspray, Woman With Eye Tick, Drake Lookalike Licking His Wife's Neck, Noisy Blonde Fivesome, Teenagers Flicking Mike & Ikes at each other until the departure gates emptied and the people got less interesting.

As I was imagining us strolling round IKEA, me wheeling

the trolley with our twins in, him struggling all muscly with the sections of a Liatorp Console Table and a HAVSTA Cabinet With Plinth, an announcement came over the PA system and his party collected up their belongings. Of all the aeroplanes in all the airports and all the flights, he wasn't on mine.

'It was nice talking to you, Maniac.'

'You too,' I said, silently hoping he'd have a shit name – something stupidly-spelled like Jaysin or Dezzmond or a duff one like Keith, so to diminish his perfection even slightly. But he didn't.

He held out his hand and I shook it. 'Rafael.'

'Rafael,' I said, ignoring the throb in my chest. Oh my God. He was the hottest Ninja Turtle. It had to be, didn't it? That had to be a sign. Days before, I'd had the conversation with Jayde and Ryan about our cartoon shag-wishes, and now here he was – a living breathing Shag Wish. He waited for me to say my name but I didn't – I was too caught up with the warmth of his hand and the fact he was named after the hot turtle.

A shiny-cheeked young woman in an orange playsuit – Fun Times at Guantánamo – made a beeline for him, linking his arm with hers.

'Shame we couldn't have hung out,' he said as he walked away.

I looked up at the TV screen. 'We'll always have Paris,' I smiled. I don't know if he heard but he smiled too.

And he left me, there alone, with nothing but the puddle of jizz to keep me company. No change there.

It could have been the parasite in me, looking for a host, but watching him walk away without a second look, it hurt. Reality shook me wide awake. I was on my own again. And I didn't like it one little bit.

Anyway, another bumpy flight, a crowded shuttle bus and a taxi ride later, and I arrived as instructed at Hacienda Santuario – sweating like a pre-war Prince Andrew. The place sat at the end of Camino Aguacate, a steep dirt track nestled in the hills above the resort city of Rocas Calientes, overlooking a golden stretch of coast.

Arturo, my cabbie, who had greeted me at the airport with a torn-off square of cardboard and a crudely-drawn flower on it, had informed me the name translated as 'Hot Rocks' and the deeper into the hills we went, the more accurate that became. Grey boulders littered a scorching hot desert of ferocious-looking thorn bushes. There wasn't another house, car or person on the horizon the whole drive up from the coastal highway. Just dead dogs. I counted four on that one road.

'Why all the dead dogs?' I asked him, who spoke way better English than I did Spanish.

He chuckled and his dimples deepened. 'There are many stray dogs in Mexico. They escape, they fuck, they produce more dogs. It's a problem.'

One of the dogs I noted looked like Tink – a little brown Chihuahua with crazy-big ears and a little black nose. She even had a white patch on her big belly like Tink. I couldn't look at her for long.

The car came to a halt in a wide turning circle at the top of a steep climb, and when the dust settled it revealed a set of tall black gates, at the top of which it read *Santuario* in spidery iron script. Beyond the gates lay an unwelcome avenue of spiky plants and bushes bearing inch-long needles.

'This looks inviting,' I said, as a sicky wash of unease crashed over me.

'*Adios, señorita*,' Arturo laughed, speeding off down the hill. I stared through the gates. It reminded me of the sight greeting the Little Mermaid when she got to the Sea Witch's lair in the book Dad read me at bedtime. It was always the bit where I'd pull the covers tight so the Witch couldn't get me. There was a button on the gate post. I pressed it and there was a click.

'Uh, I'm looking for Tenoch Espinoza?' I said, my head itching like a bitch and my throat drier than the sand beneath my shoes. No answer. 'Uh, Dannielle *me envoi*? Bobby Fairly? *Yo soy* Hilary Sharp?'

Still no answer, despite my valiant attempt at minimal Spanish. I pressed the button again. Again, no answer. I dropped my leaden rucksack to the dirt and kicked the gate repeatedly until one of my trainers flew off.

'FUCK'S SAKE!' I glared up at the endless blue sky. My sweat had formed patches and I could smell definite crevice rancidity. This was the proverbial It: the deadest of dead ends. My ire had woken up all the thought owls; as welcome as unsolicited U2 albums and almost as impossible to get rid of: I was tired as fuck, hungry, dehydrated and boiling hot.

'SOMEBODY HELP ME! IT'S NOT FAIR! IT'S NOT FUCKING FAIR!'

But it was fair, wasn't it? I'd more than asked for a bit of payback and here it was. I couldn't walk all the way back down the track in a blistering hot, *Mad Max*-esque wilderness to the coast road – I'd surely die of thirst en route. This was it. This was the end. In a few months' time, some backpacker would stumble across my skeletal cadaver complete with pile of fake extensions on the ground behind me. They'd find Richard

E. Grunt in my backpack and my fake passport. They'd put two and two together and realise it was me. Probably release a fucking book about it and become a bestseller.

And as I'm sitting there, panicking, losing the will to live and identifying which of the hook-beaked fuckers circling above was going to peck the flesh from my ribcage, the panel on the post behind me fizzed and clicked.

A deep, gravelly voice barked '*Quién está ahí?*'

I scrabbled to my feet. 'Yeah, it's Hilary? Hilary Sharp?'

'*Tu nombre real?*'

'Hilary Sharp? Hilary? S.H.A.R.P? Hilary Fucking SHARP?'

There came a laugh. 'One last chance, *señorita*,' he sang. Suddenly he was speaking perfect English with a Spanish lilt. 'What. Is. Your. Real. Name?'

'My name… is Rhiannon Lewis.'

And there came a buzz. On a deafening creak, the gates opened slowly inwards onto Spiky Plant Avenue. I grabbed my bag and shoes and raced down the track like The Little Mermaid on her brand-new legs. A white camera on one of the pillars swivelled as I entered, and once I was through the gates creaked closed behind me and met with a heavy *clank*.

The stony path wound through the forest and the deeper I went, the greener the trees became. Succulent cacti, tall *boojum* trees with curling branches like long scribbles into the wide blue sky. Palms with wide fronds, acid green cacti with fluffy white flowers up the stems and short craggy old men trees like something out of the Upside Down. I was so thirsty.

I came upon some wide steps leading up to a heavy wooden door. I knocked. A camera above swivelled my way. There was a scuffing sound, flip-flops on stone. Bolts sliding. The door opened and a tattooed brute with one arm in a blue sling stood before me. He was 60-odd but his hair was shockingly black, scraped into a ponytail, and his face smooth. He wore long grey shorts and in his good hand was a 10k gold dumbbell.

'Rhiannon,' he said gruffly, rolling the 'R'.

'Tenoch?' I said.

'*Hola*,' he said, his face brightening. 'Welcome to my little house.'

'Thank you. I think,' I muttered, stepping inside.

What followed was a tour of his 'little house' which was more of a mansion and an exceptionally tidy one at that, albeit it hideously decorated with animal skins, brown leather and gold accessories. I followed, achingly slowly because of his limp, though I didn't ask about his injury, nor his gimp arm or any of the myriad keloid scars littering his skin. I was still too thirsty.

'No visitors,' he said. 'No communications – emails, calls. Everyone and everything that comes into this house does so only with my permission.'

'OK,' I said. Glancing towards the kitchen in the hope that he'd read my mind and offer me some kind of cold liquid before I deadass fainted on the pristine earthenware tiles.

Thankfully the place was air-conditioned, and in the huge kitchen, bearing the largest oven I'd ever seen and two giant fridges, we stopped. 'You can make your own meals,' he said. 'Pop Tarts, sandwiches, whatever.'

Saliva flooded my mouth. I hadn't had a Pop Tart in weeks. 'Bobby said I'm not allowed to eat Pop Tarts, I love them but—'

'Eat what you like here, *be* who you want. There's nobody for miles.'

He led me past the fridge full of sodas through an archway into a lofty seating area with a suite of sofas and wing-back chairs draped in cow hides.

'We have Sky TV so you can watch what you want in here. We have nearly as many English channels as our own. BBC, the news, *Downton Abbey*. I watch it all the time. That why my English so good. You like *Made in Chelsea?*'

'No I fucking don't.'

The chairs were all positioned in a C-shape around a fireplace so huge I could stand up in it and jump and I still wouldn't have hit my head. On the wall above hung two crossed machetes – both with serrated edges – like the one on his massive chest tattoo – one of about fifty littering his body.

Tenoch clocked me looking. 'They cut through bone. You – no touchy.'

At the other end was a fully stocked bar with stools dressed to look like saddles. It stank of cigars, and the back wall was covered with antlers.

'Bar area.'

'Mmm,' I said, still gasping for anything wet in my mouth.

Next to the living room and bar was a small messy office and a large TV screen on a bracket split into six black-and-white images – the feed from six exterior cameras. He showed me an app on his phone where he could view the footage at any time. He had apps for everything. Apps to close and open the blinds, apps to turn the lights on, apps to adjust temperature.

'There's a camera in all the rooms, even yours. For security, I'm not a pervert.'

And I believed him. He had hands like Dad's. Boxer's hands. There was a punch bag in his home gym too – an old converted stable running along the side of the west wall. He said I could use it whenever he wasn't.

'I'm not into gyms,' I said, folding my arms.

'Use it for stress,' he said, which pulled me up. I had used the gym a couple of times on the ship when I was stressed and it had helped me in a way I hadn't expected. Maybe it helped Tenoch in the same way.

'So do I have the run of the place?'

Tenoch shrugged. I took that as a yes.

There were pictures dotted all over that ranged from the mundane – family photos, a young Tenoch chewing a cigar and wearing a ten-gallon hat with one foot perched on a giant tortoise – to the bizarre – lying across a Ferrari, surrounded by topless women, pulling a giant bear along on a chain, brandishing a golden gun in one hand and a severed head in the other.

'I'll show you upstairs to your suite.'

Ooh, things were looking up, I thought, despite my dehydration light-headedness, and as if by magic he took the hint.

'Oh, my manners. I haven't offered you a drink. What would you—'

'Cold soda,' I said without thinking. 'Would be great. Thanks.'

Gold was a running theme at the Hacienda. Anything that could be gold, was. Baths, the sinks, accents of gold on all his gym equipment. As we were going back downstairs, I noticed a large painting hanging on the facing wall – it was of a girl lying down in a large meadow of shimmering golden flowers.

The flowers framed the girl's face; her smile brighter than the gold.

'Is that a Klimt?' I asked.

'No, *I* painted that. It is my daughter, Marisol.'

'It's lovely,' I said, wanting to say something nice at that moment, rather than what I wanted to say which was *Why aren't her eyes in a straight line and why do her toes look like sausages?* I figured I needed to keep this guy on-side. I switched on Hilary. 'You're so talented.'

'Thank you. I used oils and gold leaf. It does not do her beauty justice but I try.'

'Where is she now?'

He stared back at me. 'She's dead. I haven't painted anything since.'

I followed him out to the baking hot pool terrace – a wide-open space overlooking a manicured lawn edged with empty borders. In the centre was a large stone igloo and next to the pool an ornate shed like a large Wendy house.

'It's great here,' I said, breathing in the sultry heat.

'You are only here for two months.'

'What do I do after two months?'

'The agreement was for surgery, recovery time and a new passport. You'll be gone by April. And I need your name for your passport too.'

'Can't I be Hilary Sharp again?'

'No. You must break the chain from Europe in case they tracked you.'

'How about Marisol? Like your daughter?'

'No.'

'Anne? Or Aña? At least it would be an echo of Rhiannon.'

'No, and no tilde. A white-bread name, unlinked to your past.'

'I can't pluck a new name from thin air. I need time to think.'

'Well, you need to think of it soon. In the meantime...' He gestured towards the stone igloo. 'This my temazcal. Get me your old passport.'

He held out his hand and I heaved my rucksack round and fished around for it. 'Why do you need it?'

'To break the chain,' he said, entering the stone igloo. 'You have an iPhone too Dannielle said?'

'No, I lobbed it in the Tiber.'

'Good.' Tenoch entered the temazcal. By the time I'd followed him in, a fire was alight in the central pit, lined with old ashes and charred sticks. My passport was on the pyre, bubbling.

'Oh fuck,' I said, my chest tightening at the sight of my only ticket out of Mexico bubbling and burning to a crisp.

Tenoch sat on the stone bench, cackling as we watched the last evidence of Aussie Hilary licked to death by an orange fury. And I may have imagined it but I could have sworn there was a bone among those embers.

'You can take those extensions out of your hair too. You don't need them now.'

I gingerly began unpicking them. My head grew lighter as they came out and I flung them into the pit on top of Hilary's passport.

'There,' said Tenoch, as the fake hair hissed and fizzled. 'You are not Hilary Sharp now, nor are you Rhiannon Lewis. So who do you want to be?'

I sat opposite him on the bench watching as the flames consumed the last remains of the person I had been. 'I have no idea.'

'Mr Fairly said you were organised.'

'Well, I'm not,' I said, catching my breath. 'How did you know Bobby?'

'I don't. Never met the *cabrón*,' he said, itching the cast beneath his arm sling. 'We've done some business in the past. I trust him.'

'Drug business? Coke? Heroin? I've seen *Narcos*.'

'You think because I'm Mexican I'm cartel?'

'No,' I said, unconvincingly.

'I *used* to be cartel, not anymore. Your friend Mr Fairly was a small link in our European chain. We did good business together.'

'You left it behind? You saw the light?'

The flames ignited his eyes as he stared into the angry pit. 'Something like that.'

'Why did you offer me sanctuary?'

He tapped his bad arm. 'I need some help. *You* need some help.'

'And money?'

'Of course. And I need you to do a job for me. Come see.'

'Sounds ominous,' I said, following him back outside, scratching an itchy bump that had emerged on the skin at the back of my neck.

'No, you should not find it hard. It right up *your* little alley.'

I trailed behind to the Wendy House, or 'pool house'. He opened the doors and the smell hit me. Inside, stacked up a heap in the middle of the room, were four very dead men.

Riddled with bullet holes, covered in blood, swarming with flies. Thick black bodily fluid had leaked into the blue carpet.

'Jesus!' I said, yanking my sweat-sodden T-shirt hem to my mouth.

'They broke into my house about a week ago.'

'What, all four of them?'

'They are part of a gang that I used to belong to.'

'The cartel?'

'I left them but they never left me. Sometimes, they make their feelings known. Don't worry – they were all bad. I know *you* only kill bad men.'

'How do you know that?'

He grinned – his teeth yellow, like a wolf's. 'I always know who I'm doing business with. I have eyes everywhere.'

Apart from the pile of dead men staining the shag pile, it was a nice little place, the pool house. There was a sofa bed, a table with a vase of fake marigolds and a TV in the corner. Through another door was a tiny bathroom.

'What do I do with them?' I asked, with more than a hint of *da fuh?*

'You know your way around a butcher's knife,' he said. 'Cut them up.'

'Why do I have to cut them up?'

He turned on his heel. 'Cut them up, burn 'em. Whatever.'

'I only did that once, cut somebody up. I didn't enjoy it.'

'OK, they will need to be buried down in that field over the back fence. You need to dig a hole and take them down there. And I can't see you being strong enough to carry them as they are. Even dead, they're too heavy.'

'Do I have to?'

'You want to stay here?'

'Can I at least have a sleep and a shower?'

'Oh sure,' he said. 'You go freshen up. I'll fix you something to eat and then you sleep. They'll still be here when you wake.'

'Great.' Tenoch closed the pool house doors and I followed him back towards the house. 'Over the back fence is an empty field between the date palms and the citrus orchard. It used to be for cempasuchil but nothing grows there now. You can take them down there tomorrow in my little *carretilla*.'

'Why does nothing grow there?' I asked.

He turned to me and grinned widely, showing a full row of Disney villain teeth. 'Why do *you* think?'

Sunday, 20 January –
Hacienda Santuario

1. DI Nnedi Géricault
2. Guy Majors
3. The actress on that bloody annoying hay fever advert with all the bees
4. The actor on that other ad for toilet paper who can't get over the softness of his own arse
5. Justin Timberlake. I don't know what gives him the right anymore.

SKY NEWS: BREAKING NEWS

'We go live to our Europe correspondent Guy Majors in Rome where there's a new development on the whereabouts of serial killer Rhiannon Lewis. Guy?'

Cut to bouffant-haired white guy in suit. Finger in ear. Eau de Gammon cologne.

'Yeah, hi, Sandy, I'm here in Rome, Italy, where it's alleged Rhiannon Lewis was seen a couple of days ago

and it is thought she is still in this area. She was last seen in a café by two tourists, mother and daughter Lindsay and Kaisha Debenham, who are here on holiday for a fortnight and they join me now...'

Cut to close-up of two blonde women – the same blondes I'd seen in the café at the Pantheon. Scouse accents. Deeper tans.

'Kaisha, if I can turn to you. Tell us what you saw. It was lunchtime, wasn't it?'

'Yeah, we were getting some lunch and there was this girl and an old woman sitting on a table near us. I recognised her from somewhere but I couldn't think where and I realised I'd seen her on a newspaper that morning in our hotel.'

Majors was practically creaming his chinos. *'And it was Rhiannon Lewis?'*

'Yeah, it so was! She was with this older woman, and they were chatting like and then Mum turns to me and she says, "Hey look, Kaish, she looks like that girl in all the papers." So she recognised her as well.'

The microphone switches to Lindsay. *'Yeah, she had sunglasses on and a baseball cap but I had this, like, sixth sense that she didn't want people to recognise her. And the longer I looked at her, like the shape of her lips and her nose and that, I remembered her face from the papers. And I got her picture up on me phone and I said to Kaish, "Eh that's her, that's the one the police are looking for."'*

Guy brings the mic back to him where it's most at home. *'But this was a couple of days ago that you say you saw her, why have you waited until now to tell the police?'*

Lindsay's turn again. *'We didn't know what to do, like. Cos I'd read about what she'd done and I thought, Christ, I don't wanna run into her but when you look at it, she'd only killed a bunch of paedos and dirty old men.'*

A man in blue-tinted sunglasses and a white England shirt has been gurning behind the two women throughout the interview. He has a bottle of lager in his hand and starts doing an Irish jig. The camera pans round so he is out of shot.

'You were happy that she'd got away with it?' said an appalled Majors.

'Yeah,' said Kaisha. *'We were. We thought, live and let live, like. But we heard what she'd done to that cabbie and the guy she'd had a baby with and we thought we better say something in case she'd killed the baby or something.'*

'Lindsay and Kaisha Debenham, thank you for joining me.' Guy turned back to camera with a definite jump of eyebrows. *'What we know for sure is that Lewis got on a cruise ship at Southampton Docks. The vehicle she'd stolen from Craig Wilkins' parents was found a few streets away and it has been impounded by forensics...'*

Cut to footage of Jim and Elaine's Ford Focus being lifted onto a low loader. When the footage cuts back, the England Shirt gurner is back behind Majors, making a wanking gesture. A mate in a red England shirt and shorts is laughing beside him.

'...passenger lists are being trawled through in the hope of finding the route out of the UK Lewis took – the hope being that this will lead police to her exact location.'

Cut to Sandy in the studio. *'The list of killings she*

mentions in her confession, Guy, they're horrific, aren't they? And they seem to escalate.'

'Yes, Sandy. The full awfulness of what Lewis did is only now coming to light and if everything in the confession is true, they are looking for a highly dangerous predator.' He consults his crib sheet. 'We all know the story of the man in the canal, Daniel Wells, whose penis was severed, back at the beginning of last year, several other stabbings, a suffocation, and at least one dismemberment. If the confession is accurate, this is a sick and vicious individual.' I think Majors had the hots for me.

'Are police any closer to locating her, Guy?'

Cut to Guy again, stubby finger jammed in ear, smiling knowingly. 'The police aren't giving anything away as of this evening but I do know they're putting extra powers behind this search and are keen to bring her to book as soon as possible. Members of the public are warned not to approach her if they see her and to call the police immediately if they have any information on her whereabouts.'

'What about Rhiannon's baby, Guy? Are police saying anything about what might have happened to it yet?'

'Yes, I spoke to a senior officer today who intimated that the baby was born before Rhiannon left the UK and is in safe hands. That's all they're saying at this time.'

The England Shirts holler, 'WE LOVE YOU, RHIANNON!' behind the camera.

Guy clears his throat. 'Back to the studio.'

Majors was all over my case in the UK. He popped up again on a search a couple of days later in a late-night topical news programme in the UK called *Late Night Insight*. He was interviewing DI Nnedi Géricault, the detective who'd been assigned to my case over a year before.

'DI Géricault, you interviewed Lewis twice, is that correct?' said Majors, stack of papers before him, pen poised.

'That's correct,' said Géricault, all the warmth of an ice sculpture.

'Once while she was under arrest for her part in the death of Lana Rowntree, her fiancé's lover, and once when she was under suspicion herself.'

'Yes.'

'And on both occasions you suspected her of being more involved in the murders attributed to her fiancé, Craig Wilkins—'

'Yes, that's correct.'

Majors' tongue is poised inside his cheek. 'Nearly a month since she skipped the country, you're no further on in locating her. What's gone wrong?'

'Nothing has gone wrong as such—'

'—but you haven't found her, have you?'

'—we are continuing to work with dedicated teams of law enforcement agencies both here and abroad—'

'—but you still don't have any idea where Rhiannon is, do you?'

'The teams we are working with, here and abroad, are examining the possible routes she might have taken—'

'—you had her in the palm of your hand, but didn't connect the dots?'

'She had a non-consistent MO. She'd killed various different people in different ways. It's hard to track someone like this—'

'—but you still didn't charge her with anything? And not long after you interviewed her under caution, suspecting her of some involvement with Lana Rowntree's death, she skipped the country on a false passport.'

'Yes, she did but—'

'—there've been sightings of her in Rome, Barcelona, Thailand and the Caribbean. It's like trying to find a needle in a haystack, isn't it?' Majors licked his upper lip, about ready to drop the mic.

Géricault barely raised an eyebrow. 'There have been a lot of *false* sightings. This strange and disturbing fandom is growing up alongside the Rhiannon Lewis case where *some* people, I should stress, are doing everything in their power to *keep* her at large. And they seem to think they are doing some kind of public service in hindering our work.'

Majors' left eyebrow rises. 'Why is that, do you think?'

'They think they love her,' said Géricault. 'They think they *know* her.'

'And what would you say to those people?'

'I would ask them to remember that this woman is a dangerous predator, capable of killing *anyone* who gets in her way.'

Majors ran his tongue along the inside of his cheek again, like he was trying to winkle out a stubborn bit of biscuit. 'She's making a fool of you, isn't she? She's got the public on-side and she's giving you the run-around.'

'*Some* people have ideas about Rhiannon Lewis being a sort of saviour of children and animals but this is simply not true—'

'—but she does admit in her confession that she has a special predilection for sex offenders and paedophiles, doesn't she?'

'Yes, but I must stress that she has also killed innocents.

Julia Kidner, mother-of-three – kidnapped, held for three months, raped post-mortem to plant DNA and stabbed multiple times. Daniel Wells was mutilated and drowned. Dean Bishopston, *father*-of-three, stabbed to death. Lana Rowntree was drugged and groomed into taking her own life. AJ Thompson, 19, father of *her* child, was burned, stabbed and dismembered. I mean... need I go on? This is not a woman to be put on a pedestal, this is someone to be *feared*.'

Guy flicked a glance at the monitor. 'What do you say to this – tonight's poll shows 92 per cent of our viewers think she should be left in peace.'

'Ninety-two per cent... so that would be about 184,000 people. And assuming your current ratings are correct *and* that they're all watching. That could be 92 per cent of ten people. There are 66 million people in this country, Guy.'

Clearly alarmed by Géricault's fast maths, Guy changed tack. 'But what about the others, DI Géricault? What about the convicted sex offender Gavin White? Convicted paedophile Derek Scudd? The two men who regularly patrolled country lanes looking for lone women drivers to kidnap and rape? Is it any wonder the public don't have a lot of sympathy for Lewis's victims?'

'Is that true?' Géricault frowned. 'Have you met Sarah Bishopston? Or her fatherless children? Or AJ Thompson's devastated family?'

Cue Guy's serious look right down the barrel with his steely greys. 'The consensus is that, right or wrong, Lewis killed more bad people than good.'

'That's simply inaccurate,' said Géricault. 'And I don't know how you can arbitrarily differentiate good from bad.'

'*You* have,' scoffed Majors.

'Yes, but how can you even begin to see the good in this woman?'

'Well, if we look at what happened to Rhiannon at Priory Gardens—'

'—no, sorry, I refuse to turn this into *This Is Your Life: Rhiannon Lewis*.'

'Right, and this isn't. This is about you, the British police, still not having a clue where this escaped serial murderer is, isn't it?'

'Yes but—'

'—do you know where she is, *right* now, DI Géricault?'

'We have a number of leads we are following up—'

'—but you don't know where she is.'

'Look, there are several key factors that need to be in place before we send a task force into any given region. We have worked with our colleagues at Interpol, putting out an All Ports Warning—'

'—but what if she's in a country with no extradition treaty with the UK? Does she use the old Ronnie Biggs method and stay put, have surgery and live the life of Riley?'

'Until we have reason to believe—'

'—will it be a shoot-to-kill order if you *do* find out where she is?'

'We want to bring Rhiannon Lewis to justice in the UK, that's all we want to do for the families of her victims.'

'So you don't want her dead or alive?'

'We want justice for her victims, Mr Majors.'

'You've no idea where she is, have you?'

'We're undertaking a massive search—'

'—but you still have no idea where she is?'

'—no, we don't but—'

'—no, there is it, right there, no, the British police and their law enforcement partners here and abroad have no idea where Rhiannon Lewis is. Not reassuring for our viewers but at least we got an answer in the end.'

'You didn't let me finish, how can I get a word in—'

'—we've got to leave it there. My thanks to DI Géricault for popping in today, stay tuned after the break as our syphilis test subjects return for their results, we have an appeal from the *Love Island* contestant whose pug was kidnapped and we'll hear from the YouTubers who started the Set Fire To Your Head craze which has claimed its fourth victim. See you in three!'

So the police didn't have a clue, any witnesses either weren't coming forward or were too stupid to call them and there was a fandom growing up in my honour. How the hell had I done it – got out of Europe unchallenged? That damned elusive Rhiannon – she was me. Everyone was talking about *me*. 'WE LOVE YOU, RHIANNON!' that guy had shouted. I was *adored*. My back involuntarily arched like a cat's when it was stroked. *Preen preen*.

But once the laptop lid was shut and I looked through the window at the dry, remote surroundings of the Hacienda where there was no other person but Tenoch for miles, I couldn't help feeling ever so slightly lonely.

And that never ends well.

Monday, 21 January –
Hacienda Santuario

1. *People who look at their phone when you're talking to them*
2. *People who tap their feet when they're watching TV, even when there's no music on*
3. *People who drink all but the dregs of a bottle of orange juice and put the carton back in the fridge*
4. *People who talk and eat loudly through a movie*
5. *People with body odour but who don't know it*
6. *Tenoch – thanks to all of the above*

I had settled in to the spacious en suite Bedroom 4 at the end of the upstairs corridor and into Tenoch's routine. He kept himself fit with two or three workouts in his gym every day and when he wasn't doing that he liked watching the news, *The View* and repeats of *The Golden Girls*. It was pretty funny, the first time I heard the jokes anyway. After the fifth watch of the same episode, I couldn't find the joy in it like Tenoch could.

When he wasn't watching that or pumping iron, Tenoch

would be in his office 'doing work'. I didn't know what this 'work' was but I got the impression it had to be dodgy to account for the four dead men stacked in his pool house, the clandestine phone calls at odd hours and the shadowy man in the black BMW who kept coming to the gates to exchange packages through the bars. I got the impression that the less I knew about it all the better.

Besides which, I still had a fucking gigantic hole to dig.

One morning, a few days into the big dig, I was woken around 7.00 a.m. – I was having a dream in which a man was continually yelling at me. *'Rhiannon! Come here! Come down here!'* It was my dad in the dream.

But in reality it was Tenoch. My eyes snapped open. And he kept calling.

'Rhiannon! Where are you? Get down here!'

I scrambled into my hoody and ran downstairs, across the lounge and out onto the pool terrace. Tenoch stood at the entrance to the pool house. He snapped his head round and saw me, eyes wild. 'What the fuck is *this*?'

'What?' I said, still creaking my eyes open to see what he was seeing. 'What's the matter?'

He gave me The Look – The Look people always give me the moment they find out how batshit I truly am. 'Why have you done this?'

'Done what?' I tugged my sleeve down over my hand and shoved it against my mouth. The bodies smelled real bad now they'd begun to liquefy in the already-intense heat of the morning. 'Oh, you mean the Sylvanians?'

'Why you… got the TV on for them? Why is this one dressed up in my dead wife's clothes?!'

'I found the dress in one of the bedrooms. It's moth-eaten so I figured it wasn't a big deal. He's experimenting with his gender. Nothing wrong with that.'

'They are… posed.'

'Yeah. The one with the maggots likes the baseball results, and the bloated one's having a nap after reading the paper—' Something had been nibbling at his exposed ankle. Probably a rock squirrel. 'I call him Rodrigo, and that one… John.'

'And the one on the toilet with his teeth on the floor?'

'Dwayne? He's… a binge eater. Always in the lav. I don't know why his teeth have fallen out though.'

Tenoch rubbed one hand down the length of his face. 'I don't understand. They should have been buried. Or burned. You fucking *loca*.'

'Well, yeah, obvs. I haven't dug the hole deep enough for them yet.'

'I see you coming in here. Do you. . . talk to them?'

'A bit. If you don't actually look at them, they could be alive. I mean, when I'm watching TV with them, it's like sitting there with a family.'

He stared at me. He paced. He stared at me a bit more. Then he said, 'Clean this up.' And he went inside the house.

The next few days were all about stiffs and shovels and scratching itchy bumps all over, courtesy of the damn mosquitoes. After the first day's dig, I could barely move for lower back ache and my fingernails were caked up with mud. But after a while, I paid neither much mind. My back got stronger, my shovel technique improved and the hole finally expanded.

I was allowed to cut a gap in the chicken-wire fence behind the pool house and peel it back wide enough for me to drag through each of the dead men. Some afternoons, between workouts, Tenoch would sit on a poolside-lounger and watch me struggling, sweating and swearing.

'You could help a bit, you know. They're pretty heavy,' I called out to him as one of the guy's hands came away from its skeleton.

'You shouldn't rely on anyone, Rhiannon. If you worked on your upper body strength you wouldn't need to.'

'Why do you work out so much if you don't use your muscles for anything other than showing off?' I said, squinting in the baking heat.

'I'm saving my strength for other things,' he said, which I didn't get but I couldn't be arsed to have him clarify either.

'Yeah, yeah,' I huffed, heaving the third man out of the Wendy House, across the terrace, round to the fence and yanking his feet through the gap, pushing him down into the shallow ditch at the bottom. I didn't have the strength to heave each of the bodies into the wheelbarrow, let alone wheel them all down into the field, so instead I had to rely on the old drag, roll and heave technique, muttering all the while.

'I'm supposed to be on my holidays. I've fucking paid to be here, why have I got to do this as well? Hmm? I mean, is that fair?' I was directing my questions to the vacant expression of the fourth man as I dragged his sorry ass through the fence and rolled him down into the ditch.

I clambered down into the ditch and grabbed his wrists, pulling him up into the field. 'I mean, shouldn't *he* be waiting on *me*? I've paid an arm and a leg to be here. When I kill a guy, the least I do is bury him myself. Why doesn't he do his own dirty work? What am I? Some kind of skivvy? Prick…'

I got back up to the pool house to find Tenoch waiting in the doorway. I yanked down my face mask.

'Is that what you think this is? A holiday?'

'No,' I said, sweat trickling down my forehead into my already-stinging eyes. 'To be honest, I don't know *what* this is.'

'You are helping me, like I am helping you.'

'I've paid you to help me. And I don't know if you've ever dug a grave before but it is bloody hard work in this heat. I've been at this for days.'

'So?'

'So you didn't tell me there was rattlesnakes in those fields either.'

'I don't expect they caused you much problem, a couple of little snakes. You're a serial killer after all.'

'I didn't kill them. I don't kill willy-nilly.'

'You just let Willy and Nilly bite you?' he chuckled.

'No, I stayed away from them.' He looked at me funny. 'They weren't me doing any harm.'

He shook his head. 'You are more *loca* than I gave you credit for. If you didn't do so much pissing and whining, that hole would be done by now.'

'Yeah, whatever,' I griped, wiping my brow and grimacing at the caked mud under my fingernails.

'It harder to kill when you are the one who has to dig the graves, eh, Rhiannon?'

This little exchange stayed with me all day, seeing as I had a ridiculous amount of time and space to think about it. Why did *he* care who I killed or if I killed? What did it matter to *him*? And I wondered if it was some sort of lesson – hard labour for my crimes against humanity. It didn't make sense.

It came up again a few days after when I was walking past his office.

'Hey, Rhiannon. You are blowing up in Europe.'

'What, literally?'

'Your story. You're everywhere. Every news show, it's your face!'

'Cool,' I said, settling into his swivel chair. 'Should we be looking for me online though? What about the search getting flagged by the police?'

'Don't worry about that,' said Tenoch. 'My computer has a re-routed IP address. Means the searches are coming from somewhere else. You're safe here, I promise. Take a look.'

Almost a week after my confession broke, the UK was suitably obsessed with me, and America was waking up to Ripperella too.

I was *every*where. Every thread. Every paper. All the headlines:

**BRITISH BOBBITT WHO CUT OFF MAN'S PENIS
IS CHILD BRAVERY AWARD WINNER**

LET HIM OUT:
Wilkins expected to be freed from jail this week

IT WAS ME: RHIANNON LEWIS CONFESSION
Boyfriend innocent, reveals diary. Exclusive by
local newsman who got the full confession

I was the subject of endless chats, Twitter threads, Facebook discussions, YouTube crime enthusiasts creaming their mum-ironed jeans over my 'magnificence', my 'audacity', my 'savagery'. There were more fan pages, thousands of new site members every day, memes created of my bored little face taken from one of the PICSOs' parties with the tagline *It's Monday again, kill me now.* Someone had even made a GIF of me walking across the farm shop car park from the CCTV footage with the tagline *Big Dick Energy.*

'Wow,' I said, looking up at Tenoch who had his arms folded and was squinting down at the screen over my shoulder. 'I'm famous.'

'Yeah. You are. You like it?'

I *did* like it. It had got my adrenaline pumping, my heart thumping. It had brought back that rippling, crippling can't-do-anything-else-but-kill sizzle. Every thread, fan site, and Reddit thread was a tiny back pat, a tickle under the chin, some human acknowledgement of appreciation. That I was admired. That I might even be *loved.*

Caro said I deserved to be loved. I wanted to believe that. A small group of kids in the UK were calling themselves the 'Dead Heads' and had set up a Tumblr, posting daily pics they had drawn of my killings, imagining what it was like to cut AJ into pieces. Imagining they were there standing at the quarry when I pushed Julia down, when I torched the Blue Van. They all said they hoped I was seeing this. They all said they loved me.

'It's better to be sick with someone than healthy and alone,' I suggested.

Tenoch's face was blank. Like Mum and Dad's when I swore

or did something to get a reaction – like smashing a glass or cutting Seren's hair.

But my growing crop of Dead Heads were giving me inner strength. Right or wrong, they renewed my belief in myself. Refreshed my energy for getting the hole dug. And they made me think, just for a short while, that someone truly cared about me. And that feeling is fucking addictive.

Thursday, 24 January –
Hacienda Santuario

REDDIT

Posted by rhiannonlewisiloveyou666 1 day ago

1.2k Comments

I'M IN LOVE WITH A SERIAL KILLER

OK so I know this is going to sound nuts but I think I am in love with Rhiannon lewis. i sleep with a photo of her under my pillow. the fact that her sister lives like 600 miles away from me is so incredible – i think if i met rhiannon, we would get along. like, i think she might even be my soulmate. i'm thinking of getting a sweetpea tattoo on my ankle, wdyt???

498 Comments

JoDiVaggio39 points

Check out the Wikipedia entry on 'hybristophilia'. And see a psychiatrist ASAP.

KendrickLaMarshmallow24965 points

I totally get that. She offed sex offenders so if I had the

chance to date her I totally would. I'm fascinated by her. And her diaries are so charismatic. I totally get her. Is that wrong?

TheOverlordShallCometh23 points

Anyone know where we can write her? There's a lot of fake social media accounts pretending to be her ATM but I'd love to get a message to her and tell her how much I love her.

rhiannonlewisiloveyou66612 points

Glad I'm not the only one! I've written letters to her and sent them to her bitch sister in Vermont. I know a ton of people on Tumblr who've done the same. And I sent some gifts too, but mainly letters.

BingedrinkerForLife729 points

I know a guy who once wrote to Dahmer and he got a response. A good guy by all accounts. Apart from the whole pesky murder, pederasty, rape and cannibalism thing.

JoDiVaggio4 points

Probably not to the people he murdered or their families.

MissMagickPluto96122 points

I relate to Rhiannon a lot because of the bullying aspect of her life talked about in the confession. I totally see why she did that to Julia, and why she tried to pin the thing on Greg. I think when you've experienced early trauma, it's bound to eff you up.

rhiannonlewisiloveyou6667 points

I think I do have that hybristophilia thing because I had a huge crush on Dylann Roof when that whole thing happened. I had, like, a ton of pictures of him on my laptop and my mom found them and I had to pretend they were for a school project about mass shooters. I love how unpredictable mass killers are. I never liked a female one though – until my beautiful Rhiannon.

rhiannonlewisiloveyou6662 points

Rhiannon Lewis is a hero, she never did what she did because she enjoyed it – she did it to get the scum off the streets.

JoJoMamaBaby61614 points

OMG I love her too! And I'm, like, in my forties now but she's so amazing, isn't she? In a way I kinda hope she is caught so she is sent to prison so then we can all write to her and she will see our words and know how much we love her.

Saturday, 26 January – Hacienda Santuario

1. *Every single one of the Golden Girls*
2. *The singer of the theme tune to The Golden Girls*
3. *The sadistic motherfucker who wrote The Golden Girls*
4. *Guy Majors*
5. *Tenoch*

The temperature in Rocas Calientes rarely dropped – it was sweltering all day and stifling all night. The sun went down but the heat lingered, close and uncomfortable like a scratchy blanket. Coupled with my copious mosquito bites, it made for regular bouts of irritability.

But hey, what's new?

Anyway, I got used to it all. To Mexico. I knew my place – digging the hole. I knew my master – Tenoch. By and large, he left me to my own devices but he was always there somewhere and that made me feel sort of safe. It took me a full week to finish the hole and push each of the men down inside it. And having shovelled the earth on top of them, I stood back in the fading sunlight on the Saturday afternoon, leaning on my shovel, a week to the day that I had broken ground. My spine was like jelly, my arm muscles on fire and I stank like a walking armpit. But I had finished it. I had done it, all by myself.

Tenoch had given me his little DAB radio which I had placed on the side of the pit to listen to while digging and the song playing was oddly catchy – some jam I'd never heard of called 'Ophelia'. I danced up and down the plough lines, stamping out a rhythm, windmilling my arms and laughing manically into the warm air until it echoed between the surrounding hills. It was the first time in a long time I'd actually enjoyed my own company.

And when I walked back up to the pool terrace, I dived in the pool, fully-clothed, soothing my itching, aching, dirty body from head to toe, coming out the other end like a whole new girl. Nearly.

As I slapped into the kitchen, Tenoch was browning the meat for our evening tacos in a skillet. The theme song of *The Golden Girls* trilled in from the sitting room. He didn't so much as raise an eyebrow at my soaking wet state.

'You did a good job.'

I could barely hear him over the sizzling skillet. 'Huh?'

'The field. It looks good.'

'Oh. Right. Thanks.'

'There are girl clothes in the cabinet in Marisol's room. Next to the one with my wife's dresses in. Take a few for yourself.'

'Are you sure?'

'Yes. Do you want another little job?'

My heart sank. 'How many more stiffs have you got around the place?'

'No more,' he laughed, juicing a lime. 'I see you dancing in the field. It makes you happy to be outside, doesn't it? Keeps you out of trouble.'

'I guess.'

'That why they call you the Sweetpea Killer? Because you like flowers?'

'They called me Sweetpea at work and I hated it. When I catfished men I made some of 'em carve flowers into their skin. But you know that, right?'

'You like the flowers though, yes?' He threw the spent lime half in the trash behind him without even looking. Hole in one. My dad used to do the same with apple cores.

'Yes. I love flowers.'

'I'll order you some plants and seeds. You can refill the borders out there. You do all the work.'

'Are you sure?'

'I used to like seeing them grow. Marisol loved playing in the fields of cempasuchil at the back of our house when she was little. A golden mile.'

'This house?'

'No, on our farm near Puerto Vallarta. She never saw this place.'

'What is sempa—?'

'Cempasuchil? Marigolds. The most beautiful colour you will ever see.'

'I'll need some quality manure that I can dig in. That will re-energise the ground. It has to be well rotted though or else it will scorch the rhizomes—'

'You sound like an expert.'

'My mum liked gardening. She spent all her time planting

and digging and deadheading after what happened to me. She said it soothed her.'

'After your brain injury? Well, it's cute that you used to help your mommy in the garden and all—'

'—no, I wasn't allowed to help. I watched her through the window.'

'Why you not allowed?'

'I wasn't a nice child. She said I didn't deserve nice things.'

'And you deserve nice things now?'

I dried my hands on the tea towel and slapped across to the fridge to get a soda. 'Probably not. I'd still like to plant the flowers for you though.'

It wasn't until the tortillas had been assembled and pushed towards me on a plate that he spoke again.

'You can do the little garden. Add whatever plants you want to the internet order. It'll keep you happy while you are here.'

I was excited, up until the point he said 'while you are here'.

'Thank you,' I said, more mutedly than I'd intended.

I was starting to cling, like I had with Caro. I thought maybe, if I did everything he asked, he'd let me stay. I could cook and clean, get the flowers growing, become a real asset to him. I'd suck his dick if I had to. I'm not averse to dick-sucking if the situation calls for it – it's just that my urge to bite down has always been too strong before. But I would do it, if it meant I could stay permanently. I think at that moment, I'd have done anything.

Monday, 28 January –
Hacienda Santuario

1. *Our delivery driver – Manuel – who brought the wrong fabric softener, seeded instead of plain bagels, and who banged the box down on the doorstep, breaking three of the eggs. Then laughed. Endless prick.*
2. *Tenoch's housekeeper, Celestina, who puts the scissors in the wrong drawer, folds my towels weirdly, never vacuums properly and can't wash forks*
3. *This Motherhood Dare shite on Facebook and any Motherfucker who shares it*
4. *Men who smell of BO and don't know it.*
5. *Novak Djokovic*

I didn't realise at first how much Tenoch's housekeeper Celestina did for him. I thought she was just a cleaner – swept a few floors, made the beds – but she did a ton of other things around the Hacienda like mowing the lawn, laundering the bed linen, mending anything broken, restocking the bar, replacing the tapes in the CCTV *and* chlorinating the pool.

She was naturally beautiful – the kind of woman who can just roll out of bed and get on with it without trowelling on a full face of make-up. But though she was only a couple of years older than me, her hands and knees looked twenty years older. She had a work ethic the like of which I'd never seen, certainly never experienced. Put my lazy arse to shame.

Celestina came to the Hacienda every morning dead early, around 6 a.m., and was usually gone by the time I'd surfaced at 8. One morning, though, things hit a little different. My eyes opened to see a tiny girl, no more than three, standing at the foot of my bed.

I thought I was imagining her at first, like she'd crawled out of a dream. '*Hola.*'

'*Hola,*' said the girl, moving her black hair out of her eyes and squatting back down on the carpet to play with Richard E. Grunt and the pink bunny, having helped herself to both of them from my bag.

'*Quién eres tú?*' I croaked.

'*Mi nombre es Mátilda,*' she answered and carried on playing.

Shortly, before my eyes fully opened, Celestina came barrelling in, scooping up Mátilda who dropped the bunny to the floor.

'*Lo siento, señorita,*' she gasped. '*Ella no debería haberte molestado.*'

'It's fine, it's fine,' I was at pains to say as I swung my legs out of bed. 'I don't speak much Spanish, sorry.'

'It's OK. I speak a little English.'

'She's a cute lil button,' I said, looking at her daughter sitting comfortably in her arms in her tiny dungaree dress and green T-short, big eyes twinkling, big thumb being sucked.

'Thank you,' Celestina smiled. 'I am sorry for her being in here. I have to bring them. My mother looks after them but she is out of town. Tenoch said it was OK as long as they – *mantente fuera del camino* – uh, stay out of way.'

'*Them?*' I said.

Celestina had two other kids downstairs watching TV. David and Saúl were eleven and seven respectively. David had a smile that could blind and wore a Spiderman T-shirt, while Saúl was short and tubby and, like myself, the type of kid to 'laugh if the cat's arse was on fire' as the saying goes. The TV was at the lowest volume and the boys were watching from the sofa – some badly-drawn Spanish cartoon.

'I can watch them for you, if you want?' I said. '*Uh, puedo cuidar, si?*'

'Oh no, they will be fine.'

'They look pretty bored. I don't blame them either – cartoons like this make me want to throw a toaster in a bath and take a fuckin' run-up.'

Celestina looked pained – I'd gone beyond her understanding, it seemed. This wasn't an unusual expression for me to see on someone else. Nevertheless, as soon as I started pinching out my seedlings from the trays and transplanting them into the ground, the children gravitated outside to watch me more closely. Kids are like magnets to me, I swear. I think on some level they know they are safe in my company.

'You can plant the new seeds, if you like,' I told the eldest and pointed to the new stack of packets on the countertop. 'And you can decide where they go,' I said to the younger boy.

'*Quiero ayudar,*' said Mátilda.

'OK, you get the most important job – you've got to water them. *Darles agua?*' She nodded vehemently.

Each one of them just got on with it and afterwards, I paid them in warm chocolate chip cookies. Best friends for life.

The boys they knew about the climate in Rocas Calientes so I bowed to their knowledge on where the sunniest patches were. Lavender, cornflowers, verbena, salvia and the special sun-loving shrubs all down the eastern border of the lawn; roses, passion flower, evening primrose, agapanthus, cempasuchil, osteospermum and some Mexican orange blossom all along the western edge. Mátilda mostly ate the herbs and buried Richard E. Grunt in the soil for me to find.

'Little pig man is hiding, *señorita*. You find him,' she sang at me, giggling behind her hand. 'Warmer, warmer, hotter, now you're colder.'

At the back fence, along the baseline of the lawn, went all the edibles – tomatoes, cilantro, *epazote,* chiles, *chayote* and the like. Sitting outside with the kids, a mug of real coffee in my hand, dipping our feet in the pool and laughing at the rock squirrels nibbling the sumac or watching quetzals drink from the red salvia, I fell in love with being alive. The sun warmed me through as the backs of my legs cooled against the marble. My extensions had gone, my real hair was getting longer and my fake tan had faded, replaced by one naturally browned by the Mexican sun. I allowed myself to imagine the place was mine. That this was my garden – sometimes, that these were *my* children.

Contentment fell down gently on my shoulders like feathers.

There was no backwards, no forwards, only this. I had to hold onto it, no matter what.

The only time I'd get angry was when Tenoch would remind me this was a stop-gap. Thoughts would start fizzing and I'd have to leave the room.

'Shame you won't get to see them bloom,' he said, coming back across the pool terrace from the gym one afternoon as I was planting out some honeysuckle along the back fence.

'What?'

'It'll be another month or two before they're strong enough to go in the ground. Maybe one more month till they come through. You will be gone before they get much bigger.'

And then he just walked away. No look back, no return. Leaving me still on the homeward slide towards my doom. And the feathery cloak of happiness vanished and my heart hurt all over again.

And yet. And *yet*.

One morning in early February, Tenoch noticed me scratching my mosquito bites on my neck when we were having breakfast.

'You're driving me mad with all that scratching, *gatita*.'

'I don't have leather skin like you. I'm not used to it. What's "*gatita*"?'

'It's just a name. Means *little cat*.' He smiled and as he did, Dorothy's mother Sophia called her 'pussycat' on the TV. It was like something my dad would have called me. I'd forgotten what it was like to be someone's daughter.

See, why give me a pet name if he didn't want me around? If he didn't have some affection towards me? It didn't make sense. What it *did* do was give me a tiny slice of hope.

A bite made its presence felt on my arm. 'Ugh, they're maddening.'

'You put that cream on the shopping list, no?'

'Yeah, I tried it, but it didn't work. I need something stronger.'

'There's a pharmacy in the town. I have to go down there tomorrow for some business anyway. Why don't you come with me? They will help you.'

'Am I allowed to visit the town, do you think?'

'Sure. There aren't many tourists around yet. Do what I do – keep your head down, and don't draw attention to yourself. Borrow one of Marisol's hats. Anyone asks, you're my daughter.'

And we went back to watching *The Golden Girls* and eating our quesadillas and drinking lemonade squeezed from our own lemons.

'Haha, Rose is going out with a midget,' he laughed. 'Typical Rose.' He shook his head, like he knew the woman intimately. I laughed too. He liked it when I laughed at the same time as him.

As I went up to bed that night, I caught a glimpse of the painting of Marisol on the stairs. His precious daughter, with her scrappy plait trailing behind her, lying among the golden flowers. The girl whose hat I was permitted to borrow, and who he could barely talk about without blubbing. I wondered what had happened to her. I wondered if he'd called her *gatita* as well. I wondered if I could grow my hair as long as hers.

The coastal highway at the bottom of the hill stretched far into the blue distance. It was bordered by an endless line of tall palms and sprawling hotel complexes, interspersed with *taquerias*, ice cream parlours or *heladerias,* supermarkets, tobacconists, liquor stores, boutiques and souvenir kiosks.

Tenoch gave me an hour to look around and get what I needed to at the pharmacy, and said to meet him back at a little *panaderia* to pick up some of his favourite – apple pie – for a treat that evening. I found the pharmacy in a side street off the beachfront and the guy sold me a giant bottle of calamine, some brown hair dye and a few boxes of anti-histamines. With time to kill so I browsed the other shops – I bought a Spiderman comic for David because I learned he loved comics, a football for Saúl and a yarn pig for Mátilda.

As I was walking out of one store, a swinging A-frame on the sidewalk caught my eye:

Galería de Salomé Casta
Open till late. 10 per cent off
ceramics while stocks last

There was an arrow pointing along the seafront towards the Distrito de Arte. I had to go and see if Rafael was there – to see if he was as flawless as I remembered.

I found the gallery along a wide cobbled street, nestled between others selling the same kind of stuff – seascapes, glass-blown sculptures, beach scenes, tapestries and bronzes. The original works by 'Artistas Locales' bore the most eye-watering price tags but basically all looked that looked like they'd been done by toddlers.

There was the obligatory naked sculpture – the odd bronze wang looming over me as I ambled around. I couldn't sniff out the picture Salomé had painted with her period clots, thank God, and the old nut job herself held court at the front of the gallery, giving short talks about the pieces in Spanish. She didn't *look* insane. She reminded me of Golden Girl Dorothy – tall and stern-looking in a long-sleeved blue silk dress with chunky bead necklace.

I stopped beside a huge ornate wall sculpture of shining gunmetal, formed into a shark with all these tiny suckerfish attached to its back. Two hundred and forty thousand pesos. Next to it was a drawing of a mother and child – the mother holding the infant, both their heads turned away. It was the simplest black charcoal drawing but I couldn't stop staring at it.

'Hello, young lady,' came the voice.

I ventured a peek. Salomé looked right at me, her last customers just leaving. 'Hello,' I said. 'How are you?'

'Oh, are you English?' she said. 'How lovely. We don't get many English visitors to this area anymore.'

Thank fuck for that, I thought.

'Did you see anything you liked?'

'Yes, lots of things,' I lied. 'I like this one a lot.'

'*Madre e Hija*. Yes, it's perfectly understated, isn't it? I noticed you looking at the oil paintings in the window by my nephew.'

'Rafael?'

'Rafael Arroyo-Carranza. I'm exhibiting him all this month.'

Of course he would have such a beautiful last name. But there was *one* flaw at least: he couldn't paint for shit.

'They're… lovely.' I pretended to study one that looked like a naked chalk Dolly Parton screaming into a bin.

'Isn't he magnificent? The *passion* in them. He's beginning to share his work more with me, after years of persuasion.'

'He's quite something,' I said, glancing at picture next to Dolly which looked like an irradiated cock and bollocks.

'*His* pieces are all reserved but he has plans to do a few more. What brings you to Rocas Calientes?'

'I'm staying with my uncle. Helping him out. He has a bad arm.'

'Oh,' she said, hand to her chest. 'You wouldn't be *the* English girl, would you?'

'Which English girl?' I said, mild arrhythmia just starting to kick in.

She burst into laughter. 'I'm sorry, Rafa said he met this brunette at the airport a few weeks ago and she hadn't told him her name. He was quite taken with her,' she beamed. 'He said she'd introduced herself as a maniac.'

I laughed. 'Oh, he remembered me?'

'He certainly did. He said you were beautiful and you made him laugh, two attributes devilishly hard to find in another person.'

'Well, I don't know about that.' Except I *did* know about that and I swelled with joy. The Hottest Turtle thought I was both beautiful *and* funny.

Gusset dryness = history.

She hooked her finger towards me and led me towards the back of the shop where she rooted around in her pocket for a key to unlock a set of drawers beneath the cash register. 'When he was here, he came to the gallery every day hoping you'd turn up. He said he'd told you about the place.'

'Yes, he did. I didn't think he would remember me.'

'Well, he did, and he was a little disappointed you didn't show up. I said if you ever did come in, he should leave a note for you, you know, on the off chance that you might want to see him again.' She fished out a small scrap of paper from the drawer. 'Here it is.'

She handed it to me. I opened it out:

Hey, Maniac. I came down here a few times but I must have missed you. Maybe you're busy. If you want to hang out anytime, ask Sal for my number. Been thinking 'bout you, that's all. Rafael ☺

'Oh shit,' I said, reading the message again, before Salomé grabbed it from me and scribbled down his number on the back.

'Only if you're interested, of course,' she said, going to hand it to me but withholding it at the last second.

'Yeah, yeah,' I spluttered, 'of course I am,' grabbing the note from her and holding it as though it was the map to the lost city of Atlantis.

'Good. Because if you *hadn't* been I'd have thought you really *were* a maniac. He's special to me. And he's been hurt before.'

'Me and him both.'

'He's coming here in a few weeks to help me move premises. Maybe you could spend some time with him? He'd love to show you around the place.'

'You're moving?'

'To a bigger spot, a few doors down.'

She was waiting for something – for me to commit to a definite yes. But I couldn't decide if I wanted to inflict myself on

Rafael. He seemed like a decent guy, despite obvious artistic dyslexia. And no good man deserved me.

So I said it. 'I don't know if I'm... what he needs.'

Salomé stepped back, seemingly shocked. 'Why would you say that?'

'I'm kind of high maintenance. *Every rose has its thorn.*'

'Is that Jung?'

'No, Miley Cyrus.'

She laughed. 'Well, here is another one for you – *every heart sings a song incomplete, until another heart whispers back.*'

'Ooh, that's good.'

'Plato. I think. Or the other one. Socrates. No, I think it's Plato. My philosophy is a little rusty.'

'Well, it was nice to meet you, Salomé. I hope to see you again.' I pocketed the note.

'Yes, I hope you see you again too, uh— sorry, I missed your name...'

And I said it, for the first time ever, without thinking – I said my brand-new name. The name I was going to have for the rest of my life.

All the way back to the Hacienda, the sky darkening, I chitter-chattered like an excited baby bird. Tenoch, one meaty hand on the steering wheel, one slinged-up arm leaning out of the window, kept his eyes on the road.

'You seem happier now, *gatita.*'

'Yeah, I am,' I said, dabbing some of the cool calamine lotion on my bites with small pinches of cotton wool.

'Good.' He smiled at me – a dad smile.

'And I thought of a new name.' I told him what it was.

His face bore no expression. 'Well? What do you think? Is it white-bread enough?'

'Yeah. It's a good name. A pretty name.'

'I went to this little art gallery and I met the lady who runs it.' I screwed the lid back on the calamine. 'And I said it when she asked me... that feels better already,' I said, looking at all the chalky discs of lotion all over my legs. 'Dad used to put calamine lotion on my chickenpox when I was little.'

'You had chickenpox?' he asked.

'Yeah, when I was about nine. Why?'

He looked at me before placing a tender hand to my chin and turning it from one side to the other. 'These scars, they chickenpox?' He was referring to the one below my right ear and next to my nose.

'Yeah. And a couple on my tummy.'

'You can add those to your list,' he said.

'What list?'

'For your surgery. Ask them to graft them for you. I had it done myself, it doesn't take long. Or they might use lasers now, I don't know.'

My heart dive-bombed. 'Do I have to have surgery?'

'Of course. You have paid for it.'

'But what if I... stayed here, out of the way?' I asked. 'Would I still need it?'

'You need to be gone from here by April. That's what you've paid for.'

'But if I stayed and kept you company? I can be useful to you.'

Tenoch didn't say no right away. He put his hand down into the bakery bag and plucked out a macaron. 'How can you be useful to *me*?'

'I can help you around your house. Keep the house clean.'

'I have Celestina for that.'

'Well, I can do other things, I don't know. I buried the bodies. I can bury as many bodies as you need. I'll do whatever. You know you can trust me.'

He didn't speak for a long time. I didn't think he was going to say anything at all. As the car passed the front gates of the Hacienda and swung a left onto the hard standing at the back, he switched off the engine and leaned across to remove a leaflet from the glove box. He handed it to me.

'The Xochiquetzal Clinic and Medspa Centre,' I read aloud.

'It's not far. Cabo San Lucas. I had some work done there myself. Dr Gonzales is a good friend of mine – I would trust him with my life.'

'Please, Tenoch.'

'Your first consultation is next week. They will do the first procedure the week after. If you want to be truly free, you have to change your face. It's hot property, and it's becoming more recognisable by the day, you understand?'

'Yeah, but—'

'But what?' he glared at me.

'Nothing,' I said, all fizzy in my chest again. It was useless nagging him. He was a closed door and surgery was the only one open to me. I had no choice but to walk through it.

'What work did *you* have done?'

'I had some tattoos removed. And a facelift. Rhinoplasty. A few chemical peels. I'll show you a picture of how I looked before.'

When we got inside, I sat at the dining table and flicked numbly through the leaflet. Every picture was of some scraped-face angel-white-toothed pre-pube who'd had every procedure going and felt 'fresh and ready for life's challenges'. I was *not* these women. I did not want to improve my face *or* brighten my outlook. Though the tummy tuck was worthy of a second look.

Tenoch brought in a scrap of paper and slid it across the table top. It was a mottled photo of a family sitting by a pool, raising a drink and squinting into the sun. A woman handing out slices of cake. A twenty-first birthday balloon tied to the back of a young woman's chair. The man sitting next to her had his hand behind her head, doing bunny ears.

'Can you see me?' asked Tenoch.

'No,' I said. 'Is that your daughter?'

'Yes,' he said, pointing to the birthday girl. 'And that's me next to her.'

'Seriously?' I said. 'That's you? Your face...'

'That's what a facelift and a nose job does. It changes the fundamental parts of your image.' He stared hard at the photo before lifting it to his mouth and kissing the girl, then the woman handing out the cake.

'What happened to them?'

He didn't answer that. Instead he said 'My point is – there is life for you to live after surgery. New face. New name. New people.'

'Is Tenoch not your real name?'

He didn't answer that either. 'You have given yourself a second chance. My advice – take it with both hands. Get out there and make good of it.'

'But *how*? Where do I go?'

'Not my problem.' He stood. 'You want quesadillas again tonight?'

'No please, *please* listen to me,' I said, sliding out my chair. 'I need to stay here. I don't have anywhere else.'

'This place is not for you. Do you never think why?' I frowned. 'You dug a grave for four men last week. Does it not scare you who those men were? If more men will come here?'

'I can take care of myself.'

'Not here you can't. This is *cartel* country. You may think you are brave, that you have bested your enemies in little old England but you cannot fight the cartel. You can't bring a knife to a gunfight.'

'Teach me how to use a gun then.'

'Haha, I'm not about to give a *serial killer* a gun.'

'But I can defend myself if more men come here. I can defend *you*.' I followed him into the kitchen where he started grating cheese into a bowl. 'We can be ready for them together and finish this.'

'Could be more of them next time. They will never stop.'

'Why? What do they want?'

'Revenge. Amongst other things.'

I was too busy freaking out about being flung out into the big wide world to really question what he meant by that. No matter how hard I worked in the garden, nor how many après-workout smoothies I made him, nor how many times I watched *The Golden Girls* and laughed in all the same places as he did – I was out on my ear. The thought of being on my own again made me realise how fucking weak I truly must be.

All my life I've had someone propping me up. First Mum and Dad, then Seren until she went to the States, by which time I had Craig and the PICSOs. When Craig was arrested, I had Jim and Elaine. On the ship, it had been Caro and the

Prossers. I was a parasite, a suckerfish, like the ones on that shark in Salomé's gallery. Looking for the next host.

Now here I was clinging to Tenoch, a stranger.

Something would turn up, I kept telling myself. A cunning plan. A miracle, even. I'd take anything. In the meantime, I tended the garden and kept my mouth shut and my eyes open. It always opened up my thoughts.

And a thought did occur to me, the following day.

I'd given the children their presents from town. They loved them, Saúl especially – and I got three hugs which made me so happy I could have cried. David read his comic from cover to cover. Mátilda still wanted Richard E. Grunt as well as the yarn pig I had bought her but I stole it from her dungaree pocket and said he'd run off to join a piggy circus, which she seemed to accept.

Tenoch had seen the present giving and bided his time.

'You will find new people,' he told me over breakfast, still sweaty from his workout. 'Don't get too reliant on them.'

I pushed my uneaten Pop Tart away. 'I like them. They're good kids.'

'I know, but they will not be around here forever.'

Fury bubbled in my core. I seethed as he wanged on and on.

'You could go to your sister. I can get someone to drive you over the border, if that's what you want.'

'That's *not* what I want.'

He downed the rest of his poached eggs. 'I'm gonna take a shower. Don't forget your consultation tomorrow. Paco will take you at eleven.'

'Why aren't *you* taking me?'

'I can't go to Cabo,' he said. 'Even with a facelift, I'm

a dead man walking there. Are you making my smoothie this morning or am I?'

I looked away. He set about doing it himself, chopping and blitzing all the ingredients, pouring them in his glass before he said one more word to me.

'Don't be miserable, *gatita*. Enjoy yourself while you are here.'

He scuffed out of the kitchen and headed upstairs.

I sat watching the knife drawer he'd inadvertently left open. I looked out at my little seedlings on the patio, quietly growing away. I would be here to see those flowers grow, one way or another.

Monday, 4 February –
Hacienda Santuario

1. *Virtue-signallers who barge into fan forums for the express purpose of educating people on why their fetishes are wrong*
2. *The Prossers who'd done an interview with a Sunday newspaper where Jayde agreed with the journalist that I was, indeed, 'pure evil'*
3. *Terminally gullible people who believe everything they read, including that I severed every one of my victims' penises*
4. *American true crime YouTuber and Rhiannon super-fan Dash Kuric who's got a GoFundMe page going to raise funds to travel to the UK and locate said penises*

I didn't want to kill Tenoch. It didn't feel right, just necessary. Everything was so uncertain again, like the ground had become unmoored. I was a bad, bad person and I needed to hide but he wasn't giving me any other choice. There *was* nowhere else to go. Across the pond, my celebrity was growing each day.

Several more fan sites had popped up since the last time I'd looked. Tumblrs, blogs, Facebook pages, and a couple of teenage crime enthusiasts in the UK had even filmed a video of their pilgrimage to some of my kill sites and posted it up on YouTube – it had over 150,000 hits so far. They'd rocked up at the *Gazette* offices and Jim and Elaine's house, leaving gifts of knitted mushrooms and Sylvanians on the gate. Two girls had dyed their hair blonde like mine used to be, others wore sweet peas tucked behind their ears.

People *loved* me. To the point of obsession.

And these weren't kids, by the way. These weren't K-Pop groupies giggling in kitten ear filters sucking on vanilla frappes – some were grown-assed people wearing wedding rings. One woman was even talking about having *surgery* to look like me.

Knowing that lifted my spirits briefly, taking my mind off my impending bad decision. The 'Rhiannon Stans' were causing a wildfire on the socials too. Some bragged about their 'murderabilia' – handfuls of grass ripped from the front garden at Jim and Elaine's, gravel taken from behind the police cordon at the farm shop car park, and some ghoulish website was selling blood-spattered unicorn onesies because there's a picture of me in one on some night out with the PICSOs on Facebook. Oh, I remember now – Halloween night. They were all witches and sexy pumpkins. I was a killer unicorn.

I miss that onesie. I don't know whose blood they used for the onesies. Can't remember whose blood *I'd* used.

It was like some mad genie had been let out of the bottle, like in *Aladdin*. And the magic was everywhere.

Over on Twitter, my name was still trending, as was

#TheHuntForSweetpea – there had been some hastily cobbled together BBC documentary in the UK, all about the rise in female killers with *moi* as star attraction. The amateur psychologists were the best part as I read their tweets:

@johnnystaffs6382111231
This was a sensitive portrayal of a tough subject, handled well by the producers and writers. Actress playing Rinannon Lewis in the re-enactments was fenomenal [sic]. What an evil cow!

@MaryQuiteContrary291
I think love plays a significant role in her hate. Look at the murders that occur during the time she knows Craig is having the affair – her hit count goes up, significantly. And during her pregnancy where she says the baby is 'telling her' not to kill people – her bloodlust only intensifies.

@SamSmithIsTheyOK58
I agree. She killed the love she felt. For the boyfriend and for the baby. When she feels love, she feels hate because she knows it will be taken from her. I actually feel quite sorry for the lass. #SweetpeaForEver

@GrannyKnowsBest21905
Possibly around the time of the attack at Priory Gardens, love and hate became muddled in her mind. She lost the ability to feel either exclusively and struck at random because of it. It's textbook.

@MamaCassHamSandwich @GrannyKnowsBest
Rinanon didn't strike at random – she made kill lists. But
if you look at the genetics, brain damage, environment,
you could see it coming. Her amygdala was damaged at
6. She was a powder keg waiting for a spark. Craig and
Lana lit the spark.

@GillyTurner22
You've only got to look at her childhood to see where it all
went wrong. Smashed over the head with a hammer, years
of recovery, vigilante dad. It's not rocket science. I think
she's amaaaaaaaazing. #IStandWithRhiannon

When I couldn't take any more misspellings of my name,
I switched to the #RhiannonHandwriting hashtag. I couldn't
find the clip on YouTube but apparently some posh handwriting expert had scrutinised my scribbles one morning on *Up
at the Crack*. My stans laughed him off the face of the Earth.

'*Oh yah, you can see by the way the "s" curls up that she's
a psychopath.*'

'*Mmm yah, that curl in the tail of her "y" indicates she
was into necrophilia.*'

'*If you look at the large bubble above the lower case "i",
this is a person who likes to disembowel people for shits and
gigs. It's absolutely textbook.*'

Aside from chit-chatter by Twitter-twatters, there was the
odd reaction GIF, the odd do-gooder trying to raise money
for my victims' kids, a selection of deepfakes of me with
Myra Hindley's hair, talking about how much I liked to chop
off penises and sling 'em in my NutriBullet. Some had me down

as Jill the Ripper, complete with stovepipe hat; others talked about the mental health crisis and how we shouldn't judge.

There were rumours of boiled heads in saucepans (never did that), human pubic wigs kept in a shoebox (it was actually my Sylvanian hedgehogs), several penises in abandoned kettles (nope), a chair upholstered in human skin (Jim and Elaine's leather Parker Knoll – some photographer had seen it in a skip outside their house) and even that I had once eaten a human pancreas (can't say I've ever felt the need).

And there were interviews with EVERYONE. Jim and Elaine with Tink in her arms, the PICSOs, the WOMBATs. The taxi driver's widow, the taxi driver's darts team. Everyone at the *Gazette*, even my replacement Katie Drucker who didn't even KNOW me but had found the compass gouges in my desktop saying 'Linus Sixgill's a Cunt'. I could hear them all now:

'…I always thought she was a bit funny.'

'…I never liked her.'

'…Priory Gardens. That's where it started.'

'…her dad's to blame, taking her to his vigilante parties.'

'…she'll be after her sister next, mark my words.'

'…that poor taxi driver's kiddies.'

'…she came to my hen weekend and killed a fortune teller.'

'…she chopped him up!'

'…did she cut off *his* todger as well?'

'…she's sick. It's that baby I feel sorry for.'

'…I always thought her coffee tasted weird.'

I'm amazed Tink didn't pipe up with a well-timed bark of derision.

They interviewed Jayde and Ryan Prosser too, in a little

taverna in Malta. They told the press about the woman in Florence, how I'd nearly killed her, how disgusted they were that I'd been around their kids. I spent the whole interview watching for signs of Ty and Sansa. Wanting to see *any* little faces. Ivy's face. That's whose face I wanted to see.

But she was nowhere.

I'd have killed for one picture of her but Claudia had managed to keep her out of the limelight. She was moving too – there was a FOR SALE sign up outside her house and she'd handed in her notice at the *Gazette* – some pap shot had emerged of her leaving the office holding a bouquet with a *Sorry You're Leaving!* card on it. There was a rumour she was going to London.

Caro hadn't gone to the press yet. Maybe she didn't even *know* about me yet. Where did she think I'd gone that day in Rome? I hoped she didn't know. I hoped she never would.

They hadn't interviewed Seren either. She was always a flat hand and a carefully placed hood when the journalists came knocking at her door. As a surviving relative of a serial killer and the grass who'd set the police on my flaming arse, she was hot property and the media hounded her mercilessly, especially Guy Majors, that self-important hack with the Messiah complex.

So I had to stay, that's all there was to it. If I wanted the sunshine – the stans, the adoration, the glory – I had to put up with the rain – hiding. Hiding from those who wanted me caught, raped, jailed, sectioned, dead or all of the above. Hiding from detectives like Nnedi Géricault whose constant proclamations that they were 'closing in on an arrest'. Hiding from journalists like Guy Majors who was hounding my sister for interviews, trying to locate Claudia, striving to get the first glimpse of Ivy to see if she had three sixes on her head. All the more reason to have surgery as soon as possible and stay hidden forever.

Or to see if I could reach one of those machetes on the fireplace wall.

And eye up Tenoch's jugular whenever he was close by.

The more I let the idea of killing him bud and blossom, the more it made sense. I would take down one of those machetes. I'd hide it under my pillow. I would wait until he was asleep, until the snoring started.

And then I would creep, creep, creep, into his room and slice off his head. Easy peasy lemon squeezy.

There was one teeny tiny problem: a thirteen-stone body-building cokehead called Paco.

Wednesday, 6 February –
Hacienda Santuario

1. *Mosquitoes*
2. *Cockroaches*
3. *Spiders*
4. *Rats*
5. *Paco*

As far as I could gather, Paco had been Tenoch's bodyguard from his cartel days and he had stuck around – dropping in to the Hacienda at any time of day, helping himself to whatever in the fridge, changing the channel on my radio or watching TV with his feet up on the furniture. He had the face and body of a Dream Boy but the personality of a rancid sanitary towel.

Paco did anything Tenoch told him to. And if something happened to Tenoch, like an English chick massacring him in the night, you could bet the house Paco would wreak a swift and terrible revenge on his assailant.

A tall, patronising gum-chewer, he had Popeye's forearms, fingers loaded with rings and always kept a set of handcuffs visible on his belt loop. Every time he looked directly at me, it felt like he was reading my thoughts. It was unsettling, to say the least.

And I wasn't the only one unsettled. Celestina would avoid him too whenever he was at the house early, which wasn't often. If he came into the room, she would leave it, whether she had finished her cleaning work or not. And when she *did* find herself in the same space, he *always* smacked her arse and laughed as she scampered away.

I noticed one thing about Paco above all else: when Tenoch was around, Paco didn't talk to me much. It was when he was away that the cat started to play. For example, the car ride to Cabo for my first surgery consultation:

'Why not you sit in the front with me, *chica*?'

'I prefer the back, thanks.'

'You can play with my radio.'

'I'm fine. Thanks.'

'So you serial killer, eh?'

'I used to be,' I said.

'Serial killer once, serial killer for life. They don't stop.'

'*I* did.'

'How many you kill?'

'Eighteen.'

He did the Robert De Niro mouth suggesting this was a pretty decent batting average. '*How* you kill?'

I stared him down in the rear-view mirror. 'Stabbed. Mostly.'

'Nice.' He broke stare to look back at the road, draping his right arm around the passenger seat head rest to flex it out. 'I lost count at fifty.'

'Congrats.'

He laughed and lit up a cigar that stank like feet and burnt tyres. 'You ever have *pesadillas*? You know, the nightmares?'

'No,' I lied.

'*None* of them play on your mind?'

'No.'

He puffed on his cigar, which I thought was weird because he was such a health nut about his body. 'Does *anything* play on your mind?'

'Not really.'

I thought he was done with me but after a few miles he piped up again. 'What about scary movies, Rhiannon?'

'I don't find them scary.'

'Oh no? What about *IT*? Weren't you scared of the clown in the drain?'

'Reminded me of my nan. Same shaped forehead.'

I didn't mean it to be funny but he still laughed, long and heartily, puffing his thick smoke out into the car. I buzzed down my window.

That Ophelia song came on the radio. Paco turned it off.

'You scared about your surgery?'

'No. I'm not having much done.'

'It will be fine, don't worry, *chica*. I had some done there myself. They're the best. It don't hurt.'

'I said I'm *not* scared.'

He laughed. 'Oh, you will be. You will be.'

Paco liked to dig at me about what I was afraid of, all the time. Tenoch treated me like an equal; someone who moved in underworld circles like they did, but Paco couldn't see it. To him I was a little girl – a *chica*, or worse still, *niñita*. When we stopped for gas on the way to the clinic, he even bought me a lollipop.

'Thought you'd like something to suck on our journey, *niñita*.' And he said it with a wink. A Fuck Wink? Or a Don't Fuck With Me Wink?

Was he goading me? I thought. It seemed like it. Tenoch never did that – if anything, he always tried to calm me down, but I guess Paco was one of those men who liked women, especially 'little girls' to be scared of them. I've never understood why, but they do. And if there's one thing I've learned, even as a little girl, it's that you must never show someone like that your fear. Cos the fucker will always use it to take you down.

The clinic itself was spotlessly clean, accented by azure glass partitions, pan-piped Coldplay and over-friendly staff who all looked like they'd gone through the laminator themselves and offered me cactus water every fifteen seconds.

The surgeon – a Mexican Clooney lookalike called Dr Aquiles Gonzales – came recommended by Tenoch, Trust Pilot and the many framed certificates dotted about his office. He was certified by the Mexican Board of Plastic, Aesthetic and Reconstructive Surgery and his demeanour was cheery and welcoming but ruthlessly blunt. This immediately put me at ease.

Until he started talking about cutting my face open, that is.

'So you say you want an image overhaul, a little freshening up, yes?'

'Yes, that would be good.'

A 3D image of a woman's body filled the screen – *my* body, the results of being measured and scanned.

'So take a look at this,' he said, adjusting the screen. 'Here is you. What we have here are your current dimensions, OK?

Face shape, jawline, ears, nose, mouth. Down to the shoulders, the breasts, arms, hands, abdomen, genital area, thighs, shins and feet. So you are overweight.'

Any remaining shred of self-esteem flew out the window. 'Yes, that is a scientifically accurate observation, I guess.'

'For your purposes, I would recommend liposuction to these areas here (thighs), brachioplasty here (tops of arms) and abdominoplasty (tummy tuck).' He jiggled my saggy pooch without warning. 'You were pregnant, yes?'

The dark clouds descended. 'Yeah.'

'We can get that pregnancy belly gone for you.'

The clouds parted. 'Seriously?'

'No problem at all.' He typed something in again, probably adding a few more noughts to the overall total. 'Now if we look at your face shape imperfections, I would suggest some otoplasty – we would pin back your ears slightly, because they do stick out.'

Turned out I *did* have a shred of self-esteem left but he'd just torn it off, chewed it up and spat it out on the carpet. He digitally pinned back my avatar's ears and immediately, it didn't look like my head anymore.

'Wow, yeah, let's do more of that shit.'

'Some rhinoplasty will shave off the little hump you have here.' He smoothed the bridge of my nose with the end of his pen. 'This should soften things up and change your facial dynamic. The bone at the end – we will shave it down to give you a little turn-up. It will all be incremental – little changes, week by week, until you are transformed. You will look like a different girl.'

'Good.'

He did the thing on the digital face and changed it with a quick tweak. Rhiannon Lewis had gone in the click of a mouse.

'That's fantastic. Is that it?'

'No,' he replied flatly. 'I would also recommend bringing forward your hairline a quarter of an inch as well, removing these moles here and here,' he said, pointing them out on my neck, 'and your scars, of course. You mention in your form that you are interested in permanent eye colouration?'

'Yeah, do you do that here?'

'No.' He sucked in a breath. 'There are risks with any type of surgery and this type of surgery is still under-tested. I will not touch it yet. Everything else, I can pretty much tell you what to expect, what aftercare you will need, what painkillers et cetera. In my opinion, I would not take the risk with your eyes. Continue to use lenses. Your sight is too precious.'

'That's good advice,' I said.

'So, we will do a couple more consultations to firm up all the procedures you would like to have. Are you sure you would you like to proceed?'

'Yes,' I said. 'Can we start with the tummy tuck?'

I was in a better mood all the way back to the Hacienda – level, confident, sort of excited. I had been low-key scared about the prospect of surgery but with no option to stay at the Hacienda, it was my only chance of sanctuary in this strange, unsettling new world of mine. I was looking forward to the tummy tuck in particular – for weeks I'd had to stare down at the forlorn, floppy sack of meat that had held Ivy inside me for months. And now she was gone, I wanted *it* gone too. Another step forward in my quest to forget her completely.

On the way back, now and again Paco would turn down the radio and say something provocative.

'I shot a coyote last night. Right between the eyes. Two shots.'

'Lovely.'

'Biggest animal I shot was a grey wolf. Must have been 180 pounds.'

'Thrillsville.'

'Hey, Rhiannon, did Tenoch show you the picture of the heads?'

Deep sigh. 'The what?'

'The heads on the spikes. He did it all himself. Get him to show you them.' He slapped the steering wheel in celebration. '*La bestia!*'

'Yeah, I'll be sure to check that out at the earliest opportunity, thanks.'

'Oh man, you gotta see it! He cut off all their heads. Man, did *that* send a message. You ever cut off anyone's head, Rhiannon?'

I pinched my belly fat, trying to imagine it gone. 'That's not my name.'

'Yeah, but did you ever cut off anyone's head?'

'Yes. Two people.'

That pulled him up. His eyes widened in the rear-view which he had angled so that every time he looked up he could see me. 'You did?'

'Yes. A female paedophile and my baby's father, if you must know. Though they were both dead at the time.'

'Whoa. So you Beauty *and* the Beast, huh? *La bella y la bestia!*' He laughed uncontrollably, even though again he'd failed to produce the desired response. As a last attempt, he clicked the glovebox, ostensibly to pull out a stick of gum, but gum is not what I saw. I saw gun – a semi-automatic pistol and a box of bullets. He took out the gum and shoved a stick in his mouth, looking at me in the rear-view mirror before shutting the compartment.

'Always on alert, *chica*,' he winked. 'Always ready for the fight.'

I batted my eyes. Paco still hadn't pushed the right button. But it was a ticking timebomb and one day I knew, without any doubt, that he would.

Friday, 15 February – Hacienda Santuario – the day before surgery starts

Facebook Rhiannon Lewis is our Qween
Facebook group
Public Group
Friday, 15 February 2019
Thread: Sightings of Rhiannon Lewis around the world

JoshuaBoshua wrote: So what do y'all reckon about this sighting of our qween at her sister's house in Vermont? Credible? Thoughts?

HellzBellz7888#: Well, considering there's been sightings of her in Spain, Thailand, and Brisbane in the last month, I would take it with a pinch of salt. I heard another rumour that some ex-pats saw her in the Caribbean a few weeks ago.

CastleOfDoom73297329: Probably a rumour, tbh.

Rachael544 wrote: Yeah, and she probably looks nothing

like her pictures in the papers now. She will have changed her whole identity.

CackyPants5554324: Everyone knows someone who *says* they've seen Rhiannon Lewis down the chip shop but it's most likely bullshit.

BringOutTheGimp277 wrote: Boooooooooooooooooo!!!!! It's Rhiannon Lewis. I'm coming to get youuuuuuuuu. I'm going to slaughter all of you one by one.

Sweetpea672: How do you know one of *us* isn't Rhiannon Lewis???

JoshuaBoshua wrote [to Sweetpea666]: You wish! LOL

BobbyAndEnema wrote: Bitch better not come to my town. Imma lynch her.

JesusIsAMalteaser wrote: I wouldn't use her babysitting service but I wouldn't exactly 'lynch' her.

JokesOnMe44 wrote: What's the matter with all you freaks in here?! This woman killed innocent people! She needs locking up and the key being thrown away into the deepest sea!

CastleOfDoom73297329: She killed TWO innocent people as far as I can gather from her confession. All the rest were paedophiles and s*x offenders. Good riddance to bad f*****g rubbish, I say.

FloralHydrate: I think she's in Mexico.

Sweetpea672: Who's the Freddie guy who got the confession??? Saw him being interviewed – he's so hot!

I closed Facebook and opened YouTube – a new video had popped up when I searched my name – an *Up at the Crack* interview with Dean Bishopston's widow Sarah about a week before. I didn't want to watch it but somehow I clicked play and Hate-Watched it instead, knowing exactly how it was going to make me feel. It's like, sometimes I want to make myself feel bad, feel *worse*.

Carolyn Perma-Tan was giving it the full furrowed brow and perpetually serious chin angle as she sat cross-footed on the lurid pink banquette, shuffling her papers and bulging out of her blue Bodycon.

Cue the steely look down the lens. 'Everyone will remember reading about the *horrors* of that fateful June evening when Dean Bishopston was out on his normal taxi-driving round in Birmingham city centre, as he did most nights to earn some extra cash for Christmas presents—'

Bigging up the sainthood.

'—when he took a fare from a lone woman who needed to get to a pub. And, as we now know, her full confession having been revealed, this woman was Rhiannon Lewis, the notorious serial murderer, currently on the run in connection with as many as fifteen murders.'

I prefer the term serial murder*ess* but whatever.

'Dean, who had a picture of his children inside his cab, was much loved by everyone who knew him—'

Cut to Sarah Bishopston, loving widow, washed-out skin, pinhole eyes, red hair crying out for a straightening tong, thousand-yard stare.

'Lewis says in her confession that she offered Dean sex, which he refused, and it was then that she struck, stabbing him sixteen times. She watched him die on the cold, hard ground. Dean's widow Sarah joins me now. Sarah – thank you for joining us today. Talk me through the moment when you were informed of Dean's death. It must have been horrendous for you.'

Someone had clearly drunk their Stupid Bitch Juice that morning.

'Yes, it was a horrendous morning,' said Sarah, all mono-tone. 'At the time it was a blur. It was so unexpected. We've always lived in Birmingham and we'd never even been burgled. We live in a safe neighbourhood. Dean sometimes had a few drunks in his cab but nothing too bad. I knew it was a risk him being out at night taking fares but he insisted he wanted the kids to have better Christmas presents that year.'

'But that moment you found out, take us to that—'

'I opened the front door and two people were standing there, a woman in a police uniform and a guy in a suit and they asked to come in. And I knew from their faces. And I held my breath. And when they said it, I collapsed.'

There was a series of increasingly stinging and interrogative questions all of which Sarah Bishopston answered without cunt-punching the woman into the wall, so fair fucks to her on that score.

'What was the moment like when you saw his body in the morgue?'

'How did the boys react when you told them Daddy was dead?'

'How have you coped with being all alone ever since?'

The woman couldn't stop crying. I didn't feel anything. Not until she spoke about their youngest, Anthony.

'He looks so much like his daddy, it scares me,' she said. 'And he asks for him every bedtime. And he cries for him in the night. I keep pictures of Dean all over the house – I'm afraid the kids will forget him. I'm afraid they don't have enough memories.'

'Tell me what kind of husband Dean was, Sarah.'

'He was the love of my life. He'd always forget our anniversary and Valentine's Day but he did a thousand romantic things. He'd write love notes and put them in my bag. Bring me flowers. We had so much in common – same sense of humour, same likes and dislikes. And we laughed so much – it was like we knew what the other one was thinking. We were in tune. Wherever he was, was home. I'll never get over this, never.'

Caro had said the same thing about Beatrice – being with *her* felt like she was home. The Hottest Turtle flashed into my mind, how in tune we had been during that short forty-five-minute meeting. What could have been.

And what was.

Within ten minutes, #RememberDeanBishopston was trending worldwide on Twitter, amid its usual cesspool of shouty voices giving too much of a shit about some celebrity dressing their cat in tinsel or having the wrong opinion about how to eat a Twix. I tried to swerve my brain away from Sarah and Dean Bishopston and their three boys. But I couldn't.

I'd taken their daddy. Like I'd taken Ivy's daddy.

I'd taken her place of safety, her home. Like I'd taken my own.

They hadn't deserved that. *I* deserved everything coming to me.

'What's up, *gatita*?' said Tenoch, leaning on the office doorframe. I closed the lid of the laptop.

'Nothing.'

'You been googling yourself again, eh?'

'Yeah.'

'You need to stop that.'

'Why should I?'

'Because it not make you happy. When you see all the nice things people are saying – "Oh we love Rhiannon, we love when she kill people, when she funny and cut off all the lil peckers—"'

'—one dick I cut off. One.'

'—yeah but even when they say good shit you're still all "They're not saying enough, I only have two hundred more fans than yesterday. Why did only five thousand people like that meme of me in the unicorn onesie?" And when they say bad stuff, you feel shitty too. I've been there, I know.'

'You do?'

'Oh yeah. In my day, I used to have people coming up to ask for pictures with me, to kiss me, give me hugs. But not everyone. Some would call me a murderer and spit in my face. Other times, I'd get shot.'

'Why? What did you do?'

'Cartel life,' he said, with a flap of his hand like he wasn't going to elaborate. And he didn't. 'It goes with the job – we are adored and hated. Like you. What did you see today?'

'An interview. A woman whose husband I killed.'

'She give it the waterworks, huh?'

'She's got three little kids.'

'Collateral damage.' I looked up at him. He sat on a stack of books by the door. 'It's always the little ones with you, isn't it? You gotta let that shit go. It brings out your devil. If you're serious about starting a new life, you've got to be different. This stuff – it not where happiness lies.'

Caro had said the same thing to me that day I'd destroyed those flowers in the botanical gardens.

You need to stop hating yourself so much. Leave it behind. Start anew. All this anger, it will only lead to no good...

That's why I checked the forums and threads and articles about me – I wanted the hate *and* the love. To make myself angry but to feel what it was like to be adored as well. The two sides of me, co-existing, fighting all the time like sisters. I was perpetuating a cycle, never breaking out of it.

Paco did his best to goad me, that day of all days. He knew I was jittery and he was my jitter bug, feeding off my low-level panic like a tick.

'Hey, Rhiannon,' he'd shout from the living room with the laptop balanced on his knees. 'You have a thing for fucking dead gringos. That true?'

'One dead Australian,' I called back, kneading my bread dough.

'Hey, Rhiannon, is it true you have a lampshade made of human skin?'

'Fake news.'

'Hey, Rhiannon, is it true you don't like the taste of tattooed flesh?'

'Nah, bit stringy.'

'Hey, Rhiannon, where did you hide all their dicks, eh?'

'I ONLY CUT OFF ONE DICK, ALL RIGHT? AND I DIDN'T EAT IT OR MOUNT IT OR USE IT TO PLAY PIN THE TAIL ON THE FUCKING DONKEY!'

'Paco, *basta*!' Tenoch, give him his due, knew exactly when Paco had brought me to boiling point and had the ability to call him off with one word, almost like a whistle to a well-trained Rottweiler.

Paco wasn't alone that day – there were three other uninvited guests at the Hacienda – Ming, Arturo and Stuzzy. I recognised Arturo as my driver from the airport – sent by Tenoch to ensure nobody else brought me to his secret lair. He was the least irksome of the four – bald, loud and the only one who habitually read a newspaper. He was also a boxer – I could tell by the knuckles and the ears.

Ming was shorter than Arturo with a shock of sticky-up black hair, like a hedgehog, and body odour that smelled like something between gravy and the grave. Stuzzy had shiny, floppy hair, a thick moustache and burn marks over the back of his neck. On his face sat a permanent scowl and I rarely heard him speak.

They were hanging around snorting coke and playing *Call of Duty* and *Grand Theft Auto* even when I went outside to transfer some new seedlings. There was no place inside where I could escape from their drinking games and loud conversations, deafening music, impromptu stripteases for my benefit or lines of cocaine on the coffee table.

'Why are they even here?' I snipped at Tenoch when he came out to the pool terrace where I was pinching out some new seedlings.

'They are pulling an all-nighter for me later. They're just kicking back before they go. Boys will be boys.'

'No, twats will be twats,' I sighed, throwing down my trowel and wiping my sweaty head on the edge of my gardening glove. 'What all-nighter?' He threw me his usual zipped-mouth and I went back to digging my borders. 'Well, I'm fed up. They've eaten all my Pop Tarts—'

'Paco doesn't like synthetic food.'

'No, the other Chipmunks – Alvin, Simon and Theodore.' He chuckled. 'I'll order more Pop Tarts.'

'—and the empanadas I made you. And Paco always drinks the milk out of my cereal bowl, I mean, what the hell is *that* about?'

'I said they could have the empanadas. I'll talk to Paco about the milk.'

'I don't want them here. I don't want their feet on the furniture, their sticky beer marks on the coffee table, their stinky cigarette smoke, their thumping music, their mud-spattered hatchbacks on our driveway—'

'It not your house, Rhiannon.'

'I'm well aware of that,' I spat. 'Sorry.'

'You need to cool off,' he said, his car keys in his fist. 'You've worked hard today. The flowers look wonderful. Now you should rest up, big day tomorrow, huh?'

'Thanks.' I rubbed the centre of my chest. 'I'm all acidy.'

'Come on. I'll take you to town. We'll get an ice cream.'

*

It was such a Dad thing to do – take me away from the situation and buy me an ice cream – and although it was slightly patronising, I went, if only to get out of the house for a while. He made me wear sunglasses and one of Marisol's straw hats so I could hide my face and dropped me off on the beachfront, unfolding a wad of notes and shoving it into my hand as I closed the door.

'Go shop, buy things... I got some business to take care of. I'll pick you up in an hour at the bakery.'

I looked at him. 'What's this, pocket money?'

'You've worked hard for me this week. Buy yourself some new clothes.'

'I don't want new clothes.'

'Stay out of trouble. I'll see you in an hour.'

Dad would say the same thing – *Here you go, treat yourself to some sweets, I've got to take care of some business.* Or, *Wait here in the car, I won't be long, read your comic. I'm just gonna go in here and beat this guy to a pulp with my mates, but don't tell your mother.* Nothing had changed. Nothing had fucking changed since I was in single digits.

So I wandered about the town, drifting in and out of storefronts. I bought a couple of T-shirts and a piña colada from one of the kiosks and milled aimlessly along the shoreline collecting shells. I took off my trainers and allowed the ocean water to caress my feet, sitting beneath a beach *palapa* to finish my drink and watching the world carrying on without me. I missed Caro. I missed chatting to someone. Laughing. I hadn't laughed for weeks.

After a while a van pulled up on the beachfront – a shabby rental with dirty plates. A half-naked guy jumped out the driver's seat. He wore black jeans and his chest was bare, his

T-shirt dangling from his waistband – his chest was the most magnificent specimen I'd ever clapped eyes on. And I knew immediately it was him – The Hottest Turtle. I didn't even need to look up and see his face.

I threw my plastic glass in a nearby trash can and followed him at a distance as he opened the back of the van and climbed in, coming out with two empty boxes and a huge roll of bubble wrap which he set down on the pavement. I remembered his aunt Salomé saying she was moving premises and that he was coming to help her.

I still had his note in my back pocket, the one he'd left for me.

The closer I got, the more detail I could pick out from the safety of my straw hat – a sheen of sweat on his back. White paint flecks on his jeans, in his jet-black hair. The tattoos on his side, his underarms, the base of his neck.

But I couldn't go any closer than that. I couldn't take another step towards him. This gorgeous man, who I would normally stand on heads to get a piece of, was like The One Ring – luring me in but repelling me too. Because I knew where this would go – I'd start trusting him and calming down and being all happy and when I least expected it, he'd break me. And Rhiannon would come back, full throttle, and he'd end up like Craig or, worse, AJ. I didn't want to go there again. Like Caro said, you never break your own heart. I had to keep it safe. I had to be on my own.

He put the roll of wrap inside the smallest box, putting that inside the big box and carrying them up the street. The thought owls still circled as I waited, watching that van: if that podcast was true and forming 'happy human bonds' was the only way someone like me could live a normal life, how was that going to happen if I didn't make human connections? I wanted to go towards him. I wanted him to hug me and tell me he was happy to see me. I wanted to tell him I'd been thinking about him too, especially at night.

But was I just horny? Like on the cruise when I'd fucked that steward? Had that made everything better? No. Because it wasn't the sex I'd wanted – it was the *afterwards*. The cuddle and the kissing and comfort of knowing that person would still be there the next morning and the next, on into infinity.

But people aren't like that. They drift in and out. I like permanence and reliability and you don't get that with humans unless they're dead. That's why AJ turned me on more when he was cold than he ever had warm. Coming home to him after that hen weekend to find him still blue in my bed was the most comforted I'd ever been by another person.

But as I stood there, watching The Hottest Turtle walk away with those boxes, another voice invaded the stage. A voice that overrode Rhiannon.

Give him a chance. You do deserve some happiness.

Maybe it was the after-effects of the piña colada and I was actually channelling Caro from afar, but the voice grew louder.

Don't rely on him, but don't suppress these feelings either. They're trying to tell you something.

It wasn't Caro. And it wasn't The Man in the Moon or Dad or Ivy in utero either. It was a girl's voice. *My* voice. Maybe the Me I was in that parallel universe I'm always thinking about – the Me I *should* have been.

'I don't want him to get hurt,' I muttered. 'If he's with me, that's what will happen.'

You're a different person now. You won't make those mistakes again.

'It's why I left Ivy. And why I'm glad I couldn't go to Marnie either.'

You'd never have hurt them. You can control yourself.

'If he hurts me like Craig did. . .'

Not all men... Go to him. If it's meant to be, it will be. If not, you'll be OK. You've got this far alone. You are strong.

So I did it – I walked towards the van, face carefully hidden beneath the hat, and waited for him to come back.

And he *did* come back – twenty minutes later – still half-naked, still sweaty but without the boxes and accompanied by a young blonde. She had flecks of white paint on her dungarees and an orange boob tube on underneath a loose-fitting fishnet vest – Fun Times at Guantánamo.

They were holding hands.

I edged around the van to the back, walking in the other direction towards the row of shops. When I got to the ice cream kiosk, I turned back to see her get in the passenger's side and close the door. The van did a U-turn in the road and passed me by without a second glance. They were laughing.

'Yeah. That'd be right,' I said, turning and walking straight into a wall called Tenoch.

'Hey, you ready for your ice cream?' He reached into his trouser pocket for a wad of cash. At least one of the bills had spots of red on it.

'Yeah,' I said, screwing up Rafael's note and tossing it into the nearest trash can. It no longer sparked joy. 'Rum 'n' raisin, please. A fucking big one.'

Monday, 18 February – Hacienda Santuario

1. *Men*
2. *Men called Rafael*
3. *Rafael's mum for giving birth to the dickhead to begin with*
4. *Rafael's grandmother for being horny ever*
5. *Women. For not being as fanciable for men*

The surgeries themselves, as Dr Gonzales had said, were all incremental, over the next few months and the best I can say about them was that at least the physical pain took my mind off the pain in my own head.

LIPOSUCTION/TUMMY TUCK
This was first and I was in bed for two full weeks after – swollen, grogged-up on pain meds and barely able to do anything but sleep and slurp soup. Ibuprofen and Tylenol were constant bed mates. I couldn't walk properly so I'd have to shuffle like an 80-year-old with chronic spine curvature who'd crapped herself.

Ironically, it was gridlock below. I became very constipated and when it *did* finally make an appearance, it was like excreting a concrete traffic cone.

Paco revelled in all my discomfort, of course. The car journeys were almost as excruciating as the agony of each op.

'Haha, *chica*, you wanna stop and get more painkillers, huh? You want a lil water to make those painkillers work faster? Is it burning, the pain? You wanna see your face in the mirror, all cut up?'

'Either shut the fuck up or grow the fuck up, will you?'

'Hoho, there she is! There's my serial killer! Doesn't take much to bring her out, does it?'

Whenever I complained to Tenoch about Paco, all he would say was 'You have to ignore him. This is what he does – he will delight in upsetting you. It gives him a thrill. He does with Celestina too.'

'And that makes it all right, does it?'

'No, but you are going to come across people like Paco in your life and you cannot rise to their bait. If you do, you will be in prison before you know it. You need to work on your temper.'

'Do I? I hadn't thought of that! Wow, eureka moment or what – I need to WORK on my temper! Easy peasy, lemon fucking squeezy!'

But of course he was right. I was my own worst enemy. And little by little I tried to divert my mind away from the vitriol that would bubble and brew inside it whenever Paco was around. And the more I tried to suppress it, the more depressed I became. I had noticed it properly the day Paco drove me back from my liposuction. I was lying down on the back seat, padded up in gauze and compression bandages, doped up on Percocet, tuning him out, focusing on the engine hum. It was working. He wasn't getting to me at all.

'Hey, Rhiannon, did you see all the fat they took out of your stomach? There was a lot, huh? They suck a lot of fat out of you? Did they suck it out of your ass? That's where you got a lot of fat, yeah?'

'Just drive, you absolute fist-magnet.' I chained a few more painkillers and lost myself in sleep.

I got lazy during that whole time. I think I only changed my leggings once in all the weeks I was laid up with my body wrapped in bandages – Aretha Franklin had her outfit changed four times when she was in her coffin.

I spent more and more time in my room, in bed, with the door locked during my recovery. I couldn't even find the will to pull out the weeds in the garden – I didn't want to do anything but sleep.

EAR PINNING

My ears were pinned back next, and that was a stinging little bitch of a procedure as well, though not nearly as problematic as the nip and tuck, even though initially I did want to vomit out all my internal organs with the pain. Adding insult to injury, I had to wear a compression bandage wrapped around my face for twenty-four hours which made me look like that botched art restoration, *Monkey Christ*. The results were pretty instant though when the bandages came off – I stared at myself in the doctor's hand mirror at a follow-up consultation, turning my head from right to left and back again.

'Wow,' I said. 'It's working. I'm *changing*. Externally, at least.'

MOLE AND SCAR REMOVAL/HAIRLINE LOWERING

For these, I was in and out the same day – it was all lasers and cool cream application for the moles and scars. For the hairline, I was under the impression that they somehow magically transplanted new long hair to the front of my head and all of a sudden I'd have bangs like Camila Cabello but no, of course not. They first had to shave the back of my head, remove each tiny follicle individually and then transplant them, one at a time, to the front of my head which, between doses of pain medication, felt like I was being injected with poisonous ants. I'd have to wait weeks for the hair to grow out as well so no quick thrills there. In the meantime, I'd look like a Bedlam test case for a frontal lobotomy.

But I guess if the cap fits...

David, Saúl and Mátilda brought me gifts when I was recovering – drawings they'd done, friendship bracelets and bags of avocados, pomegranates and pecans they'd picked from one of the fields over the back. Sometimes they'd sit on the end of my bed – David telling me stories in Spanish to help me learn the language. Mátilda would play with my hair and paint my nails and Saúl would run small cars up and down my blanketed legs. They were under strict instructions from Celestina to leave if I got too tired.

Tenoch left all my meals on a tray outside my room. When he did come in to see me, he kept it brief.

'How are you today?'

'Meh.'

'Your flowers need you. They need watering.'

'Water them then.'

'I think they would rather it was you. They like it when you talk to them and dance for them with your little radio on.'

Cut to me, lying there, spent from a whole day's doing nothing, trying to summon a fuck to give. In the end, I couldn't. 'Flowers don't care who waters them. They'll take it from anyone. They're sluts. Like Lana.'

'Who?'

'Just water them, will you please?'

'Anything else?'

'Have you got any drugs? Like Prozac or anything? Xanax?'

'No.'

'You're ex-*cartel* and you can't even cadge me a bit of Prozac?'

'That's not what you need. You need to get up and get busy. Breathe in some fresh air. Tend your garden. It will make you feel better.'

'Whatever,' I mumbled.

'Shall we practise your backstory again?'

'No, not yet. Later. I can't do anything right now.'

'OK. Anything else I can do for you?'

'Don't let Paco up here to use the bathroom. He took a shit yesterday and it still stinks.'

'That wasn't him, it was Arturo. He is lactose intolerant. Paco force-fed him some heavy cream for a joke.'

'Ugh. Keep him away from me. Keep all of them away.'

'As you wish, *gatita*.'

Wednesday, 6 March –
Hacienda Santuario

1. *Plastic surgeons who say procedures will 'sting a little' or suggest 'some slight discomfort' will occur. The kind of 'sting' and 'slight discomfort' he's going to feel when I boil his head in a vat of hot oil*
2. *Nosy medical receptionists*
3. *Paco and his three amigos for their constant eating of my Pop Tarts, laughing at unfunny TV shows and shitting in the upstairs toilet. The smell sticks to the walls.*
4. *That blood pressure bitch nurse who squeezes my upper arm. Never an accurate reading, always has to try again. Sadist.*
5. *People who do that cling film challenge thing to their dogs*

As time went on, with the help of painkillers, I ventured downstairs more, usually when Paco and the Chipmunks had left. I'd go out to see my flowers, water and deadhead them and stroke the leaves. Or I'd sit beside the pool listening to my radio, chucking monkey nuts at the rock squirrels who'd snuck in beneath the fencing. It brought me back to myself, a little bit more, each passing day. The smells of chlorine, lavender, the pozole cooking on the stove or Tenoch's Deep Heat on his knees became the scents of my life.

Still just temporary scents though. I was still on the conveyor belt ride to Fuck Knows Whereville.

Paco was Tenoch's eyes and ears on the cartel and, according to him, there were no more immediate threats to the Hacienda. So life became quite samey for a while. It gave me endless time to think. To wonder.

Though Paco was still deathly irritating – goading me and laughing at me and poking me playfully in eye-wateringly painful places whenever Tenoch was out of the room – sometimes, I could glean useful information from him, like what part Tenoch had played in the cartel before life at the Hacienda.

'They called him El Mago. The magician. He could make things disappear.' He sat at the kitchen island when I was mixing a carrot cake one morning, dipping into the bowl of crushed walnuts for the decoration.

'Like what?'

'What do *you* think, *chica*?'

'So what was your business in the cartel?'

'I was a lieutenant.'

'What does that mean?'

'It means I was a bad guy. We were bad people. Psychopaths. Actually, we make psychopaths look like pussycats.'

He took the opportunity to stare at my pussy when he was saying that – he took most opportunities to stare at it, either as a threat or a promise. The only thing left for him to do was to grab it but maybe he wasn't *that* much of a psychopath.

'So what kind of things did you do?' I said, taking a handful of crushed nuts myself and knocking them back.

'Beatings, waterboarding, electric shocks to the genitals or tongue. Sometimes we would order a slaughter – several people. I've seen members of the cartel chainsaw a head clean off. You know what sound a head makes as you're slicing it off? It squeal – like a pig.'

'Yummy,' I yawned.

'We made bombs too. No mercy. I saw one guy – seriously crazy motherfucker – rip a beating heart right out of a cop's chest.'

Kind of put things in perspective for me, that conversation. The worst I ever did was stab someone and chop them up. Paco's gleeful stories about his cartel made me realise there were worse people than me in the world. People even *I* couldn't best. And a sort of depression set in.

Between getting up and going back to bed, all I would do were three different things on a rota:

Eat food, garden, watch TV.

The next day: eat food, garden, watch TV.

Some days there would be slight variations to it: maybe eat food, garden, take slow walk on treadmill, eat more food, watch YouTube video – *My Life as a Truck Stop Stripper*, google *What is this dry patch on my ankle?*

Other days: treadmill, eat, watch TV, learn Spanish, watch YouTube videos of tiny animals trying to climb stairs, do Buzzfeed quiz – *Who'd Win in a Fist Fight – You or Mike Pence?*

And though I was back using the internet, I asked Tenoch to put a block on 'Rhiannon Lewis' so I wouldn't be tempted to check what was happening in the outside world. I didn't want to know. He had been right – the praise always inflated my ego and the negative stuff made me want to stick knives in things. The best thing for me was to stop looking altogether.

The children still visited whenever Celestina was there and they were a massive help in the garden when I couldn't bend down for stitches.

'We will help you, *señorita*,' said David, taking charge. 'Saúl – you need to dig up the mint today. Don't eat all the cilantro, Mátilda.'

'I'm not eating all of it! Saúl ate some too.'

'No, I didn't, I only ate some mint. You got a big fat belly.'

'No, *you* got a big fat belly!'

Some mornings, when the gardening got too political, they would play in the pool instead, with Tenoch's permission. I ordered some pool noodles and sat wrapped up in my compression bandages and dressing gown on a sun-lounger, watching them splash. It was hard not to feel left out.

'They are so happy,' said a voice behind me. Celestina had emerged, apron in her hand, finished for the morning. 'Thank you for letting them use the pool.'

'It was Tenoch, not me,' I said.

'No, you asked him if they could. I never like to outstay our welcome.' She nodded towards the borders. 'Your flowers are beautiful.'

'Yeah, they're really coming on.' I followed her gaze to the purple and orange explosions along the far edge of the lawn. 'They made you some things.' I pointed to the assortment of pressed flower pictures and miniature bouquets in tin foil vases the kids had made her on the opposite sun-lounger.

She smiled, gazing happily at her kids as they played happily in the pool. David was the first to spot her as the other two chased each other on their pool noodles.

'We going home, Mama?'

'When you are ready,' she said, settling the pictures and bouquets on her lap and sitting on the sun-lounger. 'You play for now.'

David beamed up at her and showed off his latest trick – a handstand with pointed feet. She applauded when he bobbed back up.

'Where is their dad?' I asked.

'Dead,' she replied. 'He used to work for Tenoch as a taxi driver – his car was ambushed one night outside the town. He was taking some American tourists to a club. They bombed his car.'

'When was this?'

'Just over a year ago. Emilio knew what he was getting into, but we needed the money. Tenoch has been very good to us, though. He always sees us right. He liked Emilio. And because of Mátilda—'

She stopped short. Paco was sauntering across the terrace with his jacket over his shoulder and a filthy cigar dangling from his lip. He smiled broadly at us and walked into the house. Celestina couldn't look at him.

'She's his,' she told me, quieter than she had been speaking so I could barely hear her.

'Huh?'

'Mátilda. I will never tell her that. Tenoch knows – I told

him, thinking he would help me out – he hates rapists like you do – but he needs Paco to do his dirty business for him so he tries to keep us both happy.'

'You and Paco—'

She shook her head. 'Not by choice. He makes me feel sick.'

I leaned in and lowered my voice. 'You work in the same house as the guy who *raped* you? And you've done that for... years?'

'Yes. We don't all have family inheritances and kindly drug runners to bail us out, *señorita*. That's why I come by so early, so I can avoid *el hombre cerdo*. The Pig Man.' She oinked with gusto and Saúl heard her from the pool and chuckled.

I glanced at the happy little girl on her pool noodle and couldn't quite believe something so beautiful could have come from someone so vile. 'Does he know?'

'No. And he won't ever know. He doesn't deserve something so precious in his life. He should only have pain and mayhem. And he's got it coming, *señorita*. You don't know how many times I have looked at those crossed machetes above the fireplace and thought of his neck.' She looked me straight on. 'I will dance on that man's grave.'

'I'll play a song for you,' I said. Her tired face brightened, briefly.

'Kids, come on,' she said, suddenly on her feet, '*vamos*, we must go.'

'Awww,' they all whined, right on cue.

'But if he knew about her,' I started to say, 'he might—'

But Paco appeared at the patio doors – not so close that he could hear us talking, but close enough to make Celestina drop her voice.

'He has several bastard children, all over this town. He

292

does not care for any of them. You cannot appeal to Paco's soft side, *señorita*, trust me – he does not have one.'

I was upstairs changing later that evening when I heard gunshots – a rapid *tuttutututututututututututututut*. When I followed the noise downstairs, I found Paco standing in the centre of the lawn and all around him clouds of dust and a tangled mess of petals, leaves and stems. He'd shot my flower beds to smithereens, barely a single stem left standing. I followed his gaze towards the perimeter fence where he'd placed a line of tin cans, undisturbed.

'Oops,' he said. 'I missed.'

I went back inside before I could say or do anything.

He called out, 'You angry with me, *chica*? Look what I did to your flowers!'

I reached the patio doors, taking deep breaths, before looking back at him. 'Not at all. That's the great thing about flowers, Paco. They grow back. Every single time.' And I smiled at him. Genuinely, like a Sweetpea would.

It was only when I got into the house I started muttering about what a massive piece of shit from an undouched arsehole he truly was.

I kept thinking about Celestina and the strength she had to muster every fucking day she turned up at that house, having to get her work done before his BMW rolled up. How every single time she looked at her little girl's face, she saw his smile staring back at her.

That was a mother. The shit she put up with. Ugh. I could never. I *would* never. But maybe I *should* in the world of New Leaf Me.

*

The children didn't seem that concerned about the Mexico Plant Massacre when the scene greeted them in the garden the next day.

'We will help you mend them, *señorita*,' said David.

'Yeah, we help you!' echoed Mátilda, toy trowel raised in the air.

'Where are the new seeds?' asked Saúl. 'We can plant even more.'

And they did. We ordered more plants, raked over the chaotic massacre of torn stems and shot leaves, and sifted out shell casings, building a compost heap at the bottom of the garden so they could nourish the new ones. We planted more seeds in the seed trays and added rooting powder to the younger plants we could save to give them a fighting chance. Out of chaos, we grew, we nourished and we took care of. We did it without anger, revenge and without anybody getting killed. It was so simple.

It was a whole new look for me. I was happier when the kids were around. I'm always happier around kids or animals than I am around adult humans. There's always a side to adults. Always a price to pay.

Tenoch seemed happier too, especially when his arm was fully operational again. He laughed more, joked more. Sometimes we'd sit out on the terrace together, watching the sunset or picking herbs or peppers for that night's dinner which he would be making from scratch – some nights pozole or menudo; other nights alambre with corn tortillas. We'd chat like we were related – easily and honestly.

'Did you ever kill anyone you didn't want to?' he asked me.

'No,' I said. And I meant it. 'At the time, I wanted to.'

'I've only ever wanted to kill in revenge. It was my job, that's all. If my boss said, "Kill your friend, kill your wife," I would do it.'

'You killed your *wife*?'

'No, luckily I never had to. But I would have if they had asked me.'

'So what were you, like, a hitman or something?'

'Yeah. A hitman.'

'How many people did you kill?'

'About a hundred.'

'Whoa.'

We continued the conversation over dinner. We tried to make the effort some nights to turn the TV off and lay place settings with separate cutlery for befores and afters, salt and pepper and glasses of local wine.

'That is where you and I aren't the same,' he said, slurping up his soup. 'You always wanted to kill, I *had* to or else I would be killed myself.'

'Dog eat dog.'

'Our cartel built schools, medical practices, gave people jobs, homes. We were loved. But also, despised.'

'Who by?'

'*Los federales* for one. And the army. And people whose loved ones we killed. I never felt good about the extortion side of the business. We had to come down hard on working people – *decent* people. I have done things you would not like me for. But if the order was given, it was their kids or mine.'

'You killed *kids*? How many?'

I lost him in a trance for several moments before he broke free of it and returned to his soup. '*Too* many. Eat your greens.'

It was always there, at the Hacienda – a sense that I couldn't quite relax. I had a nice house, a garden, all the sunshine I could want, daily companions in Celestina and her children and a body beginning to heal itself and which I was looking after with regular helpings of green vegetables and fresh fruit smoothies.

But there was a growing sense that bad times were never far away. That something terrifying could happen at any moment.

It may also have been my hormones.

And herein layeth the problem – because where there be hormones, there be'eth Rhiannon. Always there, under the surface, watching, waiting, for anyone to piss her off. It didn't matter how much surgery I had on the outside, on the inside, I was much the same. And men like Paco brought out the worst in me.

Take the night when I was minding my own business watching TV in the living room. Tenoch was on a call in his office and I'd been sitting there icing my homemade cookies on a lap tray watching an episode of *Ramsay's Hotel Hell* – the one with the ghost, Gordon's apple pie recipe and bedsheets covered in spunk – when they came in, Paco and the Chipmunks. He took the remote off my arm rest and chucked it to Arturo who stole two cookies and slumped on the sofa, switching over to *The Santa Clause* on Sky Christmas.

To be honest, any break from overpaid basketballers high-fiving piss-easy goals or snarky barbs from grey-haired Miami divorcees was welcome. Problem was, they didn't shut up the entire film.

'His ex-wife a tasty piece of ass. Why they divorce?' said Ming, stealing three of my cookies and making a triple-decker sandwich from them before posting it in his mouth whole.

'Here we fucking go,' I muttered.

'Why his kid not want to spend Christmas with his mom?' asked Stuzzy, scratching his junk, already on his fifth cookie. 'He not like Judge Reinhold?'

'Oh, he was the guy in *Beverley Hills Chihuahua*, yeah? He funny,' said Ming, who always sat on the floor for some reason.

Paco took Tenoch's armchair, aka The Throne. 'So he not the real Santa Claus, he a toy salesman, right?'

'Where did that fuckin' ladder appear from?' said Paco.

'There no way you could get a full-grown man down that chimney. And what about the houses that *don't* have chimneys? How does he get around all the houses of the world in one night?'

Stuzzy googled the number of houses in the world on his phone. 'It not possible. It not possible.'

By this point steam was emitting from my ears. 'OK it's not possible, you win. This film is a farce.'

'Why he grow a beard? And get fat?' said Ming.

'BECAUSE HE'S FUCKING SANTA CLAUS, ALL RIGHT?' I erupted, and the lap tray and two remaining cookies flew across the room and every lizard and rat in a twenty-mile radius scarpered. 'HE KILLED THE LAST SANTA *CLAUS* AND READ THE CARD ABOUT THE SANTA *CLAUSE* AND NOW HE'S GOT TO BE THE SANTA *CLAUS* BECAUSE THAT'S THE SANTA *CLAUSE*. WHAT'S SO BLOODY FUCKING DIFFICULT TO UNDERSTAND!?'

They all sat there, open-mouthed, except for Paco – he was laughing. A lot. After that they all stayed silent, for a long time, until near the end of the movie when Ming ill-advisedly piped up with:

'So he *was* the real Santa Claus all along? I not understand this movie.'

I walked out, and I kept walking, with Paco's shrill laughter ringing in my ears the whole time. I strode across the terrace, through the hole in the fence and down into the ditch and all the way through the field to the place where I'd buried the men. I lay down, breathing deeply for several minutes, until I had returned – back to life, back to reality, back to myself.

And I felt so stupid. That wasn't a moment to let Rhiannon fly. Why had I done it? Knee-jerk response. She was always there – caged. Primed. But no more. I couldn't let Paco win. I had to be better. Take the higher ground, like Celestina had. Even if I knew, damn well, that surgery might be able to change my appearance, but it couldn't touch my soul.

Friday, 15 March –
Hacienda Santuario

1. *Paco*
2. *Paco's mother, father, and all the ancestry that spawned him*
3. *Paco's chipmunks, Ming, Arturo and Stuzzy, who seemingly have only three 'jobs' they do for Tenoch – eat my Pop Tarts, shit and snore*
4. *Kings of Leon for not enunciating any of their lyrics*
5. *Bono*

The nose job was my last surgery and the one I'd been dreading the most – not because of the inevitable pain, but because it marked the final step. After my recovery, I would have to leave the Hacienda. That was always the plan. And every day it became harder to contain my capricious inner self.

I got pissed the night before and my mouth did not taste good the next morning. I was coming to the conclusion that I couldn't handle my drink and I'd already arrived at the conclusion I would never drink mezcal again. My vomit could outpace a bullet train.

Celestina gave me the doggiest of looks as we'd passed each other on the stairs – her with her mop and bucket of suds.

'I think I got most of it in the bowl,' I mewed. 'I can clean it later?' but she still batted her eyes and headed for the bathroom on a slosh of water.

I attempted a small bowl of cereal to settle my growling stomach. Paco was already at the Hacienda 'doing a job for Tenoch'. He didn't even say hello, just sauntered into the room, flexing his muscles in his too-tight vest and sliding his iPhone across the kitchen island. A news article. The headline:

SWEETPEA SISTER ATTACKED ON
DOORSTEP BY CRAZED FAN

'The fuck?' I said as he attempted to take back the phone.

'Oh, you wanna read it, do you?' he said, snatching up the phone and holding it away. 'You wanna read about your sister? What's it worth, huh? What's it worth, Rhiannon? What you gonna do?'

His breath stank of those tarry cigars and as I reached up high for the phone he pressed his hard chest against me like we were playing basketball.

I pulled back, seeing it was clearly turning him on. I walked away.

'That laptop's encrypted, remember?' he said, sliding the phone back onto the countertop. 'Go on. Look at it.' He held up his hands in surrender.

BBC News – SWEETPEA KILLER'S SISTER ATTACKED ON DOORSTEP BY CRAZED FAN

Thursday, 7 March 2019
STAFF REPORTER

THE SISTER of serial murderer Rhiannon Lewis, who is wanted in connection with the murders of thirteen people, has been attacked at her home in Vermont.

Seren Gibson, 34, had been receiving as many as twenty-five phone calls a day from a woman claiming to be her sister Rhiannon, and has had her home broken into twice in the last month.

Lieutenant Linda Cordell of Vermont State Police says stalking has high penalties in the state. 'This woman thinks she has a responsibility to punish Mrs Gibson for informing on her sister. She says she is speaking to Rhiannon Lewis who is telling her what to do – to call Mrs Gibson, go to her house, to make her paranoid and to eventually, cause her physical harm.

'We do not believe Lewis is in contact with the assailant but we are taking this case seriously. She is now the subject of a restraining order and cannot go anywhere near Mrs Gibson, her husband or her children.'

When asked about the rumour of the woman turning up at her daughter Mabli's school and trying to collect her, the Lieutenant was similarly non-committal.

'We are working closely with Mrs Gibson and her family to ensure their safety and that the maximum punishment is exercised should the subject break the terms of the order.'

Mrs Gibson was unavailable for comment last night.

'You got some serious fans, *chica*,' he said, sitting down on my still-warm breakfast stool and picking up my spoon. He finished the bowl and tipped the dregs into his mouth. 'Did you tell them to go after your sister?'

'No.'

'Do you *want* them to do that?'

'What's it to you?'

He took my bowl to the sink. 'Nothin'. I heard a rumour your sister called the cops on you. If it were me, I'd want her fuckin' barbecued.'

'I'm not you.'

'So you forgive the bitch for what she did?'

'I didn't say that.'

'But you don't want her dead?' He sat back down on my stool.

'There are other people more deserving of that outcome than her.'

He snickered. 'Is that a threat?'

'Not yet.'

Paco didn't respond to that, just left the room, nodding. He wasn't done though. He had another trick parked up his sleeve to needle me with and it came later that day as he drove me home from my four-hour nose job. There weren't enough painkillers in the world.

'What happened to your baby, Rhiannon?'

My head throbbed all over and my voice was croaky. 'None of your business.'

'She called Ivy, yes?'

'Say what you're gonna say.'

'I was just asking.'

'Why?'

'Because. We are friends, yes?'

'No.'

'Well, what are we?'

'We are nothing,' I spat, resisting the urge to sniff up my nose plugs. 'You are a vaginal polyp. The pus in a festering boil. A cancerous tumour. And the sooner you're cut out, the better.' It would have sounded a lot more threatening if my voice hadn't been so whispery,

'Your baby's going to die without you, without her mother's milk,' he sang after me in his strange, immature way.

He was like a live-in troll. He'd say anything for a reaction. And as soon as I realised that, it became easier to ignore him. Don't feed the trolls. Pretend they don't exist. They hate that.

I didn't look in the mirror until I got up to my bedroom – I looked as though I'd been on a skid pan with Stuntman Mike. The surgeon had broken my nose for the procedure so I had chronic head pain, puffy eyes and purple bruising around the centre of my face for two weeks. I peeked behind the compression tape to see if the swelling had gone down – I kept doing this so that was probably why it took longer to heal. My nostrils had to be packed out with gauze plugs and I lost my voice completely for a few days because of the breathing tube they'd shoved down me during the op. I was so tired, all the time, and they recommended that I sleep upright which didn't help matters.

The boys didn't recognise me when they first saw me that following morning. Saúl wouldn't even come into my bedroom.

'It's OK, I hurt my nose so I had to have it mended,' I told him. 'I won't look like this forever.'

'Does it hurt?' asked David, gingerly sitting down on the edge of my bed.

'Yeah. Like a son-of-a-fuh— ...yeah, it's pretty painful. *Mucho dolor.*'

'When will we see your face again?' asked David.

'I have to go back to the doctor's office in a few days and have this stuff taken out of my nose. And the nose cast can come off in two weeks. But I'll still be a bruised for a while. I miss being able to sniff.'

Mátilda climbed up onto the bed and with the lightest touch kissed the tip of my nose. '*Bésalo mejor,*' she said. Kiss it better.

Paco took a different approach.

'Hey, Rhiannon, nice face. Imma have to stop drinking soon cos I sure as shit don't wanna see two of *that*!'

'Hey, Rhiannon, you fall out the ugly tree again this morning?'

'Hey, Rhiannon, I've eaten taco meat that looked better than you.'

But I had to Bruce Lee this shit and not have an emotional reaction to every little thing. I had to breathe and allow shit to pass me by because my anger was his fuel and I had to starve that fire.

I tried to take my mother's approach – *Go through the motions. Pretend she's not there. Ignore, ignore, ignore. Maybe she will grow out of it soon.*

But he didn't.

It got to the point where I thought my face would look like that forever – a mangled, swollen, purple mess of tiny eyes, enormous nose and incurable agony. But as long as I stayed away from Paco, I knew I could ride the storm. Aside from having to endure the aftercare trips to the doctor's office to remove the packing and have my stitches taken out, I could live my life, grow my flowers, chow ibuprofen and give my body all the right foods it needed to heal.

In short: I started looking after myself. I started looking after my mind too. Tenoch got me into meditation – ten minutes every morning.

'I've done this every day for forty years,' he told me as we sat cross-legged and facing each other on the lawn one morning, early, as the sun was rising. 'To have a healthy body, you must also have a healthy, calm mind that will help you make the right decisions.'

He bored the arse off me going on about the importance of the breaths and mindfulness but some things still got through.

'The more you do it, over weeks, months, years, the more space you will create in your mind.'

'What do you mean, space?'

'Space between thought and action.'

'Yeah,' I said. 'I do need that. I've been trying to do that when Paco pisses me off.'

'Is it working?'

'Sometimes. It's getting better. But I don't think it's going to work for me, Tenoch.'

'Try it.'

'You think a few minutes of meditation and a bit of

camomile tea is going to make me stop wanting to punch cunts in the face?'

'Worth a try, isn't it? If you want to be better?' I closed my eyes. 'Good. Focus on the breaths. You have too much random shit in your head, it will create a mess.'

'Do you actually like that rapey bastard you hang around with?' I breathed deeply, held it, and let it out, too quickly.

'I've known him a long time,' he replied, on the breath.

'Yeah, but do you *like* him?'

'Like I said, I have known him a long time. Paco knows me.'

He was as trapped around Paco as Celestina. He couldn't do without him. That was why he kept him around. Kept him sweet.

'Don't rush it, concentrate on holding and releasing those breaths,' he exhaled. 'A little of this every day will help you to carve out some space between your bad thoughts and acting on them.'

'Meditation is going to stop me wanting to kill people?'

'No,' he said flatly, opening his eyes. 'That will remain with you forever. I can't get rid of that. But I *can* help you to make better decisions about who you kill. Focus on those breaths. Allow them in naturally. When your mind is fleeting to those random places again, bring it back to those breaths. Hold them. Release slowly. You are here. You are breathing. You are loved.'

I snapped open my eyes. It was what Caro had said to me, another lifetime ago. No, not another lifetime – two months ago. *Being alive is enough. We're here, we're breathing.* 'Who loves me?'

'The universe,' he said, his eyes still closed. 'The sun, the animals, your flowers, they love you. They grow for you. Mexico loves you.'

It did cheer me to hear that. It felt like my feet were touching the ground again. I had a bedrock to work from – as long as I had the sun and the flowers, the salt and scent of the ocean, blue sky and the whispering flight of unidentified birds of all colours overhead each morning, it didn't matter who else was there. That could be my Enough.

Later that morning, I'd turned on my shower and went back into my bedroom to grab some clean pants when I heard loud voices downstairs – the Chipmunks were in the living room watching TV and eating the contents of the snack cupboards, no change there. But Celestina and Paco were outside, behind the house, arguing.

'...*mas dinero.*' More money.

'...*de ninguna manera...*' By no means.

Paco wanted to do something, but Celestina wasn't having any of it.

Or as she put it, '*No hay manera en el infierno.*' No way in Hell.

Paco stormed into the house, rallied his Chipmunks and they all left. I watched from my window as the black BMW sped off from the front gates on a cloud of dust. Celestina went back inside and a while later came upstairs with a pile of my folded washing. She normally had her hair scraped back in a messy bun, but it was down, almost covering her face.

'*Gracias, señora,*' I said as she placed the pile on the end of my bed. 'Are you all right?'

'*Yes, gracias,*' she said, vanishing as quickly as she'd arrived. There was no way she wanted a conversation.

When she'd gone, I wrapped a towel around me and went down to the office to speak to Tenoch.

'Paco and Celestina were arguing.'

'What about?'

'I don't know. She doesn't usually speak to him, though. She always leaves as soon as he gets here. He must have cornered her.'

'Celestina can handle it. She's not a scared girl around him anymore.'

'She told me what Paco did to her.'

Tenoch sat back in his chair. 'How do you feel about that?'

'I don't know why you still employ him. He's a rotten apple.'

'He has not touched a woman since.'

'So?'

'So... maybe people deserve second chances. Working for me, maybe that's his second chance.'

'He's a rapist. Fact.'

'And you're a serial killer. Fact.'

'I'd rather employ a cockroach than a rapist.'

'Good job you are not the one who has to employ him then, isn't it?'

I scuffed my foot into the hallway carpet and hurt my big toenail in the process. 'Can I kill him yet?'

Tenoch snickered and sat forward in his chair. 'No, you cannot.'

'Well, you know where I am.' I made to leave, stopping to check my nose for the millionth time in the hallway mirror – it was so nice being able to breathe properly again without my teeth aching.

'Your sister's getting a hard time, isn't she?' he called out.

'Yeah.' I leaned on the door frame. 'I don't like it.'

'If my sister had called the cops on me, her head would be on a spike outside her house right now.'

'Paco said the same thing.'

'But you *not* say that. You not like us. You care about her, don't you?'

'I don't want her dead. So yeah, I must do.'

He spun the laptop towards me and clicked play on a video from my niece Mabli's vlog – she was crying on camera. Her brother Ashton's rabbit had got out of its hutch and been killed on the road and the pig had got too big and had to be sent to a farm. Her dad Cody had bought them both Tamagotchis to replace them but hers had died after she took it swimming.

'Poor kid,' I said. 'I didn't realise Tamagotchis were still going. I used to have one myself until I set fire to it.'

'Wait,' said Tenoch. There was another reason Mabli was crying – some woman had attempted to abduct Mabli after her dance class a few weeks ago – by that 'woman who said she was Auntie Rhee'.

'Some woman's pretending to be me?'

'And attempting to abduct your niece, yes.'

Mabli was still crying on the video.

'*Everything's getting on top of me,*' she said as her Stranger Things-inspired fairy lights twinkled on the wall behind her. '*My pets keep dying. And my friends are ignoring me. I feel like there's a lot of pressure at the moment. And I worry about my mom. Like, that video that's going round of her and the supermarket and stuff. Even my friends are sharing that video and they think it's funny. I'm like, dude, that's my mom...*'

'What video is she talking about?' I said, to no one in particular.

Tenoch tapped 'Supermarket' into YouTube and it came up as a suggestion before he'd finished writing her name. The footage had been watched over four million times – two women had followed Seren to her local supermarket and one had filmed as the other had straight up accosted her.

'*Why d'you do that to your sister, yo? Why d'you do that? You a bitch, girl. That chick ain't done nothing wrong. She's a fucking hero compared to you.*'

Seren tried to front it out, wheeling her cart along the aisle, staring straight ahead. She looked washed out. Grey hairs at her dark temples. They were pulling at her coat, trying to get her to turn round to face the camera.

'*My daughter was taken from a burger bar when she was five by one of those assholes and he molested her, yo. He didn't even get fuckin' jail time!*'

'Get off me!'

'*You think I don't want Rhianna to finish him off? You think if I had the courage I wouldn't do that myself? She's saving kids' lives, you stupid bitch. What kinda sister are you for ratting on Rhianna to the cops?*'

'Some fan. Can't even get my fucking name right,' I seethed.

At this point, Seren dumped her shopping cart, grabbed her bag and marched out of the store. But the women followed her into the sunlit car park.

'*Yo come back here. Why d'you do that to her? She wan't doing nothin' to you. Rhianna's ten times the woman you are, bitch!*'

The camera got juddery as the women ran after Seren and all I could hear was her screaming, '*Let go! Let go of me! You're hurting me!*'

And they tripped her up and they beat her, right there in the car park. People surrounded them. A couple of them cheered. And there's one image of Seren's face as the video stops – blood streaming from her nose.

My fingers lengthened. That's what got through to me – seeing her like that. If I'd have been there, I'd have slit both of their throats. You don't attack my sister and live to tell the tale. Grandad didn't. Neither did Pete McMahon. I felt the same as I did then – lustful. Hateful. Ferocious.

Tenoch snapped the computer lid shut. 'That makes you want to kill again, doesn't it?'

'No,' I lied.

'You have the hot sauce, *gatita*. Watching someone you love in pain or fear brings it out of you.'

'I thought it had gone, when I had Ivy. The need went, overnight. But some things do bring it back.'

'Like your sister.'

'Yeah. And children. And animals being hurt. I think I can handle everything else now. But that still does it for me. I still get irritated by everything. I... don't want to kill every last person I meet who moves my Pop Tarts or sneezes too loudly or says they prefer the British *Office* to the American one. It's sort of polarised things. *She's* polarised things for me.'

'Your little Ivy?'

'Just Ivy. She's not mine anymore.'

'It is a good thing for you to say that. What about your sister?'

'There's nothing I can do, is there?'

'No,' he said. 'This is one battle she will have to fight without you.'

Friday, 29 March –
Hacienda Santuario

1. *Rich people – you do realise a fifty grand watch and a £50 watch tell the same time, don't you?*
2. *John Cena and The Rock – who said you could act?*
3. *Noel Gallagher*
4. *Liam Gallagher*
5. *Overly woke people – sometimes, you put me to fucking sleep*

When I finally looked at myself in the full-length mirror in Marisol's bedroom that late March morning, without the bandages, without the compression suit or corset, when the scars on my stomach had crusted over and the bruising had diminished enough to be able to tell what I actually looked like, I saw what I'd wanted to see for a long time – someone who wasn't me.

The waistband of my knickers had finally seen the light of day for the first time in years – flatness from tummy to mons pubis. I had a neat, thin scar spanning the length of said knicker line, but the saggy pouch of before had gone. It was tight. Bumpless. Like she'd never existed.

My nose was smooth to the tip. Forehead smaller than before with a faint regrowth starting where the follicles now sat. My ears were nestled at the side of my head, all identifying moles had vanished. If you asked me whether I'd ever had chickenpox, I could say no with the full certainty that no tell-tale scar could be found anywhere on my person.

Once I put on a bit of slap, my lenses and hair dye, I crept into the room next to Tenoch's and sifted through the clothes in Marisol's wardrobe. I put on a white *huipil* dress embroidered with golden flowers all around the neckline and waist, sprayed on a bit of perfume and practised the knowing, overbitey Marisol smile from the gold staircase painting. I slotted on her straw hat and helped myself to a bit of jewellery from a trinket box – some silver rings that fit my fingers and a gemstone necklace that looked like a flaming orb when it caught the light. I flicked my short brown plait from one shoulder to the other. It was a facsimile – by no means perfect, but good enough.

I sauntered downstairs to where Tenoch was watching the episode of *The Golden Girls* where Rose inherits a pig. I stood under the crossed machetes, waiting, until I had to kick the metal fender to get his attention.

He flicked me a classic double take and his face went flat, like I'd smacked it with a tray. He bounced to his feet.

'Well?' I said, twirling. 'What do you think?'

He couldn't close his mouth. '*Santa madre de dios,*' he kept saying, quietly, whispering. Rubbing his face. 'I thought you were Marisol.'

'Your daughter?' I said, playfully chewing the chain of her necklace. 'I look like… your daughter?'

'That is her dress. And she used to wear her hair like that.'

He came closer and frowned. 'You smell like her too. That is her perfume.'

'You said I could, didn't you? I found it at the back of that wardrobe. Oh, this is bad, isn't it? I've offended you. I'm sorry, I'll go change—'

'—don't be sorry.' He cupped my face gently, like I was priceless. He had tears in his eyes but blinked them away. 'She wore that to her prom. The opal necklace too – I bought her that for her sixteenth. It suits you.'

'You approve?'

He wiped his cheeks. 'Yes. It make me so happy but so sad to see that dress. To smell her perfume again.' He reached out and pulled on my plait playfully, before dropping it. '*Dios mio, la extraño mucho.*'

'I'm sorry, Tenoch.' I *wasn't* sorry and I knew exactly what I'd done. But something he said did get to me. When he hugged me and breathed in her perfume. He couldn't let go. 'I'm *not* her, Tenoch.'

He nodded against me. 'You are the nearest thing.'

It took me straight back to Ivy and how much I hadn't wanted to let go of her little pudge hand in that incubator. I did the same thing sometimes with Mátilda when we were playing – I'd hold her hand, like some creep. Ugh. I was doing what he was doing – coveting something that wasn't mine, merely because it bore the slightest resemblance to the thing I'd lost.

'What happened to her?' I asked, as we broke out of our hug.

He turned away from me and marched back to his chair where a new rerun of *The GGs* was starting. He turned up the volume.

I sat on the footstool.

'Stop looking at me like that,' he sniffed.

'You said we're not the same, you and me, but we are, Tenoch.' I muted the TV. 'You feel your daughter's loss like I do. We can only forget them for so long. The men I buried, did they kill Marisol?'

He shook his head. 'No. But they rolled with the ones who did.' He said it more to the muted Golden Girls than to me. 'They thought I was informant for the drug police. I was not. Their minds had been poisoned. They tried everything to get me to confess. But I did not do it. I was set up.'

'By who? Paco?'

'No. Paco may be an asshole, but he has proved himself to me time and time again in business.'

'What did they do?'

'They started with the animals, one by one. Chickens, goats, pigs. My dogs. Then Errol, my tortoise since I was five years old. They cut off his head. Then they started on my family. My wife, and then my daughter. I had to hear their screams. For two days. I wanted them to kill me, but instead they left me with the pain. Revenge became all. I went crazy.'

'What did you do?'

'I went to the desert and tried to die. But God or Santa Muerte made me live. I got water, found food and I got strong. And when you are strong, you can think clearly. Body strong, mind strong. I've been the same ever since. I decided I wanted to kill more than I wanted to die.'

'I can understand that.'

He looked at me, the glint of a smile in his eyes but not on his lips. 'Paco was the one who found me – he told me where to find their warehouse. I know you hate him, but you do not know him like I do. He loyal. We learned their movements, their weaknesses. That's what you do when you want to get the better of someone, *gatita*. You don't rip a book down its pages, you break its spine. The *weak* point. We got some guns and went to their warehouse – they were expecting a shipment from Europe. Probably from your friend Bobby.'

'Was this when you cut off their heads? Paco told me about it.'

'I shot all of them first, and I watched them bleed out. When they were nearly dead, I cut off their limbs with those two machetes, right there. And I burned their arms and legs in an oil barrel, right before their eyes.'

I looked back towards the fireplace where the gleaming knives sat on their presentation nail, unmoved and unstained.

'And I made sure my face was the last each of those *hijos de puta* saw. I cut off their heads and I stuck them on long pikes, and I planted them in front of the warehouse so their associates would find them the next morning. It sent out a warning that nobody could fuck with me. They looked like your little flowers. Dead heads.'

'How many did you kill?'

'Seventeen. But worse still, I took their money. A *lot* of money. And I hit the road, eventually ending up here where I build my little house with my bare hands. And I started my business again. Those men you buried are from a splinter group of the same gang. They have been looking for me these past twelve years. They have better comms now so it was only a matter of time before they got lucky. But they still have not cracked the code of El Mago.'

'Not *yet*.'

'You're right. Another cell will come, another day. But for now—'

'You're safe.'

He shook his head. 'Never up here,' he said, tapping the side of his head. 'Up here, I am forever in the depths of Hell. Where I belong.'

'The revenge didn't make you happy?'

'How could it?' he said. 'Revenge is a temporary thrill, like sugar. You want it, you crave it, but it does you no good. Celestina told you what Paco did to her?' I nodded. 'It makes you want to kill him more?'

'Yes.'

'But you have not killed him yet.'

'He's a big guy. And he has guns. And friends. And you.'

'You know when to strike and when not to strike. You are clever.'

'No, I'm not clever. I'm just not stupid. I've always relied on speed and surprise. I get the impression with Paco he'd always know I was coming.'

'You are learning, *gatita*. Your instincts are good. You can read people. Sometimes it is necessary to read between the lines.'

'I thought about killing you for a while.'

'I not doubt that,' he said. 'Because you wanted to stay here?'

'Yes.'

'I had a gut feeling I could trust you to make a different choice. You a little wiseass and you got a temper as fiery as *chilate de pollo* but I knew you wouldn't betray me.'

'I still wouldn't.'

'Do you still want to stay here?'

'Yes. I do.'

He shrugged. 'Then here you stay.'

'Seriously? Even though I wanted to *kill* you?'

'Thought and action. You *thought* it but you didn't do it, even though life has given you every opportunity to do so. You have been here three months, you've done everything you've been told, you have put colour and scent back into my beautiful garden, and despite all Paco's efforts, you haven't stabbed him yet even though I know you want to.'

'Yeah, I do want to do that.'

'Well, now you have your reward. This is your home. You can stay as long as you wish.'

I couldn't hold back my smile. 'Thank you,' I said as he pulled me into the safest hug. 'There's really no catch?'

'No catch. But I want you to promise me that you will try and curb those... impulses of yours, especially around Paco.'

'I still think he's up to something. What if he's a double agent? Like, he could be working for them *and* working for you? Didn't you see *Homeland*? It could happen, Tenoch.'

'Why don't you let me worry about Paco and you worry about yourself, eh? I want you to try for a life without killing. A *normal* life. Maybe at some point you will want to leave here of your own accord.'

'Is there such a thing as a "normal life" for a serial killer?' I asked.

'If you want it bad enough, yes. I think so.'

*

After that, the subject of my leaving the Hacienda didn't come up – Tenoch kept to the contract of providing me with a brand-new passport, backstory and papers for my onward life, but it was tacitly understood that I didn't have to leave. He trusted me and I cherished that. He even showed me his artillery.

At the back of his office was a wall covered with books. Once all the books and the bookcases were removed, the wooden panels behind became visible. Tenoch gently pressed on the panel in two separate places at the same time and the panel shifted up and out and to the left, revealing behind it a cubbyhole full to the brim with guns, knives, bullets and even hand grenades.

'Touch the panel gently here and here,' he reiterated, 'two hands and the panel will slide away. But this is for emergencies only, OK? If we get any more assholes showing up here, you come in this room, lock the door and get behind this book-case as quickly as you can. You hide in the box till I whistle. Nobody knows this is here but me and you.'

'Not even Paco?'

'Not even Paco.'

'Where did you get all this from?'

'I've amassed it over the years, some is army surplus; other things stolen from rival cartels. It varies.'

'Will you teach me how to fire a gun? I've never done it before?'

'You haven't?' I shook my head. 'You're missing out.'

He set about teaching me how to load and fire every piece. I practised on the empty tin cans Paco had lined up along the fence at the end of the lawn. The first time I fired a pistol, I recoiled – the sound reverberated around the whole valley, like it was ricocheting off the walls of the world.

'Steel yourself, *gatita*,' Tenoch would say. 'It's you or them. Two shots, aim for between the eyes and the hairline.'

'Have you got any earplugs?'

He laughed. 'They're coming to get you, you're gonna stop and find your earplugs before you fire back? Do it again. Reload.'

And I did. After several more attempts and multiple wipes of my sweaty palms on my shorts, I got quite steady with an AR-15 and a Glock 22. And I discovered that getting praise felt better than getting a shot on target. Like when Dad used to praise me. Like all the praise I got when I got stronger on my legs after rehab. I'd get paid in Sylvanians for every big milestone – walking more steps, completing a full sentence.

Tenoch didn't do that, of course. He'd just holler 'Good girl' or 'Well done' and with practice my hold got steadier and my shot got closer to the red bullseyes he'd painted on the sides of the cans. Blandishments, compliments, hugs, carrots not sticks, worked wonders. Happiness found me again.

'My girl's a sharp-shooter, eh?' he would laugh and clap when I'd hit my tenth can in a row off the fence. 'How are you doing this?'

'Thinking about Paco,' I smirked, aiming again and hitting the bullseye. 'Makes me shoot straighter.' I fired but my shot went off course and hit one of my plants, shooting the centre of it clean out. 'Well, it *did*.'

He cackled. 'See? You're allowing emotion to get the better of you. Killing is a business – clean, efficient, necessary. Try again.'

'I still hate the fucker.'

'I will tell him to leave you alone.'

I clicked the safety back on the gun and stared at the plant I had hit, still swaying in the breeze. I shot it again and it completely exploded, roots and all, out of the earth.

'It's OK,' I said. 'I know how to handle him.'

Friday, 5 April – Hacienda Santuario

1. *Anyone who drives a car in Mexico – complete nutters*
2. *DJs who talk over the end of the song and don't say who sang it*
3. *Broadband providers in Mexico – it's all shit*
4. *Celebrities who crave fame at all costs one minute, then have the cheek to ask for privacy the minute they have kids*
5. *Infomercials. They're like the fucking mosquitoes. Everywhere.*

'Hey, *gatita*, that your boyfriend?'

Tenoch was at his desk in the office when I walked past, dripping wet from the pool. He turned the laptop towards me – the screen showed Sky News UK – Craig had been released from jail.

Kay Burley was outside the prison in a pink anorak, screeching down the mic in the howling wind. Jim and Elaine were there too, Tink was in Jim's arms, wearing a little Arran knit. My heart pulsed.

'Your old man, eh?' said Tenoch.

'Yeah,' I said, moving closer to the TV.

Elaine was clutching Jim's arm and a load of other people were standing behind them wrapped up in coats and scarves, holding up signs saying things like, *Innocent of all charges* and *Let Him Out!*

Finally, the tall heavy doors of the prison slid open and out walked Craig. The Pink Anorak went into full screech meltdown.

'Here he comes now, this is it, this is him – Craig Wilkins finally, after so many months of agonising wait and stress for him and his family, here he comes, a free man at last!'

They got the money shot of him with his bulky plastic bag of clothes and his grey face awash with tears, trundling towards the gates and all the adoring people cheering and *About Time*-ing. Cut to Elaine, sobbing. Cut to Jim, biting his quivering lip. Cut to Tink, shivering in her Arran knit in Jim's arms. Cut back to Jim saying to her, *Look, there's your daddy.*

That's what broke me, Jim calling him *Daddy*. And as Craig walked closer to the camera, I saw his face but he didn't look sad. He looked… dismantled. He practically fell into Elaine's arms and she cradled him like a large baby. Tink licked his cheek, Jim mouthed the words *It's over, It's over, You're safe, You're safe*. The Pink Anorak screeched on in the punishing wind.

'Well, it's a momentous day here where a man finally gets the justice he's waited so long for. Craig! Can you give us a few words? How are you feeling? What's it like to have your freedom back?'

To Craig's credit, he didn't say one word. Jim grabbed his hand like he was a little boy again and swerved his family away from the line of cameras, across the road, and out of sight.

And I have to admit I was jealous. Jealous of *Craig*, of all people. Jim would protect him now like fucking Batman, like he'd protected me when he thought I was carrying their grandchild. Craig could live his life now, free of jail. Free of me. He could probably sell his story. Get a bestseller, do the talk shows. But did I still want all that? Did I wish that was me? More fame? More adoration? The Pink Anorak screeching *my* name?

No. That was all frilly ribbon around the gift. The gift of being able to go home now. Having a normal life. That was the gift.

The lucky bastard.

'What is it like to see him again?'

'I dunno,' I said as he licked away from the screen. 'I'm glad he's out.'

'You are?'

'Yeah. I only confessed for him.'

Tenoch sat back and stared me down – an expression I couldn't read.

'What?'

'You never fail to surprise me, Rhiannon.'

'I'm not Rhiannon anymore, remember?'

'Oh yeah,' he said. 'I keep forgetting. Those brownies I smell cooking?'

'Yeah. I'm making some for the Chipmunks. Trying to be a better man.'

'That's my girl.' He smiled with an avuncular wink.

When the oven timer sounded, I scurried downstairs to find Paco taking the smaller tray out the oven.

'These are ours, right?'

'Yeah,' I said. 'Save some for Tenoch.'

'He won't mind.' He took all the brownies, piling them up high on the centre of a plate, into the living room for the boys. Some football game was on TV – they'd eaten the lot by the end of the first quarter.

Tenoch scuffed in from the office. He saw the trail of chocolate sludge left on the counter and baking tray. 'They didn't save me any?'

'No,' I said, removing a smaller tray from the top oven. 'These are yours.'

'Ah, you too good to us.' He picked up one of the brownies but it was too hot so I wrapped it in kitchen roll for him. 'Far too good to us. Thank you. Listen, we got to do our own cleaning for a little while – Celestina has left us.'

'She's *left*? Why?'

'I don't know. She left a note on my desk this morning, saying she had gone to work at one of the hotels in the town.'

'Oh, right,' I said, barely hiding my disappointment. 'I guess that means the children won't be coming anymore either?'

'You guess right. I told you not to rely on them,' said Tenoch, the brownie finally cool enough to nibble at. His face collapsed into ecstasy. 'These are good. You are an excellent baker.'

'Thanks,' I said.

'So, how would you feel about taking over Celestina's job now that she has gone? Just the basics – cleaning, vacuuming, laundry. I would pay you a wage—'

'Yeah, that's fine.'

Paco returned to the kitchen with a crumby plate. 'Did you say Celestina has gone?'

'Yeah,' said Tenoch. 'Found a new situation in town.'

'Where'd she go?' he demanded.

'Didn't say.' Tenoch began tucking into his still-warm brownies.

Paco looked directly at me. 'Because of *her*?'

'No, she just has a new situation.'

'It is, it's because of her, isn't it?'

'It's nothing to do with me,' I said. 'Maybe it's something to do with you, Paco? How 'bout dat?'

Paco looked back to Tenoch who was still non-plussed and boshing his brownies, one by one.

'She's a broken arrow, *jefe*. She could talk.'

'She won't,' said Tenoch.

'You sure?'

Tenoch stopped eating, wiped his mouth and began talking to Paco in fast Spanish that I didn't understand. Well, I understood one part of it – *falta de respeto*. Disrespect. And I understood Paco's response.

'*Si, jefe.*' Yes, *Boss*. Tenoch was shorter than Paco, by a clear foot. Even so, Paco sort of shrank before him.

Paco sloped back towards the living room, affording me his filthiest glare yet.

Wednesday, 17 April – Hacienda Santuario

'*Hola, señorita,*' came the little voice as I was reeling up the hose on the pool terrace one evening. It was David, Celestina's eldest, clinging to the other side of the chicken-wire fence behind the pool house.

'Hey!' I cried, delighted to see him until I got closer and saw his lip was cut and his face badly bruised down one side. 'What's happened?'

'We have to leave town. Paco has been threatening Mama.' He eyeballed the pool terrace.

'It's OK, he's not here. He did this to you?' A small flame ignited in the centre of my chest. 'Where's Celestina? What about Saúl and Mátilda?'

'They're OK. But we're scared. He found out we had gone to *la casa de mi tía* and he followed us there. Mama took Saúl and Mátilda into the forest and I ran but he caught me and he beat me. He wanted to know where Mama was. He said he was going to kill all of us.'

'Why? What's his problem with her?' The flame expanded.

'I heard them arguing. He wanted her to break into Tenoch's study and find a clue.'

'What clue?'

'A clue for where he keeps his money. Tenoch has a lot of money but it not in a bank. And Paco wants it. He was planning to steal it and cut her in. He told Mama to spy on Tenoch but she would not do it. She is scared, of both of them. I came here to warn you. Paco will hurt you to get to the money.'

'I know, don't worry.' I touched his hand through the wire and he gripped my finger. 'I'll be OK.'

'No, no you won't,' he said, starting to cry. 'Paco is... *un hijo de puta*.' He scuffed his trainer in the dirt. 'A bad, *bad* man.'

Tenoch could tell my mood had dipped later that afternoon when I'd tripped over the mop bucket and hurled both mop and bucket into the pool. We went down to the beachfront again for ice cream. It was on the tip of my tongue to tell him about David's visit but I knew he wouldn't believe me and even if he did, maybe it would get David in trouble. I didn't know what to do for the best.

An open-air *tianguis* was in full swing along one of the side streets – the stalls selling fruit and veg, second-hand clothes, street food sizzling away on hot griddles. A lady with a tray handed out slices of mango drizzled in tajin – a chilli sauce. Divine on every level. Brought my tongue back to life.

'This is what it will be like for you now,' he said as we bought our ice creams and headed for a vacant beach palapa to sit down. 'No need to cover your face. See that vendor? He's only giving you a second look because he thinks you're beautiful.'

'Am I?'

'What?' he said, licking the chopped nuts from his strawberry sundae.

'Beautiful?'

'Of course my girl is very beautiful.'

That made me feel like the sun was shining just for me – like everything there was for my happiness. The dazzling sea. The thumping *musica norteña* coming from the bars and souvenir shops, the rich sweet smells of the panaderia and fried camarones (shrimp) and whole pulpo (octopus) wafting up from the beach barbecue. We practised my backstory again – *Where did you go to school? What job did you do up until the age of 21? What was your mother's maiden name?* – until I'd answered every question without stuttering.

'You are ready for your new life now. Start living it.'

People walked dogs, jogged, milled about buying souvenirs and conversing with friends. The *fonditas* and beachfront cafés thronged with people sitting out eating some of the largest bowls of soup and stuffed tortillas I'd ever seen. I ate half of my ice cream and tossed the rest in the trash – my heartburn was biting too hard to enjoy it.

'You are too quiet this afternoon,' Tenoch said, as we watched a boat drift into shore and two fishermen bring in the day's catch.

'Am I?' I said, stabbing at the sand with a pointy rock. One of the fishermen began cooking on a griddle on the water's edge and a small crowd, mostly locals, ate them on paper plates and chatted easily. 'Pescado zarandeado,' Tenoch informed me. That's what they're eating. Grilled snapper marinated in spices and Guajillo chillies, with warm tortillas. They pay what they think it is worth.'

'Nice.'

'Aren't you happy about being here anymore?'

'Are you kidding?' I said. 'I love it here.' I kept looking towards the art district and thinking about Rafael. Even though I had seen him with the girl, I still wanted him. I wanted him to appear again and ruin my life completely.

'You have a heavy mind. What is on it?'

'David came to the Hacienda this morning. To warn me about Paco.'

'What did he say?'

'He was covered in bruises. He said Paco had been threatening his mother, forcing her to search for your money. She refused.'

Tenoch nodded, but carried on nibbling his ice cream cone and watching the fishermen.

'He beat the crap out of him, Tenoch. He's only 11.'

Tenoch continued to stare out to sea, but still didn't say anything.

'They're not safe.'

'They will be,' he replied, finishing his cone and wiping his hands on his jeans. He got to his feet and helped me to mine. 'Thank you for telling me this.'

'So you believe me?'

'Yes, I believe he came to the Hacienda and told you that.'

'What about David?'

His mouth twitched. 'David's mother was raped by Paco, this you know. Celestina has been waiting for three years to strike back at him. A serial killer who hates rapists and loves children comes to live with Paco's boss – she thinks she has found the perfect solution. David appears with bruises – tells you it was Paco and then, like magic, no more Paco.'

'No, that's not it. It can't be. The boy was black and blue, Tenoch.'

'I do not doubt that. But are you telling me it's not even a little convenient that he came to you this morning to "warn you"?'

'No. I believe him.'

Tenoch laughed. 'I pay Paco well. Why would he steal from me?'

'Because he's greedy. Because he wants to be you. Take over your home, your business.'

He shook his head. 'Paco has never let me down.'

'You can go through a lot with someone and they can still let you down.'

'This is true.' He took my pointy rock and lobbed it across the sand towards the sea where it skimmed the water. 'You should come down here on your own sometimes. It is a safe area. It's good for you to mix with people.'

'Don't change the subject—'

'They will be fine. I will see they are protected.' But he was so flippant with it – he didn't really care. And I don't think I could force him to. Sometimes he could be a real prick.

'Come on, we have to go.' I didn't move until he looked at me. 'I give you my word, Celestina and her kids will be all right. I'll keep Paco away from them.'

As we reached the car in a parking lot at the back of an electrical store, a stray dog puttered over to us, sniffing the air for the macarons Tenoch had bought for supper. It was in my nature to fuss it and want to take it home but the dog didn't want to be held for long. Most of the shopkeepers left out water bowls and he lapped greedily at one at the front of the store.

'I miss having a dog,' I said as I got in the car, watching it pad away in the wing mirror as the engine started. I was so focused on him and reminiscing about the way Tink used to snuggle up under my armpit in the mornings, I nearly didn't see it – the black BMW that turned out of the side street and sped off in the opposite direction. The unmistakable arm dripping in gold bracelets and rings, resting on the driver's open window.

'That was him,' I said, just as a large van clattered past. 'That was Paco.' I don't think Tenoch had heard me, but I didn't say it again.

Monday, 29 April –
Hacienda Santuario

1. *Vapists*
2. *Rapists*
3. *Pedestrians who have no concept of the word 'car'*
4. *Fitness freaks who take protein supplements when they're already getting all the protein they need – we get it, you're special, now fuck off*
5. *People who can't construct a sentence and/or tell a joke – e.g. Paco when he's pissed and/or drugged up to the eyeballs*
6. *People who shove my face into a cold pie at seven in the morning*

'Happy birthday, *gatita*!' Tenoch announced as I came down the stairs. He was leaning against the kitchen counter and staring at his laptop screen, surrounded by the aforementioned jollity and decorations.

'How did you know it was my birthday?'

'I know everything about you. And I wanted to get you some things to celebrate. Everyone should have a birthday.

Though this will have to be your last 29 April birthday. Your new birthday is 25 September.'

'Oh. Right.'

'And I got you a cheesecake from our favourite bakery. They just delivered it.' He scuffed over to the fridge and brought out a flat white box, lifting the lid to show me a creamy yellow cheesecake with *Happy Birthday* scrawled over the top in red sauce. 'It is vanilla and coconut and they use real vanilla pods and organic coconuts and fresh cream cheese. Smell it.'

It was early and I was naïve, granted, and as I leaned over and inhaled the cheesecake and it got the saliva glands flowing of course, he struck, pushing my face clean into the wet pie with a resounding *splat!*

I emerged to the deafening sounds of Tenoch's screeching laughter. 'Now it a party, eh? Hahahahaha!'

'Mi Gente' came on the radio – the Beyoncé version – and he turned it up extra loud and we danced around the kitchen, chunks of cream cheese plopping from my face to the floor tiles. I scraped the mixture off my cheeks, tasting my delicious fingers. We danced until we couldn't breathe for laughing.

He gave me the day off my cleaning duties and we ate the rest of the cake watching a *Golden Girls* marathon beginning with Blanche going through the menopause and ending with her, Dorothy and Rose going to a nudist hotel.

'The children sent things for you as well,' said Tenoch, bringing in a small bag full of treats – pictures drawn by Saúl and Mátilda, a whole heap of candy, and a comic book David had drawn and illustrated all by himself.

'Did you see them?' I asked him, as I took the box.

'Yeah, I saw them yesterday. They are all well.'

'And Celestina?'

'She is well too.'

'So did you find out what was going on?'

'No, not yet. But I will. And I almost forgot your main present...'

He disappeared out to the broom closet in the hall and he returned moments later wheeling in a brand-new mountain bike with a big purple bow tied to the handlebars.

'Wow, what's this?'

Tenoch beamed. 'Yeah of course. Go ahead, ride it around *la terraza*. See if the saddle needs adjusting for you.'

I rode a bike for the first time in years. I rode it round the lawn and once I'd got my balance and found my speed, it was the most fun I'd had for ages. It was the best present I'd been given, apart from Tink.

When I rode back indoors, there was another present waiting for me on the kitchen island – a large brown envelope, wrapped in another purple bow. Tenoch patted it and slid the parcel towards me. 'One more for you.'

Inside was a slightly worn American passport with a new photo of myself post-surgery, plus new paperwork. I had a social security number, Part A and Part B medical insurance, even a brand whole birth certificate.

'I fulfil my promise to you, *gatita*. You cannot get better documents. They are state of the art. And they all check out, I promise.'

'Thanks,' I said, staring down at my official new name, 25 September 1990 birthday and whole-assed new parents. 'Although, technically, I paid for this myself, didn't I?'

'Yeah, you did. But I bought you the bike.'

'So you couldn't make me any younger than twenty-nine?'

'No, but you have a new birthday. How does it feel to be a year older?'

'It's different this year. I don't think I feel like *her* yet – the new name – but I definitely don't feel entirely like my old name either. I guess I'm… somewhere in between the two.'

Paco turned up about eleven, on his own this time, and tried his best to keep needling me about stuff – about the doppelgangers showing up on my sister's doorstep, harassing her in the street and outside her son's school, about Ivy again and he even showed me a news article where some obsessed fan had sent a detailed letter to the *Bristol Evening Post* claiming to have killed the guy found in the sand dunes in Mallorca.

She had signed it 'Sweetpea'.

But the information in the letter was in the public domain and, therefore, could not be verified.

'You should write your own letter, Sweetpea,' Paco grinned, following me as I walked my bike down Spiky Plant Alley. 'Tell the world in detail how you killed that guy. Give them details only the killer would know.'

'Why would I do that?' I said. 'I'm not proud of it.'

'I would be,' he smirked.

'I'm not you. We are not the same. I can stop this at any time.'

'It doesn't matter how many times a snake sheds its skin, *chica*. It always gonna be a snake.'

I stared into his eyes – he was a clear foot taller than me but I held my ground. 'Is that so?' I said, swinging my leg over the saddle as the gates opened for me. 'Well, have a nice day.'

'You don't mean that,' he said. 'I know you want to kill me for beating the shit out of that kid, don't you? You don't like it when I hurt kids, do you?'

One foot on the pedal, one on the ground, I stared out at the bright Mexico morning, inhaling the breeze. I looked back at Paco and I could see it there in his face – how much he wanted me to leap off that bike, run back to the gates and barrel into him. To beat him, to swear, to strike, to stab.

How many times had Celestina wanted to do that? I wondered. But she hadn't. She was still biding her time. Serving it ice cold. And I would too.

I was pedalling into the distance when I heard him scream after me. 'I don't know what he sees in you, fat skanky English puta! You'll fucking get yours!'

Sunday, 5 May –
Hacienda Santuario

Most mornings, after I'd done my chores, I rode down to the beachfront on my bike. One day I ventured into an organic market and bought some vegetables for our *pozole*. Another day I visited a bird sanctuary where I lost myself to the beauty of hundreds of parakeets, quetzals, toucans, white ibis and vultures and a tiny hummingbird who drank sugar water from my cupped hand. It was probably trained to do that but still, it was a happy moment I'd remember forever.

IKR? It's all getting a bit Julia Roberts, isn't it? But I swear, that's how it was. It's like my birthday had heralded a new era – an era where I chose to be happy, no matter what else was happening. It was a rebirth-day, you might say.

I visited a sculpture garden and an aloe vera plantation, as well as more of the museums, shops and art galleries I'd only previously walked past but had never gone inside on my own.

I ate freshest calamares tempura, fig and arugula salad and tuna carpaccio at the seaside cantinas, drank the rummiest piña coladas, and collected handfuls of tiny white shells in the cool waters of the Sea of Cortez at the end of a long hot day.

And it was great coming home and telling Tenoch, bringing him little gifts – shell necklaces I'd watched being made, tacos from street vendors, and a little craft *gatita* – a handmade yarn kitten with black-and-white stripes, blue button eyes and a smiling mouth that I thought he would like.

'I love it. My little *gatita*, just like you.'

Mexico gave me freedom and a friend and it made me like the world again. I liked *myself* again. My killing urge all but disappeared, but not in an unsettling way like it had aboard the cruise – in a natural way. I was nourished. Bedded into Rocas Calientes like one of my plants. Fed, watered, appreciated. No need for this Venus flytrap to bite.

One evening, I hung around Playa Tortuga – the beach – reading a book beneath my usual *palapa* and soaking in the last vestiges of sun with a fresh piña colada. 'I so don't deserve this,' I chuckled to myself – the realisation had dawned as the sun went down. I was in fucking paradise when, by rights, I should have been in jail.

A party had started up on a hotel terrace. A family danced and laughed, spinning themselves around a dancefloor surrounded by large umbrellas decked in fairy lights. Some children spilled out of the throng and scampered down the steps, all crowding around an iPad. I crunched up the seashells I'd collected, breathing in the salt and smoke air, trying to ignore the hubbub but it kept filtering through my consciousness. One of the kids, a boy with long eyelashes framing his chestnut-brown eyes, came running over to see what I was holding.

'Hola niño,' I said. He waved. I showed him the shells and he toddled over and peered into my hand. '*Cuántas conchas?*'

'*Uno*,' he began, his fingertip poking each shell in turn. '*Dos, tres, cuatro, cinco, seis... siete!*'

'*Ahh muay bien!*' I applauded him. We chatted for a while – me in only basic Spanish and him saying a lot of shit I didn't understand.

I locked eyes with a guy standing on the steps behind him – this severe-looking Mexican with equally dazzling brown eyes and a jawline for days. I recognised him instantly as he called out for the young boy.

'*Mateo! Ven aquí!*'

It was *him*. The Hottest Turtle, backlit by patio heaters and strings of fairy lights hanging from a multitude of outdoor umbrellas. A breeze whipped up the ends of his flapping white shirt as he stood there, one hand in his pocket, the other rubbing his stubbly chin, looking like something between boybander and angel. I'd forgotten how beautiful he was.

And I rationalised that the boy must be Tiny Turtle and taking one look at his clothes and the marigold tucked into a buttonhole, I realised the party was a wedding – *his* wedding. Hot Turtle and Fun Times at Guantánamo. She was there, on the terrace, in a bride's dress, laughing and spinning round like a heroin-addicted hyena.

I tipped my shell collection into the little boy's hand and he giggled, scurrying back towards the other kids on the steps. And I walked away.

'Hey!' Hot Turtle walked towards me. I walked faster, back in the direction of the railings where I'd chained up my bike. I couldn't speak and my chest hurt. Heartburn from too much piña colada. Or the churros I'd necked in the supermarket

– they'd been hot, straight out the oil – and my fat ass couldn't wait. They'd burned my oesophagus en route.

But the damn sand was shifting under my bare feet and I couldn't move fast enough. 'Hey!' he called again.

I stopped and turned around. His white shirt flapped open to reveal an acre of stunning chest. 'Oh, hi.'

'I recognise that smile but I remembered you a whole other way.' He squinted. 'Hello, Maniac, it is you, isn't it?'

Immediate jelly knees. I didn't know which part of him I wanted in me first. But first things foremost – I hated him and he was a Judas who had just got married to another woman. 'OK, bye.'

'I almost didn't recognise you.'

I'd been so hell-bent on disguising myself, I'd forgotten the one person who I *did* want to see me.

'I had some work done. Better or worse?'

'Well, you looked beautiful before. But now you're kinda spectacular.'

Oh my God – that moment. If I could have bottled it, I'd have showered in it for the rest of my life. Goosebumps raked my body like a violent storm. 'Flying Without Wings' was playing inside my head and Westlife were about to get up off their stools for the big finish. I glowed from the inside out.

'You were talking to my nephew.'

'Oh, I thought he was your son,' I said, gesturing to the boy. 'I had some shells and he was admiring them. I wasn't hurting him.'

He looked back at the boy who was dispensing the shells around his gaggle of friends. Then back to me. 'I didn't think you were hurting him.'

'Well, *felicidades* on your wedding,' I said, nodding towards the party.

He frowned, big eyes shining in the fairy lights around the railings. 'It's not mine. It's my sister's.'

'Your sister?' I said, stupidly relieved. 'The bride, with the blonde hair?'

'My sister Olivia, yeah.'

'Oh right.' Another of my world-famous boo-boos. Fun Times at Guantánamo was his *sister*. Who he was most definitely not having sex with, so my jealousy was entirely misplaced. 'Well, I have to go. Sorry for... sorry.'

'I thought I might see you before now.' He stepped closer.

'Huh?'

'Sal gave you my note?'

'Yeah,' I said, scratching a new mozzie bite on my wrist, recalling the day I'd screwed up said note and chucked it. 'I didn't think you were serious.'

'It was just hanging out, no biggy. It's cool if there's another guy or—'

'There's no other guy. I wanted to see you too.'

'I thought about you yesterday at the supermarket. There was this dude getting his blood pressure checked and he had this cough that was driving me crazy. And I kept thinking—'

'—just fucking die already?'

He stared. I knew that look. It was the same one everyone gave me when I'd crossed the line. But the most astonishing thing was that he didn't berate me or walk away or gasp like most people do. He laughed.

'You took the words right out of my mouth.'

We were laughing then. And adding more irritants to our

imaginary kill lists – the guy yanking his dog's lead when it was trying to sniff a trash can, tourists who wore sombreros, tourists who are surprised that Mexican food tastes better than the shit they've always eaten back home, and tourists who slam their tequila. He had it in for tourists in particular.

'You wanna go grab a bite somewhere?'

'Don't you have a wedding to get back to?'

He looked back at the terrace where 'Despacito' had kicked in and every single couple was up slow dancing. 'They won't miss me. Come on.'

Rafael knew the area well and chatted to a number of people as he led me through the streets and up the rickety back steps of a bar down the street from Salome's. The bar was on a roof terrace, decked in fairy lights – a theme carried over to the tables where clusters of lights sat in shallow bowls. The place was packed with people and body odour was the aroma of the night. Rafael didn't smell bad though. He smelled of lemons.

'What aftershave is that?' I asked him as we waited in line for a table.

'I don't wear it. This is my natural manly scent.'

'Liar.'

'Tom Ford, Venetian Bergamot.'

'Knew it.'

'Like it?'

'Bit.'

'Good.'

His shirt flapped open again on a holy night breeze, showing a tattoo on his chest over his heart – stars and stripes, and a bird perched on a cactus, its beak clutching a snake.

'What is that?' I said, pointing it out.

'Mexican-American flag. My buddy did it before I joined up.'

'Joined up what?'

'The army.'

'You're in the army?' I said.

'*Was*,' he corrected. 'Left a couple years ago, before I made Sergeant First Class.'

I didn't know what to say, not having had any military interest myself, other than what I'd gleaned from watching one ep of *SAS: Who Dares Wins* and even then I switched over halfway through to *DIY: SOS*. It was just a lot of shouting and being denied bacon sandwiches. I'd crack on the first day.

After an age of waiting, which for once I didn't mind as my fat ass was well entertained by bowls of free coconut prawns being handed out, we were shown to a table by the roof's edge. Rafael pulled my chair out for me.

'You wanna try the gins?'

'No, can't stand gin.'

'Why d'you let me bring you to a gin bar if you don't like gin?'

'Dunno. I wanted to go where you were going.' My face heated up. Even serial killers get embarrassed, you know. I realised that the day I was aggressively scratching my minge and the postman was watching me through the window. 'I'll have whatever you are.'

'I'm having a beer. What you wanna eat?'

'Surprise me.'

And so he did. He returned to the table with six Pacificos in a bucket of ice cubes and cut limes, followed by a waiter with a large tray heaving under several different little bowls and plates of piping hot food.

'Oh, I love this!' I squealed. 'We did this in Spain, me and my friend. I tried jamon and fried sardines and baby squid and pintxos. It was great!'

'Well, here you got manta ray and yellowfin *taquitos* with pico de gallo, Caldo de Siete Mares, which is a kind of fish stew, chiles rellenos – stuffed bell peppers – duck croquetas, chips and guac, grilled broccoli and a chocolate and pecan brownie to share.'

'This... this makes me so happy. That's so sad, isn't it?' I laughed. 'How much do I owe you?'

Rafael wouldn't hear of it. 'Buy me dinner tomorrow, we'll call it even.'

'Deal.' We clinked bottles.

We chatted long into the night. I told him about *The Alibi Clock,* my ill-fated attempt at writing a book and getting it published; he told me about his army career and his dabbling in oils and watercolours, as evidenced by the artworks on display in Salomé's gallery.

'Yeah, I saw those,' I said, swerving around what I wanted to say – that they were shite – and instead opting for the less offensive 'They're all sold'.

'Did you like them?'

'I don't know anything about art.'

'But what did you think of them?'

'So colourful and... you're incredibly talented.'

The lie stuck in my throat like a bone but he beamed at the compliment. I'd tell a thousand lies to make him look at me like that all the time.

'I was nervous to talk to you before. At the airport.'

'You were?' I sank half my beer in one go to get the butterflies drunk. 'Why were *you* nervous, Army Boy?'

'Some women have that effect on me.'

'What women?'

'Ones I like. Ones I want to like me back.'

I sank the other half of my beer. 'So you *like me*?'

'Maybe.'

We'd got so flirty, all of a sudden. 'Good. Well, feel free to check out my arse again any time you like.'

'What?'

'When I was coming up the stairs and you were behind me – you were totally checking out my arse.'

'I was *not* checking out your ass,' he said, all faux-annoyed.

'Oh, all right. I was checking out yours earlier, that was all.'

'When?'

'In Salomé's gallery. You were putting my bike in her store room and you bent over.'

'Well, I *wasn't* checking out *yours*.'

'All right.' I held up my hands in surrender. 'Whatever you say.'

'I was *actually* studying a tropical bird that had flown into the bar,' he explained. 'And if I *did* happen to glance up at—'

'—stare at.'

'—your ass, it was completely by accident.' He couldn't help smiling.

I couldn't help it either. 'I don't know where we stand anymore on arse-checking. I mean, can we do that?'

'I guess so,' he shrugged. 'If the ass-checkee doesn't mind.'

'I don't mind. I quite like it. I've done a lot of squats so

I kind of like people looking at my arse. Actually, I want people to look at it. I want people to queue up and buy tickets to fucking *worship* it.'

I had him laughing then, loud and unabashed, head back. And if I thought his smile was great, his laugh was glorious. Like Christmas bells.

It had all gone a little bit too Kate Hudson for my liking.

We got onto the less important shit like our favourite colours, swear words and best/worst movies. His were yellow, motherfucker and *Saving Private Ryan* but he couldn't think of a worst movie.

'What's yours?'

'*The Devil Wears Prada*,' I replied. 'No question.'

He laughed. 'Why?'

'Ugh, I just hate it. Everything about it irks me. Like, if I worked for a woman like that I'd be lacing her coffee with arsenic and shitting in her bed. Minimum. But Hathaway puts up with it.'

He delighted in my irk and I couldn't help comparing him to Craig. He'd have told me to shut up or ignored me until I'd finished. Raf seemed to find me fascinating. 'What else don't you like about it?'

'I hate her unsupportive curly boyfriend. I hate that whole glow-up makeover montage. I hate that speech Streep does about the colour of the jumper. I hate that mean Mary Poppins bitch. I hate that smug *Mentalist* guy. I hate that she leaves the steak. The whole thing sucks endless ass.'

'But it's got a positive ending, right? She goes on to better things.'

'Yeah *right* at the end though. You have to sit through an eternity of chronic Ugh to get to that bit.'

He chuckled. 'I see what you mean. So what's your *favourite* movie?'

'*Rocky.*'

'No hesitation. Why that one?'

'Reminds me of my dad. He was a boxer. He died, a few years ago now.'

'Shit, I'm sorry.'

'I adored him. Daddy's little girl. I don't have much family left so… when Uncle Tenoch said I could come out here for a few months and help him on his… farm, I jumped at the chance.'

'You like it here?'

'I do,' I said. 'Well, I do when my uncle doesn't invite his stupid friends over for constant beer nights and belching competitions. I like it down here though. The people are so friendly. And the men are so hot.'

'So you're on the prowl, are you?'

'No, I'm simply appreciative of male beauty. Before they open their fucking mouths and ruin it.'

'I'm glad I found you again.'

'I came down a few times and went to Salomé's gallery to look for you.'

'I came down here too, in January. And again in February when she moved premises, I came to help and—'

'—I saw you. Heaving boxes. And walking hand in hand with a girl.'

'What girl?'

'Your sister. But at the time I thought she was your girlfriend—'

'Ah shit. You shoulda talked to me.'

'I should have done a lot of things. I just protected myself until I was strong enough to deal with it.'

'Deal with what?'

'Being let down. I can't go through it again. I can't go through a *relationship* again until I know I can handle it ending. A tough girl is what I have to be.' I started singing 'Daddy Lessons' by Beyoncé but he didn't smile.

'I would never cheat on—'

'It doesn't matter,' I smiled. 'I can't rely on you or anyone else to make me happy. It has to come from me. I've been hurt before.'

'I get that.'

'You know what it's like to have your heart broken?'

'Big time.'

I reached for another beer. 'Show me some more of your tattoos,' I said, leaning forwards. He pulled back his shirt sleeves to reveal another eagle with a sparkling 3-D blue diamond in its claws on his right forearm and a crescent moon on his left. I was lubricated enough by this point to touch him on the arm. 'I get the eagle and the flag but what's the jewel for?'

'My mom's nickname for me. Joya. Means jewel in Spanish.'

'I grazed over the ink with my fingertips. 'That's... nice.'

'*Mi corazon, mi luz y mi joya preciosa.*' He rolled his eyes but his mouth smiled. 'That's what she calls the three of us, me and my brother and sister. My heart, my light and my precious jewel.'

The more we chatted, the more I just wanted to be in his company. Not even touching. Being near him was enough. I could have stayed all night. But there was a point when my stomach rolled over like a manatee in custard.

'Ooh God, I don't think I should drink anymore. Or eat. Or speak.'

'Do you wanna go home?'

I swallowed hard. 'I think I better. Where's my bike?'

'Salomé took it into her store room, remember? Let's go get it.'

Not only did he not let me cycle back up to the Hacienda half-cut and vomitous, but he put my bike on the back of his dad's car and drove me up there instead, allowing me to hang my head out of the window like a spaniel. 'Thanks for dinner,' I said when I got out, five minutes away from the Hacienda. He got out too and unhooked my bike. 'Sorry I got so pissed. I haven't drunk in a while.'

'It's cool. I can't see a house here. You sure we came the right way?'

'It's just over the brow of that hill. There's a red security light on the gate post. I would invite you in but I'm not allowed visitors.'

'How come?'

'My uncle... is a private person.' I swallowed down an over-eager surge of vomit, desperate not to puke in front of him on our first date.

'OK, well, if you're sure you're gonna be OK?'

'Yeah, I'll be fine,' I said, wafting him away and wheeling my bike in the vague direction of the gates. 'Honestly, go. I'm good.'

'Can I see you tomorrow?'

'You sure you want to?'

'Yeah. You're buying me food, remember?' By this point he was a white blur careening round my vision on a background of stars. 'I'll pick you up at noon.' He wrote the time on the back of my hand and walked back to the car. Didn't even try to kiss me, the chivalrous prick.

'Noon. OK. I'll see you at noon,' I said, forcing myself to imprint his handwritten note to memory as I edged away from him, vomit rising.

The next thing I remember is waking up in my bathroom with one side of my face on the toilet seat, mascara smudged and a long string of orange drool dangling from my lip. I'd been there all night.

Tuesday, 7 May – Playa Tortuga, Rocas Calientes

Note: no Kill List again. Where there's no Kill List, there's no reason to kill. There's balance in my mind. There is Happy. And with Raf, I was permanently, irritatingly, sickeningly happy. Honestly, if I'd seen us out and about holding hands, kissing necks, stroking hair, *I'd* have wanted to smash us in the face.

I didn't tell Tenoch about him – for some reason I wanted to keep him as my secret for the time being. And I don't know but I thought maybe he might throw a spanner in the works.

I spent the next few days with Raf – each morning after chores I'd ride down to the hotel and we'd hang out with his family, mostly eating, playing drinking games, swimming or wandering the town desperately trying to learn more Spanish so I could join in with all the conversations.

Raf and I talked a lot, and we laughed a lot too. We licked ice cream off each other's noses, watched sunsets from the shoreline like two bloody idiots. The only reason I'd watched sunsets before was to gauge how dark the sky was before going out to stab a rapist.

We were now on a Kate Hudson schmaltz level, bordering on Meg Ryan Tier. And I wasn't used to it. I wasn't used to how often Rafael would kiss me, hold me, reach for my hand in a way that let me know he was glad I was there. My cheeks would ache every day so I knew I must be enjoying myself, but I couldn't convey it as easily as *he* could. Raf and his family conveyed emotion the same way they danced – freely and easily. No holding back at all. I conveyed emotion like a typical Brit – rarely, painfully and only then once accompanied by a shitload of alcohol.

And I told him that. I had to. I'd pulled back from him too early when we had hugged on the beach one evening, watching said sunset.

'If I'm coming on too strong—'

'You're not, you're absolutely not. No, I love it. I think I'm stopping myself feeling too much. Does that make sense?'

He laughed. 'No. It's not because of your uncle, is it?'

'Why would it be because of him?'

'Well, he seems a little… over-protective of you. Not letting you bring people home. Not letting you stay out.'

'I can stay out. I can stay out all night if I want to. He's not protective of me – he's just protective of his house – but it's not just that. I think I'm protecting *myself*. Guys come along and ruin stuff. Or make *me* ruin it.'

He gently dropped my hand, but he said the perfect thing. 'Well, I don't want to ruin anything here. I can try and like you a little less?'

'No,' I said, taking his hand again. I didn't like the emptiness when he wasn't holding it. 'Like me a lot. I think I need you to.'

'You got it,' he winked and my stomach flipped over as he pulled me closer and ran both his hands through my hair, leaving me breathless.

I wasn't thinking about Craig. And I wasn't thinking about how much Rhiannon didn't *deserve* this. I was simply content. Being with Raf and his family made me feel like the person I *should* have been: Parallel Universe Me.

I liked his family almost immediately, once they'd all stopped kissing and hugging me upon introduction – I thought that was weird but only cos I'd never had that reception before. Salomé closed her gallery for the evening and came down to the beachfront to join us – she hugged me like an old friend. But it was his parents, Mike and Bianca, who particularly fascinated me.

'They were childhood sweethearts,' Raf told me as we sat around one of the outdoor tables. 'Grew up on the same street in Chihuahua. They've been like this since they were teenagers. I don't think they've ever even argued.'

I watched them; Michael stroking Bianca's arm; her nuzzling his shoulder as they listened to an uncle telling a story. Sometimes Michael would say something just for her and her eyes would close slowly, as though it was the most gorgeous thing she'd ever heard, then they'd kiss, and rejoin the conversation. It was like they'd stepped out into their own little world, only for a second, before stepping back in. Bianca would present him with little gifts – a napkin folded into the shape of a bird or a heart bitten out of a slice of cucumber. Silly shit, too pure for even the likes of me to take the piss out of.

I started doing the same with Raf, to show him all his loving gestures weren't in vain. I'd kiss him when he wasn't expecting it. I'd present him with little gifts – a shell I'd found, a grey pebble in sort of the shape of a heart, and a little wooden turtle with a nodding head I bought from Salomé's gallery.

But unlike his parents, me and Rafael didn't know each other inside out. Rafael hadn't known me long at all. We hadn't even had sex by this point. He didn't know anything about me, except my name. My *fake* name. And that was the difference. With him, I could be anyone I liked. I didn't have to be Rhiannon. Nobody knew me as Rhiannon in that family.

And if I wanted it to last, that's the way it would have to stay.

Thursday, 9 May – Holiday Inn en el Agua, Rocas Calientes

Rafael invited me to join him and the fam at their hotel for a pool party – they had taken over the whole place, it seemed, and the men were in the water playing a particularly violent game of volleyball. There had been three nosebleeds so far, one of them an elderly aunt.

There were a lot of people on the pool terrace when I got there, all different family members from the previous two nights, so I had to endure another punishing round of hugging and kissing but I was strangely used to it by this point. I almost welcomed it. I met his older brother, Nico, who was an older, more hench version of Raf, and his wife Ariela with their three kids, Ana, Elijah and Mateo – the little dude I'd given the shells to.

'Ah so *you're* the girl who's brought the smile back to my little brother's face, eh?' said Nicolas, enfolding me in a gentle chokehold with his enormous Popeye arm. 'Well, you were a little late in getting the good-looking brother, sadly. I'm afraid I'm already taken by this old ball and chain.'

'Don't listen to him,' said Ariela, giving her husband

a playful shove, her arms dripping in bangles, hair all knotted up in a scrappy bun. 'Come and grab a drink and something to eat before these guys snag all the chicken wings. And word to the wise – don't eat too much of Abuela's capirotada – you will not float in that pool afterwards!'

'Good advice, thank you.'

I properly met Raf's older sister Olivia too – Fun Times at Guantánamo – who was more strikingly beautiful than I'd given her credit for. I noticed she wasn't joining in too much with the conversation when the rest of the aunts and uncles were doing their Getting To Know You bit and she was the only one who didn't smile as easily.

During the second half of the volleyball contest, I was staring into the void, wondering where Raf had got to, when an iPhone was thrust before my face and a picture of a teenage boy with buck teeth assaulted my eyes.

'He hasn't always been that gorgeous, just so you know,' said Liv. 'So start praying your kids get *your* teeth, not his.'

I grabbed the phone from her and stared hard at the picture. 'That's him? Jesus. I didn't know he was Bugs Bunny's understudy.'

'Yeah, he really beat the shit out of puberty, huh?' she chuckled darkly.

I handed her back the phone. 'He really did.'

'So you and him for real?' She tossed the piece of melon from her cocktail towards an iguana basking on the deck.

'Yeah. I like him a lot.'

'He's had a tough few years,' she explained, shifting round to face me on her lounger, top boob teetering perilously out of her bikini; one hand behind her head revealing a line of dark bruises. 'He was kicked out of the army, which hurt him a lot.'

'He doesn't talk much about that.'

'It's cos he's ashamed. He regrets it big time. We *all* do. Fucking idiot.'

'What happened?'

She reached back to pick a hibiscus flower dangling over us from a planter. 'He beat up his buddy – the dude who slept with his wife.'

'He's *married*?'

'Oh no, they finally divorced about a year ago. But it sent him into a spiral. We were worried we'd never get him back. Anyway, the asshole who slept with his wife happened to be his best friend *and* his lieutenant colonel.'

'Oh. Shit.'

'Raf beat up the guy pretty bad. Army kicked him straight back to San D. Cuntasaurus Rex left soon after. We were all glad to see the back of *her*.'

'Where is she now?'

'Headless down a fuckin' storm drain, I hope.' I could tell me and Liv were going to get on like a house on fire. 'But now he's got no pension, no references, and he's living back with Mom and Dad.' She sipped her drink, like she was sipping the proverbial tea. 'He's desperate for someone in his life. Someone he can protect, look after. Do you really like him? Honestly?'

'Yeah. I do. Honestly.'

'But?'

'There's no but.'

'He said you wanna take things slow. We talk. He tells me stuff.'

'I don't… want him to let me down.'

'You mean you've been fucked around before and you don't want him to do the same thing to you?'

'Yes.'

'Well, he has trust issues too. But I haven't seen him this in love with someone since Cuntasaurus. And look how *she* treated him.'

'I want to be better for him. I didn't… handle the last break up well.'

'Don't let one bitch colour the whole scene,' she said, her green-taloned hand emphatically slicing the air between us. 'Don't let it ruin you for all other relationships. Trust me, I've been there. I tried to find someone as devoted and loyal as my brothers for years and I thought: nah, they're regular one-offs, like my dad. This was before I met Edouardo at Nico's gym. I wanted to be better for him too. He helped me get down to my goal weight.'

'You mean thinner,' I muttered.

Her husband climbed the pool steps and grabbed his towel from a sun-lounger and gave her a wink. They fist bumped.

'Imma grab a cold one,' he said.

'OK. I'll be in soon, babe.'

'Don't be long. And don't drink too many cocktails – it's empty calories.' He blew her a kiss. She smacked her cheek with it.

I could have smacked him sideways.

Liv turned to me when he'd gone. 'Since meeting you, Rafa's actually *smiled*. I'd forgotten what his smile *looked* like! We've all seen the change in him. Sal says he comes down here all the time, looking for you.'

'I know.'

She put her arm behind her head again, a different arm, revealing another batch of bruises. She saw me looking at them and lowered it quickly to scratch her thigh. 'Mosquito bites. Little shits can't get enough of me.'

My stomach flipped over.

'So,' she said, pointing a long green fingernail at me as she sat up on the edge of her lounger, 'I'll only say this once to you: if you break my brother's heart or mess him around or act all demanding and shit – like, if you are *Cuntasaurus 2: Reloaded* – let it be known that I *will* take your life.'

'Seems fair to me.'

'Oh, I mean it, English Girl. And our mom? She'll spit on your dead body and stamp her stiletto hard into your eye socket.'

'OK.'

'And our brother Nicolas? He'll set your fuckin' bones alight. And our uncles are cops and they'll prolly help us hide your body.'

I laughed. She didn't. 'I wouldn't want to hurt him, Liv. Unless he hurts *me*. Then I'll probably have to... I don't know, cut off his dick, slice up his torso in a bathtub and bury the bastard in the flowerbeds.'

She threw me a look which I couldn't read before bursting into laughter which bounced off the hotel walls. She reached for my hand and squeezed it. '*You* get me, that's a good start. You fuckin' get me. Cuntasaurus never got my humour.'

'You want to track down the old C-Rex and tie her to the back of a truck, maybe drag her around for a while?' I suggested.

She pursed her lips. 'Gimme the keys, Thelma. Just gimme the keys.'

Friday, 10 May – the beachfront, Rocas Calientes

'Hey, try this,' said Raf, handing me a bag with six warm dough balls inside it when I met him on the beachfront that morning. 'Freshly baked.'

And even though I was full, the warm ball was, indeed, all of the noms and a few hundred more. Chocolate oozed out of the centres.

'Oh, my Christ. You could kill me right now and bury me inside a giant one of these and I'd probably wake up and thank you.' We were sitting on the low wall separating the beach from the sidewalk and I kicked my feet against the concrete. I was like a kid again.

Raf laughed, way more than people usually laugh at one of my jokes. He laughed at a lot of my jokes. This helped the fancying thing a lot.

'How the hell do you eat so much and not put on weight?' I asked.

'I work out, not to excess just to trim off the extra. I enjoy it. My mom says, *Si no estás comiendo, no eres feliz.*'

'What does that mean?'

'If you're not eating, you're not happy. Food brings us together. We eat, we grow, we share, it makes us strong. It enriches us.'

'She's not a fan of dieting, I take it, your mum?'

He frowned. '*Ninguna perra flaca te va a complacer, mijo.* Basically, don't truck with skinny bitches, son. She never liked my ex-wife Tina so I guess she was right. Says they starve their brains like they starve their men.'

'I like your mum.'

'She likes you too,' he said, feeding me one of the little doughnut things. 'She wants you to come and celebrate with us in November, for Dia de los Muertos. We come down here for that to be close to our grandma, Dad's mom. *Then* you'll see us eat some food, holy shit. We eat like we're about to go to the chair.'

'What happens for that?'

'We all meet at the hotel, we dress up, paint our faces, walk up to the graveyard with all the stuff. We sing, we dance, we get sad. We scatter petals on the ground, make flower garlands. And we stay with the ones we've lost, all night long. Big crowd of us.'

'We don't do anything like that in the UK.'

'I think every culture has their own way of dealing with grief. We believe during the festival that our loved ones come back to us. We put pictures of them all over their tombs. Trinkets, bottles of perfume, stuff that belonged to them in their lifetimes. Tequila, cookies. To lure them.'

'So, they come back and eat the cookies and drink the tequila?' I asked.

'No,' he laughed, 'it's all to let them know we remember them. To let their spirits know they're not alone.'

I rested my head against his shoulder. 'That's so nice. I should do that. I miss my dad.'

'He knows you do,' he told me, stroking my hair. 'He hears you. You're not alone you know, not if you don't want to be.'

I held him around his waist and put my head on his shoulder. 'You wait till I get crazy. I won't see your ass for dust.'

'So you'll still be lookin' at my ass, huh?'

'Maybe.' I sat up straight, wondering if I should quit while I was ahead – before I got closer to him than was healthy for either of us. 'Maybe this is too good to be true. Or too true to be any good.'

'*Siento que atrapé un rayo. Pero tal vez ella no quiere ser atrapada.*'

'Translation?'

'I caught a lightning bolt. But maybe she doesn't want to be held.'

'You're wrong,' I said. 'I *do* want to be held. But I'm so bad for you, Raf.'

'Why don't you let me be the judge of that, huh?' He started laughing. 'What are you doing to me, girl? You got me lookin' so crazy right now.'

That pulled me up. 'Did you just drop a Beyoncé lyric in there?'

He was still laughing. 'I may have done, yeah.'

And that was all I needed to hear. 'Take me to bed. Right now.'

The second he put the sign on the door handle outside his hotel room, we were tearing into one another. We didn't think, we did what our bodies demanded. We were more or less fully-clothed the first time, I was desperate to feel him inside me as deep as he could go, and he came so quickly but it didn't matter. Because we had the whole night to do it again.

And again.

And do it properly. To take in every section of each other, to allow our skin to bead with sweat and watch each other's tongues and fingertips smooth it away. And weirdly, I liked hearing his heartbeats when I was on him. I thought I could only get that kind of comfort from a cold body. I'd only been turned on like that before by the *lack* of warmth, the certainty of death. But heartbeats, warmth, cuddles with Raf – that shit became addictive. I've never been made love to in that way before. I've had good orgasms with Craig and with AJ too – at least one while he was still alive – but this was brand *new*.

Time was when I'd needed sex and Craig hadn't been home or hadn't been up for it, I'd settle for porn and the biggest dildo in the LoveHoney catalogue. I'd feel *better* – sated but not loved.

With Raf, I felt *loved*.

He was worth all the dick pics, wolf-whistles, insults and crushingly awful Plenty of Fish, Match, Snatch, Bumble, Fumble and Tinder dates I'd ever yawned through. As he lay beside me, tracing the length of my body from my shoulder, down my arm, across my scar and back along, over my hip and down and back again, he said, 'I love that part of you the best. It's like a sculpture. Like you're carved out of marble.' I raked his hair back away from his sweaty forehead and he closed his eyes.

'I'm sleepy.'

'Me too. But I don't wanna sleep.'

We both started singing Aerosmith, right on cue.

'We are so in sync!' I chuckled and we kissed again. Meg Ryan Tier = level completed.

'What's turtle in Spanish?' I asked.

'*Tortuga*,' he said, deeply, sending a little heartbeat to my nethers.

'Oh, like the beach? What's *hot* turtle?'

He frowned. '*Tortuga caliente*.'

'Oh right.'

'Why?'

'Just wondered.'

'Yeah, that's what any right-minded maniac would wonder, I guess.'

'Does that make me weird?'

'Beautifully weird,' he said, flicking my earlobe. I cuddled against his chest. He didn't seem to want to be anywhere else. That was the best part.

'Can I ask you another weird question?'

'I wouldn't expect anything less.'

'Your sister. Those bruises on her arm—'

He fell back against the pillow. 'She says they're mosquito bites.'

'Can mossie bites give you bruises?' I said, resting my head on his bicep.

'Yeah, they can apparently. I looked it up.'

'Do you believe her?'

'No. None of us do. But till she says otherwise, we gotta go with it. She defends him to the hilt. One time she came round for dinner – lip all swollen. Swore she'd tripped on a bathmat and smashed her face on the sink. She won't say a word against him. She wouldn't speak to Mom and Dad for months last time they accused him. Gotta play it real careful when it comes to Edouardo.'

'I like Liv,' I told him, stroking his arm up and down. 'I'd hate to think of her being hurt. Makes me wanna – put Edouardo on our list.'

'Yeah, me too,' he said. 'He's king of the fucking list. Believe me, we've all said our piece to her on this and it never goes well. But we gotta follow her lead.'

'For now.'

'For now.' He pulled me in and kissed me again. 'Hey, why don't you come back to San Diego with us on Sunday?'

'What?'

'Come back with us. Stay for a while. See if you like it. Just be with me.' He could tell I was squirmy. 'It's all right. Forget I said anything. I'll settle for coming to see you every few weeks.' He cuddled me in. 'If you want me to.'

'I *want* you to,' I said. 'But—'

'But what?'

I swallowed my answer – it's what Rhiannon would have done, hiding her true self. But I didn't want to do that – the new me had to be different. Well, as much as she *could* be.

'I need to know I can be without you first.'

'How do you mean?'

'Well, you're going home the day after tomorrow and I'm gonna miss you like mad. But I need to know I can handle that. I need to know I can be all right on my own. Do you know what I'm saying?'

And the stupid idiot said the perfect thing:

'Yeah. I think we *both* need that.' His kisses were slow and gentle and I couldn't get enough of them.

I think I knew for sure how he felt about me the following day: the day he did the David Guetta Face.

Lemme explain:

The David Guetta Face is how I test whether someone is genuinely happy to see me or whether they want me to fuck off – it's the face David Guetta pulls when he sees Kelly Rowland for the first time in the video for 'When Love Takes Over'. Now, I'm not great at assessing people's moods – sometimes people can be pissed off with me and I don't see it. Sometimes people are scared but unless they tell me, 'Hey, you know what? I'm pissing my pants right now,' I wouldn't get the hint. But I do know pure joy and I see it in David Guetta's face when he sees Kelly in that video.

Kelly's walking through the wind machine towards the beach party, looking boss, and Guetta's pushing his trolley along, setting up his decks, plugging in his amps, and the wind whips up and the seagulls are all flocking around Kelly and she's got her stilettos off and she's parading up the sand in this stunning dress like the total qween she is and she's walking through the water, hair all blowy, and it turns night time and Guetta's decks are all set up and the music's blasting out and he's having it large and Kelly finally reaches him at the decks and David Guetta looks at her with this face –

This *I'm so damn happy to see you* face.

My point is I never get a David Guetta Face from anyone. And yeah, I know why, I'm a miserable beeyotch, is it any wonder, right? My mother hated me. Bullied at school. Colleagues all thought I was a weirdo. Craig couldn't wait to bury his clam hammer in the nearest acre of blonde that wasn't me. Nobody's ever pleased to see *me*.

But when I came down to breakfast at the hotel that following Saturday morning and I saw all his relatives in the dining room, and Raf helping himself to eggs, he turned to me and he did the David Guetta Face.

And that was when I knew. I knew he was genuinely into me. And he made me believe I was something I never thought I could be: normal. I don't think I stopped smiling all day.

At least until I got on my bike and rode back up to the Hacienda after we'd said our 'Goodbyes' and 'I'll Miss Yous'. It was only then that the contentment started to ebb away from me and a new feeling slid into my DMs.

The strangest, coldest feeling that I was being watched.

Monday, 13 May – Hacienda Santuaria

1. *The creator of the #CutForRhiannon hashtag on Twitter – I'll do the cutting, thanks.*
2. *Guy who punched his dog to death in the latest animal abuse video doing the rounds. I'll find you one day, Mark Cordero. You mark my words.*
3. *That British comedian turned criminologist who tries to psychoanalyse me on his true crime podcast. Seems confident but you put me or any of the inhabitants of Monster Mansion in a room with him and you wait for the smell of pissed pants.*
4. *Rafael's brother-in-law Edouardo*
5. *Edouardo again. He deserves to be on here twice.*

Whenever someone you love leaves you, or you leave them, it feels like they've taken a piece of you with them. And the place where that missing part is, it always hurts.

Sadness consumed me like a shroud all that day after Raf had left for San Diego and I knew it would be a month until I saw him again. I kicked around the Hacienda, on my own for once as Tenoch and the Chipmunks were out, but I couldn't even take advantage of that because there was nothing I wanted to do. After all my chores were done, I opened the lid of the office laptop, retreating to the affection-starved millennial's equivalent of a cuddle – the internet.

Is it possible for a serial killer to fall in love? was the first thing I googled. I learned a whole lot about hybristophiliacs – people who fall in love *with* serial killers purely because they are serial killers – but next to nothing about myself and what *I* was feeling.

The hybristophiliac search led to recent articles about the Rhiannon Lewis stans who were still out there, still with me in spirit, still loving the Sweetpea Killer and all her darkly devious deeds. There were more interviews with names from my past – Lucille from the PICSOs, Daisy Chan from the *Gazette*, White Nancy from WOMBAT, the family of Troy Shearer, the rapist I killed in the alley in Cardiff. More think pieces on why I did what I did, what might have caused it and an updated documentary about Priory Gardens, skewed towards 'the creation of a monster'.

An 'At Home With Freddie Litton-Cheney' piece in *Hello!* mag.

And a wedding announcement in *The Times*.

Mr and Mrs P.D. Proudlove are pleased to announce the marriage of their daughter Claudia Margaret Gulper to Mitchell Aaron Silverton. The marriage took place on Saturday, 27 April at Southwark Cathedral. The Proudloves are pleased to welcome Mitch into their family.

This linked to a small news article:

Sweetpea's Baby Gets New Family Months After Killer Gave Up Child For Adoption.

Claudia was married. Ivy was five months old and she had a family. A mum and a dad. There was no mention of her anywhere else and still no pictures online but this news gave me an uneasy realisation: a sense that my daughter really did belong to other people now. She had a daddy now too. I hoped he loved her like the one I took away from her. I couldn't dwell on it for long – the gnawing in my chest grew the more I thought about it.

I closed the laptop and went outside. Right about now, having hit such a peak of frustration, I'd have gone out and catfished some pervert or stabbed Tenoch's punch bag or something. But, for once, rage wasn't the feeling that crackled through me. I was just sad.

I went to my plants. I sat on the edge of a raised bed, between two poinsettias, resting my face on the cool petals.

'Calm minds make better decisions,' I said, getting myself into a cross-legged position. 'Focus on the breaths... focus on what matters. Deep in... deep out. Focus on what matters. I am here. I am breathing. I am loved... deep in... deep out... she's safe now. She's safe.'

Monday, 3 June (early) – Hacienda Santuaria

1. *People who use the phrase 'a hundred years young'*
2. *People who bang on about hot box yoga*
3. *People who don't let you know when you have something in your teeth*
4. *Paco*
5. *Paco*
6. *Paco*

I lay there, in between sleeping and waking, searching for an explanation for the noise. Sometimes a *caracara* would be chirping in a cactus somewhere and that would wake me up. Or a brush rabbit would trip the security lights. Other times, like that night, a noise couldn't be explained. Hearing voices, I crept downstairs. In the living room was your average midnight vision – my 60-something Mexican renegade roommate Tenoch, wearing a Kevlar vest and brandishing an assault rifle.

'Get back upstairs,' he whispered. 'Lock yourself in the bathroom. I will whistle when it's safe.'

'What is it?' I whispered back, pulling my dressing gown tight.

'Uninvited company.'

'Who?'

His phone app security system had nudged him in the early hours to let him know someone had been captured on video climbing over the front gates. 'Paco said we would get a warning this week. He couldn't be sure when.'

'The cartel? They're here?'

He didn't answer. 'Take the Glock from my desk and get back upstairs, go now!'

'How many of them?'

'Enough. Now go!'

I caught a movement on the pool terrace and hunkered down. A figure had crept out of the bushes and hid behind the stone temazcal. I caught the flash of a white skull bandana in the glint of the security light and I saw he had a gun as well, and not a little one either – an AR-15, like Tenoch.

'I can help you,' I whispered. 'I can reload or something. You can't fight them with only one good arm.'

'I've done it before, now get out of here. I can't protect us if I'm worrying about you. For the last fucking time, *gatita*, GO. NOW!'

So *that* was frustrating. I had to grab the Glock as directed and scurry back upstairs like a good girl, waiting for Papi to rescue me from the toilet.

It was pathetic. *I* was pathetic.

And I sat on said toilet, like a pathetic girl would. I waited an age, freezing my feet off on the cold tiles.

'This is ridiculous,' I huffed, crossing my legs. Nothing happened for a long time. Until it did.

Even from upstairs, through two closed doors, the gunfire was deafening – glass breaking, men shouting, guns *rat-atat-atat-atat-atat* rattling off rounds like a fucking Clint Eastwood movie. I flicked off the light and jumped in the bath, crouching low, holding my Glock close like a teddy bear.

And I admit it – I was terrified. In my head I was sent right back there – to Priory Gardens, when the mad man smashed his way in. When I was helpless and small and all the babies were screaming. I was more scared than I had ever been in any situation I had put myself in. *Before* I'd had the upper hand – speed, surprise, a knife, scissors. But with guns, it was no contest. The odds were stacked, threatening to tumble down and crush me completely.

The worst part was when all the noise stopped and it was still dark in the bathroom and all I could hear were my own quickening breaths. Not knowing who was still alive. Not knowing if Tenoch would come up and get me. It felt like hours. I listened out, trying to calm my breathing. And there came the distant but definite sound of a whistle.

I ventured out of the bath, unlocking the door and manoeuvring down the stairs, one at a time, the Glock held out shakily before me. I tried to remember every film I'd ever seen with the same scenario – tried to keep my back to the wall, gun pointed, watchful for movement, making swift transfers from corner to corner. There came a noise from the kitchen – deep breathing.

The room was a fucking mess – windows smashed, furniture upended, two large lumps motionless on the floor. And Tenoch stood there, his back to the refrigerators, sweating profusely, clutching his side.

I flicked on the light. 'Shit, are you OK?'

'We're gonna need new windows,' he wheezed.

I looked out across to the living room to a sea of broken glass and smashed wood. The bodies of two men, all in black, skull bandanas wrapped around their faces. The security light on the pool terrace illuminated another. They'd shot up my flower beds too. Again.

'Bastards.'

But I couldn't dwell on that – Tenoch's grey T-shirt was half red with blood from his pecs down. He'd been shot in the belly and again at the top of his leg. His *good* leg. The blood was spurting.

'Jesus Christ,' I said, placing the Glock down on the island and taking his weight. I manoeuvred him over to a stool to locate the first aid kit. 'This is not good, this is not fucking good.'

'Yeah,' he panted. 'I sorta guessed. Look at my back... is it clean?'

'No, it's pretty fucking messy from where I'm standing,' I said, opening and closing cupboard doors.

'Exit wound, *gatita*. Did the bullet come through?'

'I don't know. I can't see a thing, it's all so fucked up. I don't think so. What do I do?'

'Ahhh,' he winced, delving into his pocket. 'Paco... will send a car.'

'I'll call 911, give me the phone.'

'No, you not call anyone, *I* call.' He put in his number achingly slowly and scrolled his contacts with a shaking thumb. 'I call Paco.'

His face was losing colour by the second – all his life was seeping out of him. He made the call to Paco, spoke a garbled mess of pain-edged Spanish which I half-translated as 'send the helicopter' – *envía el helicóptero* – then he ended the call and sank down against the cabinets. 'He'll… be here soon.'

'Can I get you anything? A cup of tea? Hot towels?'

'That's childbirth.' He took my hand with his free one – the other holding his stomach in. 'I am glad you are here.'

It was only when I helped settle him against the cupboard and stood that I saw the man, standing by the windows. A *fourth* man.

'Oh, shit.' I ducked behind the island as shots rang out above my head.

'Shoot!' Tenoch wheezed, scrabbling for the Glock on the countertop.

I waited for the next round of bullets and when it had stopped I reached up for it and wrapped my hand around it.

'HE'S RELOADING. DO IT NOW!'

He was right there, feet away, creeping towards us when I pointed the gun and aimed and fired and *WHAM* – half his fucking head exploded – half against me, half against the cabinets. His body crumpled and I staggered backwards. It wasn't a delicious kill, like some of the others had been. I was removed from it, using the gun, and I saw death for what it was for once – messy and bloody and final. And not in the least bit sexy.

Tenoch struggled back to his feet. 'I must… get to Paco.'

I was still standing there with the gun shaking in my grip, mouth open, wiping blood and skull fragments from my face. A horn sounded outside. As I helped Tenoch outside and along Spiky Plant Alley towards the front gates, he stumbled to the ground and I fell with him.

'What do I do with the bodies?' I asked.

'Bury them like the others,' he wheezed. 'Burn everything broken. I will send Paco and his boys to fix the windows.'

The black BMW waited – headlights on, engine rumbling. I got him through the gates before we both stumbled to the ground. Two men got out of the car and ran to help – Ming and Arturo.

'How did you get here so quickly?' I said but neither of them answered and Tenoch yelled out in pain as they bore his weight and lifted him back onto his feet. 'Is he going to be OK?'

'You need to look after the place, *gatita*,' Tenoch wheezed as they eased him into the back seat.

'I will, I promise, I'm not going anywhere,' I told him.

'Good girl,' he said, stroking my cheek with his whole hand, like my dad would. 'Keep yourself safe... you know how everything works.'

Tenoch took one last look at me as Ming closed the back door on him and ran round to the driver's side as Arturo got in the front. There was this look in his eyes as the door closed: the same one Sandra Huggins had before I brought down the axe. The same look Derek Scudd had before I mounted him with that pillow – fear he was about to die.

The car sped off down the dirt track, disappearing into the dust on the dark road until all was silent.

And I was left there, alone, in the middle of the night, with a man's liquefied head contents still running down my face.

Thursday, 6 June –
Hacienda Santuaria

1. *People on TV shows who order drinks then leave them, mid-conversation*
2. *Soap operas or TV dramas with domestic violence storylines that imprison the woman the moment she fights back*
3. *People who slurp their drinks, on TV or in the same room as me*
4. *Everybody Loves Raymond – I don't*
5. *Size Zero models who claim to eat like pigs. Fuck off.*

Three days I spent at the Hacienda alone. After Ming and Arturo came to replace the smashed windows the following morning, there were no other visitors. There was no news on Tenoch's condition either. I missed people. I missed David and his drawings. I missed Saúl's fat little belly jiggling whenever he laughed and the way Mátilda always held my hand when we were looking for insects in the borders. I missed Raf so much I could barely think about his face without bursting into tears.

I buried the dead men in the back field, like I'd done before, taking my radio out for company, and doing little else but dig and ache for the full three days. Except this time, the hole took less time and was almost big enough at the end of the second day. Maybe I was stronger or maybe it was the old school Madonna marathon one radio station was playing that put fire into my arms one afternoon, I don't know, but it was a lot less arduous than before. It was even kind of enjoyable.

I'd almost reached the bottom of my trough when my shovel clanked against something hard – another stone, I figured at first, scraping around it to reveal and dislodge it. But the more I scraped, the bigger the stone got.

Turned out – not a stone, but a skull.

Fuck knows how many people were buried in that field. But here's a weird thing – the sight made me puke. Made me scramble out of the hole and leap over the side and barf right up. Like, for once, the sight of death was abhorrent to me. It was a *normal* person's reaction.

And I got to think that perhaps there was such a thing as a normal existence for me. That the Hacienda wasn't where I belonged at all.

Early on the morning of the third day, I was awoken by the sound of a key in the front door. It was Ming, closely followed by Stuzzy and Arturo, and all of them were carrying in a piece of medical equipment – a trolley stuffed with new packets of syringes, bundles of clean bandages, IV bags and a defibrillator and a cool box labelled 'SANGRE HUMANA' and plastered in a load of warning labels – taking it all upstairs to Tenoch's bedroom

379

'What's going on?' I said as they all walked past me. 'Where's Tenoch?'

'I'm here, *gatita*,' said a voice at the door. And there he was, uneasy on his feet and leaning heavily on Paco who was helping him from the back seat of the BMW, looking much paler. 'I'm here. I'm home.' He reached out and cupped my face as I went to greet him.

'What's going on? How come they let you out?'

'I wanted to come home,' he panted, obviously in some pain.

'This is his house, remember?' said Paco, with his doggiest glare, practically carrying Tenoch straight past me.

The last man in was one I instantly recognised – my surgeon, Dr Gonzales from the medical centre.

'Rhiannon, it's so nice to see you again!' he beamed, shaking my hand with both of his. 'I only wish it could have been in better circumstances.'

'What's happening? He doesn't look well enough to be home so soon.' Paco helped Tenoch up each individual stair in turn.

'He insisted,' said the doc in hushed tones. 'Said if he was going to die, he wanted to be here.'

'He's going to die?'

'It's early days. He needs complete rest and some new blood in his system. We did a midline operation to clamp a slow leak in his abdomen and we have stitched him up but we have to keep a close eye on him. Regular scans and monitoring so he doesn't develop an infection. Two of the boys are matches for his type – they will donate what he needs.'

'But he's going to *die*?' I said again.

'Don't worry about him, Rhiannon – this isn't his first

380

rodeo. These were the twelfth and thirteenth bullets I've taken out of him. He's a fighter. There's no doubt about that.'

They were all fussing and flapping about Tenoch in his bedroom all day and I couldn't get close to him until about seven o'clock that night. Only then did Paco and his Chipmunks exit stage left – another 'little job' they had to do for Tenoch – but which I wasn't told anything about.

When the doctor was happy Tenoch was bedded down for the night, he announced he was going to get some shut-eye himself.

'I will be next door, Tenoch. If you need me, press your button.'

Tenoch lifted his wired button and pressed it, causing a small device in the doctor's hand to vibrate and flash a red light.

'Great, it works. I will see you later.'

Tenoch patted a vacant spot on the bed beside him. 'Come.'

'You should have stayed at the hospital,' I told him as he held my hand. 'What's wrong?' He had that pained look again – the fear face.

'I thought you would have gone.'

'You asked me to look after the place. I've cleaned, I mowed the lawn. The Chipmunks put new windows in...'

'What about the men? What did you do with them?'

'I buried them. They're in the back field with the others.'

'You bury them straight away? No dressing them up or reading them bedtime stories this time?'

'As soon as it got light. My back didn't hurt as much this time. Think I got into my groove a bit more.'

Tenoch smiled. 'Good girl.'

'I missed you.'

'Did you?'

'Yeah, of course. I didn't know what was happening.'

'Neither did I,' he said. 'Your soldier boy been visiting, has he?'

'What? How did you—'

He chuckled. 'You still have much to learn about me, *gatita*. Remember what I said – as far as you're concerned, I have eyes everywhere.'

'I knew it. That why Paco's been following me to the hotel, isn't it?'

'Not always Paco. They take it in turns. I told them to be discreet.'

'Have you been bugging me too? How did you know he was a soldier?'

'It was easy. Facial recognition app, cross-checked his army records. But I want you to know – I did it to protect you. I wanted to know he was a good influence.'

'And is he?'

'From what I know about him, yes he is.'

'Good. Because I think I might… love him.'

He patted my hand and his face brightened. 'Good. And you happy?'

'More than I thought I could be.'

'I am glad. I wanted this for you.'

'What if it doesn't work out though? I haven't seen him in almost a month and he's supposed to be coming down here next week and maybe he won't still feel the same about me.' His TV was warbling on in the background – Blanche was being necked by some octogenarian lothario on the lanai.

'Have faith,' he wheezed, reaching for his pill bottle and twisting off the cap. He tossed back a few of the pills, forcing them down his throat with a swig of a smoothie. 'It will work out because you will make sure it does.'

'What about if Rhiannon, you know… comes back?'

'She's your dark side. Everyone has one. You cannot be whole without her. But I think maybe you have tamed her now. She will not come out unless you open the door to her cage.'

I squeezed his hand. 'Thank you for everything.'

'Thank *you*…'

'Don't you dare say "for being a friend".'

He laughed and the laugh turned into a painful cringe that he blew out, clutching his stomach. 'I could not be prouder of you than if you were my own Marisol.'

A shot of adrenaline went straight to my heart and bloomed in my body – from my heart and outwards. 'Whoa. That means a lot.'

'You must travel. Go places, do things. Be happy. You are like your flowers – you will only last so long in this world so you need to make the most of your life. I wish I had a second chance to be better.'

'Why are you saying this? Is this like a deathbed thing?'

He squeezed my hand and looked at the little yarn kitten with button eyes I had bought him from the market. He put it on his chest and stroked it. 'My *gatita*. You have been good to me.' He noticed I was wearing the necklace I'd taken from Marisol's jewellery box, lifting it away from my chest and studying it in the dying light. 'This is a fire opal,' he said. 'It was mined in the hills near here. It's beautiful, yes?'

'Yeah,' I said. 'I saw it in her jewellery box and I was drawn to it.'

I followed his gaze out to the corridor where the gold leaf painting of Marisol shimmered in the dying light of day. 'She was beautiful too.' He'd never stop missing her.

That's what children do to a person. They rip you wide open, forever.

'Tenoch? Tenoch?' And with my little yarn *gatita* on his chest, he fell into a deep, snoring sleep.

Friday, 14 June – Holiday Inn el Agua, Rocas Calientes

Tenoch grew stronger by the day and was up and about again by the time Rafael had come back to me that Friday, like he'd promised.

Me and Raf spent a blissful few days together, barely leaving his room. And each morning when we'd appear late for breakfast, both burning with afterglow, his family would lead the hotel dining room in a round of applause which ordinarily would have been hella embarrassing but we just laughed.

With Dr Gonzales permanently at the house to look after Tenoch, I didn't have to concern myself with his care at all so I could stay at the hotel indefinitely, joining in with the dancing, the late-night drinking games, the deep philosophical and political debates. And Rafael would kiss me and hold me as the night grew colder on the terrace and lend me his Venetian Bergamot-scented hoody when I began to shiver.

Seriously. It was like a fucking Hugh Grant movie, without the irritating posh friends and floppy hair.

Early that Friday evening, we headed out on the beach to feed the strays some of the scraps of our sandwiches at lunch.

By chance, a group of biologists from a local conservation project were releasing buckets of hatched baby turtles into the ocean and we were invited to help. We took two Olive Ridley babies each and placed them on the sand about ten metres from the water's edge. And we watched them all scurry up the wet sand, heading for the water, disappearing into the tumbling waves, never to be seen again.

'They're so tiny,' I said, holding Rafael as we watched them all go, little black dots, swallowed up by the waves.

'I wonder if any of them'll make it. I overheard one of the volunteers saying only about one in a thousand get to adulthood.'

'Seriously?'

'Yeah. But the ones that do live to, like, a hundred years. Like tortoises.'

'That's pretty cool.'

We sat on the wet sand, watching the sun go down and the turtles swim away and the volunteers picked up their baskets and walked back up to their vans.

'How come you never talk about your army career? I asked him.

'Huh?'

'We talk all the time. You ask about me, I ask about you. You tell me about your ex-wife, your favourite films, songs, pizza toppings. But you never ever talk about the army.'

'Not much to say. I got kicked out.'

'Yeah, but what was it like? Did you get to kill people?'

He looked at me. 'Yes.'

'Tell me about it.'

'I don't wanna put those images in your mind.' He kissed the centre of my forehead.

'If they're in your mind, I want them in mine as well,' I said.

'The last tour I was on,' he sniffed, 'I was burnt out. We were a contingent of ground combat troops supporting coalition forces against ISIS in Syria. It was my third tour. I'd seen some things on the last one I couldn't process. Psych nurse said it was "part and parcel and I had to compartmentalise it" but I didn't know how.'

'Compartmentalise what?'

'Seeing a woman stoned to death. Finding the charred body of a 12-year-old girl, set on fire for *talking* to a boy. On my second tour, our battalion came across a quarry in the desert where these people had been crucified. A few of 'em were kids. One was still alive. He'd been there for days. They haunt my dreams, these people.'

'Did he live, the boy?'

He shook his head. 'Another time, there was this house where an explosion had gone off – we were sent in to clear it – and I moved a couple planks out the way and there was a baby under the rubble. Covered in blood.'

'Holy shit.'

'My parents were so proud when I joined up,' Raf continued. 'It's a big deal when a Latino gets honours in the American military. My dad has some crazy-assed debts on his business that he doesn't think I know about but even so, they threw the biggest party. Then I found out about Tina and… I lost my shit. I don't think I've ever fully got it back. Salomé says I wanted to get kicked out. She says I'm an artist with paint, not blood. She might be right. I thought it was for me but … I've still let them all down.'

'No, you haven't. They love you no matter what. I bet there

are a lot of other military families who'd love to have their sons or daughters back home with them.'

He laughed, holding my face with one hand and kissing my cheek. 'You're talking like a mom.'

'Am I? Oh.' That pulled me up.

'It's OK, baby. You don't need to make me feel better. I know I've fucked up. I'm 33 years old and I buss tables in my dad's restaurant. I put up shelves and paint walls for my aunt. I fitted my sister's wardrobe.' He stared out to sea. 'I don't have a clue who I am now.'

'Guess what,' I said to him, bringing him back to face me. 'I don't know who I am either.'

'You wanna find out who we are together?'

I nodded. 'Big time.'

I liked how I was when I was with him – he smoothed the hate out of me, and I tried to hug and kiss the sadness out of him. But sooner or later he was going to see the real me – and that would be the ultimate clincher. He didn't have to wait long either.

The following night, in fact.

We'd spent the perfect Saturday together at Campo A Mesa, a sunny, field-to-table restaurant up in the hills, eating lunch and petting ponies, lying in long grass, drinking bottomless mimosas and falling asleep in each other's arms. And that evening we came back to the beachfront and ate fresh crab on the griddle, cooked by one of the fishermen, and Rafael and he got into an easy conversation which he translated so I could join in. It was a magical one-of-a-kind sort of day.

'You have cilantro in your teeth,' he said as we walked back to the hotel.

'Do I?' I said. 'I don't have a mirror.'

'I'll be your mirror,' he said, turning to me face on.

'You'll need to get it out for me then, won't you?' I said as he leaned into me, holding my hands and kissed me slowly, deeply, edging his tongue inside my mouth and licking across my top teeth. I pulled away. 'Did you get it?'

'Nah, I'll have to try again.' And he did it again, this time all along the bottom set instead.

'Got it now?'

'Yeah, I got it,' he said. I kissed him again. I didn't ever want to stop. 'Are you good at getting cilantro out of other places?' I asked. 'Cos I got some in some other places too.'

He got all embarrassed and dipped his head and I nudged him, giving his ass a little kick as he strode out in front of me.

'It's been a nice day, hasn't it?'

'The best,' he said, putting his arm around me.

'Don't let's stop having days like this.'

'OK, if you insist.'

But, of course, there came the banana skin. They don't just stop dropping from the sky because you're in love. At least, not for me.

We were walking across the car park at the back of the hotel and two guys were sitting on a low wall, drinking.

'Hey girl, you got some good titties there,' the blond American shouted, followed by the laugh of his tall, red-haired friend.

'Keep walking,' said Raf, squeezing my hand a little tighter.

'I'm not afraid of them,' I said. 'I'm afraid *for* them.'

'Yeah. Me too.' Rafael tried to laugh but he was winding tight.

The comments carried on, all across the parking lot. 'Hey girl, come back and show us those big titties. Come on. You can do better than him!'

God knows why he'd said that. Rafael was a walking-talking Aztec god and he was skinny-assed dick crust in ill-fitting jeans.

'Come on over here and suck on this big ol' dick, babe!'

His mate was even worse – a ginger belch on legs wearing Letterman sweats and puffing out his chest to appear more hench than he actually was. I'd seen more hench on Judi Dench.

We were almost at the back steps to the sun terrace when they got in front of us. Raf squeezed my hand tighter and stepped in front of me.

'Girl, come on, you got a twofer here. Where you going? Will you let us suck on those big titties?'

Hurr-hurr-hurr. In stereo. They proceeded to make suckling noises. I was strangely calm, God knows why.

Raf's hackles were up. '*Podrían cerrar la boca y tener un poco de respeto ese, huh?*'

This only made them laugh louder. 'OK, Beaner, whatever you say,' said the blond.

'*Chinga Tu Madre!*' Raf yelled and spat on the ground before them. This only caused the red-haired one to unzip his fly and grab his package. He thrust it forward.

'How about you watch us take your girl, *cabrón*? I'll take the pink, and my boy here can take the stink. Then we switch.'

'Yeah, let's cuck the fucker!' said Blondie.

'Uh, do I get a say in any of this?' I said, craning my neck around Raf's broad shoulders. *Hurrr-hurrr-hurrrrrrrrrrrr.*

I was getting bored by this point. I did not want to fight

– I just wanted to leave. I leaned into Raf. 'Why don't we go to my place and fuck each other's brains out, hmm?' I didn't want to rise to their bait nor their flaccid penises which were, by this point, dangling quite openly in our general direction.

But Raf was steaming. 'Yeah. Before I do something *they'll* live to regret.'

We turned on our heels away from the hotel and towards the beach.

'Hey, you gettin' angry with us, *pendejo*?'

'Keep walking,' I said.

'Girl, we're not giving up on you!'

We headed down the steps to the beach. The walk seemed endless and made all the more difficult in the shifting sand, but after a short while, we couldn't hear them anymore. Thought we'd lost them.

But they'd followed us. We got to the second set of steps along the beach and there they were, on the steps with their bottles, zips still undone.

'Hey baby girl, where you been all my life?' *Hurr-hurr-hurr.*

'I've had enough of this,' said Rafael, marching up the sand towards them and yanking the beer bottle out of the blond one's hand, smashing it on the steps. The ginger one grabbed him to hold him back as the blond started punching him in the stomach.

By the time I got to them, Raf had straddled the blond on the ground and was punching his face as the redhead choked him in a headlock. My boy was fighting two guys at once – I'd never seen anything hotter. It was like live gay porn. Even so, I steamed in, picking up one of the bottles, and smashing the ginger guy over the head. Beer and blood spurted.

'I got it!' Rafael puffed as the ginge staggered backwards.

But I couldn't let go. New Me wanted to do the right thing and leave it to the trained soldier, but Rhiannon didn't want to be left out.

'Take him,' I said, nodding at the blond. 'I got this one.'

I lurched my head back and nutted him square in the face, the way Dad liked to do, kicking him backwards into a plastic table and chairs. I was on him like a panther, mounting his trunk and grasping his head with one hand, half a glass bottle in the other, stabbing his face, his neck, his eye sockets. *Stabstabstabstabstabstabstabstabstabstab.* Just like old times.

The man screamed and beat my arms, smashing into my throat with his fists as he writhed on the sand. I didn't know what was happening until Rafael had hold of me, shouting

'Let go, baby! Let *go*!'

I turned my attention to the guy's shorts and yanked them down, grabbing his cock in one hand and the broken bottle in the other but before I could get stuck in, Rafael had pulled me away. The blond guy, now covered in blood too, scrabbled for his screaming, blind friend and dragged him up the beach, away from us.

'We've gotta get out of here,' Rafael panted, pulling me to my feet and taking my hand. 'Come on.'

I dropped the bottle and we ran through the streets and didn't stop until we had reached the cemetery where we could hide amongst the trees. We were both covered in blood, shaking like leaves and laughing like maniacs.

'Fuck!' Raf shouted, grabbing an empty jug from one of the graves and filling it with water from a nearby tap. He poured it over my hands first then his own to wash away the blood. 'Fuck, fuck, fuck! Where are you hurt?' He held my face with his free hand.

'I don't think I am,' I panted. 'Nothing hurts. I feel amazing!' And I laughed, hysterically, almost in his face. I was so happy – it was the first time ever something like that had happened and I hadn't risen to the bait until I had to. And I had done it to protect Rafael. It was for him, not for me. I loved him. I loved *me*. I loved us.

'Your lip's bleeding,' he said, caressing my face so gently.

'So's yours.'

He pulled off his shirt and tore it right down the sleeve, soaking it with water and padding it gently over my mouth. We caught our breaths and wiped our faces and he sat beside me on a tomb.

'My God, you can throw a punch, girl.' He dabbed at my mouth with the torn cloth, making a face I couldn't read.

'What's that face for?'

'Doesn't that hurt you?'

'No. It was fun beating someone up with you tonight.'

'You really *are* a maniac. Where'd you learn to fight like that?'

'I did warn you. Daddy made a soldier out of me.'

'Your eyes went black, baby.'

'They were hurting us. That's all I could see. It's like everything became loud in my head.' I touched his lip. 'Does that hurt?'

'No, I'm good. I'm just thinkin' 'bout you. What if *he'd* had a knife?'

'I didn't think about that. I would have killed for you tonight.'

'I'd kill for you every night.'

And he held on tight to me – tight enough that I felt secure, but not so tight I couldn't leave if I'd wanted to. When he pulled away, he removed the hair that had become stuck in the blood and looked me face on. 'You know, my grandmother said something to me when she first met my ex-wife. She said, "*Ella te debilitara*, Rafael." You know what that means?'

'No.'

'She will weaken you. You know what she said about *you* when she met you? "*Ella te fortalecerà*." She will strengthen you. Abuela's 98 and she's never been wrong about anything.'

And we kissed so fiercely, blood trickling into my mouth, until I couldn't tell whose I was tasting.

Sunday, 16 June – Holiday Inn el Agua, Rocas Calientes

1. Paco

I decided to go back to San Diego with Rafael and his family that Sunday evening – they had a flight booked for 8 p.m and I was going to join them to cement my fresh start. Raf had told them all about the men who'd attacked us and I'd won some major fam points for stepping up to defend him and Bianca had cuddled us both for the longest time, before clipping Raf around the ear for 'starting a fight'.

'I didn't start it, Mom, they started it. We—'

'—finished it,' I added. Raf winked at me as his mother scanned his face, probably doing the X-ray thing for signs of internal bleeding.

'She's going to come back with us tonight, Mama.'

'You are?' said Bianca. 'That's wonderful! We will book your flight.'

'No, it's OK, I can do that, don't worry.'

'I insist, we pay for your flight. Nicolas can do it on his app. Let him know your passport number.'

'I'll have to get it – it's back at the house.'

'We have to be out of the rooms at noon, then we will go down to the beach for the afternoon until we have to go to the airport. You come, yes?'

'Well, I should go back and spend some time with my uncle, I think, say goodbye. But thank you. I'll meet you back here later.'

'The cars will leave at six,' she said before kissing me on both cheeks and grabbing a plate from the stack and reaching for the serving spoon in the scrambled egg.

'I'll pick you up about five thirty,' said Raf as he saw me out of the hotel after breakfast and walked me back to my bike along the beachfront. He gripped my hand. 'I'm real glad you're coming back with us.'

'Yeah, so am I.'

'You got something on your mind?'

'How did you know? *I* didn't even know something was on my mind until you said it.'

'I can tell with you. You go all quiet and you sort of do this staring thing. It's, like, momentary but I see it.'

'I'm gonna miss my uncle, that's all. He's been good to me.'

'It's not forever. You can come back whenever you want.'

'I don't think I can,' I said and fell against him into a hug.

'Why not?'

'He's not going to be… with us much longer,' I said.

'Oh baby, I'm sorry,' said Raf, rubbing his hand up and down my back in long strokes, which was so soothing I almost fell asleep against him as he held me there. 'Why didn't you tell me?'

'I've been trying to block it out. Pretend it wasn't happening.'

He didn't seem to want any further explanation. Must have thought I meant cancer. 'Do you want me to come back with you and get your stuff?'

'No, I'll be OK.' I stood on my tiptoes and kissed him. 'Go have a good day with your fam. Say bye to Salomé for me. I'll see you later.'

'Five thirty,' he said, not letting go of my hand. He pulled me back in as I tried to leave.

'What's up?'

'Are you gonna be all right?'

'Yeah. I got my bike.'

'I can take you up there in the car. It won't take ten minutes.' I gave him the eyebrows. 'I know. We gotta survive apart to be better together.'

'Something like that.'

I gave him one final lingering kiss and unchained my bike from the racks near the ice cream shop. He waved me goodbye and I rode away.

When I got to the Hacienda, I suppose it was around 11 a.m. My plan was to pack my bag, say my goodbyes, and be back down with him for a one o'clock lunch. That isn't what happened.

For a start, when I got inside, the house was silent. I ran upstairs to tell Tenoch I was leaving but he wasn't there – his bedroom was empty. All the medical equipment had gone, there was no Dr Gonzales, the bed was neatly made, and the little yarn *gatita* I'd bought him sat alone in the centre. I picked it up and called out to him again, louder.

'Tenoch?'

No answer, came the reply.

He hadn't been outside for weeks so it was odd that he was nowhere within earshot. An uneasy thought arrived – what if he'd taken a turn in the night? 'Tenoch?' I called again. But there was still no answer.

I went into my room and started packing my rucksack, gingerly, without much thought, still listening out for him. Maybe he was in the gym. Or maybe he and the doctor gone for a walk. I didn't want to go without saying goodbye. But I didn't want to miss lunch with Raf's family either.

When my bag was packed, I got to the top of the stairs and an uneasy feeling washed over me. I looked back at Tenoch's bedroom – just as a shadow passed below me in the hall.

'Tenoch?'

Footsteps paced to the bottom of the stairs – it was Paco. Unshaven. Greasy. Black vest, black jeans, heavy black boots. He looked up at me, swigging a Pacifico, face peppered in sweat. 'What are *you* doing here?'

'Waiting for you,' he said, gesturing to my packed bag with the little yarn *gatita* poking out of the top. 'Going somewhere?'

'Yeah,' I said, descending and side-stepping him into the living room. 'Where's Tenoch?'

'Gone. Where are *you* going?'

'What do you mean, gone? Where's he gone? When will he be back?'

'You tell me.'

'What?'

'*Papi ha desaparecido, chica.* He's gone. Vanished. In a puff of smoke. And if he's taken *my* fucking money, I'm going to rip his fucking heart out.'

I carried on down the stairs – Paco watched as I took every one. I attempted to walk past him but he grabbed my chin in his iron grip. 'Ow, the fuck are you doing?'

'Where's he gone, you little bitch? Tell me or I'm going to fuck you up.'

I dropped my bag, attempting to prise his hand from my face. 'Get off me! I don't know where he's gone, I haven't *been* here, have I? Last time I saw him he was bedridden!'

He dropped the bottle and drew his gun from his pocket – the pistol I'd seen in his glovebox. He held it against my temple. 'Where. Is. My. Money?'

'*What* money?'

'I've seen you two talking in corners, all quiet so I won't hear. You know where it is. It better be here.'

'Why the hell would he tell me where his money was?'

'You know,' he seethed. 'You fucking know everything. And you're gonna tell me, one way or another.' He pulled me into the living room by my hair – it had been trashed again, like before when the men had shot the place up except this time the windows were intact – it was everything *else* that wasn't. Kitchen cupboards spewed open, drawers were pulled out, the TV was riddled with bullet holes and most of the sofa cushions lay ripped and torn. There were even some large, raggedy holes in the walls.

'What the f—'

But before I could blink, his fist smashed into my face.

'*Todos ellos, los niños. Tráemelas. Todos ellos, los niños. Tráemelas. No me importa. Llega aquí ahora, rapido.*'

I stirred slowly, my face stinging, brain throbbing. Paco's

voice – a one-way phone conversation. He was pacing the kitchen.

'*Esperamos a que la rata tome el queso.*'

I lay on the rug, my vision all blurry, watching him from the floor, pacing up and down, opening the fridge, tossing stuff down on the counter, tearing packets. The *click-hiss* of a soda can.

'Hey, you're awake!' said Paco, tossing his phone onto the kitchen island and coming back towards me. 'I made you a sandwich.' He settled a plate next to my head and placed the soda can beside it. 'We're gonna be here a while.'

There was a short wheeze of air behind me and I tilted my head to see Arturo, his cheek smushed into the floor, dead eyes staring, blood pumping from his neck into the rug.

'He wanted to untie you,' said Paco, crunching through an apple.

I went to stand up but my left arm was tethered – he'd cuffed it to the fender. 'The *fuck*?'

Paco pulled over footstool and sat beside me, still crunching through the apple. I tugged on the cold bracelet but it was locked solid. I wasn't going anywhere. He ran his thumb over my top lip and showed me my own blood. 'You start talking, I'll unlock it. You stay silent, you bleed more, understand?'

'Talk about what? I don't know anything!'

'OK, lemme explain it like the baby you are.' He threw the apple core into the cold fireplace and gripped my chin again. 'I come here yesterday to find the house empty and both Tenoch and the doctor gone. And I want to know *where* they went and *where* my money is. I worked with that man half my life, and half of what he has is mine. So if he's taken it, that's on you.'

'He didn't tell me he was going, let alone where to. I only came back to say goodbye to him and pack my bag.'

Paco laughed, glancing over at Arturo's body. 'I don't believe you.'

'Tenoch trusted you.'

He got up and kicked Arturo in his ribs. 'Everyone has their price, *gatita*.' He didn't say it like Tenoch – he hissed it, like a rattlesnake. And he kicked me in my own ribs. Pain radiated and I curled into myself like a bean.

'CALL ME A FUCKING PRICK, *GATITA*!' he screeched, kicking me again. 'COME ON, WHO ARE YOU? YOU JUST SOME LITTLE BITCH? WHERE IS MY SERIAL KILLER? WHERE THAT HOT-BLOODED *CHICA* NOW, HUH?' He grabbed my hair and pulled up my head. I could barely see for the strings of pain in my skull but I would not give him what he wanted – Old Me. The Hot Head. The Killer. The Weak One. I would show him how strong I really was.

'WHERE IS YOUR *PAPI*, *GATITA*? EH?'

Paco dropped my head and shouted a bunch of loud, sweary Spanish. Before I could see it coming, he'd kicked me in the face.

He must have knocked me out again.

Next thing I knew, the light had dimmed, the sandwich was dry and curled up and the soda can had vanished. Arturo's body had gone too – just a bloodstain on the rug remained. Paco was sitting in Tenoch's armchair; a bowl of nachos on the armrest, watching the blank, shot-up TV screen.

'You ready to talk yet, bitch?' he said, through a mouthful of chips.

My mouth was swollen and all I could taste iron in my spit. 'I told you, I don't know anything.'

'He gave you cash when you two went into the town. Where was he getting it from?'

'I don't know, his office?'

'I've checked there. I have checked this whole fucking place and guess what – nothing. He cannot have taken it all – he *must* have left some for me. Or you, huh? Did he leave it to *you*?' He sprang out of his chair to threaten me with his boot again but this time I was ready for it and curled into a ball, shielding my head with my one free hand.

He sat on the footstool and lay one of the machetes across his knees, stroking the blade back and forth. 'I've seen you down at the beach with your boyfriend. You going to him today? That where you're going with my money?' I didn't like how he was stroking the blade.

'No. I don't have your money.'

'You sure about that? You leaving so suddenly. You going to Tenoch—'

'NO, I DON'T KNOW WHERE TENOCH IS AND I DON'T KNOW WHERE HIS MONEY IS. PLEASE, LET ME GO! WHY DON'T YOU LISTEN?'

'What do you know about Celestina?'

'Nothing. Tenoch said she got another job. That's all I know about her.'

'Bullshit,' he spat. 'Tenoch treats you two like his daughters. You're protecting him. You both knew what he was planning.'

'He doesn't say shit to me! Why would he say shit to *me*?'

Paco shook his head. He got off the footstool and paced towards the kitchen. 'That *pendejo* you've been fucking coming here to pick you up?'

I stayed silent.

'Or you meeting him at your little hotel? Cos if he comes up here looking for you, I'll be ready for him. Then you'll fucking talk.'

'He's not coming here. He's not picking me up.'

'In that case, I will go down to that little hotel and Imma bring him up here to you, and Imma make you watch as I pull his guts out of his body.'

'FUCK YOU!' I shouted in his face.

'No, no, no, Sweetpea. Fuck *you*. You're in *Paco's* house now. And you will lick shit from my shoes if I tell you. Eat your sandwich.'

And me, being me, hoyed it Frisbee-style towards him, missing him completely but creating a satisfying crash against the wall, sending corners of bread and shredded lettuce outwards in a mini-explosion.

'There she is,' he grinned. 'There's my Sweetpea.'

'FUCK YOU, YOU FUCKING CUNT!' I shouted again, flinging my shoe at him. And then another shoe. And then a sofa cushion, which was a really shit thing to throw but there was nothing else within reach.

'You ever hear that expression "We have ways to make men talk"?'

I tugged at the cuff with all my might, yanked at the fender to loosen it but I was stuck there good.

'Well, I have ways to make *you* talk.'

I prayed earnestly to a god I didn't believe in that Raf didn't show up at the gates, looking for me. He had no idea what I was up to my neck in.

'YOU TOUCH HIM, I WILL—'

'You won't do anything, *chica*, because I have a gun and a machete and you are a girl chained to a fucking pole,' he said, high on his own hysterics. 'But if you tell me where Tenoch has gone, I will think about letting you go. All I want is my money. You tell me where that is, you go free.'

'I DON'T KNOW WHERE HE IS!' I screamed finally. 'I DON'T KNOW WHERE HIS MONEY IS. I DON'T KNOW ANYTHING ABOUT ANYTHING! HE DIDN'T TELL ME JACKSHIT!'

Paco checked the time, sighing dramatically. 'You'll talk. Soon enough.'

My head was in a tailspin – how long would I have to sit there, protesting my innocence, trying to wriggle out of the cuff before he believed me? What else could I do? Every time he left the room, I was practically breaking my own wrist to get free but it was just getting sorer. All hope was lost.

Hours I sat there – he kept coming back in, checking his watch, checking I was still there. Like, where the fuck else would I be? He'd tucked the machete into the back of his pants but clutched his pistol tightly, pointing it straight at me at regular intervals.

'Need a piss yet?'

'Yes.'

'Piss your pants.'

He'd never have shot me – he needed me too much and he knew it. The worst he could do was torture me – shoot my legs, maybe rape me. Get the remaining Chipmunks, Ming and Stuzzy, in to rape me too until I confessed. But I *couldn't* confess. I truly didn't have anything *to* confess. I kicked out at the fender whenever I'd summoned some more strength but as hard as I tried, I couldn't get the cuff over my hand.

I watched the clock on the oven display tick down – one, two, three thirty. At four fifteen, Paco sat on the armchair nearest me but not so close that I could touch him. I was waiting for another threat or at the least for him to start cutting off my fingers one by one. And I'll be honest, I felt sick to my bones. I had no plan in place to stop him. No cunning plan, or even a snarky retort. I was at whatever mercy he was about to throw down.

'Last chance. Where has Tenoch gone and where is my money?'

'I. Don't. Know.'

'Yes. You. Do.'

'Go. Fuck. Yourself,' I spat. 'Hard.'

My mouth betrayed me where my body was paralysed with fear. This was me as I hadn't seen myself for a long time – a victim. Helpless. Trapped. I was the six-year-old sitting on the rug again at Number 12 Priory Gardens, watching Fireman Sam, drinking milk and munching a custard cream. Seeing the man in the garden. Hearing Alison scream. Him running at the window. The smashing glass. Kimmy's high chair falling over. The screaming in the crib. Ashlea calling for her mummy.

'You think I can't break you?' he hissed in my ear. 'You're wrong, Sweetpea. You are so wrong. *Conoce a tu enemigo.* That is what we say in the cartel. It's time.' And he licked me all the way up the side of my face.

I think that was the moment I realised I was broken – my wrist certainly felt like it from all the wrenching. But Paco strode out of the room without a second look. I heard voices, distantly. I couldn't make out words or tones but the next thing I knew, a sweaty-looking Ming strode in, heading towards the refrigerator. He clicked open a soda, gulping it right down and belching unapologetically. Then he saw me on the rug. He knew I'd be there.

'You're not gonna let me out either, are you?' I said.

He shrugged, like it was more than his job was worth and I wrenched and pulled at the fender again to at least try and get one of the legs loose, kicking out and screaming and wailing like the mad woman I was always pretending not to be. It still didn't budge. And my wrist ached purple.

'Fuck—' said Ming, placing his soda can on the counter. At first I thought he'd meant me, then I saw what he was looking at.

Paco and Stuzzy had entered from the hall, holding two wriggling sacks.

It was the screams that did it – when they wrenched open the sacks, one by one, a small dishevelled child tumbled out, whimpering. Mátilda and Saúl, their mouths bound, hands and feet tied. Paco went outside and brought in another bundle without a sack – David. But although he was tied too, David wasn't moving. I couldn't see him *breathing*.

I couldn't speak or scream, it was all backed up in my throat. Saúl and Mátilda saw me, bloody, swollen and chained to the fender. Their noses were bloodied too, their eyes full of tears.

'You'll talk now,' said Paco. 'Or I will kill them all, big to small.'

All I could do was cry. Like a child. I wanted someone to come to me, hold me. I wanted my dad. I wanted Seren. I wanted Rafael.

'I can't tell you anything, Paco, because I don't know. I would tell you if I did, you know I would. Please... please don't hurt them. I'll do whatever you want. I... don't... please don't hurt them.'

Outside, a scream – distant but definite. It came again and again – the scream only a mother could produce. It tore a fire right through me—

Celestina.

Her distant screams grew louder and more desperate. She was rattling the front gates ferociously, screeching, roaring – a ravenous lioness separated from her three cubs.

'Go and quiet that bitch,' Paco yelled at Stuzzy, along with something else in fast Spanish. 'If you can't quiet her, put a fucking bullet in her.' Stuzzy nodded shortly and left the room.

And then Paco came to me.

I was still crying, and peeing too by this point. Nothing had changed. But *everything* had changed.

'This is how I get to you, huh?' he said, carrying Mátilda and bending down to grab my chin hard. 'This is what I have to do to get through to you? This is what makes you piss your panties?'

He placed the child on the rug next to me and grabbed her throat. A gunshot rang out somewhere and all the screaming stopped.

'Who's next, *gatita*? Come on, I give you one more chance. And for every single fucking minute more you keep me waiting,

I will kill them, one by one.' He squeezed the child's throat, tighter. Her face bloomed red, little wet cheeks bulging with the pressure.

'I DON'T...' I sobbed. 'I DON'T KNOW WHERE HE IS! HE DIDN'T TELL ME! PLEASE, PACO! I'LL DO ANYTHING BUT I SWEAR I DON'T KNOW. I'LL HELP YOU, I'LL HELP YOU FIND HIM. AND THE MONEY.'

Quick as a flash, he pulled his pistol from his jeans and pointed it at Ming, standing in the kitchen. As Ming tipped his head back to drink his soda, Paco called out, 'Yo, Domingo!'

The trigger clicked as Ming turned to face him and a hole blew clean through his forehead. He lurched back against the refrigerator, the soda can flying from his grasp in a shower of his own blood and he slumped to the kitchen floor in a big, fat heap.

Saúl screamed and huddled next to his brother's body on the floor, hiding his face in his neck.

'Big to small, Sweetpea. You ready for the next one?'

Mátilda passed out cold in Paco's hard embrace. Saúl started screaming and Paco barked at him to be quiet, eventually dragging both him and Mátilda out into the hall. I heard the broom closet door creak open and Saúl screaming still behind his gag as Paco threw them both inside, ordering them to stay quiet. He shut the door and came back into the living room, kicking David's lifeless body as he passed. The boy groaned. A small chink of light cut into me – David was *alive*. I hadn't failed him.

Where there was life, there was hope. But Paco pointed the gun at his head and—

'NO!' I screamed. 'WAIT!'

He came back towards me, tilting his head like he hadn't quite heard. 'Did you say wait?'

'The arrr-artillery,' I stammered. 'S-s-ecret room.'

'Secret room?' smiled Paco. 'There's a secret room? I fucking KNEW you knew something. Where? Where is it?'

'I'll tell you if you let them all go. *Please*, Paco.'

'No, no, you tell me *now*. I check, *then* I let them go.' He aimed the gun back at David.

'Off-office. In the office. Behind the b-b-b-bookcase. There's a hidden p-p-panel. If you press the wall in two places, east and west, gently, it will open. It is behind there, a secret room, I swear.'

Paco glared at me, holding the pistol to my skull.

'It's in there. Go look. I promise you.'

He grinned, scratching his temple with the muzzle of the gun. 'If I not find what I'm looking for in there, I will blow holes in all three of them. And then you.' And he left the room.

Everything I had been keeping back, meditating out of my palms for the past few months, it was all gathering again in my head and my chest like storm clouds. It was all coming at me – too much, too much. But I needed it. I had minutes until Paco had moved those books and that bookcase out of the way and found the panel and pressed it only to discover the secret room only had guns in it – no money.

And that was *if* Tenoch had left any. Maybe he had taken everything.

All of those kids were going to die, one by one when he came out of that room. I needed Rhiannon. I needed the Rhiannon I had been in Florence when Ty had been kidnapped. I needed the Rhiannon I had been when I was suffocating the paedophile, Derek Scudd. The Rhiannon who had kept Julia all those months in the back bedroom and sliced off her fingers one by one. The Rhiannon who had watched her grandfather die in agony.

Because they had hurt children.

It was my only chance – Rhiannon had to do the unthinkable. And I lay on the floor as flat as I could and reached out with my foot to hook it around the nearest armchair leg. And with some difficulty, pulled it towards me, close enough so I could grab the cushion. I aimed it up at the wall behind me.

Again. And again. And again.

I kept missing, at first by a lot. But I did it again, and again, until it touched it, a glancing caress but enough to make it wobble from its hook. I tossed the cushion up again and dislodged it so it dangled precariously above my head like a guillotine. And several attempts later, the remaining machete wobbled violently on its hook and clattered down to the hardwood floor.

I looked to the door – I could hear Saúl and Mátilda crying in the cupboard. David's face still unmoving on the floor, metres away from me. A trickle of his blood snaked along the grouting in the floor tiles.

'*Está bien, bebés. Está bien*,' I kept saying. It's all right babies, I'm going to save you. *Te voy a salvar*.'

Three more children would die if I didn't do it. Three more children would die when I could have saved them.

And as small as I was at Priory Gardens, was as big as I became now. I flooded my head with rage, with the stark awfulness of the situation, and the urgency of getting to Paco before he could get to them. I was their only chance. And I took that machete and I raised it high above my head, lining it up with my wrist. And I swung it out wide.

And I thought of Priory Gardens.

And I thought of Ivy.

And I heard Mátilda scream. And I heard Saúl scream in the cupboard.

Don't look, darling. Don't look back in there.

And I smashed the machete down. And the pain was immediate. Scorching, endless pain. But it hadn't worked – it didn't come away. So I swung it round and smashed it again. And I screamed so loud I could no longer hear the children. I tried every trick in the book to make it hurt less – it was someone else's wrist, someone else's blood. It took three attempts. Again. And again. And again. On my own wrist. I sent the pain to Blackstone. I sent it to Grandad. To Derek Scudd, to Gavin White, to the Men in the Blue Van and Troy Shearer and Patrick Edward Fenton, to the two guys who'd attacked us on the beach, to Ming and to Stuzzy.

And I sent it to Paco.

And the blade hacked through my skin, flesh, veins, ligaments, bone, and after three excruciating strikes, there was release – my arm came away, gushing blood. It was intense agony but I was free and my ragged, severed hand dropped to the rug, limp in its dangling cuff.

Sweating hard, vision still swimming, I staggered to my feet and lurched into the kitchen, puking into the sink, before grabbing some tea towels and wrapping them tightly around my horrific stump. The kids were crying in the broom closet, more muffled now. It was my one window of opportunity. I picked up the machete again, heading for the office.

But I could feel myself slipping away – my eyesight blackening around the edges. White-hot pain scorched up and down the length of my left arm and I felt my blood pump out of me.

Paco had moved the bookcase away from the wall, still trying to find the parts of the panel to push. He was a bulldozer, going at it with his fists, thumping it all over – he didn't have the lightness of touch Tenoch had.

He turned to face me and did a classic double take. Saw the blood-drenched tea towels. The dripping machete in my one remaining hand.

'The fuck?!'

He backed against the wall – his gun on the floor, closer to me than him and before he could lunge for it, I grabbed it and pointed straight at his groin, firing twice. He flew back against the panel with a roar of pain, sliding down to the carpet, clutching his package, blood streaming through his fingers, screaming obscenities at me. I stood over him, watching him scream.

But both my legs buckled from under me and I dropped down too. I couldn't stand. I reached for the door handle to pull myself up but I couldn't grab it. I was like a marionette – all strings down. And Paco was getting up.

'*Morirás, perra*,' he snarled. '*Morirás, perra!*' You will die, bitch.

I was done. The gun was clicking empty. He came for me again, groping across the floor for the machete, and my focus swam so much I couldn't grab it. It wasn't in my hand anymore – it had gone. I scrabbled out of the office, into the hall and he slithered after me, spitting venom. I had to get to the broom closet. That's all I could think. Those kids would not die while I was there, not this time. He would have to cut me into tiny pieces first.

There was a loud crash upstairs and fast footsteps on the landing. I got to the closet when a hand grasped my ankle. I waited for blade and pain.

But there were heavy footsteps on the stairs and down them tore Celestina, a blur of red and white. Eyes wild, her face and hands all covered in red. She kicked Paco hard in the face and he rolled away from me, cursing and yelling. And she kept kicking him, his ribs, his spine, stamping on his wrist until he dropped the machete.

She didn't hesitate. She didn't give him a second chance to rise. Her scream tore through the room like an electrical fire as she brought the blade down hard on Paco's neck, twice before it detached, tumbling to the carpet. He had squealed, only briefly. She kicked the head away and it stopped rolling beside me – face tilted up. Eyes flickering. Mouth still gasping. Blood oozing. Clean, efficient, necessary.

Even when she held it up by its hair, there was no extraordinary surge of pleasure from seeing his still-blinking eyes and open neck. It was like something had been lifted away from me, like a heavy stone, and thrown clear. God knows how it felt for her. She dropped both head and machete to the floor. I could have sworn I heard the mouth groan.

'My babies?' she cried, wiping her hands on her formerly white broderie anglaise dress and kneeling, her hands on both my cheeks, slapping me awake. *'Donde estan mis bebés?'*

I banged my head against the closet door and crawled out of the way. Black spots had appeared in everything I tried to focus on. The tea towels around my stump were sodden

413

through. I could no longer feel the pain of it, I just wanted to sleep. My eyes rolled – I had to stay awake.

By the time I staggered to my feet, Celestina was consoling Saúl and Mátilda inside the closet. '*Está bien, está bien. Tu mami esta aqui.*'

'How did you get in?' I said, forcing myself to my feet using the doorframe and swallowing down another urge to puke as I caught sight of my blood-soaked dressing. My left arm was completely numb.

'Climbed up the drainpipe, smashed a window upstairs.' Her face shone with sweat. She looked down at herself. 'I don't know which blood is mine.'

Through the hallway window, I could make out a body lying on the doorstep. A man with a gun limp in his hand and his throat torn out – Stuzzy, who had gone to 'quiet the bitch'. I booted Paco's head into the office and closed the door so the kids wouldn't see it.

Celestina and the children ran into the living room where their brother was unmoving on the tiled floor. His mother rubbed his back and smacked his cheek to wake him. 'Wake up, Davey, wake up!' Mátilda yelled.

'Is he dead?' I said, leaning clumsily on the back of the armchair.

'No, he's breathing,' said Celestina, cradling him in her arms. She gave Saúl an order and he ran to the kitchen to get a glass from the cupboard. He filled it at the sink and ran back with it, throwing it over David's face.

David stirred, momentarily, but he couldn't open his eyes. He groaned in pain – he had a head wound, a bad one.

'He's going to die,' I said. 'He's going to die, isn't he?'

Celestina rocked him in her arms and gabbled copious prayers to someone above. 'No, he will be all right. We will get him help. I will call for help.'

Both Saúl and Mátilda cuddled their brother's waking body. I was so weak I couldn't stand.

'We need to get that on ice,' said Celestina, gesturing to my stump. She ordered the two little ones to look after their brother and hold up his head to keep taking sips of the remaining water. Her mouth and teeth were red with dried blood.

'What did you do to Stuzzy?' I asked.

'Tore out his throat,' she said, sitting me down on a cushion-less chair and grabbing some clean tea towels from a kitchen drawer.

'With your *teeth*?'

'He gave me no choice. I had to get to my babies.' It was then she saw my dangling hand still in the cuff on the fender.

'I'm going to faint,' I said as some feeling came back into my arm.

She wrapped my stump tightly. 'Hold that on tight, don't let it go. I can't believe he did this to you. *Un puto gilipollas!* He chain you up to cut it off?'

'No, *I* cut it off. I had to get to him before he got to them.'

'You did it to *yourself*?'

'He was going to kill them.'

She cupped my cheek, briefly, then sniffed. 'Ugh, that animal. OK, we need to get you out of here.' She went to get my hand. 'We put this on ice, they may be able to stitch it back on for you. How long has it been—'

'I really think I am gonna faint.'

'Come on,' she said, helping me to my feet. 'You need some air. You've lost a lot of blood.'

Outside, colours were so much brighter. The air was easier to breathe and the sun was beginning to dip in the sky, a violent orange glow that bathed everything beneath it in gold. I walked towards my flower beds. I'd almost reached the salvia when my legs went from under me and I thumped down to the grass. There was no way I was ever getting back up. I was dead weight.

Celestina knelt beside me. 'You are a mother too? I can tell.' She tilted the glass of water to my mouth. The intoxicating scent of the cempasuchil swirled around my head like a choir. 'We are given a super strength when we become mothers. A strength we don't even know we have until we need it.'

Mátilda brought me out a blanket and covered me with it – it was a hot day but I was cold, close to shivering. My eyes opened, momentarily, and I saw their faces. The two children, leaning down, crying. Asking if I was OK.

'David?' I said. 'Is David all right?'

'Mama is putting a bandage on his head,' said Saúl.

'Is he awake?'

'Yeah, he's awake now,' said Mátilda.

The adrenaline had begun to leave me, along with a fair amount of blood. I kept counting them – one, two, three, one, two, three, and their mother. All alive. Definitely all still alive.

'It's OK. It's all OK now,' I whispered.

I tried hard to stay awake, forcing my eyes open to see the vast blue sky, mosquitoes dancing across it. Children's faces. Snatches of conversation – Spanish and English. Voices. Children. Men. A woman. Three men.

Someone saying my name, my *new* name. Again and again and again.

Fuck, they cut off her hand? Jesus Christ—
Policía. Did you call them? Call them...
Where is it? Don't lose that bag.
It's here. Are we gonna make it?
We will if I drive.

I felt the ground leave me – I was being moved. In my mind I thought this was death. This was what happened – you were scooped up by an angel or something. Your brain activity still registers stuff – voices, last confessions, the life support machine being turned off. You have a vague sense of what's happening but you're down the tunnel and you can't turn back. I couldn't see. Couldn't open my mouth to speak. I heard Nico's voice, Raf's brother.

'Hospital, *vamos. Yo manejare.*'

'Stay with me, baby. Please stay with me. I can't lose her!'

That was the voice I'd needed to hear. We were moving – in a car. My head in Raf's lap. I still couldn't open my eyes. But I found my voice.

'Is it still there?'

'What did you say, honey?' said Raf, stroking my head. 'She's awake!'

'Is it still attached?'

'Is what attached, baby?'

'My head,' I said.

'She's not making sense.' I felt his kiss light on my head. He snivelled.

'Why are you crying?'

'Shit, she's so cold. Try and stay awake, baby. Keep looking at me. It's gonna be OK. I'm not going to leave you. I got you now, I got you.'

It was the last thing I remember hearing. But it was all I needed to hear.

Wednesday, 19 June – St Christopher's Hospital, Colonia Centro, San Jose del Cabo

Raf's face was the first I saw when I opened my eyes. I was lying in a bed and he was asleep in a chair beside me. It was night outside. I didn't know where we were, I was just glad he was with me.

A short nurse with thick calf muscles came in and drew the curtains.

'Hey, you're awake!' she said spryly. Her badge said María del Carmen. She knew what I was thinking. 'The doctor will be in to see you soon. I'll let you come round a little first.' She looked across at Raf, still sleeping. 'He's barely left that chair in three days. He must like you a lot.'

I went to speak but no words came out.

'It'll be a while before we know if the operation has worked. You might not feel anything in your fingers immediately but that's normal. You're going to need some rehabilitation but there's every chance it will function again. You were lucky it went on ice so quickly.'

I stared at my left arm, resting in an elevated stirrup, all bandaged up and nowhere to go. Last time I'd seen it, it had been dangling in the cuff in front of Tenoch's fireplace. My sides ached and I couldn't move my fingers – they wouldn't respond to any command but it was there. I didn't know *how* but it was there.

'Yeah, you got some cracked ribs too. They did quite a number on you, hun. But you're here, and you're gonna be all right. Can I get you anything?'

I willed her to read my mind that I needed a wee. And again, she just knew.

'You've got your bag all connected up so don't you worry about getting up and going to the bathroom.'

Fucking hell, I thought. She really was a mind reader. I willed my mouth to speak but the words were lost, somewhere between my brain and my face. She walked over to Raf's side and flicked on the light. That woke him up.

He immediately roused himself and looked over to me. 'Hey, baby, there you are,' he said, forcing his eyes open wider. 'How are you doing?'

I couldn't even smile at him. I could blink, that was about it.

He frowned and looked up at the nurse. 'She's still a little woozy with all the pain meds so give her time,' she said.

This had happened before, me waking up in hospital and not being able to speak except this time, my mum and dad weren't there. Seren wasn't there. And I wasn't in England. I was a million miles away from everything, including parts of my own body. I could move both my feet – that was something. I could wiggle my toes – I could slide my foot back and forth across under the sheet. And I could hold Raf's hand with my right hand and I could squeeze it. But my left hand was useless. And I couldn't remember how to speak.

'Her eyes look … different.'

'We had to take out her contacts,' said María del Carmen. 'They're right there.' She pointed to a little pot on the bedside cabinet.

The nurse explained to Raf what she'd explained to me in a hushed voice, like I couldn't hear. I was 'probably in delayed shock' because I'd 'experienced a massive trauma' and I 'had a lot of medication' in my system. Raf held my head against his own, stroking my cheek. He smelled of coffee and fabric conditioner. I wanted to go to back to sleep in his arms.

When she had gone, he sat there looking at me.

'Hey, you. You scared the crap out of me. When you didn't show up at the hotel I went on up to the house to find you. And boy did I find you.'

I looked at him, willing him to read my mind.

'I can't believe what they did to you, *mi niña hermosa*.' He kissed my face. 'Can you remember anything? Me, Dad and Nico found you. And that woman, Celestina and her kids. She put your hand on ice. She saved it.'

I blinked, hoping he'd read my mind again, like the nurse had.

'You gotta be real careful with it for a few weeks. You were in surgery for a whole day. Celestina said you saved her kids from that guy Paco? Was it him who chained you up? Are you in any pain? He beat you up pretty good. Did he make you wear coloured contacts? Was it like *LA Confidential* and you had to dress up like … How the hell did you even get involved with a cartel?'

I closed my eyes and nuzzled into his neck.

'I'm sorry. You don't have to talk about all this now, I'm sorry.' He kissed me all over my face. 'You're safe, that's the main thing.'

My throat was so dry and I looked behind him at the cabinet where there was a water jug and a cup. I reached out to it and he poured me some. I drank two whole glasses before he spoke again.

'Hey, I found this little guy in your bag when I was looking for your MediCare papers.' He reached down and handed me the little yarn *gatita* that I'd bought for Tenoch. 'Do you want it?'

I did a grabby hand for it and held it against my chest. It smelled like Tenoch's deep heat spray.

'I better make a call. Everyone's worried about you.' He stroked my hair and left.

I have no explanation for the mute thing – I swear I wasn't putting it on. I guess I was reverting to type. I'd been mute for ages after Priory Gardens and I wonder if my brain had gone into some area of regressive trauma.

After Raf had gone, in came Celestina. She was wearing a hospital gown like I was and there were sore red rings around her wrists and ankles but she was clean of all blood, her hair pinned back in a neat bun.

'Hey, how are you?' she whispered, checking behind her at the door and creeping in. 'I wanted to see you without your boyfriend. To thank you.'

I nodded. I wanted to ask how the children were.

'The children are fine. David has a sore head but there is no problem inside him, *gracias a dios*. The other two won't leave his side.'

I nodded again.

'My mother is here. We are going to stay at my aunt's house. The children will be happy there. I just want to thank you again.' She touched my withered, dead hand in the sling.

You are such a good mother, I wanted to say but my mouth wouldn't say it. Couldn't say a word.

'I have spoken to the police,' she continued. 'I told them everything. What I did to Stuzzy. And Paco. And what Paco did to me. Detective Beltran is a good man – he listened to me. He says the law is on our side but they will still want to talk to you. I cannot tell him where Tenoch or the doctor went, though. Do you know?'

I shook my head.

She located the clipboard at the base of my bed and removed the pen, tearing off a small strip of paper from the bottom.

'I give you my number and address at my aunt's. If I can help you in any way, you will find us there.' She scribbled it down, enfolding me in a hug which I could only partially reciprocate. I wanted to thank her too for saving my life but my voice wouldn't come, no matter how much I willed it. I gripped her hand properly with my good one and hoped she understood. If it wasn't for her... my eyes welled up.

'I go now,' she said, releasing herself. 'Thank you, Sweetpea.'

I didn't know how to process what had happened at the Hacienda in any logical way. But as it turned out, the mute thing helped massively. Doctors, police, Raf's family, they all came into my room one by one and in pairs, firing myriad questions at me about what had been going on, why the children were there, who the men were, where Tenoch was, whether I had been kept as a sex slave. I had my backstory, signed and sealed already. I just had to fill in a few blank pages.

The police seemed content that Paco and the Chipmunks had been wiped off the Earth and the ballistics report matched mine and Celestina's story of what happened that day at the Hacienda. Ming and Arturo had been shot by Paco and she had killed Stuzzy and Paco in self-defence. Tenoch and Dr Gonzales had done a bunk at some point two days before. But where to, that was unknown. There was a rumour, just a rumour mind you, that Tenoch had in his possession over a hundred million dollars. Maybe more. No wonder Paco had been blinded by greed.

For once in my life, I hadn't killed anyone. Well, not recently anyway.

As far as *my* side of the story was concerned, that checked out too. It was all there on the system: a young woman with my name, aged 29, originally from England, who grew up in the care system and had moved to New York in her early twenties to study at NYU. Birthdate: 25 September 1990; Blood Type: B+; Civil Status: single; same social security number. She'd ditched her course, due to stress, and gone on the road. The next time she'd shown up on government computers had been in Odessa, Texas a year later where she'd got a library card and a job as an administrative assistant for a realtor in El Paso.

If reincarnation *does* exist, knowing my luck I'll *still* come back working in fucking admin.

Anyway, in October 2016, the girl left her home in El Paso and hit the road again, went off the radar. Presumed dead. Until now.

'I got in with a bad lot,' I said, as though that would explain where I'd been for the past three years. 'I was hitchhiking along the Baja Peninsula one day and Tenoch picked me up, gave me a home, a job. He was good to me.'

Beltran bought it. They *all* bought it, even Raf's family.

I was a runaway, who'd showed up at the home of an ex-cartel hitman. There I'd been put to work as a cleaner and that was that. But Raf's mother Bianca knew there was more to it. Why else had I been at the airport that day we first met?

She sat by my bedside and leaned in tight when we were alone. '*Cariño*, you can tell me, it's OK. I do not judge you. Did those bad men force you to… travel to places to… be with other men?'

She meant was I sex trafficked. My subsequent silence spoke volumes for her and she collapsed into tears, gripping my hand, rubbing it as though rubbing me clean. She pulled me into the warmest hug, stroking my hair, rocking me gently. '*Esta bien cariño. Nosotras te cuidaremos.*'

It's OK, darling. We will take care of you.

As I drifted into sleep I heard hushed voices muttering.

'That must have been why she was at the airport that day.'

'Probably pimped out to some drug lord in the city.'

'He had acres of poppy fields.'

'He'd been a hitman, they said. Made her change her eyes and have surgery.'

'Black tar. Unrefined.'

'The detective said there's no bank account. Lord knows where he kept it.'

'She cut off her own hand to save those kids?'

'What makes a person do that to themselves?'

'Poor, poor girl. . .'

The bottom line was that Raf's family all felt sorry for me. I'd been used and abused by the rich and wealthy of Rocas Calientes and I was a broken, shattered soul in need of their care. And they would care for me, no question. It was like being lifted up by a thousand hands. I even volunteered to have an AIDS test, to further enhance the lie.

It was just like after Priory Gardens. *Get Well Soon* balloons, presents, cheek-strokes, cuddles and more kisses than I'd had in my life. I'd saved those children. That, at least, was true. And the Arroyo-Carranza family would be there to save *me*. And that was all I wanted.

None of them left me alone for an instant – except a single ten-minute slot, last thing at night when Raf was snoring in the chair beside me and turned to the wall. I picked up the little yarn *gatita* on my cabinet, intending to further investigate the small hole that had become unstitched. I'd noticed it a few days before, when the doctor had been wanging on to me about physio facilities in San Diego. There was something white rolled up inside the cat's rear end. A scrap of paper. I waited for the next snore to mask its unravelling.

A scrawled note in pencil: it read...

NYC Vaults. Box 23-25. Go live your life, gatita. Tx

426

PART 3: New York State

Wednesday, 22 January 2020 – Sluggers Bar, Fifth Avenue, New York City

'So that's why you're here,' says Freddie, turning to the last page in his notebook. 'That's a safety deposit box number here in the city, right?'

'Yes.'

'So what did he leave you? In the box? What did he put in there? Is it money? It's money, isn't it?' He nods towards the cardboard box next to me.

'Oh, this isn't it,' I say. 'I haven't checked it yet. This is something else.'

'Oh God, this is amazing. Can I come with you? To open it?'

'Nope.'

'Aww come on.' Freddie sat back in his seat, staring at my crap hand. I held it out so he could inspect it more closely.

'Occupational therapy is helping a lot. I can do this now.' I lift my second finger a juddery inch off the table top, then slowly another inch, until it falls by its own accord. Freddie looks at me before carefully moving back my sleeve to see the raggedy scar all along my wrist. 'I know, Frankenstein much?'

'I can't believe they stitched it back on.'

'I got lucky.' The diamond shone on my fourth finger, right on cue. 'We went back down to Rocas Calientes in November, for the Dia de los Muertos celebrations... that's where we got engaged.'

'Congratulations.'

'It was incredible. The road all the way up to the cemetery was paved with a thick carpet of orange marigold petals and lit by tiny candles. They all sang in Spanish. Everyone brought gifts for the dead and painted their faces and dressed up in colourful clothes. We hung paper decorations from the trees and danced in that cemetery all night long. Every tombstone was lit with candles and colour. Kind of reframed death for me. Having a family has reframed *everything* for me. People I love. People who love *me*. Killing isn't as important anymore. I know what's important now.'

'Any sign of Tenoch?'

'Nope. The Hacienda's all boarded up and there's talk of auctioning it off for the locals. Rumour has it he escaped through tunnels he'd dug out beneath the temazcal – where he'd buried his stash.'

'Wow.'

I can't help smiling. 'I know. Total Shawshanker.'

'Did you hear that Craig got engaged too?'

'Yeah,' I said. 'That weathergirl, wasn't it? Soapy Titwanks.'

Freddie laughs. 'Sophie Cruikshanks.'

The accompanying picture to their exclusive interview on the *OK!* site was of a bride and groom jumping on a trampoline – the bouquet in mid-air between their cheesy expressions, her subheading that Craig was 'her world'. I barely recognised

Craig – he'd put on *so* much weight. I knew he was getting his dick shined by some ho cos I'd seen him on *Up at the Crack* weeks earlier, going all coy about the 'new lady in his life'. I hadn't realised it was so serious.

'How do you feel about that?' asks Freddie.

'I was a bit miffed to begin with, I'll admit it. He'd nag the life out of me for buying the expensive dishwasher tablets not Lidl own brand and moaned on like a bitch about the four-star hotel I'd booked for that Beyoncé concert when the 'Premier Inn is next door to the venue' and that bitch got a fucking Cartier? Livid.'

'He's becoming quite ubiquitous in the UK. Done a few interviews, got himself a publicist.'

'He'll be on *Ready Steady Cook* next, you mark my words.'

Freddie shakes his head. 'Happy human bonds, huh? You've totally got away with it, haven't you?' He reached into his bag and pulled out his phone, clicking onto YouTube. He gave a furtive look around and slid the video across the table towards me. 'I mean, you're home and dry, now this has happened…'

It's a WCAX News report from two weeks ago. I'd seen it before – serious-faced newsman in grey suit looking down the barrel of the camera. Blonde in blue anorak, standing in the pissing rain at the end of a darkened street lit only by blue and red police lights. The tickertape headline:

WOMAN SHOT DEAD AT HOME OF SERIAL KILLER SISTER

'We're getting information about a shooting in Lawford Heights. Early reports are suggesting that a woman has been shot dead at a house on Old Mill Road. Mark Weppler

is live from the scene. Mark – what can you tell us about this unfolding story right now?'

'Yes, Cindy, I'm here at this beautiful, unassuming house in Lawford Heights, a short distance from the main highway in the town of Weston and what we know about this situation right now is that in the early hours of the morning, sometime around 2.15 a.m., a person attempted to gain entry to this property behind me and that person was thought to be serial killer Rhiannon Lewis, who has been on the run from justice in the UK for the past year.

'This house belongs to Lewis's sister, Seren Gibson, and her husband and two children. Fortunately, the Gibson children are away staying with their father at the present time – it's understood the couple have separated under the strain of the situation – so the children and their dad were not present when the incident took place.'

'So do we know the status of Mrs Gibson, is she OK?'

'It's not clear at this time who was shot – whether it was Mrs Gibson herself or the intruder, Cindy, but one thing we do know is that not five minutes ago, we got these pictures of a body bag being wheeled out of the house and into the back of a private ambulance so somebody's dead for sure.'

'What was it like for you to see that headline?' asks Freddie, stopping the video in its tracks.

'Weird,' I tell him. 'I thought someone pretending to be me had shot her dead inside her own house. I had a panic attack on the spot, right in my mother-in-law's living room. Luckily no one else was home.'

'And what about this...' Freddie clicked onto a news article, this time static, and enlarged the headline:

WOMAN SHOT DEAD IN VERMONT CONFIRMED AS SERIAL KILLER RHIANNON LEWIS:

Sister IDs Body

'I didn't get it,' I tell him. 'I didn't understand why Seren had said the woman was me. It was obviously, judging from the news reports, some doppleganger who'd been hanging around her place, breaking in, scaring her kids for months. But Seren had shot her stalker in the face and told the police she was me. She identified the body. She wouldn't have got it wrong – she's my only relative.'

'Right,' says Fred. 'But you don't look like you used to anymore.'

'Even so, my own sister would know. She just *would*.'

'But she's made the whole world believe it *was* you. Any idea why? Every news outlet, every Tumblr thread, every Twitter tag, everyone believes Rhiannon Lewis is officially dead.'

'Except Géricault,' I snort.

'Yeah well, she's a detective. She's programmed to look beyond the obvious. But it looks like the American police are taking it as self-defence, doesn't it? They haven't jailed Seren yet at least. She's done you a big favour if you ask me.'

'Well, she did owe me one. Or two.'

Freddie shook his head. 'If I were you, I'd want to know more. I'd want to know why she's identified that body as you. Are you on your way to Vermont to see her?'

'No, I'm here for the safety deposit box, I told you.'

He glances at the cardboard box. 'So what's in there?' He has that look in his eyes – his journalist look, the one he was always sidling up to me with on my doorstep. He knew there was more to this visit than met the eye.

'Just… souvenirs.' I pat the top of the box to tantalise him. It works – he licks his lips.

Freddie's eyes thin and he bites his lower lip. 'What kind of souvenirs?'

'*My* souvenirs,' I tell him.

'Vermont is only a few hours away. You sure you didn't engineer this trip just so you could pay your sister a visit? You sure this safety deposit box thing is on the level?'

'Quite sure, Inspector Clueless.'

He laughs. Sluggers is significantly quieter now – all the baseball and basketball games have finished and only the hard drinkers are left at the bar, like on *Cheers*, mumbling world views to the barman who looks nothing like Ted Danson. More like Charles Manson. 'So… I guess that brings us up to date.' He closes his notebook and clicks off the pen.

'I guess it does,' I say. I make the universal sign for *Can we get the check, please?* to a passing waitress.

Freddie reaches into his jacket. 'I'll get this.'

'Was that the kind of sequel you were waiting for?'

'No,' he says, shaking his head. 'I was expecting something completely different. You've… changed. 'You've turned it around, Rhi— whoever you are.'

'Or so I'd have you believe,' I say, placing my hand around the box.

Freddie looks at it. 'You still haven't told me what's in there.'

'Oh yeah. So I haven't. And you know what?'

'What?'

'I'm not going to either.'

I slide out of the booth and slip back into my coat as Freddie slips into his. It's gone 2 a.m. 'There's another bar down the street that stays open till four,' he says, glancing at Google Maps as we gather our things.

'No, thanks. This has been fun but I have a connection to make.'

Freddie shakes his head, helping me sling my bag over my shoulder and picking up my box before I can. I stare at him and he hands it to me. In the darkness of the bar I see the box is dripping at one corner.

Outside, he clicks on his Uber app – I hail a yellow cab.

'You wanna share a ride? I can take you anywhere,' Freddie offers. 'If you're going to the vaults now—'

'No, thanks.'

'It's the least I can do. You've given me another whole book here. You didn't tell me anything about Seren though. Or Ivy. What about them? You haven't given me anything about *them*.'

'Nothing to give. The best I can do for them both is to stay away.'

'So you're definitely *not* headed to Vermont now?'

'Nope. Definitely not. Seren Markled me out of the picture long ago. And Ivy's with Claudia. Safe. Secure. Claudia's new husband seems to love her like a real dad. I'm letting sleeping dogs lie. I can't afford not to.'

A cab pulls in and I open the back door, Freddie stands beside it, keeping it open while I put all my stuff inside. He hands me his business card. It's a quality document, hard and gilt-edged – he has his own logo and everything – FLC. No company name. He *is* the company.

'Wait,' he says, 'if you're dead, how am I meant to persuade people that this is your true story?'

'Not my problem, is it?'

'Maybe I could say I met you just before you died, how about that? Rhi—? How about that? Wait, come back!'

I leave him standing there on the street, all frowny and lost, as I step inside my yellow cab and disappear into the night.

'Greyhound bus station, please,' I tell the driver.

Thursday, 23 January – Greyhound bus from JFK Airport, Queens to Manchester, Vermont

The bus leaves the hanger at 3.50 a.m. and, as with all journeys involving other human beings in confined spaces, it is predictably irritating, long-winded and, at times, makes me wish I was dead. My phone runs out of charge four times, *that's* how long it is. But I pass the time sleeping, texting Raf and checking out the contents of the envelope Tenoch left for me in the safety deposit box – he really has seen his *gatita* right.

It was good to have got the story out. I don't know what Freddie will do with it – maybe he'll make up some shit that I visited him before Seren shot 'me' dead, I don't know. I don't actually care. I think I wanted to get it all straight in my own head. There are so many rumours about where I'd been, what I'd done, how many dicks I'd severed en route, I want the truth to get out as well. Maybe I just wanted to talk to someone who had known the real me. The real me before I became the *new* me.

*

It's an express service terminating at Rutland, so there aren't too many stops – Ridgewood, Albany, Walloomsac, Shaftesbury. I alight at Manchester, half an hour away from the house according to Google Maps. I've scribbled the address down in my Notes app, swiped from an old Facebook post of Mabli's, inviting all her classmates to her birthday party before she changed her security settings. I jump in another cab and arrive as the big yellow school bus pulls away from the kerbside at the bottom of their drive.

The box is still dripping and one corner is saturated to the point that the cardboard has begun to sag. I clamp it with my gloved hand and begin the gravel-winding, woodland walk up to the house.

Seren told me once it was 'just like Honey Cottage', our grandparents' house in Wales. But it isn't. For a start it's about three times the size and it's not stone-washed-white but clap-board white with a cobblestone path leading to an ornate green door. A Christmas wreath sways in the breeze. There are green-and-red fairy lights wrapped around the porch pillars and a sign stuck in the dirt saying, *Santa Please Stop By*. As I wend my way along the cobbles, I notice several mismatched flower pots beneath the porch. I put down the box on one of the pots and as I'm about to knock, the door flies open.

'Oh, hey there, I was—' She's holding a watering can and it's dripping from the spout. Intended for the pots, I presume. There's no flicker of recognition as we stand face to face, sister to sister – me under the porch, Seren on her *Welcome to the Gibsons* coconut mat. 'Oh sorry, I thought you were the mailman! Can I help you?'

I don't speak. Whole seconds tick by. She doesn't recognise

me at all. Me and her in the same space and time, feet away for the first time in years.

'How about a toastie? Extra salad cream?'

Her eyes become hooded. Her face darkens.

There it is. The flicker.

'Jesus! No! No! Christ no!' she screams, like she's being led towards the Wicker Man.

She drops the watering can with a clatter and the door flings back. She runs into the hall, skidding on another coconut mat which slips beneath her feet. She screams for her life.

'Somebody! Help me! Help me!'

There's nobody around, she's made sure of that, moving to somewhere no other sod lives. She runs, up the wide, winding staircase two at a time. A distant door slams. I retrieve my box from the flower pot and place it down beside my rucksack and the shabby chic wooden sign that reads *Home Is Where The Heart Is* in curly script. The hallway is peppered with photos – skiing, Christmases, pumpkin-carving, first day at school. Ashton laughing his head off at some clown; Mabli cuddling one of her dearly departed rabbits.

The place is magnificent – I can tell that from the hallway cos you can see in to all the other ground floor rooms – the enormous pine kitchen with white marble island, the sprawling family living room with its gigantic squashy cream chairs. On a thin table in the hallway sits the most ornate bunch of flowers I've ever seen – funeral flowers, it looks like – blue hydrangeas, cream roses, white carnations and Asiatic lilies stretched wide open like they're laughing. It looks like it's been stolen from Liberace's headstone. I pick up the card. *My offer still stands. In Deepest Sympathy – FLC.*

Freddie. Litton. Cheney. Same gilt-edged card.

I close the front door behind me, checking momentarily outside for signs of heroic lumberjacks or maple syrup sellers who have heard her screams, but seeing signs of neither, I climb the stairs. There are many doors on the first-floor landing but it's obvious which one she's behind – the closed one, at the end of the cream runway – I hear her breathing heavily, a muffled high-pitched wheeze, and the door judders, like she has her back against it.

'Seren?' The wheezing stops, like she's clapped a hand over her mouth. 'I want to see you. Let me in.'

'The police are coming,' she says with a shaking voice. 'They'll be here any second. And I've got a gun.'

'What are you going to tell them? Your dead sister's ghost has come to attack you? Come on, I want to talk. You owe me that at least having shot me in the face and buried me. I don't have a weapon. And I only have one hand. You're properly in the driving seat here.'

It's minutes before the door opens the tiniest crack and an eye appears through said crack. A wobbly voice says, 'I have a gun.'

'Yeah, you said.'

'Why are you here?'

'Isn't it obvious?'

'You've come to kill me.'

'If I wanted to kill you, I'd have killed you by now.'

'So why are you here?'

'I want to know why *you* killed *me*. Or why you *said* you killed me.'

It takes an age, maybe seven minutes, but she does eventually open the door fully – a small handgun, pointed straight at me. Still crying, still unable to control her breathing or her shaking hands.

I pick up my crap hand with my good one and wave at her with it. She stares at it, like everyone does. And there we are, a Mexican standoff, her inside her bedroom door, me out on the landing. 'I'm going to stand here until you talk to me or kill me again. Your choice.'

'I *will* shoot you if you come closer.'

'I don't doubt it.'

She has on a typical Soccer Mom outfit – pink hoody, boyfriend jeans, brand-new Converse and her hair is longer. It used to be all sharp bob and angles but since she's had kids it's gone to shit – somewhere between the Rachel cut and Tarzan.

The distant peal of sirens alerts us to life outside these walls again.

'You better see to that. I'll wait up here.'

I take a seat on the little baseball glove chair in what I presume is my nephew Ashton's bedroom, even though I've never met him. She points the gun at me all the way down the stairs until I can't see her anymore. I overhear the convo. But for once in her life, amazingly, she doesn't rat me out.

'Uh yeah, it was that trophy-hunter pair who were here last week. Same ones. They got in through the living room window and they stole a... candle, a Yankee Candle, and... some holiday cards. And then they left.'

'Just left?' A man's voice. The front door closes.

'Yeah, I'm so sorry to waste your time. I guess I'm still a little jumpy after you know... everything.'

I sneak into Mabli's room – see her desk where she films her vlogs, her Stranger Things fairy lights on the wall behind her bed, her shelves full of toy animals and trophies she's won for spelling bees and writing competitions.

'Ma'am, you still seem a little scared, would you like me to check around the place for you? Make sure everything's secure?'

'No, I saw them drive off, they're long gone. It was a different car to last time only I didn't catch the plates, I'm sorry. I'm fine, honestly. A little shaken up but—' She did the nervous laugh I knew well from our phone calls.

'Is there anyone you'd like me to call? Your husband?'

I linger at the top of the stairs, leaning over the bannisters. 'No, we're separated,' she says. 'He doesn't need to know about this. Nobody was hurt. Can I get you a coffee or something?'

'No, ma'am, thanks all the same. If you're sure you're OK?'

It takes a few more questions and a guided tour of the downstairs before the officer is happy enough to leave her, at which point, I venture back down myself. I find her in the living room, locking her knives in the safe behind the overlarge family portrait. Even walking slowly into the room, I make her jump.

'Is that necessary?' I ask her.

'I think it is,' she says, turning the combination on the safe and settling the portrait back in place. The room is heavily decked out in Christmas fluff, fake snow and feathery boas and a large tree stands proudly in the corner, already trimmed with popcorn, gingerbread figures and an angel that a child has made. Either that or they bought it from a blind cobbler.

'You and Cody are separated?'

'Yeah,' she says, removing her gun from the back of her jeans but not pointing it at me, just sort of holding it. 'We're in touch.' It's as though she resents every word she utters; like each one costs her money.

'I'm pretty hungry. Any chance of that toastie?'

She doesn't answer for a while but when she does she says *Kitchen* and points the way with her gun.

The ceilings in all the downstairs rooms are white with fake wooden eaves to make it look olde-worlde even though the place was probably only built in the last ten years. The kitchen countertops are spotless white, flecked with shards of glitter, and there are two sets of bi-fold doors looking out over a huge flagstone sun terrace. Beyond it is a vast, sloping green valley. Seren sets about making the toastie while I pull out a stool at the opposite end of the breakfast bar.

'It's a nice place, Seren. Great for the kids. Whereabouts did you kill me?'

She stops unwrapping slices of fake cheese, momentarily, before starting up again like she's been rebooted. 'Out there.'

I hop off the stool and look out onto the terrace. The table and chairs are gnarled metal, the same green as the door. It's the only thing about the place, apart from Seren, which looks stark and uninviting. I stare out at the flagstones. She knows what I'm doing before I do.

'We had it jet-washed when the police were done.'

I nod, looking past the terrace down to a sloping lawn and an area where there's a veg patch and some chickens peck about inside a large wire pen. 'The papers said it was on the doorstep.'

'Papers lie.' She stops peeling squares of plastic cheese from plastic wrappers and stares at me. 'How do you do it?'

'Do what?'

'Kill someone? How do you do that and not feel anything?

I haven't slept a full night since it happened. Why can't I be as nonchalant as you are?'

'Because you're not supposed to be,' I say. 'I killed because my brain is wired up all wrong. I killed because I liked it.'

'Liked? Past tense? You've stopped?'

'Well, I think I'm in what psychologists call the "period of de-escalation".'

'How long does *that* last?'

'No idea. I'm happy though. And I'm letting that be enough for now. How come you're not in prison for my murder?'

'We've entered a self-defence plea because the woman – *you* – had been hounding us so much.'

'*I* had?'

'Several times over the past year. She'd been violent. Followed my kids to school. Tried to take Mabli coming out of a dance class. She broke in and stole my purse, all my cards. Found out where Cody worked, stalked *him*. Sent threatening notes. All she wanted was you.'

'Nightmare,' I say.

'A living Hell,' she smiles, but her eyes don't. She tries to tug open the bread bag. 'And now *you're* here.'

It's the most she's said so far, and it says everything. 'Did you know it was her when you shot her?'

'Of course I did,' she spat.

'So why did you do it?'

She sighs, deep into her chest. 'I guess I snapped. I thought it would get rid of you for good. Didn't fucking work though, did it?'

'How is killing a perfect stranger going to get rid of *me*?'

She throws down the bread bag, unable to get her fumbling fingers to twist off the plastic tie. I reach across and open it – her hand moves towards the gun. I remove two slices of bread, throw them towards her, and tie up the bag. I sit back down.

'My life for the past year has been on hold, waiting for this day. Waiting for you to come here and finish me off. I don't sleep anymore – I doze and I wake with up with heart palpitations. I don't work, I *can't* work. I'm on anxiety medication. I've driven my husband away, my kids'll be next cos I snap at them all the time. And it's all because of *you*.'

'You don't sound anxious now. You sound... angry.'

'That's because I *am*. The fear of you has always been bigger than *you*. And now you're here, I can see you're just... a woman. A woman who doesn't even look like my sister anymore. You've lost those lines between your eyes and you're not scowling. It's weird... this is the calmest I've felt in a long time.'

'I had surgery.'

'Obvs.'

The griddle smokes and she lifts it up and slides my toastie out onto a plate. I don't even remind her to put the blob of salad cream on the side – she just remembers. Except it isn't salad cream. It's called Miracle Whip.

'The fuck is this?'

'It tastes the same.'

I dip my toast point in the blob and lick it. 'You've been living here too long. It tastes like shit.' I look up at her. Her hand goes straight to the gun.

'You never said anything. In the diaries. About... me,' she says.

445

'You read Freddie's book?'

'He sent me a copy. He wants me to talk to him for his sequel. I won't.'

'I said plenty about you.'

'But you never mentioned... what you saw at Honey Cottage.'

'I told you I wouldn't.'

She tidies up the condiments, wipes the counter, even though it doesn't need wiping. 'It's the one question he keeps asking me. All the journalists ask me – *Why does Rhiannon go after sex offenders? Why paedophiles? Is it because she was molested as a child?*'

'And what do you tell them?'

'Nothing. I think that's what I find so hard – is it my fault you turned out the way you did?'

'Why would it be *your* fault?'

'Because that's when you turned. That summer when you saw what Grandad was doing to me. Yeah, you did bad stuff to me before that, your personality changed after Priory Gardens, but we were bringing you back, me and Mom and Dad. It was working. You were coming back to us. Then we went to Honey Cottage that summer and... you flipped.'

'Do you remember that conversation we had that night, lying on top of the hay bales in the back field?'

'I've blacked a lot of those summers out.'

'You said to me, "While he's got me, he won't touch you." That's when I knew, one way or another, Grandad was going to die. I saw him hit you that morning when you forgot to bring in the eggs. And later when he was doing that stuff to you in the barn...'

She scrunches her face like she's got sudden brain freeze.

'I was going to push him down the stairs, or stab him when we went on that picnic at Ogmore – I hid the kitchen knife in my bag. I was going to do it. I was planning to lure him into the long grasses, saying I'd found a dead bird.'

Seren's fully crying by this time. 'And you'd never have said a word, would you?' I shake my head. 'Nanny was so mad at you. "Why didn't you help him? Why didn't you call for me?"'

'You smiled at me, at his funeral.'

'You'd killed my monster,' she said. 'I felt good.' She wiped her eyes roughly on a piece of kitchen paper and threw it in the sink. She was angry again. 'But I felt bad about feeling good because he was dead.'

'He raped you, Seren. I couldn't let him get away with that. I'd kill all your monsters for you. I always will. Cos I love you. I *am* capable of feeling love.'

She shook her head, not looking at me. 'What about the calls, the silent messages, all the emails you've sent me? If you love me so much...'

'I didn't send you anything.'

'What about that letter to the *Evening Post* about killing that woman in the farm shop? And the letters to the *Gazette* and the *Mercury*?'

'Not me, not me, and what's the *Mercury*?'

'What about my birthday last year and that horrible thing you sent to my office?'

'What horrible thing?'

'Oh come on. The... turd in a Tiffany box?'

'I didn't send that.'

It dawns on her face, and her eyes search mine. 'The dead cats?'

I shake my head. 'I wouldn't kill cats.'

I tuck into my sandwich and she stands there, hands resting on the island, gun behind the butter tub, thinking things through.

'No, you wouldn't, would you?' she says, more to herself than to me. 'You didn't do *anything*? Send anything to me or Cody this past year?'

I shake my head. 'I've had better things to do than dick about with you, Seren. My stans just messing with you, I expect. It didn't mean anything.'

She sits down on the stool opposite. 'Like when you used to set fire to my clothes as a kid. That didn't "mean" anything, either, did it?'

'I only did that twice. I was bored.'

'Stealing my stuff?'

'You never shared.'

'Cutting off my hair when I was asleep?'

'Two times I did that.'

'Stabbing me with the scissors?'

'Yeah. All right. I was a bitch to you, whatevs. You've shot me in the face and sent me to a morgue. I think you more than got your own back.'

She nods and sort of laughs and looks to the ceiling as though someone up there will help her.

'I *did* love you,' I said. 'I still do. I don't kill people I love. I kill *for* them. And I killed *twice* for you, if you remember.'

'Don't you put Pete McMahon on *me*.'

'That's not what I'm saying. It's about *me*. It's *in me* forever, has been since, I don't know, Priory Gardens, maybe since birth. Maybe it was Dad taking me to watch him beat up those guys on the register or Grandad molesting you. Or Julia cutting off *my* hair and burning holes in *my* school uniform with the Bunsen Burner when the teacher's back was turned because a mute wouldn't tell anyone. Maybe it's *all* of those things. Maybe it's *none* of those things. Maybe it's fucking Maybelline.'

'She looked like you. The woman... the woman I killed. She had your hair, your eyes. She'd even had a nose job. I mean, how insane is that?'

'Whereas I was already insane and had surgery to *not* look like me.'

'I wanted her gone. I wanted *you* gone.'

'But you still aren't sleeping. Or working. Or happy.'

'No. Not at the moment.' She looks at my hand. 'What happened to you?'

'You wouldn't believe me if I told you.'

She puffs sharp air like a whale coming up out of the ocean. I see the flicker of a smile before it vanishes. There's a noise outside and we both look to the window to see a van pulling away from the mailbox at the end of her drive. 'Probably more fan mail for you,' she says.

'What do you mean?'

She leads me outside to the garage, lifts the door and shows me over to a pile of boxes labelled *RL gifting* and a date. A whole pile of them. She opens the first, dated last year.

'Presents. From your fan club.'

'What?'

She shows me the edited highlights of what she's been sent

– Sylvanians, letters containing everything from death threats to marriage proposals, teddy bears, friendship bracelets, packets of Maoams, boxes of Pop Tarts, and a picnic hamper containing everything I'd need for life on the run – wet wipes, socks, charger, bottles of water – basically a festival survival kit.

'I'd be touched if it wasn't so pathetic. Why have you kept all this?'

'Police told me to. I started off by reporting it every time I was sent something but there was so much and every day I'd get something new so they asked me to keep hold of it, label it and store it for them. Once they'd guaranteed none of it was from you.'

'They thought I might send fan mail to *myself*?'

'They were covering every eventuality, I guess.'

One of boxes is labelled with two large red letters – *KC*. She lifts it down from the top shelf and brings it over, standing it on the floor between us.

'This is from your head cheerleader – Kacey Carmichael.'

'The woman you killed?'

'Yeah. Your doppelganger.'

I can't help but laugh. The box contains countless letters and parcels of books, teddies holding hearts, more Sylvanians and handmade soaps.

'That's what she did, made soap.'

'From the ass fat of rich widows by the smell of it.' I closed the box.

'It's not funny. They're obsessed. They dress like you, talk like you. Travel far and wide to visit your murder sites. Two of your fans were actually sectioned, did you know that?'

'No.'

'One of them was prank-calling Dean Bishopston's widow, saying she was *you*. She told her how her husband's last words were about his kids.'

'No, they weren't.'

'Whatever. But that's the kind of sicko fan you have. In some ways they're *worse* than you. They love you. They want to meet you, marry you, *be* you. Some of them actually want you to kill them.'

'Then they should be careful what they wish for, shouldn't they?'

When we're back in the hallway I remember my gift.

'Oh, I forgot, I brought a present,' I say, looking around for the box, but it's not there.

'I moved your things when the cop came,' she says, striding into the lounge to retrieve them. She shows me where they are behind one of the chairs. I pick up the box and hand it to her.

She frowns. 'What is it?'

'Well, it's for the kids.'

'Why's the bottom damp?'

'Just open it. It's not a bomb.'

She still isn't sure around me, probably remembering the end of *Se7en* and thinking I've done a Paltrow on her, but she lifts the flaps of the box anyway and peeks down inside.

'Oh my God.' She scrabbles around gently. 'A tortoise?' she says.

'*Two* tortoises. They're babies. I read on Mab's blog how her pets kept on dying so I got to thinking, What will outlive *her* so she won't have to be sad again? And I knew someone once who said they had a tortoise for, like, sixty years or something so I knew they'd make great pets. And I had this layover in New York and I passed this pet shop and… voila.'

She stares down into the box and shakes her head.

'They don't take much looking after. I think they're hibernating at the moment. Guy at the pet shop didn't seem sure. I put a little bowl of water in there in case and a head of lettuce. They hibernate for ages apparently.'

She looks up at me. 'You never forgot one of their birthdays.'

'Why would I?' I stare up at the picture of them dressed as pumpkins.

'Do you want a picture of them? To keep?'

'Yes, please.'

She leads me back into the kitchen and points to the fridge where there were an assortment of lists and photos and children's drawings. There's a photo of Ashton holding a football trophy.

'He's got Cody's grin.'

'Yeah, he does.'

'Is there a way back for you two? You still love him.'

'Yeah, of course but—'

'If you love him, that's enough. Put yourselves back together.'

'For *their* sakes,' she says.

'No, for yours.'

She takes down two photos – the football one and one of Mabli on a small horse. She hands them to me. 'Thanks.'

I look back towards the fridge. Ashton on his bike. Mabli and her (now dead) ginger cat. A shopping list, a school flyer for a Christmas fair, and a picture of a child I don't recognise; it's not Ashton *or* Mabli. A different little girl, a toddler, sitting in a small wooden chair before a Christmas tree and a mountain of presents, wearing a tartan dress. Big hazel eyes, hair like soft caramel, a one-toothed smile beaming enough to light up the room.

'Who's that?' I ask, as the picture pulls me towards it.

'Oh God,' says Seren. 'Yeah, uh… that's Ivy.'

'*My* Ivy?' I take the picture down off the fridge and stare at it. The last time I saw her, she was a blob in an incubator, eyes like tiny black lines in her face. Now they're wide open, the colour of tiger's eyes. Like AJ's eyes. She's the most beautiful child I've ever seen. But she would be – she's *mine*.

'I totally forgot that was there, I'm so sorry.'

'Why have you got this?'

Seren clears her throat. 'Claudia sent it to me. We've kept in touch.'

'Why?'

'She friended me on Facebook a few months ago. Started sending me progress reports on Ivy. That picture came with her Christmas card.'

'She's got a tooth,' I smiled.

'Claudia wants me to be in Ivy's life, if only from a distance. She looks *so* much like you. Well, like you *used* to look at that age.'

'Does she?'

'Yeah. Mirror image. Can't you see it?' I shake my head. 'What do you feel when you look at her?'

'Sick.' I can't take my eyes from the picture. 'Sad.'

'Is your heart thumping?' I nod. 'Do you want to cry?' I nod again, unable to see the picture through water. 'Do you want to touch her face, smell her hair, give her a hug? That's how I feel when I look at *my* children. They don't want hugs so much

453

anymore but I'll never stop loving them, wanting them near me. I even ache when they go to school some days. *That's* love.'

I wipe my cheek and hand her back the photo but she hands it back to me. 'No, you can keep that one too, if you want. You did the right thing, giving her to Claudia. She loves the bones of that baby. Ivy wants for nothing.'

I can't stop staring at her. 'Claudia married again. Are they happy?'

'What time's your flight?'

'I have a few hours. It's a direct one at least. I had to get the bus here from New York because of the tortoises. What's this Mitch like?'

'The kids will be thrilled with their tortoises, thank you. Mabs will probably want to call them Jimin and J-Hope. Ash prefers the Yankees—'

'Seren, you didn't answer me. Is Claudia happy? Is Mitch good to her?'

'Yeah,' she says. 'They're very happy. I'll see you out.'

She's holding something back, I know she is. I stand in the porch facing her, like I did when I first arrived, waiting for it. She grabs something from a short fumble through the drawer in the hallway table and hands it to me.

It's a picture of two little girls in a swimming pool. Us in Madeira on the pool noodles. Sun shining. Bobby Fairly chatting to Dad in the background. 'I always liked this one too.'

'Thanks.'

'Mum did love you, you know. She... didn't know how to help you. Nor did Dad. Nor do I.'

'Yeah, well, I can help myself now.'

She wants to say something else, I know she does, and I wait for it.

'Ivy is fine, OK? You don't need to worry about her...'

'But?'

'Claudia's sick. That's why she got in touch with me. She has breast cancer. They've caught it early but she's scared. If something happens to her, Mitch is going to adopt Ivy.'

'Oh.'

'I didn't want to tell you. You're settled and happy and I'm so pleased.'

'Why would Mitch getting Ivy be a bad thing?'

'It wouldn't,' she says, guardedly.

'You said Claudia was scared.'

'Well, she's asked me to take Ivy if the worst happens. She's going to put it all in writing. It's just belt and braces. That woman who arranged her adoption, Heather—'

'—Wherryman?'

'Yeah, she's going to help her.'

I can't speak. I'm losing myself. Rhiannon's rising up from her resting place, like a zombie from the dead. 'Why doesn't she want Mitch to have her?'

'Well, Mitch isn't really a... dad type.'

'What do you mean, "a dad type"? Why marry him then?'

'I don't know, she fell in love, I guess.'

My heart thumps in my ears. 'What about Claudia's sister in Australia, AJ's mum?'

'Claudia fell out with her when they heard about AJ's death and she kept them from seeing Ivy. It escalated and they lost visitation rights.'

'What happened?'

'I don't really know. But Mitch was supposed to be the glue that kept them together. Claudia's desperate to have the perfect family, and they almost have it. They've got this wonderful house in London, in a nice area, Claudia got a terrific job at this publishers but Mitch is a little—'

'WHAT?'

'A bit of a fly-by-night. Unpredictable. He was married before and he did some jail time but he's a reformed character. He's turned himself around—'

'—my baby is in a house with an ex-jailbird? What did he do?'

'Well, his sentence was commuted to two years from six—'

'—WHAT. DID. HE. DO?'

'It was a long time ago, twenty years or more. He was a young teacher. And he was... having a relationship... with a student. Claudia knew about it, well, she didn't know how old the girl was—'

'How old?'

'Old enough to know better if you ask me but—'

'HOW. FUCKING. OLD?'

'Thirteen.'

'THIRTEEN?'

'But this was years ago, and the girl admitted to leading him on—'

'THIRTEEN?'

'It's history, Rhiannon, ancient history—'

'IT'S RAPE.'

'I'm sure he's—'

'—you're sure what, you're sure he doesn't have a taste for pre-pubescent girls anymore? Jesus Christ, Seren. WHY DID

YOU TELL ME? How can I leave her with him now I know that?'

'I will do my best to help Claudia, I promise you. You don't need to get involved with this. Listen to me – you *have* to stay away from her. For her sake. For *mine*. I could go to jail if they find out you're still alive.'

'Ivy's my *daughter*. And she is living with a *paedophile*.'

'Calm down, Rhiannon, please.'

'Calm down? Calm down?! You tell me my kid is living with a convicted sex offender and you don't think I'm gonna flip my fucking wig?'

'You gave her up,' she said, pleadingly. 'She's not your responsibility anymore. And Claudia is an amazing mom, I promise you. And she loves Mitch but— oh God, I shouldn't have told you this. Why did I open my fat mouth?'

'Maybe on some level you *wanted* me to know.'

'Oh shit. No, no, Ivy wants for nothing. While Claudia is alive, Ivy is fine.'

'Claudia is *dying*.'

'We'll figure it out, OK? I give you my word. I will make sure Claudia has support, as much as she needs. As far as the authorities are concerned, you are out of the picture now. You're free to live your life. Stay away from this, Rhiannon. *Please*. Please?'

Thursday, 23 January – Burlington International Airport, Vermont

1. *Journalist of the moment Guy Majors who called me a 'depraved, evil maniac who needs burying in a lead-lined coffin'*
2. *People with fully workable legs who stand still on travelators*
3. *People who huff and puff about taking shoes and belts off at the cattle grid, I mean, security gates. Get a fucking mooooove on*
4. *People who spread viruses and cause planes to be delayed*
5. *Mitchell Aaron Silverton*

I google Mitch Silverton in the cab on the way to the airport. Everything Seren said was true. I find a picture – blond hair, dazzling blue eyes, bit of stubble, thin mouth, broad shoulders, sharp dresser, ever so slightly rapey about the eye.

There's an article from five years ago about the girl he would take home to his place on a lunchtime. A maths whizz without many friends. How she adored him. How he made her feel loved when her dad walked out. How he'd groomed her over many months. How he had hit her only 'once when he'd lost his temper'.

The rage crackles inside me – the pain intensifies, like I'm being cut open at the breastbone. Storm clouds gather in my head. I can't catch my breath. He's in the same house as Ivy.

A message pings through on my phone from Rafael when I'm in the line for security. I need to hear his voice. I call him back as I'm redressing on the other side. I don't think it even rings before he picks up.

'Baby? Oh, thank God you're OK.'

His voice is the soother I need. Like ice cream on a chilli burn. 'Yeah, I'm fine. Sorry, the meeting went on longer than I expected and after they wanted to take me out to lunch to discuss a sequel. I've missed you so much.'

'Oh baby, me too. I can't wait to see you. So you think they're gonna publish you? If they're talking about a sequel already, they must want you.'

'Yeah, I think so. They said they will probably change the title to *The Alibi Girl* or something. "Girl" is a more sellable word than "clock", apparently.'

'Ahh well, that's OK isn't it? Not a deal breaker?'

'No, I guess not.'

'You don't sound sure. Had something happened?'

'No, I'm OK.'

'What's up? Talk to me.'

'No, I'm just tired, honestly. And my hand aches a bit.'

'You been doing your exercises?'

'I forgot. I'll do some on the plane. Do you want any Toblerone?'

'No, I'm all set,' he laughs.

'Is everyone OK there? How's Liv?'

'She's… OK,' he said. A hesitation between the noun and the adjective – I was picking up on this more and more where Liv was concerned.

'Raf? What's happened?' My skin prickles. Heat all up my neck.

'I got back from the restaurant and she was talking to Mom in the kitchen. Wouldn't let me see her face – she says she "fell over". She won't come out of the bathroom.'

The chilli burn in my heart returns. 'Get your dad and your brother and your uncles, grab your blow torches and go round to that fucker's house and end it for her.'

'She wouldn't thank us.'

'*I'll* fucking do it then.' I can't keep the fork out of my tongue, the hiss out of my spit. Can't keep my chest cool or my legs still – they're jiggling about like I'm about to run.

'We miss you.'

His brother calls out, '*He's pining for you, Ophelia!*'

I laugh, despite myself. 'I miss you all too. More than you know.' I grab my things, tucking my passport into my coat. 'I've got a direct flight this time. I'm walking to the gate now. It's so busy – a lot of flights from China have been cancelled so there's a backlog.'

'Yeah, I saw something about that on CNN. Some virus going around in the Far East.'

'I'm sure it won't affect us. Look, don't worry about picking me up from the airport. Traffic will be a nightmare.'

'I don't want you taking the bus home by yourself.'

'You don't need to worry about me.'

'I know but I do. You sound out of breath.'

'I've been running,' I say. I stare up at the Departures boards. All the gates are open. My Delta flight to San Diego is *Preparing*. People are getting in line. The flight at the next gate is going to London – it's carrying a two-hour delay. The gnawing in my chest is never going to go. It's with me forever, like she is. Knotted up, tangled amongst my vital organs like bindweed. Like ivy.

'What time do you think you'll be home?'

'I'm not sure,' I say, checking my boarding card. *Ophelia Jane White. Booked on the 7.15 p.m. flight from JFK to San Diego International.* I stare hard at my name – the name of the person I am now. The name of the person I so desperately want to be.

But my baby girl needs me. My baby girl's in danger.

'I love you, OJ.'

'I love you too.' My eyes flick up to the Departure boards. They go from one to another and back again. San Diego. London. San Diego. London. San Diego. London. My legs are still jiggling.

'Come home soon, won't you?'

My heart picks up its familiar *thump thump* rhythm. My fingers lengthen. I can't catch my breath. Everything outside is chaos. Suitcases rolling. People running. Announcements blaring.

But everything inside is suddenly so simple.

'I'll be with you soon, baby, I promise. I'm coming home.'

Acknowledgements

Jon Appleton, Roxie 'Joan Wilder' Cooper, Georgia 'Rhiannon' Maguire, Emily Metcalf, Laura Myers, Jenny Savill and all at Andrew Nurnberg Agency, Katie Seaman, Lisa Milton, Joe Thomas, Becca Joyce and the whole team at HQ, Penny Skuse, Maggie Snead, Matthew Snead, Kirstie Swain, Sensitivity Reader Melissa Vera at Salt and Sage Books, Patrick Walters at See Saw Films, Magda Wasiczek for her beautiful cover designs and my lil Teddy Bear who has walked me along many a field, furrow and pavement until all my plot knots have been thoroughly unpicked. Yes, even my dog got an acknowledgement. This is what happens when you hit 40 and you don't have kids – you namecheck a Jackahuahua.

My Bath Spa buddies, namely Lucy Christopher, Steve Voake, Jo Nadin and Sue Bailey-Sillick and all the BA and MA students I have had the pleasure of regaling with my writing advice that was all stolen from Kurt Vonnegut anyway.

I'd also like to thank all the bloggers, reviewers and murderous darlings who are still buying, borrowing or stealing *Sweetpea* and *In Bloom* and shouting the bad name of Rhiannon from the rooftops, namely: Ashlea Dunstan, Bookie Tracey, Brian C, Charlotte Lucy @ Books and Bargains,

Chloe's Reading Room, Emma @ Book Love Life, Em @ Faffing At Life, Gaby @ GNTxReads, Gem Loves Books, Jade @ Best Books to Get Buried In, Jen @ PrettyMachine, Jessica @ IlanaReadsBooks, Joanne Easton, Karen JK Hart, Karen's Reads, Kayleigh @ Once Upon a Thriller1, Kayleigh's Reading Corner, Killer Reads, Kirsty @ Kirst Edition, Laura's Book Corner, Lucinda Is Reading, Melanie's Reads, Mia @ Turning A Page, My Bookish Life, Rebecca @ Bookworm Rebs, Sara @ My Bookworm Life, Sarah Hardy, Sarah Jane Huntington, Shona Louise blog, Sophie @ So Little Time for Books, Soph's Bookshelf, Terri and Catherine @ Haribo Reads, The World of Sophie, Tracey Gibson @ Tea Please, Tracy Fenton @ Compulsive Readers, Victoria Loves Books, What Ella Reads, What Victoria Read, Zooloo's Book Diary.

Consider yourselves ALL off The List.

Thank you again all for your hard work, support, enthusiasm and/or time in helping me to bring *Sweetpea*, *In Bloom* and *Dead Head* to life. It is massively appreciated more than mere words can say.

**Make sure you've read the rest of the
Sweetpea series featuring everyone's favourite
girl next door serial-killer, Rhiannon Lewis.**

Book 1

Although her childhood was haunted by a famous crime, Rhiannon's life is normal now that her celebrity has dwindled. By day her job as an editorial assistant is demeaning and unsatisfying. By evening she dutifully listens to her friend's plans for marriage and babies whilst secretly making a list. A kill list.

From the man on the Lidl checkout who always mishandles her apples, to the driver who cuts her off on her way to work, to the people who have got it coming, Rhiannon's ready to get her revenge.

**Because the girls everyone overlooks might
be able to get away with murder...**

Book 2

Rhiannon Lewis has successfully fooled the world and framed her cheating fiancé Craig for the depraved and bloody killing spree she committed. She should be ecstatic that she's free.

Except for one small problem. She's pregnant with her ex-lover's child. The ex-lover she only recently chopped up and buried in her in-laws's garden. And as much as Rhiannon wants to continue making her way through her kill lists, a small voice inside is trying to make her stop.

But can a killer's urges ever really be curbed?

**Don't miss the standalone funny, twisty
thriller that will keep you guessing**

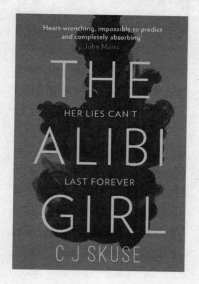

Joanne Haynes has a secret. That is not her real name.

And there's more. Her flat isn't hers. Her cats aren't hers. Even her hair isn't really hers.

Nor is she any of the other women she pretends to be. Not the bestselling romance novelist who gets her morning snack from the doughnut van on the seafront. Nor the pregnant woman in the dental surgery. Nor the chemo patient in the supermarket for whom the cashier feels ever so sorry. They're all just alibis.

In fact, the only thing that's real about Joanne is that nobody can know who she really is.

But someone has got too close. It looks like her alibis have begun to run out…

ONE PLACE. MANY STORIES

Bold, innovative and
empowering publishing.

FOLLOW US ON:

@HQStories